the DEVIL can be KIND

ELENA LUCAS

To all those that feel powerless: You are seen. You are heard. You are loved.

And on the days where you feel like the world is against you - find the Adalyn in you. I promise she is in there.

A NOTE FROM THE AUTHOR
TRIGGER WARNINGS

The Devil Can Be Kind is a dark mafia romance novel that explores challenging themes that may not be suitable for all audiences.

The novel contains explicit sexual scenes, strong language, references to drug and alcohol misuse, addiction, violence, firearms, threats of harm, injury and, in some instances, death. Additionally, there are references to sexual assault throughout, with particularly sensitive material in **Chapter 25.** If this topic is likely to affect you, please consider avoiding this chapter.

Whilst these themes are integral to the characters' stories, your wellbeing comes first - please read with care and reach out to someone if you are struggling.

Reader discretion is advised.

CHAPTER
ONE

ADALYN

W*ell thank fuck for that.*

I sighed and threw my head back, letting the warm breeze wash over me. By now it was early evening, and the setting sun had begun to cool the blazing Nevada air. Off in the distance was the familiar chatter of Friday night crowds gathering on the infamous Las Vegas strip. The excitement was contagious, and I was more than a little excited to throw away the stresses of my day at Pretty Penny Loans and join in.

Tonight, my friends and I were going out on the town to celebrate Bonnie's birthday. Through a connection, she had managed to get us into one of the most exclusive nightclubs in town—The Venetian Prince. The waiting list alone was over three months long, with private booths costing well into the thousands each. Bonnie, the bloody brilliant Bonnie, had not only managed to get us into this fortress of a club, but had also landed us a booth with VIP passes. We were practically *guaranteed* to be rubbing shoulders with the social elite and maybe even a few celebrities...if we were lucky.

1

I cannot wait!

I pulled out my phone and read through my texts from Bonnie and another friend, April, as I made my way to my car to the rear of the building. Pretty Penny Loans was one of my family's many businesses and where I unfortunately worked Monday through Friday as part of my 'identity'.

Let me explain what I mean by that exactly...

My name is Adalyn Mannino, but I go by Adalyn Parker these days. My family is one of the wealthiest in the continental US with an assortment of bars, restaurants, casinos and loan companies to its name, as well as a great deal more...*illegitimate* business ventures, too. My father is none other than Alberto Mannino, or as he is better known, Don Mannino. He is the head of our rather *large* family and has a reputation for ruthlessness. No one in our family so much as breathes without his say so. And while it was true I was his only child, it was rare that details of the family *business* were ever shared with me. My primary purpose was to be amiable and look pretty as my Mamma had once insisted. But from the little I did know... I knew that we weren't nice people.

My new identity came about after one of my family's many 'deals' went horribly wrong seven years ago. Forcing us out from our beautiful white mansion in Las Vegas and into the dregs of upper middle-class suburbia, where we were bestowed the name 'Parker'.

Thus, 'Adalyn Parker' was born.

A twenty-five-year-old ex-cheerleader who works full-time as a receptionist in Las Vegas and still lives with her insufferable parents. *Yawn.*

For the most part, I was pretty committed to my new 'normal' identity, even going so far as having my raven hair dyed shit-bright blonde once every other week. Gone were my expensive designer clothes, Tiffany necklaces and *ah...my beautiful Chanel handbags.* It was thoroughly depressing, and my patience was wearing thin after all these years... Which is exactly why I was going out partying tomorrow night. *Zero fucks given.*

I approached my car and buckled myself in, fiddling with the control panel until my music started blaring obnoxiously through the speakers. My car was perhaps the only indication left of my former life and was definitely not the kind of car a receptionist earning minimum wage would be able to drive: a custom black-out Dodge Challenger Hellcat complete with extra wide fenders and red calipers.

Hands down, it was the love of my life.

I screeched out of the lot and made my way onto the I-eleven to Boulder City, which was a little over half an hour away from my work. I took a call from April on the way and confirmed our plans for tonight, before pulling into the driveway.

Our house was halfway up the hillside on the outskirts of town and was easily the nicest on our street. What with its light grey walls and large ornate windows, the house was deceptively upper middle-class. The average onlooker couldn't detect the multitude of security cameras, the high-tech fingerprint recognition panel by the front gate, or the extra thick bulletproof windows. Nor could they know that the neighbouring house was also owned by my father and housed at least ten Mafiosos at any given time.

That was the beauty of it.

I killed the engine and made my way inside. As I entered, I could hear my father on a conference call in his study while my mother lounged on the sofa shopping on her laptop. It was just like any other typical day in the 'Parker' family.

"Hi, Mamma." I called out.

"Hello," she greeted absentmindedly, her long dark hair pulled into an immaculately messy bun at the top of her head.

3

"How was work?" I asked, heading toward the kitchen to get a drink.

"Average."

Part of our 'Parker family' rouse was that my mother owned and managed a designer boutique in town. Not only was it used to justify the *fabulous* middle-class life we had, but it also helped keep her from getting too bored. My father was never around during the day, either constantly locked away in his study or traveling somewhere for meetings. There was a lot of time to kill in the 'Parker' family.

"That's good," I said mutedly, grabbing a coke from the kitchen.

"Hm."

With that riveting conversation over with, I headed up to my room to plan my outfit for the evening in the lull before dinner.

I spent the next hour or so trashing my room and trying on various dresses and outfit combinations. I finally settled on a midnight satin slip dress paired with a well-loved pair of black stilettos. Satisfied with my choice, I put away my discarded clothes and headed downstairs for dinner.

Our housemaid, Mabel, was serving some spaghetti by the time I took a seat at the table. I was the first to arrive, but my mother followed soon after with her laptop still in hand. We ate in silence until my father arrived, taking his usual seat at the head.

My father, even to me, was an imposing man with a short stocky build. His greying black hair was always perfectly slicked back into his preferred style, and he rarely wore anything other than a designer suit.

"How are my ladies doing?" he asked in his deep, gravelly voice before tucking into his food.

"Great, dear," my mother responded bitterly, clicking away

on the laptop still. She was long since past pretending to enjoy her family's company.

"Adalyn, how was work?"

"It was fine." I smiled and gulped down another mouthful of spaghetti.

He nodded and continued eating.

"Papa, I was thinking... Maybe I could work at one of our other businesses now that I have more experience. I was thinking maybe one of the casinos? Doing something less admin related maybe..." I looked over at my father who was still chewing his food.

"I don't think that's a good idea," he dismissed. "Instead of working, your efforts should be focused on learning how to keep your own home and how to cook."

"It is a blight on this family to be as unskilled as you are," my mother remarked sharply. "It has certainly done you no favours in attracting a husband so far." Her piercing gaze settled on me with a dissatisfied grimace.

My father waved his hand absentmindedly, "We will have Mabel teach her the basics."

"And if that doesn't work? What husband would want her then?" my mother sneered at him. "Perhaps we send her to a proper cooking school. I told you giving her that job was a waste of her time."

It wasn't within my power to protest, so I tuned their bickering out as I continued eating instead. Any hope I'd had of attaining a proper career had long since been snuffed out.

It wasn't my place to want control over my life. I was a woman... and women in the Cosa Nostra had no power. We were meant to be docile, submissive characters performing in a drama of violence directed by men. Nothing more. And while the rest of civilization had inevitably marched on with the times, our little corner of society had remained stagnant in the name of tradition.

My father's phone began to ring and after looking at the caller ID, he picked up his plate and answered, marching off to his study. I gritted my teeth in quiet frustration.

"Stop frowning, Adalyn. You look ugly." Mother muttered, taking a gulp of her wine.

"Thank you, Mamma." I sneered.

"Right, I'm off," She suddenly jumped up and slammed her laptop lid down.

"Going anywhere interesting?"

"There's a new bar in town, so Sally and I are going." She stalked off to the hallway to grab her handbag, heels clicking on the marble floor. "Goodbye!" she called before leaving.

My mother has always been about as motherly as a block of ice.

I quickly finished my food alone and went back upstairs to wait for April to arrive.

Thankfully, she arrived only half an hour later, armed with more than half of her closet in order to get ready for the evening.

April and I became instant best friends back in high school, what with her fast quips and devil-may-care attitude. She was stunningly beautiful with bright green eyes and a tall willowy frame, my absolute opposite in every way.

"I cannot believe it! How the fuck did Bonnie get us into The Venetian Prince?" she gushed while dumping her stuff in my room.

"I know, she's a gem. She had to sleep with that guy Brad, though, to get us in." I took a seat at my dresser and began priming my face.

"Brad, the bartender guy? Wow." She took a seat on the floor and got out her makeup bag.

"I know, I think they are dating now though, so it worked out for the best." We chuckled at the unlikely love story.

"Let's hope to God he has some hot-ass friends then," April cheered.

We spent the next couple of hours getting glammed up, dancing to shamelessly loud music and sinking a few pre-drinks. April had selected a short emerald dress, while I'd slipped on the thin satin number I'd chosen earlier. I threw on my shoes, grabbed a golden clutch bag and declared myself decent.

We walked arm in arm to the car waiting for us in the drive-way. To April's unassuming eyes, it would have seemed like a normal rented chauffeur car, but in reality, it was one of our security cars complete with tinted ballistic windows. She didn't even take note of the gun tucked into the driver's waistband as we sang horribly along to the music. People outside of the Cosa Nostra rarely did look too closely in my experience. They were always more trusting.

Not tonight! I stopped that train of thought and brought myself back to April's bad singing.

A short while later, the car pulled onto the infamous Las Vegas strip and to our only destination for the night: The Venetian Prince.

When we arrived at the colossal new building, we were greeted with crowds of hopefuls waiting in line at its entrance. Desperation hung thick in the air as we exited the car and walked through to the VIP section. We flashed the doorman our fancy laminated passes and within minutes were beckoned inside, much to the irritation of those still waiting in line.

The flashing lights and roaring music of the nightclub perfo-rated our senses as we wandered through the entranceway to the heart of the club. An expansive dance floor dominated the club's center, with wall-to-wall bartenders and seats surrounding the space. We were directed to our left and up a short flight of stairs, which led to a balcony overlooking it all. I saw no less than ten luxury black booths as we reached the top, each trimmed with gold filigree. We wandered over to the furthest of them after spotting some familiar faces amongst the crowd.

"Bonnie!" I shrieked as she came running out of the booth. "Happy birthday, beautiful!"

"Addie! April! This is fucking awesome right? Look at these booths!" She lounged over the side of our lavishly designated alcove.

"Come take a seat!" Brad, who was already sitting beside my friend, called out to us.

We slipped into the plush velvet booth and helped ourselves to the bottle of champagne on ice at its center.

"Girls, these are my friends Louie and Jack." Brad gestured to the two men sat to his right.

The man I assumed was Louie was dressed in a fitted blue polo and was undoubtedly handsome, with 'All-American captain of the football team' vibes. Jack on the other hand looked a bit more rebellious with visible tattoos and a low-cut black top. Neither one was particularly my type though. *Great.*

Bonnie sat on the other side of Brad with her other two friends, who I had only met a handful of times. They were all engaged in an enthusiastic debate on what shots to order, while April was making quick work of getting to know Louie and Jack.

"Are you in college?" Jack shouted across to me.

"Uh, no. I work at a loan company." I smiled, downing a mouthful of champagne. "What do you do?"

"I work in advertising." He pushed out his chest proudly.

"Cool."

"And you?" he asked, turning to April.

"I'm in retail," April said cheerfully. "Pays like shit, but at least I get discounted clothes." She shrugged and we giggled.

The idle chatter continued for several minutes as the men figured out their odds on leaving with us tonight.

I internally rolled my eyes as Jack made another play in my direction, and I shirked away from his hand as it came to rest against my leg under the table.

"I'm going to dance!" I declared, suddenly standing up and pulling April up along with me.

She shot me a knowing look as we walked the short distance down to the dance floor, weaving through a small break in the bodies packing the LED tiles. Hand in hand, we began swaying salaciously to the music.

One song morphed into another, and I found myself lost amongst the heavy bass and thuds of the track as it bled from the speakers. After a few more songs had ebbed away, Louie decided to join us with a goofy smile on his face. It was clear that he was trying to put the moves on April, and she was only too eager to accept the attention. Deciding I didn't want to become the third wheel to a tongue bath, I stepped away after a few moments and went over to one of the bars lining the room.

The place was jammed, and my five feet one inch didn't stand a chance of getting the bartender's attention, even with my VIP badge. After about ten minutes of trying and failing to get a drink, I turned back to the dance floor watching the gyrating bodies and pulsing strobes overhead.

"Excuse me, Ma'am?" A polite female voice broke me from my reverie.

It was one of the bartenders.

"This is for you." She placed a large cocktail in front of me on the bar.

"Um... I didn't order this," I admitted, looking at the drink.

It wasn't just any drink. It was a coconut lime spritzer—my favorite drink.

"It's from the gentleman over there." She nodded to her right, but I couldn't see anyone I recognized in that general area.

"Which gentleman? And this isn't spiked, is it?" I looked at the glass quizzically.

She snorted and looked in the direction she had nodded trying to locate the man.

"He was over there but now I don't see him..." She shook her head, giving up. "And no, the drink isn't spiked, I just made it."

"Well thanks, I appreciate it." She nodded and left, turning to serve the man next to me.

I picked up my cocktail and elbowed my way back to April and Louie, who were still dancing...or rather *groping* each other.

"Did either of you order this for me?" I shouted at them over the music. They both shook their heads 'no'.

I frowned.

"Someone else you know must be here; isn't that your favorite?" April shouted back over the music.

I looked around the room thinking perhaps one of my security guards had decided to enter the club despite my specific instructions to stay out, but to my confusion, I didn't see any of the familiar hulking men. Deciding it was probably a fluke, I gulped down my cocktail and started dancing alongside April. Louie looked just about ready to piss himself with the attention of two females on him, and I couldn't help but laugh at his ridiculous face as we enjoyed the music.

At some point a while later, we decided to head back to the balcony, and as we reached it, I felt my phone start buzzing in my clutch.

I fished it out and glanced at it as I continued up the stairs: 'No Caller ID'.

I didn't bother answering, stowing the phone away again as I re-joined the group. They had begun playing a risqué game of truth or dare, and I motioned to join in.

I sighed when my purse began buzzing again, but I ignored

it... until I couldn't anymore. Whoever was calling me was doing it *constantly*.

Irritated, I pulled my phone back out and slammed my finger against the green button.

"Hello?"

I couldn't hear much over the thudding of the speakers, but I knew whoever was on the other side wasn't speaking. Bored with whoever was spamming my phone, I hung up and took another sip of my cocktail.

Within two seconds, the screen lit up again with 'No Caller ID'.

Right—now I'm annoyed.

"Someone is trying to call me. I'll be right back," I shouted to April, who nodded and waved as I left.

I quickly headed back down to the main floor, and followed the signs to the smoking area located at the back of the club. By the time I pushed open the door and stepped out into the cool evening air, my phone had logged eight new missed calls. I ground my teeth in frustration and headed away from the thundering music.

"Who is this?" I demanded as the buzzing began again.

Instead of getting a response the line immediately went dead.

What the hell?

I stared at the blank screen stupidly, expecting them to call back.

They didn't. The phone remained silent.

"Unbelievable. I bet it's that damn security team..." I started mumbling.

I turned to head back toward the door, but the moment I did my body slammed against something hard, and I immediately felt hands pinning my arms harshly to my sides.

I opened my mouth to scream...

But the world had turned utterly and completely black.

———

THE NEXT THING I KNEW, my head was throbbing like hell and my mouth was as dry as sandpaper. I squeezed my eyes closed tightly, trying to block out the blinding sunlight, desperate to fall back asleep. I was exhausted and my body ached like I'd been laying awkwardly for—

Wait, sunlight?

My last memory was walking into the smoking area at The Venetian Prince.

I lurched forward with a start.

It took me a solid minute to realize that I wasn't at the club anymore, my mind struggling to keep up. I was, in fact, in a quiet room, on an enormous emperor sized bed... in a place completely unfamiliar to me.

The walls were painted a muted deep grey, interposed with chaotic abstract canvases. It held little in the way of furniture besides a modern leather chaise Léon and an eighty-inch flat screen facing the bed. It was cold and masculine...and unnerving.

Where the hell am I?

I threw myself out of the ridiculous bed, but my body was much less obliging than usual, and I ended up in a heap on the floor. My satin dress tore from the sudden movement.

"Ow! For Christ's sake!" I muttered in outrage.

"You're awake then."

I jumped at the sound of a deep, unfamiliar voice.

Apparently, the room wasn't as empty as I had thought.

Footsteps quickly rounded from the other side of the bed, revealing a six-foot-six man that resembled a dark-haired Adonis. He was immaculately dressed in a black suit, and his hair was pulled back into a bun with expertly shaved sides. He was beautiful...and a complete stranger. *Who in the actual fu—*

"My name is Jesse," He greeted, flashing me a handsome smile.

I immediately tried to heave myself up off the floor in a vague attempt at preserving my dignity, but my throbbing head made black spots dance in front of my eyes with each movement.

"Let me help you up, Adalyn." The man—Jesse—lifted me effortlessly from the floor and placed me in the center of the bed.

"H-how do you know my name? Wh-who are you?" I stammered.

He folded himself onto the nearby seat as he answered, "Lots of people know your name...and I already told you, my name is Jesse."

"Well...*Jesse*, can you tell me where I am?" I asked, letting an edge of frustration seep into my tone.

"Ah, I can't tell you that. That's better off coming from the Boss." He answered, unaffected.

"Boss? What boss?"

He immediately jumped up with his hands raised in the air as if he were speaking to a wild animal.

"Nope! I am not answering that question."

With surprising grace, the man wandered over to a sideboard and opened it, revealing a mini fridge packed with an assortment of drinks. He pulled out a water bottle, grabbed something from a nearby drawer and handed it to me.

"For your head." He said after I didn't take the box he offered. "You probably feel like crap. You've been sleeping for over twenty-four hours."

I gaped at him in shock. *Twenty-four hours? Who the hell are these people?*

"Drink up. Over there, you will find a walk-in closet. Everything in there is yours. The other door is to the bathroom." He gestured to the doors on the opposite side of the room, but my brain was stuck on the word 'yours'.

"I'll come get you in thirty. You look like shit, so probably a good idea to take a shower before you meet the Boss."

I audibly gulped, and he laughed at my anxiety.

"Oh, don't worry Adalyn. I'm your assigned bodyguard now, so I'll protect you." He winked and exited the room, locking it behind him.

As soon as the room stilled back into silence, questions raced across my groggy brain like a flame dancing on gasoline.

Boss? The club's boss? What the hell did he mean by bodyguard? And who in the hell are these people? I threw myself back onto the bed and growled in frustration, finding absolutely no answers.

I took the pills Adonis—I mean *Jesse*—had passed me, and after about ten minutes, my groggy head felt considerably better.

I made my way out of bed and slowly meandered into the bathroom on unsteady feet. It was bigger and grander than any bathroom I had ever been in before; simple yet ornate in design. An oval bath stood at the room's center before an illuminated panel of pure white marble. It was stunning.

One look in the mirror over the vanity and I almost died of embarrassment. The man had been right—I looked like complete and utter shit. My blonde hair was matted to the sides of my head and my makeup would have given the Joker a run for his money.

I quickly did my business and then stripped off my clothes, jumping into the spacious shower. With each minute under the hot steam the unease in my stomach grew.

Once I was finished, I dressed myself in a towel and headed to the closet next door in search of clothes. Clearly, my ripped dress was less than ideal, given I had no idea who I was supposed to be meeting imminently and didn't know where the hell I was.

I all but drooled on the floor when my feet hit the plush carpet.

The room was fitted with floor to ceiling cupboards stocked with racks upon racks of designer clothes, shoes, handbags and everything in between. Chanel, Gucci, Alaia... I spotted all my favorites amongst the colorful rails. A matching white dresser sat beside a comfy round pouffe, and I stumbled to it. Overcome with curiosity, I carefully pried open one of the drawers and swallowed back a gulp as my eyes settled on a beautiful array of glittering jewelry.

What is *all this?*

Frustration washed over me—I hated being so clueless.

Realizing I had taken my sweet time in exploring the room, I pulled out a pair of black leggings and a white Balmain graphic tee. After spotting the heavy bags under my eyes, I applied a quick layer of powder foundation I found, scooped my wet hair back into a ponytail, and called it good. Whoever the 'boss' was, he wasn't going to care about my appearance anyway.

I walked out of the dressing room to find a bored looking Jesse leaning against the other, now open, door across the room. He looked me over and grinned before gesturing, for me to lead the way out of the room.

After a few minutes of walking, I realized that the place we were in was in fact a house. A very *large* house.

Well, I'm definitely not in the club anymore. I gulped as cool tendrils of fear curled in my stomach.

We walked through a warren of tunnels before emerging on a large balcony overlooking an entrance hall. A perfectly polished imperial staircase connected the curved balcony to the room below. It was beautiful...and far too ostentatious to be in someone's home.

Jesse led the way as we descended and passed through various hallways, eventually stopping at a closed door. He knocked quickly before opening it and motioned for me to enter.

I gingerly stepped inside and was greeted with a large study, lined with bespoke walnut units and a matching polished desk. The room was somewhat similar to the bedroom I had woken up in and painted with a similar shade of muted grey.

All of this, however, was far less eye-catching than the young man sitting behind the desk and gazing at me with indifferent black eyes.

This man exuded nothing but power and wealth to an intimidating degree. From the stubborn set of his lightly stubbled jaw to his perfectly proportioned nose and the arrogant glint in his dark eyes, the man reeked of it. His crisp Armani suit and the gold Rolex on his wrist set my teeth on edge and senses on high alert. My earlier fear unfurled itself from my stomach and slivered down my spine at the sight.

The unfamiliar man's eyes dropped, scrutinizing my appearance, and I immediately regretted the casual clothes and wet hair I was sporting.

"Adalyn Mannino. It's nice to finally meet you."

CHAPTER
TWO

ADALYN

Hearing my real name from the beautiful man's lips made my heart pound furiously with adrenaline. My body tensed, preparing for an inevitable onslaught.

This is not going to be good.

"My name is Don Marco La Torre." He announced, eyes slicing to mine with an indifferent intensity that sent shock rolling in my stomach.

I had never heard the name before—but I didn't have to.

He was a Don. *Cosa Nostra.*

I was in the home of a rival family.

And they knew who I was.

"I've been watching you for a while now, Adalyn." He continued after a moment. "You see, the Mannino's double-crossed my family a long time ago and took something irreplaceable from me. So...when the opportunity presented itself, I decided to take something in return. You."

With a deliberate slowness that spoke of power and authoritarian control, he rose to his feet. Coming toward me with a predatory stalk that sent a chill down my spine. He languidly leaned against the rich mahogany before me, shooting me a gaze that was more predatory than it was human.

My God, the man was huge.

Not Adonis's level of huge, but *still*... He was right around the six-foot mark, and while his muscle density paled in comparison to the other man's, the Don had a more aggressive physic. A testament to a lifetime of discipline, persistence, and countless hours spent training, I was sure. Even to the most untrained eye, he looked the epitome of lethal.

I swallowed the frog in my throat and forced myself to look away from the man that more closely resembled the devil himself.

His fingers drummed absentmindedly against the desk beside him. "You belong to me now, as my hostage, and until your father meets my demands you will stay my hostage indefinitely."

Dread and fear leaked into my blood in equal measure. The hair on my arms rose as the realization of my situation hit me.

Shit.

I didn't know how I had found myself trapped here, who the hell this man was before me, or where in the godforsaken country I even *was* right now... but it didn't matter. Not really. All that mattered was the very real possibility of torment, pain, and brutality that awaited me until my father paid their ransom.

Assuming they would let me leave at all.

Unfortunately, I knew how Mafia men operated and knew that the odds of me leaving this situation unscathed while waiting for my ransom to be paid were dwindling by the second.

If I was going to survive, I had to think of something.

The only problem was I didn't have *anything* to offer him. I had been kept away from the family business my entire life, and I didn't have even the smallest bit of information that could help save me from this situation.

But I *had* to think of something. If I didn't... I didn't want to think about what could happen to me.

I had heard too many men being tortured by my cousins to not know what was coming for me. But, I had also watched the men of my family navigate conflict, master manipulation and perpetually act with an often-false sense of bravado, too. I had seen many men play this game every day of my life... Now my survival was going to rest on how well I could play that game, too.

I bit back my fear as an idea cemented itself in my head.

Here goes nothing.

I sighed loudly in irritation. As if being held a hostage was merely annoying as opposed to terrifying. "Have you even made contact with my family yet?"

The Don's expression darkened in what I was certain was insult. "*Obviously.*"

Clearly this man didn't like being questioned. Couldn't say I had met many Cosa Nostra men that did...but I filed that piece of information away for later anyway.

"Then I'm unconcerned." I dismissed. *Liar.* I shoved away my fear and forced myself to shrug with a nonchalance I didn't feel, "This will all be over soon enough."

"You seem oddly sure of yourself." The Don remarked, unimpressed.

A bead of sweat tracked down the back of my neck, keenly aware of how my next words could mean the difference between living, dying, or torture.

I didn't know what kind of man stood before me now or what he might be capable of, but I knew his type well enough to know a monster lived beneath his skin.

My lie was going to have to be a good one.

I hid my fear behind a smile, "Oh, *I am.* You see, you haven't just stolen some random Don's daughter that doesn't stand to inherit anything. You've stolen one of my father's greatest *assets*. Whatever ransom you're demanding, he'll pay it. And I wouldn't be surprised if he would pay you more if that meant my *safe* return."

A second ticked by in silence. My heart beat in my throat as the man seemed to evaluate me, weighing up my words and searching for something in my expression.

I prayed to God he didn't see the cracks in my façade.

I had never been a very good liar.

Eventually, he smirked.

"And, how exactly, are *you* an asset?" A cruel, calculating trace of humor colored his tone and I bristled.

"Because *I* can be used to negotiate alliances in a way few other deals can. Marriage is a very powerful institution in our culture, is it not? Through me, my father plans to expand his empire and forge alliances that are not only built on trust, but are *legally* binding. I would consider that an asset... Plus there is only one of me."

The Don's expression darkened, and his face hardened at my words as he saw the logic in my answer.

It didn't matter that it was a bold ass *lie*.

It was true that marriage contracts were the most powerful way to forge agreements, adding weight to even the most tumultuous business deals...but it wasn't exactly like my father was rushing to expand his empire, and I hadn't even caught so much as a whiff of a marriage contract being drawn up with my name on it. As far as I knew, my father wasn't that bothered about expanding the Mannino's reach outside of Las Vegas or about using me to broker an alliance.

But *he* didn't need to know that.

I crossed my arms and shot him a look I was hoping he would interpret for cool indifference.

"It goes without saying, but if you so much as lay a hand on me during my time as a hostage... *Well*, my father won't take too kindly to that. He would consider it an act of war and your family will be hunted long after the ransom's been paid. You'll all be dead within a year."

I prayed to God he didn't detect the subtle quiver in my tone.

"What makes you think I give a shit about starting a war?" Anger hit me the second I registered the *boredom* in his tone. Like he would much rather shove nails into his eyes and drink battery acid than continue speaking to me.

"Are you really that stupid?" I bit out.

And instantly regretted it.

Cool tendrils of dread coiled in my chest, culminating into fear when he took a step toward me. Within a second the man was in my face, towering over me with a large hand latched hard around my jaw. He wrenched my head up, forcing me to meet his furious gaze.

I winced at the pain but met his glare head on, refusing to show him any fear and desperate to cling to the facade of self-importance I had constructed.

"Not very smart for a mafia princess, are you?" He spat. The muscle of his jaw ticked as his fingers branded themselves against my skin. "Your family are *nothing* to players like me. I could exterminate every one of them before the end of the week if I wanted to. Your threats mean nothing." He promised.

Shit.

I *needed* him to think my family posed some kind of real threat—it was the only chance I had.

"Perhaps. Perhaps not. Let's just say you'd have more than only my family to exterminate if that was the case." I hissed back, fighting against the tightness in my jaw to get the words out.

His lips curled, flashing perfect white teeth.

"Bullshit." He said, calling my bluff.

Fear curdled my stomach.

I had to up my game. Double-down. I *had* to convince him. I didn't want to consider the alternative. *Couldn't* consider it.

Fortunately, I did know the name of one business associate of my father's... even if I had spent the last seven years trying to forget it.

"Not sure my father's deal with Arturo Lopez constitutes bullshit, but okay. I would be very careful not to underestimate your enemy, Don La Torre. After all, it is harder to fight a war that comes at you from both sides."

The muscle ticked in his jaw again but after a handful of seconds more, his hand released my face and he stalked away, preferring to glare at me from a distance. The material of his shirt pulled taunt as he crossed his arms, ever the picture of indifference.

"Fine." He said the word like it disgusted him.

Potent and consuming relief made the weight of my lies melt away the second the word reached my ears.

He believed it.

The story I had fabricated and spun to my advantage...it had been enough to protect me from the very worst this situation had to offer.

He wasn't going to hurt me.

"You will remain here, *unharmed*, until negotiations conclude with your father. The room you woke up in will be yours for the duration of your time here and you are free to move about the house, but you are not permitted to leave it."

I fought the urge to sink to my knees in gratitude, and I did my best to keep my expression neutral and cold. Much like the man's before me.

Our eyes fell into a kind of deadlock across the room. The stoic silence gnawed at my insides, making me feel all kinds of discomfort. I forced myself to ignore it. He was sizing me up, much like a predator sizes up his prey, and there was no way in hell I was showing him any weakness. Not *now*. Not after the foundations of my ruse had been poured.

"You are free to leave."

I didn't need telling twice.

I spun on my heel and walked out the door as swiftly as my legs could carry me.

————

MARCO

My earlier conversation with Adalyn had echoed between my ears since the second the door had snicked shut behind her.

From the moment I saw her across the bar at The Venetian Prince, I had been blindsided...and I hated it. Almost as much as I hated her blatant self-assuredness.

Adalyn Mannino was not what I had expected.

Her doe-like eyes and petite stature had inexplicably duped me. She had looked sexy as hell back at my club, and yet, she had carried herself in a way that told me she didn't know it. There was a distinct shyness about her that all but screamed *Cosa Nostra*.

But appearances were deceiving.

There was nothing innocent or submissive about the woman that stood before me in my study. Nothing doe-like about the woman who had threatened war against my family if I so much as touched her. My blood boiled into a rage at the memory.

Never in my life had I been shown such insubordination or contempt by someone who lacked any sort of power. Even those who were considered my rivals never dared. She was a Mafia Princess and had been keenly aware of who I was *before* the word 'stupid' had left her pretty little lips...and yet she hadn't hesitated to call me it. Just as she hadn't shown fear when I'd glared at her, her small jaw consumed by my hand.

I hadn't decided yet whether she was the bravest woman I had ever met or the most insolent. Either way, her disrespect had gotten to me. It pushed my buttons in a way few things ever did.

"Brother."

Jesse's voice broke through my internal dialogue, and I flexed my hand from the fist I had unknowingly formed.

I looked up at the two men who had entered the room.

"Communications with the Mannino's has started to decline." Benny informed me.

Benny was my consigliere and had worked for my family as an advisor for over thirty years, having served my father before me. He was a stout old man these days, but his advice had always been as sound as his reasoning.

He leaned forward in his chair to place a black phone on the desk between us. "I have proposed a meeting with them in the coming days. The location, for the time being, is undecided."

"Fine. I would suggest somewhere close to Las Vegas, but not close enough for them to band together should they need too. We don't need a bloodbath before the talking begins."

"Agreed. I will look at available options with Wyatt and Jesse this afternoon."

The older man rose from his chair, tipping his head in a show of respect before departing the office.

Jesse hauled himself down into the recently abandoned chair, "Looking a bit worse for wear there, Brother." He observed.

I dragged my hands down my face, feeling the tension in my forehead.

"She's a beauty, isn't she?" Jesse grinned.

"She is insolent and headstrong. A mafia princess should be raised better." I retorted.

Jesse just shook his head, "Well, I think it's admirable."

"Admirable?" I questioned, rising to my feet, and pouring some whiskey from the decanter nearby. I slid a tumbler over to Jesse as I re-took my seat. "How so?"

Jesse only deigned to answer after he had chugged back some of the amber liquor. "There's not many men in this world, let alone a *woman*, who would stand up to you the way she did today. Any other person would have cried, begged at your feet, or accepted their fate without a word. Instead, Adalyn stood before you and threatened *you* with her family's worst. She has more balls than I have for doing that."

"Or she's just stupid." I muttered.

He tipped up his glass with a smile. "You and I both know her GPA says otherwise."

It was true; it was in the file Jesse had compiled on her and her entire family.

I sighed. "She is going to be a challenge."

"And you thought the hard part would be these negotiations." He laughed and tipped back the glass, downing the rest in one. "Which reminds me, I have an inmate to take care of."

My lips quirked in a smile as he got to his feet and promptly departed the study.

The moment the door snicked shut behind him, I let out a heavy sigh I'd been holding since the moment Adalyn Mannino had walked into my life.

I took a mouthful from my tumbler and retrieved the phone from across the desk. The screen lit up with a picture of Adalyn and the friend I had seen her dancing with the other night at the club. I clicked on the messages and call history, reviewing the communications between us and the Mannino's.

Benny was right—they were dwindling. Their responses had started coming slower over the last two days and were increasingly sparse. Irritated, I put the device on the desk, and I glared at the phone.

Adalyn's phone.

Lured by curiosity instead of reason, I retook the device and began scrolling through its contents for an entirely *different* reason.

Her photo album was surprising in that it told me almost nothing about her. The images were entirely ordinary, consisting of her friends, her car and outfit ideas she clearly liked. Nothing of any real note.

I gritted my teeth in frustration but quickly calmed back down when I noted the numerous apps for social media. I scrolled through them all, seeing the things she liked or followed. The conversations she had been having.

There was one in particular that caught my attention.

Seems my hostage has a naughty side.

I scanned through some of the pictures she had sent to someone called 'Jason'. Anger tinged with arousal pooled in my gut as I stared at a risqué photo of Adalyn in some intricate lingerie. Her delicate face pulled into a timidly patient smile.

My dick instantly hardened and began throbbing.

I quickly clicked on the other two images she had sent, skirting around the dick pictures also present amongst the chat history.

I almost creamed in my goddamn pants.

Fucking hell.

The final picture was of Adalyn in a sexy black lace outfit complete with suspenders. Her nipples were like hardened beads against the tight strip of fabric cradling her chest. Her panties mere spindly little scraps of material at her sides.

I'm going straight to hell for this.

Not that I cared one tiny bit. Someone like me was going to go straight to hell anyway... Might as well enjoy the descent.

I retrieved my own phone and air-dropped the images across to it, saving them.

I was going to need them for later when I was in the privacy of my own room... For *research* I told myself.

―――――

ADALYN

The second I had reached my room that afternoon, I had started devising a plan.

I pressed my face against the glass of one of the windows and sighed upon seeing the steep drop to the ground below. It was steep enough that I wasn't confident I could walk away from it. There wasn't a perfectly manicured bush, ledge, or anything else I could use to break the fall either, and I all but cried with frustration.

I have to get out of here.

If I was wholly confident on my family's ability to pay the ransom, then I would have barely considered trying to escape. But the truth was... I wasn't counting on it. On *them*. What if Don La Torre wanted something my family couldn't give them? What if they wanted my father dead as part of the exchange? They were things my family were never going to deliver on and whether I liked it or not, I wasn't worth *that* to my family.

I was just a Don's daughter. I wasn't even an heir.

I was going to have to find another way to save myself... and the window had looked like my best option up until five minutes ago.

I threw myself back across the expanse of bed.

I need a new plan.

―――――

By eight o'clock that evening I found one.

I had spent hours listening to the movements of the house and keeping track of how busy the halls of the mansion were. It wasn't the best reconnaissance mission I had ever launched, but it was better than being totally blindsided. No one would be expecting me to run on the first night anyway... It was the best shot I had.

When dinner was brought to my room shortly after eight, I wolfed it down to build up strength. I didn't know what I would do if I did make it out of wherever-the-hell-I-was, but I sure as shit didn't have any money on me to buy food for a while if I did.

At about ten, Adonis—*Jesse*, knocked on my door to say he was turning in for the night and said if I needed anything he was in the room across the hall. I was going to have to be extra quiet while leaving, given how close his door was to mine when I sneakily took in its proximity. *Fantastic.*

By eleven, I had found a travel bag in the dressing room and loaded it with a few water bottles, my medicine that I—albeit unnervingly—found in one of the drawers, and two Chanel handbags.

What? He said they were mine, I reasoned.

With my essentials packed, I threw on some new leggings, an oversized top, and a jacket before sitting on my bed and waiting for the clock to hit twelve.

The moment it did, I eased the bedroom door open and listened for any signs of movement from either Jesse's room or further down the hall.

After waiting a few minutes and hearing nothing but ominous silence, I tiptoed down the passageway and descended the steps.

Deciding that the front door was probably too obvious an option, I edged through the halls until I came to the furthest room in the house. I pushed open one of the windowpanes and all but squealed with excitement as it opened fully. I threw myself through it and ended up head-first in a pile of leaves and sticks.

"Ow! A fucking bush?"

I tried to make as little noise as possible while disentangling myself from the spindly branches, swallowing back a few yelps in the process. Eventually, I landed on the grass on the other side.

After finding my feet, I headed across the patio and ran across the grass with no idea where the hell I was heading. My initial excitement at escaping the house was short lived when after a few short minutes of running I was greeted by an imposing eight-foot-tall brick wall.

Bollocks.

There was definitely no way I was getting over *that* monstrosity, so I followed it around hoping it would finally lead to a gate or entry point of some kind. After walking a while and seeing nothing, I came across a break in the brickwork. It was a solid double gate, positioned at the end of a tarmacked road leading away from the house.

Knowing I needed to move quick to avoid detection, I felt for any ridges I could get a leg over. To my dismay, the wood was totally smooth.

With climbing over it out of the picture, I dropped to the floor to see if I could squeeze myself under—I fit, but just barely. It was going to be tight, but not impossible.

I tossed the duffle bag over the top of the gate and edged my way under, scraping myself along the tarmac and stones. I wiggled myself free on the other side and stood up, brushing away all the dirt as I turned to face the road.

"Good evening."

"Fuck!" I screeched, jumping out of my skin.

Jesse was leaning causally against the front of an all-black armored Mercedes G-Wagon, parked up not five feet from the gate.

The engine wasn't even running—like he had been there for a while.

"You do realize that the gate was unlocked, right?" He laughed, clearly enjoying himself.

"Yeah right." I sighed and picked up my bag up from the floor.

My escape plan was foiled. Bitter disappointment weighed on my shoulders.

"It was. I opened it for you to see what you'd do." He chuckled.

"Just shut up."

He walked around to the passenger side of the car and opened the door, gesturing with a hand for me to get in.

"Get in, Bandit. I'll take you back."

I scowled at the new nickname and tossed him my bag, getting into the SUV before slamming the door behind me. A few moments passed before Jesse climbed into the driver's seat, shaking with laughter.

"Something funny?" I demanded, turning my whole body to face him as he turned the key.

"Your get-away bag literally has nothing but handbags in it." He eventually managed to get out.

"They are *Chanel* handbags! What was I supposed to do?" I answered furiously as he started the car.

With a ghost of a smile lingering on his lips, he pressed a button on the dash and the gates swung open to allow us to pass. We followed the tarmac up a slight incline for a couple of minutes until the front of the house came into view, illuminated by hundreds of exterior lights.

I say house, but in reality, it resembled a palace much more than any house I'd ever seen. It was regal to an intimidating degree. A beige stone palace right smack in... *Where the hell was*

I? Whoever Don La Torre was, he almost certainly had more money than God.

The SUV rolled to a stop in front of a stone portico that framed the main entrance. I sighed, resigning myself to the fact that I wouldn't be leaving the house again for God-knows how long... *maybe not ever.* Something clutched painfully at my chest.

I might die here.

The realization that my death was a not just possible but potentially inevitable, hit me like a bucket of ice. Whether my ransom was paid or not, whether my ruse was believed or not, my odds of getting out of this situation alive were slim to none. And based on the apathetical Don that lived behind these walls, there was a chance I was already living on borrowed time.

Attempting to run away was surely a punishable offence by the Don's standard, ransom or not. What was going to happen to me now?

Nausea rolled in my stomach and my ears rang painfully.

"Are you going to get out? The front door is unlocked," Jesse prompted.

"I-I—" My chest constricted again, and I couldn't catch a breath.

I started shaking uncontrollably, and black spots danced in my vision. My breathing coming in fits and starts—a panic attack. I was having a panic attack.

Out of my periphery I saw Jesse jump out of the car but barely recognized I was being moved until he was crouched in front of me through my now open door. His mouth opening as if he were speaking, but I couldn't make out the words over the incessant ringing in my ears and fear clutching at my chest.

I glanced at the intimidating man before me, his hands

capturing mine as he tried to get my attention. Trying to calm me.

With a harsh tug on my hands, I finally began hearing his voice amongst the suffocating silence, "Look at me, Adalyn. Everything is okay. You are well. You are safe." He kept repeating the words over and over.

I concentrated on his voice, slowing my breathing to the words until the tightness in my chest subsided enough that I could let in a breath of air. Slowly, my breathing became steadier and stronger as the seconds wore on. The tightness lifting infinitesimally with each breath.

When my head cleared and my senses eventually returned, I looked down at our entangled hands in embarrassment.

"I'm sorry. That was pathetic." I croaked, pulling my hands away and swatting some of my escaped tears.

"Not pathetic."

"Yeah, it is. I don't know what happened." I admitted. "I think it just hit me that I'm probably going to die here. Or worse." I shrugged, faking nonchalance with the statement.

Jesse just chuckled and shook his head as he stood up.

"You aren't going to die here or anything else." He said seriously. "Don La Torre is not a monster."

I laughed in disbelief. "You don't know Don's very well then."

"I'd say I do. The Boss and I grew up together and I knew his late father very well too. Marco is no monster." He pulled the door wider and gestured exaggeratedly between the SUV and the entryway. "Now are you going to get your ass out of my car or are you planning on running away again?"

I climbed down from my seat and walked back into the house dejectedly.

I turned just before I started up the stairs to my room.

"Jesse," I called after the retreating man's form already halfway across the foyer, heading further into the house.

He paused. "What, Bandit?"

"Thank you for helping me...in the car."

He winked and smiled up at me. "No problem. Saving damsels in distress is kinda my thing. Now get your ass in bed before you get into any more trouble."

I nodded and did as he suggested, going back to my room.

I immediately stripped off my clothes and crawled under the silk sheets.

Well, that didn't go to plan. I thought bitterly.

Although my escape attempt had been a colossal failure, it had given me comfort to know that at least *someone* here seemed friendly... Perhaps even kind.

I tried to ignore the voice that told me that that *someone* also happened to be best friends with my captor.

CHAPTER
THREE

ADALYN

O ver the next few days, I didn't so much as stray from the confines of my room.

To my surprise, no one came to punish me on the first day after my escape attempt and by the second one, Jesse had even come to keep me company. If he had known I was about to be killed, tormented or beaten, he certainly wasn't showing signs of it. By that afternoon I was feeling considerably better about my chances of being alive the following day and fell asleep without barricading the door like I had the previous night.

The next morning, with the birds chirping and the halls of the mansion silent, I felt the last of my immediate fears die away.

If I was going to be punished for attempting to flee, he would have done it already.

Dons were never the type for delayed gratification anyway... or at least they *rarely* were. Perhaps my warning had held more sway than I had originally thought?

Half wanting to test the theory, half wanting to get the crap away from the monotonous four walls of my room, I decided to bite the bullet and head downstairs, silently praying my confidence had not been misplaced.

Quietly, I managed to retrace the steps I had taken with Jesse when meeting the Don for the first time. Not stopping until I found myself confronted by a familiar vacant hallway with a single door housed at the end of it. The door was now left partially ajar, a sliver of light glinting against the polished tile flooring.

I hesitated at the sight, not sure what my next move was going to be.

I wanted to know what was going on with my ransom but... did I have enough power in this situation to just go sauntering into his office and demand answers?

I was caught between marching down the hall like I owned the damned place and skulking back to my room like the submissive I normally was, when the indistinct sound of voices floated to where I was standing.

Sucking in a quiet breath, I tiptoed the distance between my spot and the door, the voices becoming clearer with each step.

I shoved aside every instinct that screamed at me I was going to get caught—I needed answers.

"You cannot just send them away!" a male scoffed. The voice was unfamiliar and gruff as if with years of experience.

"I can and I will." Jesse responded cooly. "If they can't put aside their own personal hatred then they can't be here. It poses too much of a risk."

"It is not as if their hatred is unjustified." another male voice responded.

"*Layton.*" another said, warning coloring their tone.

"Regardless of their reasons, allowing them near her is too much of a risk. It could cost us everything," Jesse argued.

Her? *Me.*

They're talking about me.

The hairs on the back of my neck rose as fear laced with dread weaved its way across my skin.

"Hasn't it cost us everything already?" the older man spoke again, triggering the responses of numerous men—around ten I'd have guessed—and sending the room into complete chaos. Each man shouting to be heard over the other.

"ENOUGH!" The Don's command rang out at the same time a loud thud echoed about the room, causing the men to fall into silence.

"I will not have any of my men putting this negotiation at risk and causing an all-out war for the sake of misplaced retribution. Adalyn is not the enemy—Alberto is. The sooner you all realize that the sooner I can be done with this stupid conversation and begin sorting out this mess with the Manninos. *No one* is touching her. If I hear so much as a taunt, a threat or learn of *anyone* defying that order then they will have me to fucking answer to."

The distinct sound of a chair being pushed back and then the clinking of glassware trickled out from the door. The only noise amongst the otherwise silent room.

"Hunter and Ross will be immediately removed from the property as Jesse has suggested, and anyone else that isn't onboard with the program can be reassigned as well. Everyone in this room should heed that warning. If any of you betray the trust I have placed in you, then you will pay for it with your life."

Shit.

I swallowed thickly as I stepped back. Away from the sliver of light and away from the lethality of the voice that trickled out of it.

I didn't linger long. The conversation swiftly moved on from me and my ransom to the logistics of where the displaced men would be assigned to and the practicalities of moving other men onto the property in their place.

I quietly crept back down the hallway and eventually found myself by the front entrance. I took a seat on one of the marble steps at the foot of the elaborate staircase, the stone bitterly cold as it bled through my leggings.

He isn't going to hurt me, I realized.

In fact, he had just threatened his men with death if they so much as touched me.

That meant that I wasn't about to be tied to a chair, beaten or shackled to a cellar wall, and even if I were, wouldn't they have done that already? My botched escape the other night would certainly have given them justifiable motive and yet... they hadn't taken it. They had left me alone.

He was worried about the repercussions.

A small smile pulled at the corner of my lips.

That meant I wasn't just a hostage to them anymore—I was someone of *value.*

And that changed everything.

———

THE NEXT MORNING, I woke in a cautiously optimistic mood.

My father had been told of my capture and would pay my ransom soon enough. It was just a matter of time before it would be paid... I hoped. Family was family. It didn't matter that I stood to inherit nothing or wielded next to no power, we were the Cosa Nostra. We *never* turned our backs on family.

All I had to do was bide my time until my family came for me...and that meant not only maintaining the ruse I had fabricated during my first day of captivity, but it also meant trying *not* to make Don La Torre want to kill me anymore than he already did.

This is going to be tricky.

Allured by the strong smell of bacon and eggs wafting through the mansion, I got dressed and padded downstairs in search of breakfast at a little after nine the next morning. I followed my nose until I came across an extravagant white kitchen and the source of the smell: a small dark-haired older woman. She was merrily bouncing around the kitchen with various pots and pans in her hands, cooking up a storm.

She smiled kindly at me as I appeared in the doorway and quickly hurried over.

"Good morning, Miss Adalyn. I'm Lucia, the housekeeper and cook. Your food is out there in the garden room, but please let me know if there is anything else you would like," Lucia said kindly and gestured to the glass double doors on the other side of the room.

Before I could mutter my thanks, she quickly scurried back to her station and continued flipping the bacon sizzling away in a pan. Curious, I wandered over to the doors she had referred to as the garden room.

Peeking through them, I was met with a bright and airy room, adorned with floor to ceiling arched windows and glass doors that led out onto a veranda. The room was decorated in an array of different shades of cream and accented with gold filigree that beautifully caught in the bright morning sun. A selection of ceramic pots at the room's edge housed various towering species of plants, their leaves a startling green against the tameness of the room. It was both peaceful and spectacular.

A small table sat nestled beside one of the ornate windows and I was surprised to see Jesse already seated, shoveling bacon into his mouth as if he hadn't eaten in a week.

"You'll catch flies with your mouth open like that, Bandit." I rolled my eyes at the nickname he had bestowed on me since my escape attempt but took a seat opposite the hulking man.

The table was covered in various fruits, yogurts, pancakes, cooked meats and pastries. There was something for even the pickiest of eaters. My mouth watered as I stacked a couple of pancakes on my plate and drizzled them with maple syrup.

"This is a bit much, isn't it?" I asked, gesturing to the food.

"Boss didn't know what breakfast you'd like so he ordered some of everything." Jesse shrugged, as if enough food for eight people being served for just one wasn't ridiculously wasteful.

"I normally have granola and yogurt for breakfast, but if I have a choice then I choose pancakes." I forked a piece into my mouth and smiled at him.

"Gottcha." He nodded, faking seriousness before gulping down some orange juice.

"Has there been any news?" I asked, knowing he would understand my meaning. I hid my gaze, trying hard not to look too interested in the answer.

Jesse just shrugged. "Not sure."

My gut told me he knew more than he was letting on, but I didn't push it. I was starting to warm up to Jesse after the last few days, and I really needed someone on my side.

I bit back my disappointment and changed the subject instead. "What's on the agenda for today then?"

"Your schedule is wide open." He flashed me a grin. "*I,* on the other hand, have some urgent errands to take care of today, so I'll have to leave you to your own devices."

A spark of hope lit in my chest.

Catching my expression, he quickly added, "But before you get any ideas...you are *still* under house arrest. There are harsher people around than me, Bandit; just remember that."

———

THE REST of breakfast passed by in silence, and soon enough, I found myself in the confines of my room, aimless and looking for something to do.

Realizing I had yet to fully explore my *temporary* wardrobe,

I decided to spend a few hours reorganizing the many colorful rods to my taste and removing things I was certain I'd never wear. Once happy with my work, I moved on to explore different outfit options and hung them all separately for future use—not that I was particularly enthralled with the idea of spending a significant amount of time as a captive.

Lucia brought lunch to my room and after scarfing down the delicious caprese salad, I played around on the television, watched a few shows, and then snooped through the cabinets in the bathroom.

When the sun started drifting toward the horizon, I threw myself against the bed with a huff. Bored and irritated, I allowed my mind to drift.

It was now well over seventy-two hours I had been away from my family. *Would they be looking for me? Did they know where I was?* I hated not knowing.

Growing frustrated with the lack of news and being left alone for most of the day, I decided I wanted answers.

The halls were silent as I marched through them, retracing my steps to locate the Don's study. After a couple of wrong-turns, I eventually located a door with two men stationed either side of it.

"Can I speak to Don La Torre? It's important," I directed to the taller and burlier one of the two.

They both appeared late thirties or early forties, judging by the fullness of one of their beards and frown lines marring the other's tanned skin. One gave me a stoic once over, while the other knocked on the door and disappeared behind it. After waiting half a minute in tense silence with the bearded one, the other re-emerged from the room and resumed his post.

"Don La Torre is currently unavailable," He said gruffly.

Excuse me?

"This is important," I argued, knowing from the bored expression on his face that my words were futile.

When I didn't get another response, I sighed in exasperation and stormed back upstairs to my room, furious.

Don La Torre not only had the audacity to kidnap me, but he was now set on totally ignoring my existence. I might be his hostage, but I had a right to know what was going on. It was my freedom at stake.

I paced about in frustration, trying to come up with a plan. What would someone with the upper hand do?

They would make *the Don talk to them.*

A wild grin contorted my face as an idea cemented itself in my head.

I switched on the speaker bar from under the flat screen and scanned through the channels until a heavy metal music station flashed on the screen. I adjusted the volume to the max and music instantly screamed through the room so loudly I had to put my hands over my ears.

Chuckling to myself, I ran into my closet to find the fluffy earmuffs I had spotted earlier when organizing. I threw them on to dampen some of the sound and perched on the bed, waiting for the inevitable scolding.

A minute ticked by.

Then another.

I frowned, disappointed that yet *another* plan seemed to be failing.

This time I wouldn't give up so easily. I adjusted some of the settings on the television, cranking up the bass until the whole room started rattling to the beat. *This will do it.*

I laid back on my bed and waited, trying to contain a maniacal laugh.

One minute... Two.

Sure enough, the door slammed open with a whoosh not a second later.

I was instantly surprised to see the Don stalking into the

room instead of one of his lackeys. He stopped at the foot of my bed, glaring at me with absolute fury in his eyes. I gulped.

Perhaps I have bitten off more than I can chew...

"What the fuck are you doing?" He yelled.

I just shook my head and gestured to the music, pretending I couldn't hear him. A muscle in his jaw twitched and he turned, storming over to the source of the noise. The television turned black, and the sudden absence of sound was painful.

The Don then turned back to me, face tensed in anger as I removed my ear muffs.

"I'm sorry, what were you saying?" I asked sweetly.

"You are playing with fire, Adalyn. If there is one thing I do not tolerate it is insubordination." He spat.

"Insubordination? I was just listening to music." I insisted innocently.

I'll damn well show him insubordination! My temper bubbled.

"And the other night?" He demanded.

The innocent smile on my face faltered and the words I wanted to shout at him suddenly caught in my throat. Jesse must have told him...

That rat bastard!

"And before you ask, no Jesse didn't tell me. I had five other people watching you *escape* into a bush." He mocked darkly, approaching the bed once more.

I thought I saw a smile twitch on his lips, and I glared in response. Color flooded my cheeks in embarrassment.

"Try it again and you will be punished." He promised.

My heart spluttered with the threat, but it was somewhat short lived. Hadn't he just said no one was allowed to touch me yesterday?

Guess it's time to test the theory...

I swallowed back my lingering unease, "You won't hurt me."

The Don folded his arms across his chest with indifference,

glaring at me with dark, impenetrable eyes. "That sounds oddly like a challenge."

"It isn't—it's an observation. Hurting me *will* cost your family and mean war." I shrugged, and his jaw ticked in obvious frustration. "It seems like a high price to pay for a bit of retribution." I added, playing to the comment he had made to his own men just the day before.

His voice was cool like steel, "Do you really think I give a fuck about preventing a war? I do what I want. If I wanted you dead, you'd *be* dead. Remember that."

His harsh words sent a chill down my spine and a tingle through my blood that wasn't entirely unpleasant.

The Don's indifferent glare burned into me for a moment longer before he turned on his heel and stalked out, slamming the door behind him.

———

That evening, I kept my head down and ate dinner in my room, deciding it was probably best *not* to piss the Don off twice in one day. As much as my lies appeared to be working... I wasn't sure they were going to be enough if I pushed the Don too far.

Instead of causing any more trouble, I threw on some drama series on Netflix and tried to forget about the real-life dramas of being held hostage by a rival crime syndicate.

It was working until Jesse waltzed in and announced he wanted to watch a movie. Initially, I blew him off, not wanting company, but eventually, I relented to his constant pestering and easy-going humor.

After a considerable amount of bickering, we decided to put on 'The Silence of the Lambs', and much to my dismay, Jesse ate his way through my entire mini fridge, pointing out plot holes as he went. Not only provoking my irritation, but also my sincere amusement whenever I managed to prove him wrong.

By the time the credits scrolled across the screen, it was late evening, and Jesse excused himself for bed. I took a quick shower before turning in myself, feeling completely exhausted.

Despite being groggy and tired, I tossed restlessly for a few hours but never seemed to quiet my mind enough for sleep. Thoroughly annoyed, I eventually gave up and pushed on my slippers to walk downstairs in search of my sleep medicine— hot chocolate. I made my way quietly through the vacant halls until I found the familiar white kitchen. I flicked on the light and rummaged around in the cupboards until I located some milk and cocoa powder.

A few minutes later, and feeling a small sense of achievement, I had a delicious smelling mug of hot, chocolaty goodness.

I padded back to the hallway and climbed the stairs to my room. My foot had just grazed the top step when a soft noise made me pause.

Was that...

Another moan drifted from the hallway to my right.

Before I even registered that I was moving, I found myself walking toward the source of the sound—a closed double door. I got within two meters of it before freezing.

Yup, that's definitely sex.

I was close enough now to hear that the moan was from a female, though whether that female was of the human species I had no clue. She squawked like a fucking gremlin.

My cheeks reddened when the word "Please" bled from behind the door in a awfully high-pitched voice.

"Please what?"

Shit.

The rough, masculine voice that followed was unmistakable.

44

My heart fluttered violently in response, and the cup in my hand shook so much it threatened to spill.

It took two seconds for me to process exactly *who* was behind that door before I sprang into action. Half tiptoeing, half running, I sped back past the balcony and down the hall to my room.

I placed the mug to the side and breathed out a heavy sigh, relieved I hadn't been caught.

It was then that I decided I was angry.

Angry that I knew nothing about what was happening. Angry that I was trapped in a gold-gilded cage with no way out, and angry that there was not a damn thing I could do about it. I was also angry that despite having so many things to be angry about, I was angriest of all that the great Don La Torre was getting his kicks across the hall while my life hung in the balance.

Fury curled in the pit of my stomach.

If he thought I would just accept my fate and play the role of powerless little hostage, he had another thing coming.

I would make him regret the day he ever decided to take me captive.

A wicked smile crept to my lips.

Oh, it is so on.

CHAPTER
FOUR

ADALYN

"Wow, you look like shit." Jesse whistled as I walked into the garden room the next morning.

"Thanks, asshole." I muttered on reflex.

My lifetime of submissiveness seemingly smothered in only one hundred and twenty hours.

Part of me said it was survival, but a bigger part of me knew I had always been this way—audacious and strong-willed. It had just been beaten out of me. Trampled on until my instinct was no longer to assert my opinion, but to bend to the wills of others. It wasn't tolerated in the Cosa Nostra: women having an opinion on their lives. After all, who were we to question the will of men?

It was why I had always felt like I didn't belong. Like I was a square peg being forced into a round hole half its size. It's funny how being trapped in this cage had also made me feel free. Perhaps not physically...but in other ways.

Troubled by that thought, I settled into the same chair I had commandeered the previous morning and poured myself a coffee.

"Couldn't sleep? You didn't have nightmares about Hannibal Lecter, did you?" Jesse mocked, bringing his own cup of black coffee to his lips.

I flipped him the bird and took a bite of the warm, syrup covered pancake that was already laid out for me.

"You need to try and keep your head down today, Adalyn." Jesse's serious tone caught my attention. "There are visitors coming to the house this afternoon, and it would be wise to stay out of their way."

His tone was ominous enough for me to decide that the meeting wasn't going to be a good one.

"Does it have something to do with the ransom?" I tried my best to sound nonchalant.

"Yes and no," He responded airily, shoving a load of bacon into his mouth and refusing to continue.

Realizing that Jesse had already told me more than any other person in this godforsaken house—or rather *mansion*—I dared to ask another question. "Do you know what is going on with it?"

"We're in talks. That's all I know."

I nodded and pretended to look bored while a small bubble of hope erupted in my chest.

Jesse finished up before jumping out of his seat and shrugging into his black blazer. "Right, I've got to get security tightened before the visit. If you need me, just ask someone to radio me."

"Tighten security? I thought you were my babysitter," I yelled after him. He stopped at the door to shoot me a look.

"Babysitter? No, Bandit. I'm head of security." He winked at me before exiting.

I sighed into the now silent room.

My babysitter was head of security...

It felt a bit excessive but made sense given I was effectively a fugitive within the Don's family home. It also wasn't that surprising given the death-glares I frequently got from the meat-head Mafiosos that paraded the halls.

A chill ran down my spine realizing that most of them probably fantasized about killing me.

I ate the rest of my breakfast alone, running through fictional scenarios on how to defend myself should any of the lackeys decide they'd had enough of me. Even if Marco had given them a direct order...one could never be too careful.

After about half an hour, Lucia came in to clear the table, and I jumped on the opportunity to ask her for a tour around the mansion, secretly praying she would keep me company for at least some of the day. To my intense relief, she accepted the invitation.

As it turned out, the mansion was set over three main floors. The basement housed a cinema, commercial kitchen for events, a gym, and indoor pool complete with a sauna and jacuzzi area. On the first floor, there were four beautifully decadent living spaces, a formal dining hall as well as numerous other rooms, some of which I had already been in. The top floor consisted of over six guest bedrooms with luxury on-suites, without Jesse's or mine included in that figure.

The entire upstairs East wing housed rooms belonging solely to Don La Torre. Lucia only gestured to the ornate, polish wood doors I had stood before the previous night, and I was somewhat grateful we didn't venture inside.

We then stepped outside, exiting through the garden room veranda to walk the grounds of the home. There was an outdoor pool, numerous formal garden spaces, as well as a large, terraced area that was designed for hosting large family gatherings. By the end, I was in total awe of the place—not only by the sheer size of the property, but by the eye-watering wealth that saturated its walls.

I had once considered my family extremely rich, especially prior to our move from Las Vegas to Boulder...but this? This made my family look like mere street peddlers.

This was wealth in a league unto its own.

I was surprised to find that I enjoyed my time with Lucia. She had a motherly, warm way about her, and I couldn't help but feel reassured with her mere presence by my side walking through the mansion's halls. If someone as gentle as Lucia could survive here, then it meant there was a chance Jesse was right about Don La Torre not being entirely monstrous in how he managed the family business.

When she left for the kitchen, I skipped upstairs to 'my' room and found a neon pink bikini amongst one of the many drawers in the closet. I quickly changed and threw on a sheer black cover up with some sandals before raiding the bathroom for a large towel, content to spend my day by the pool. I headed back outside to one of the rattan loungers by the pool and set down my various items, stretching out and basking in the blazing midday sun.

After only thirty minutes, the heat had started to become suffocating, and I decided it was time to take a dip into the water. The pool was cool and refreshing as I swam several laps along its length before floating idly along the surface a while.

After I had cooled down sufficiently, I heaved myself onto the side and laid back against the hot stone.

I wonder if there are any inflatables—

A shadow stretched over me.

"What the fuck are you doing?"

My eyes jolted open in surprise.

I gulped when I saw whose shadow it was.

The Don stood over me, hands on his hips in an obvious display of exasperation. He was glaring and if looks could kill... then this man could have had the world on its knees in less than thirty seconds.

Heat that *didn't* entirely originate from the sun lit my skin ablaze.

"Do you ever say anything else?" I asked absentmindedly, like my stomach wasn't doing nervous somersaults at his sudden presence.

Despite the heat, he was wearing the same outfit I had seen him in before: black slacks and a black, collared shirt. The only difference now was that the cuffs of his shirt were rolled to his elbows, revealing two muscular forearms that were covered in intricate black ink.

I pulled my sunglasses down slightly, raking my eyes over his body in a way that was intended to unnerve him.

"You know you would be quite handsome if you ever stopped scowling." I said as acerbically as I could.

Men rarely looked bored when surveying me. I wasn't exactly *Margot Robbie*, but my toned waist and bubble butt weren't wholly uninspiring, especially when I was in a skimpy-ass bikini like I was right now...and yet, I had seen flies look more interested. I swallowed back my irritation.

"I wouldn't have to scowl if you just behaved." His voice was as bland as his face.

"What is your problem? I'm not doing anything!"

He was being completely impossible.

"The problem is that I have some...*difficult* visitors arriving in a few minutes and you are pissing about in a bikini." His words were calm, but I could hear an undercurrent of anger seeping through.

I looked down at my bathing suit, inspecting it. It was a cute pink string set and while it did leave little to the imagination, it concealed all the important parts of my body.

"There is nothing wrong with my bikini." I protested, crossing my arms angrily while glaring up at him.

"Oh, really? Because that there,"—he pointed over his shoulder to one of the nearby windows—"is my office and I can assure you that it hasn't covered up a whole lot since you got out here." His lips twitched as if he found that information humorous somehow.

My cheeks burned with embarrassment.

The Don's gaze suddenly dropped from my face, roaming down my neck before settling on my chest. He quirked a brow and I glanced down.

Frustratingly, my crossed arms had disturbed the material of my bikini, revealing the dusky pink of my nipple.

"Perv," I muttered and yanked the material back into place.

His gaze fell to the side, and he smirked before picking up my towel and tossing it at me.

"Go inside. Now." He ordered, smirk vanishing as quickly as it came.

I huffed, lifting my legs out of the pool and rose to my feet. I marched over to the lounger to collect my things, anger simmering to a boil when I felt his judgmental glare brush against my skin.

Unable, or perhaps unwilling, to restrain my searing temper, my smart mouth opened before any sense of self-preservation could kick in, "Whatever, Marco. Fuck you."

I held my breath and prayed that the ground would swallow me up and take me straight to hell, or perhaps a plane would fall out of the sky and hit the yard, but it was too late. The words were out of my idiotic—apparently *suicidal*—mouth.

Moron.

One second. Two sec—

His hand latched onto the back of my neck, yanking me around to face him viciously. The Don's furious face was suddenly only inches from my own. His depthless coal eyes piercing me to my soul.

I didn't dare meet them, dropping my gaze to his prominent and closely shaved—but stupid, definitely *stupid*—jawline.

"What was that?"

His words were as lethal as a razor and in that moment, I got a flavor of what it would feel like to die by this man's hand. It felt like all-consuming power and smelled like rich spice.

"Speak to me with disrespect again and I'll—"

"Kill me?" I interrupted.

I knew that he couldn't. That he needed me alive in order to broker this deal with my family and to avoid an all-out war... and if Jesse had been right, too...then that meant the hot-headed Don before me didn't have any real intention of hurting me. It was an empty threat...and judging by the muscle ticking in his jaw, my guess was right, and he knew it.

"There are fates worse than death, Ada."

Ada?

My heart stuttered at the word, but I quickly recovered. I couldn't allow myself to analyze *that* right now. Not with his firm hand still wrapped around my throat and his threat lingering in my ears.

"Yes, there are," I agreed. "But you wouldn't do that to me would you, Marco?" I cooed, much like a lover would.

I did it to provoke him, to set him off or make him uncomfortable, but once again, his expression remained unaffected and cold.

And yet... hidden away in those opaque irises swirled something. Exactly *what* that something was though, I didn't know.

I wasn't sure who was winning this game, but I felt an odd sense of satisfaction seep into my blood as his hand dropped from my neck, falling to his side.

It was made all the sweeter when I felt his gaze lingering on me as I pulled away and walked the path back toward the house.

I was getting under his skin whether he liked it or not.

Trouble was, he was also getting beneath mine.

———

AFTER MY ENCOUNTER with Don La Torre at the pool, I stayed in my room like he had asked. Thankfully, Lucia brought up a delicious, toasted ciabatta roll to keep me from starving, and I washed it down with some fresh lemonade. I took a bath shortly after, pampering myself with some lotions I found in a cupboard and stuck on the television while I lounged on my bed.

Three episodes into a new true crime documentary, Jesse came barging into the room and collapsed unceremoniously beside me.

I laughed at the stupid expression he wore. "Meeting over?"

"Over," He confirmed. "What the fuck are you watching?"

"It's a true crime documentary. You should really try watching things other than porn sometimes, Jesse," I teased.

"Na, I'm good." He grinned. "Boss wants to see you in his study." He added, picking up the remote and flicking off the show.

I sighed.

Guess I'll be going now then.

Jesse's eagerness told me that the meeting had been about my ransom, which meant there was a good chance my family could be coming for me, and I would be free soon.

The thought made me both excited and nervous at the same time.

I walked somewhat slowly to the study door, stopping and waiting patiently outside the familiar room for the guards to let me in. It was the same two as before... Layton and Wyatt I think Lucia said their names were. I kept my eyes surreptitiously away from the one I thought was Layton, recalling his snarky remark in the study a few days previous. The other, Wyatt, held open the door and gestured inside.

Just like the first time I came into the room, Don La Torre was sitting behind his desk as I entered. The room smelled of him—like sandalwood and spices.

It was pleasant and masculine...so I breathed through my mouth instead.

A small smile graced the Don's face as I took a seat opposite him, sending a tingle along my skin and my earlier confidence dithering. That smile made him look boyish and charming... and was infinitely more dangerous than his usual indifference.

"What?" I asked, suddenly nervous.

"Nice hot pants. They are better than a bikini though, I suppose." He said sardonically.

Crap.

I hadn't even considered what I was wearing—a pair of gray shorts that more closely resembled underwear and a black crop top. Once again, I was completely underdressed and mentally kicked myself for not realizing it sooner.

I scowled and muttered an insincere "Thanks".

A moment of uncomfortable silence bubbled between us before I couldn't stand it any longer. "Is there any news from my family?"

His face soured and his eyes grew tight. "We are still in discussions."

"Discussions? It's been days," I scoffed bitterly.

"These things take time."

I shook my head in disappointment. I knew my family had enough money or property to pay whatever price the man before me could demand. It meant that there were other factors at play besides that...didn't it?

I eyed the man before me suspiciously, "You are dragging your heels then. My father would have paid anything to have me back by now. You must want more than money," I accused.

He let out a cold, humorless laugh. "I wouldn't be so sure about that. There seems to be some resistance between your family members."

I wasn't entirely surprised by the news. My family weren't

exactly a harmonious bunch at the best of times. But this...this was undoubtedly the fault of my cousin Leon.

My cousin was an asshole that had infuriated me since the day I was born. To be frank, he was an idiot who used our family's money to get away with whatever he wanted. Despite that, he had a reputation for being reckless that no amount of money could bury. He was forever bragging about 'holding the keys to the kingdom', what with him being the closest male heir and my chances of inheriting being as possible as aliens landing on the pentagon. After all, I was *just a woman* as he so eloquently put it.

In essence—I hated his ass.

But unfortunately for me, my father didn't. He doted on my moron cousin as if he were the son he never had. Of course, *Leon* would be the one to question paying. I had no doubt any resistance was coming squarely from him. He probably got my uncles to weigh in on it, too. It was no secret he'd been trying to push me out of the family or marry me off since I was eighteen.

I guess he saw now as his opportunity.

"Fucking Leon," I muttered.

"There should be more progress in the next few days," The Don offered. His rough voice sounded softer somehow, but then a scowl marred his features, and I thought maybe I'd imagined it.

He collected his phone from the desk and started texting away on it.

I pursed my lips. "Is that it? Is that all you called me in here for?"

"Yes," Came his terse response as he continued on his phone.

How would someone who was valuable to them respond to that?

I swallowed back my anxiety and levelled my gaze, determined to maintain my ruse.

I forced indifference into my tone. "I've been here for days, and I'm bored. I want my phone back."

"No." His response was immediate. No hesitation whatsoever.

"It's not like I can ask for help, I don't even know where I am!" I protested, getting to my feet.

"You're in Chicago and you can't have your phone back because I'm using it."

Chicago? How the hell did I get to Chicago without realizing it? Then I remembered how groggy I had felt on my first day here, and it all made sense. *They had drugged me.*

Then my cheeks warmed as I processed the second half of his sentence. If he had been using my phone to broker the ransom...hopefully that had been *all* he was doing on my phone.

I turned on my heel to leave, unable to hide my embarrassment.

"Your boyfriend Jason hasn't called if that is what you are worried about."

I froze mid-step. Dark humor lilted his words, and I all but choked on the oxygen in my lungs.

"*Not* my boyfriend," I corrected.

"All these pictures suggest otherwise."

I swung back round with a jolt.

He now had what was obviously *my* phone in his hand and was scrolling obnoxiously through it. That stupid, heart fluttering smile of his pulling at the edge of his lips.

My heart thudded in my ears as I fought to control my unease. I had no need to feel it. There wasn't anything on my phone but naughty lingerie shots... and I knew I looked hot as hell in them or else I wouldn't have sent them to Jason. The thought was enough to allow my unease to ebb away into a languid self-assurance.

I crossed my arms, with faux annoyance. "Pervert. And it's called a *fuckbuddy*."

His eyebrow raised in quiet question.

Clearly, he wasn't expecting me to be so flagrant about sex, but I wasn't in the mood to play the Virgin Mary when on enemy turf—even if it was frowned upon. He also didn't have to know that it was a bold-ass *lie*.

"Well, enjoy rubbing one out over my nudes," I said sardonically. "Oh, and speaking of weird sexual fetishes, please tell your pet banshee to keep it down in future. I thought an animal was dying in the halls. Terrible noises…"

I turned back on my heel as I saw his head fly up in surprise.

My comment had caught him off guard and hit its intended target.

Feeling very much like I had won another round with the most powerful man I had ever encountered; I smirked the whole way back to my room.

CHAPTER
FIVE

ADALYN

Days passed at the mansion, and I spent a lot of my time by the pool, reading a book or lounging about watching television in one of the various living rooms. I was biding my time and trying to keep my head down. My confidence in the ransom being paid soon had started turning sour, and as the hours trickled slowly by, I couldn't shake the feeling that my faith in my family had been misplaced.

The only time I didn't sit brooding on the thought was when I was eating breakfast with Jesse, and thankfully, after a couple of days we started to eat our dinners together, too. He would always disappear during the day though, and soon enough, loneliness had started setting in.

On the fourth day, I plucked up enough courage to ask Lucia for help teaching me some basic Italian recipes. Cooking had never been something that came naturally to me, and with an ample amount of time on my hands, it seemed like a good opportunity to learn from a woman who made the best food I had ever tasted.

The days quickly morphed into weeks—two to be exact—and I hadn't spoken to another person outside of Jesse and Lucia for the entirety of them. All the usual busyness of the house was notably absent and apart from the odd Mafioso or maid here and there, the halls were unusually vacant.

It seemed that the Don was elsewhere, and I couldn't say I was sad about it. Something about the man made my head hurt and my blood smolder...and I wasn't entirely sure that was a good thing.

————

THE CLOCK in the kitchen read twelve forty-five when I pulled a steaming pan of chocolate brownies from the oven. Not ten minutes later, Jesse appeared from god-knows-where he spent his days, with a plate in one hand, and I rolled my eyes at him. I cut him a piece before stacking the rest onto a plate.

"Everything okay, Jesse?"

He seemed quieter than usual as he ate. I had grown somewhat accustomed to his mannerisms over the last two weeks, and his silence now was unsettling.

He just shook his head and downed my glass of coke from the counter.

"Boss wants to see you." He nodded in the direction of the study and rose to his feet as he spoke.

Apprehension suddenly made me edgy.

I hadn't realized the Don was back again.

I wiped my hands on the kitchen towel and took the plate of brownies with me as I followed Jesse to the study. He didn't knock as we entered, going straight in and standing beside the corner window rather than leaving like he normally did.

My stomach churned when I observed the Don and an older man I didn't recognize opposite each other, engaged in quiet discussion.

Hesitantly, I moved forward and placed the plate at the edge of the desk before sitting in the only available seat. I didn't miss how the Don's gaze followed the movement, nor the way he seemed to study the plate as if I'd put a pig's head on his desk instead of a pile of gooey chocolate brownies.

"Ada, this is Benny. Benny is my consigliere." There was that nickname again.

I did my best to ignore the sudden sputter of my heart and turned to the man beside me.

"Hello," I offered, returning the older man's smile.

I couldn't help but notice the air in the room was tense. Benny's smile was clearly forced, and Jesse's reticence was out of character. Only the Don looked unaffected by it, though I had a suspicion that it was rare to find him affected by anything.

"Our discussions with your family have concluded," Marco began, bringing his hands together in a pyramid over his lap. "They have been unsuccessful. Your father is refusing to meet our demands."

My stomach fell to the floor.

What?

My mind swirled like a hurricane, confusion and anger obliterating all rationality.

They wouldn't do this to me, would they?

"You're lying!" I'd hoped my voice would come out furious and accusatory, but it just sounded hollow.

It surprised me when Jesse stepped forward to answer instead of the Don, "Adalyn, just listen to him." I met Jesse's eyes and saw nothing but concern in them. "It's true."

"H-how much was it?" I asked, not really expecting an answer but asking the question anyway.

To my complete surprise, the Don responded. "One hundred mill."

My stomach knotted with his answer.

Admittedly, I didn't know much about the state of my family's finances...but I knew that we *had* one hundred million dollars. My family owned an assortment of clubs and casinos, many of which were situated right off the infamous Las Vegas strip itself. If we didn't have that kind of money lying around, then it really wouldn't have taken that much effort to raise the funds Don La Torre was demanding.

They just didn't want to.

My chest constricted and my breathing suddenly became labored.

Not only had my family turned their backs on me and left me inside enemy territory...but by doing that, they had told Don La Torre just how worthless I really was to them. To him.

The Don now knew I was a liar...that nothing and no one was going to protect me now.

Panic started spreading like frostbite.

It suddenly didn't matter that I was in a room with three very powerful and emotionless men. Tears welled in my eyes, and I hid my head in my hands as a quiet sob caught in my throat.

I vaguely heard Marco's firm voice ringing out in Italian. I didn't know the language well enough to understand what he'd said and frankly in that moment, I didn't care either way. I felt Benny and Jesse move slowly toward the door in response to whatever it was though, disappearing with a gentle click of the handle.

His desk chair creaked, and I flinched.

I was scared. Terrified.

He's going to kill me now.

A sob tore out of me.

My heart stammered and my breaths were coming in pants as I finally lifted my head. I was met by the cool black eyes of the Don, as he leaned against the desk.

I fell to my knees before him instantly, the ground biting into my knees.

"P-please don't kill me," I cried. "I'm so, *so,* sorry I lied. I didn't know they wouldn't pay. Please, Marco, *please* don't hurt me. I'll do anything. I'm s-sorry. I'm so, *so,* s-sorry," I begged, my voice garbled by my tears and sobs, making me sound nothing short of pathetic.

I didn't care. I was begging for my life.

"I'll do anything. *Anything.* Just *plea*—."

"You aren't in here so I can kill you."

What? Why?

I didn't understand the words that hung between us.

Why wouldn't he kill me?

My sobs died in my throat and acute relief made the pounding in my ears almost painful. I swiped at the tears tracking down my face, breathing in uneven gasps as a new wave of terror quickly constricted my lungs, my relief suddenly short-lived.

If he wasn't going to kill me...*did that mean a fate worse than death?*

I tilted my head to look at the Don, meeting his dark eyes with nothing short of terror.

"T-t-then what are you going to do to me?" My voice came out a trembling whisper. Tears hot and heavy staining my cheeks.

"I'm not a fucking monster, Ada. *Jesus,*" The Don bit out, taking in my expression.

He laughed once without a single trace of humor and straightened to his full height, walking away. He stood and looked out the window like Jesse had earlier.

"W-what?" My brain struggled to process what he had said around the pounding of adrenaline and remnants of fear clutching at my chest.

He turned back toward me, shoving his hands casually into his pockets. His Rolex glinted with the movement.

"Unlike a lot of men in my *profession,* I am not the kind of man that sells women into torment. So quit looking at me like I am."

Surprise had me searching his face and meeting his indecipherable eyes with my own. He let out a heavy sigh.

"You are to remain here for the foreseeable future. Until I can figure out the particulars," he said measuredly. Once again, the picture of ease and stoic detachment.

"Now, get *up*," he ordered.

I immediately complied, unsteadily finding my feet and heaving myself back into the chair. The cool leather instantly stuck to my over-heated skin as I contemplated what he had said.

"I'm to remain here," I muttered to myself, as if checking I had heard the crux of his words correctly. "I'm not going to be killed. I'm not going to be sold..."

"No, you're no—"

"Why?" I blurted out, cutting him off.

His eyes found mine again, but this time there seemed to be something else swirling within them. Something I wasn't sure I could place.

"Because I don't punish innocent people."

His sentence hung heavy in the air until a loud knock sounded against the door. Wyatt stepped inside and judging from the look on his face, I knew my time alone with the Don had come to its end.

I seized the opportunity and fled the office, not stopping until I was in the confines of my room.

With the door firmly locked behind me, I curled up on the windowsill and listened to the gentle pattering of rain against the glass. Sobs bubbled up from my chest, breaking through the relative silence.

My family didn't pay the ransom.

The words burned deep within my chest, burrowing into my bones. Rejection and hurt crashing into me with equal ferocity.

I may not have been the heir or had any kind of power...but blood was supposed to run thicker than water. That was ingrained into the very heart of the Cosa Nostra. The whole institution was founded on blood, loyalty and family.

Loneliness and an impending sense of dread consumed me as another sob tore free of my chest.

I was stranded in enemy territory and there was no longer a way out.

My family was not coming.

———

THE SUN HAD MEANDERED to the edge of the horizon, casting the room in a gentle golden glow as I was roused from sleep. A swift knock vibrated on the door, and I shifted against the leather chaise lounge, righting myself from the awkward position I'd fallen into.

I cleared my throat quietly, "Come in."

A sliver of light trickled in from the hallway outside and I glanced toward it, expecting to find Jesse. With a start, I realized that the Don had entered the room instead, and I watched cautiously as he stopped a few yards away.

"Are you alright?" Marco's deep voice, despite being gentle, was loud against the silence.

"Do you care?" I challenged, then immediately regretted it. I needed to tread carefully now, with my safety no longer guaranteed by my lies. "I'm sorr—"

"Save it." He dismissed, putting his hands in his pockets like he had done earlier. "Simpering and weak doesn't suit you, Ada."

My mouth slackened in shock.

I could feel his eyes burning into me and I made the monumental mistake of meeting them, unwittingly trapping myself in his predatory gaze.

He didn't say anything further. It was like we were locked in some strange little stand-off where only he knew the rules. Another minute ticked by.

Then another.

My patience finally snapped. "Can I help you with something? Or are you just going to stand there like a creep staring at your new slave?"

Shit.

I didn't really know what the repercussions for my outburst were going to be, but I certainly didn't expect him to *smirk*.

"An intriguing idea...but no." His tone was almost...*playful.* "As you are aware, I already have people for *that.*"

He scratched at his chin as a smile ghosted across his lips.

The motion was telling.

Suddenly, I understood why he had stared at me silently before, declining to speak. He had *wanted* me to challenge him. To lose my temper. To snap at him.

He was provoking me.

What. The. Hell.

I didn't have time to process *that* as he was already speaking again.

"Like I said before, you are to remain here. But you are no longer a hostage."

He crossed the distance between us slowly, his footsteps silent against the plush carpet as he stopped less than a foot away. The Don reached a hand into his trouser pocket and pulled out an unfamiliar white phone, holding it out.

"Abuse it and you will lose it." He warned ominously.

"You're giving me a phone?" I questioned cautiously. Tentatively taking the phone from his outstretched hand.

"Not a hostage, remember?" He responded dryly, stepping away and seemingly surveying the room.

Allowing me some privacy, I quickly realized.

I pushed at one of the buttons on the device and the screen immediately lit up in response, opening on a home screen. It had already been configured.

It took me less than thirty seconds to determine that despite the phone in my hand, there was no way for me to contact my family. I didn't have their numbers, and even if I could somehow miraculously remember the digits, they would have been changed the moment the La Torre's had made contact. The only other hope I had was through social media...if that hadn't also been deleted already and I couldn't be sure. I tried to check anyway, but the permissions on the phone were all denied, blocking me from accessing any of it.

It was disappointing...but did I really want to make contact with my family? The fact that my initial response to that question was *no*, unsettled me more than anything else.

I clicked on the contacts list and found two numbers already keyed in.

I snorted out a laugh, "You are such an ass." I muttered, then contemplated how sane I was for insulting him.

He was just provoking you though, remember? He wants you fiery...

The Don turned back around, facing me once again.

"That's funny, I could have sworn I just bought you a new phone." He scowled, but it seemed like with fabricated annoyance this time rather than genuine irritation.

"I don't mean the phone. The phone is actually... Thank you." I coughed awkwardly.

His gaze shot toward the window behind me as he muttered a nearly inaudible, "You're welcome."

I had to force myself to swallow before continuing. "It's

just... You saved your name as 'Don La Torre' in my contacts. That's a little formal, don't you think?"

He let out a dark, low chuckle that sent tingles dancing down my spine.

Holy hell.

That sound was dangerous.

"What else would I call myself?" He asked somewhat rhetorically, but curiosity and challenge seemingly battled away in his eyes. He *wanted* me to answer.

He wants me to challenge him, I realized.

"I can think of a few names better suited." I offered cheerily and he scowled with faux irritation.

Adrenaline mixed with fear trilled through my system. I doubted he allowed many people to challenge him like this... and it was exhilarating.

He turned and walked back toward the door. Then stopped. I pretended not to notice his pause, though in reality I was always too keenly aware of this enigmatic man's presence.

"Ada?" The word sent my heart racing into overdrive.

"Marco." I responded dryly, keeping my eyes on the phone.

His silence told me he wasn't happy about my omission of his title, but he didn't comment on it like before.

"I have a meeting at one of my clubs tomorrow night. You will attend."

What?

It took me a moment to process what he'd said, but then an excited smile pulled at my face.

"So, you're really not going to kill me then?" I asked, only half joking.

When I looked over to him, he was already smirking to himself. "Maybe later."

He pulled open the door and stepped out, closing it gently behind him.

The moment the door snicked shut, I let out a heavy breath of air, the rational part of my brain finally flickering back to life.

I was no longer a hostage.

I would have to remain behind the stone walls of enemy territory, but I was no longer here to broker a deal between families. I was just...*here*.

Don La Torre certainly wasn't what I had expected.

Most men in his position wouldn't have thought twice about putting a bullet between my eyes or carting me off to the highest bidder at the earliest opportunity...and yet, this Don had done neither. He had even given me a phone for Christ's sake!

He had actually *wanted* me to actively challenge him. To lose my temper and push his buttons...even going so far as to *provoke me* to do it.

Simpering and weak doesn't suit you, Ada.

I'd thought that the many years I'd spent around dangerous men had sharpened my instincts and made me a good judge of character...but Don La Torre was something else entirely.

I just didn't know what.

CHAPTER
SIX

ADALYN

The next day I was in a surprisingly good mood, though that probably had a lot to do with the fact that I was finally leaving the house for the first time in almost four weeks. I had also recently found out that the meeting was an overnight thing, and it only added to my excitement. A night away from the mansion was just what I needed.

I had settled on a deep, smoky look for the occasion, pairing it with a gorgeous black dress that ended at the knee. It was completely backless and featured an exaggerated waist-deep V at the front that showed off my curves. A pair of strappy black heels and matching clutch completed my ensemble. With a final spritz of hairspray on my meticulously pinned hair, I heaved my stuffed duffle downstairs to meet Jesse at eight o'clock on the dot.

He let out a low whistle as I descended the stairs.

"You look...hot as fuck." He wasn't exactly reticent with his gaze, and I felt a blush creep across my skin.

He took my bag as soon as my feet kissed the floor and led

the way outside to his SUV. I climbed into the front and messed about turning on something upbeat while Jesse climbed into the driver's side.

It took a few minutes to exit the grounds of the house but then we were cruising through the streets with lights flashing past us.

"Don't try anything stupid tonight, Bandit." Jesse warned after a few minutes.

"I wasn't planning on it." I said truthfully. I knew it wouldn't get me anywhere even if I did. *He would probably just drag my ass back here anyway.* "I like having some freedom."

"Good." He sighed. "When we get there, Alonso and my team will stay with you."

"Where are *you* going?" I questioned, feeling a bit worried about being left with Mafiosos that would undoubtedly want to kill me.

"I am accompanying Marco in the meeting," Jesse answered, a sly smile on his face. "Why? Gonna miss me?" He winked.

"Who is Alonso?" I asked, ignoring his jibe.

The lights on the dash illuminated his smirk. "Alonso is my number two. Don't worry, you'll be in safe hands."

We drove until the small brick buildings had turned into towering stone ones, interspersed with skyscrapers built of glass. Streetlights and glowing neon signs lit up the darkening night sky as pedestrians littered the streets, collecting in groups and making their way to various restaurants or nightclubs for the evening. My excitement began to grow as we pulled out in front of a particularly luxurious building with crowds of people queuing outside.

The car rolled to a stop and numerous people ogled the vehicle, craning their heads to see who was inside.

Jesse promptly came around and opened the door, escorting me onto the sidewalk. A security guard standing beside the club's private entrance came forward as we approached, and Jesse tossed him the keys without so much as a glance.

"You get used to it." Jesse whispered after seeing my discomfort, and I let him pull me the rest of the way inside the building.

We walked into a grand entryway, lined with black mirrors and a few steps that led down to the members only area. It was classy and totally unlike the stereotypical nightclub I had imagined we would be going to. Everything was modern and black, lit up with deep purple LEDs that emanated from hidden parts of the ceiling and lined every surface.

We made our way to the bar and the mingling crowd parted around us. Fear and awe painted on every face we passed, and it didn't take a genius to work out what word would be on their lips: *Mafia*. Clearly Marco's clientele was used to the spectacle of handguns and designer suits. I forgot just how intimidating Jesse looked to someone who didn't know him...

We stopped opposite a Goliath of a man and Jesse slapped him on the back by way of greeting.

"Bandit, this is Alonso. Alonso, Bandit." He introduced us.

Aside from being incredibly tall, Alonso was built like a brick shithouse and absolutely covered in muscle. He looked to be mid-thirties and had a distinctly rugged look about him, like he cut down trees or something in his spare time. Though, surprisingly, his eyes seemed kind and friendly.

"Bandit, Tom and the others are also here to keep an eye on you." He gestured to three or so other burly young men standing behind Alonso. "Now, for the love of God, behave!"

He started to walk off, but I grabbed his arm.

"Where are you going?" I huffed, suddenly nervous to be away from him.

He patted my head condescendingly and I smacked him on the arm. He grinned.

"Over there." He pointed to the corner of the room.

It was only then that I noticed a small, raised platform in the corner that housed a simple and very luxurious seating arrangement. Layton and Wyatt stood either side of its entrance, which meant that Marco was somewhere amongst the various people crowding the space. My eyes scanned the unfamiliar faces until my eyes landed on him. He was off to the side talking with another man who seemed slightly older, but my attention was quickly drawn to the scantily clad women sat on either side of them. Lapping at their stomachs and stroking down their legs seductively as they talked.

I scowled at the sight.

"Be careful you don't catch anything," I muttered, disgusted, and he grinned mischievously before heading off toward them.

I sighed, slightly annoyed I'd been left but happy to get a drink and try to enjoy my relative freedom.

I stood by the bar and settled in for the long wait for service, but all of twenty seconds passed before the bartender placed a coconut lime spritzer in front of me. I didn't even have to ask.

I shot Alonso a curious look and he just smiled.

"Alonso, I don't have any money to pay for this." I admitted, leaning closer to him to shout over the music.

The poor guy had to lean halfway over just to hear my question, dwarfing me in the process.

"They know who you are, it just goes on the Boss's tab."

"One of the perks of being a captive, I take it?" I rolled my eyes, and he laughed. "What are you having?"

"Not allowed alcohol while on duty, Ma'am." He smiled, holding up his bottle of water.

"Fantastic." I groaned.

Drinking alone always sucked.

Not knowing exactly what to do and *definitely* not drunk enough to start dancing, I hovered by the bar drinking.

Half an hour later and my third cocktail finished—I was bored.

I glanced over to the booth where Marco was having his 'business' meeting to see if it showed any signs of finishing soon. Unfortunately for me, discussions seemed to still be in full swing with no end in sight.

The only thing I could think of to keep myself entertained was to get out onto the dance floor, but to do that by myself I needed to be drunker. *Much* drunker.

I ordered three shots of tequila, downed them one after another and then handed Alonso my clutch bag.

"I'll be on the dance floor!" I yelled and sashayed off.

I quickly mingled with the crowd and started moving to the beat. The numbness of the alcohol started to bleed its way through my system, erasing all my worries and boredom with it as I moved.

God, I've missed this!

I rocked my hips to the heavy rhythm, and after a couple of songs, my dancing seemed to attract a fan. He was easy on the eyes in a typical bad-boy way and had an air of confidence that made me smile. We gravitated toward each other until he stood behind me with his hands on my hips. I began moving against him seductively, in time with the music. The guy definitely had moves and it was sexy as hell.

When his hands dropped, gripping dangerously low on my hips, I leaned my head against his shoulder and flashed him my best flirty smile. His head dropped and his lips pressed against my throat for a split second before he jerked away from me.

I stumbled forward violently and closed my eyes, knowing I was falling but incapable of stopping it.

"What the—" I half spluttered.

A strong arm wrapped around my waist, heaving me

upright and pressing me against the side of a spicy scented chest.

"Guys, chill out! We were just dancing!" I heard an unfamiliar male voice yell.

I quickly peaked over my shoulder to see the guy I was with being dragged away by Alonso and Wyatt toward the exit. "Speak to me again and I'll snap your fucking neck," a powerful and, unfortunately, *familiar*, voice shouted back.

It was only then that I realized exactly whose side I was pressed against.

Shit.

My dance partner didn't have time to answer as he was pulled through the crowd. His drunken eyes going in and out of focus as he went.

"What the fuck are you doing?" Marco demanded, pulling me away enough to glare down at me.

It took me a second, but I recovered from my initial shock. "I was dancing."

"Like a slut?" He snapped. I scowled and tried to push away from him, but his grip was like an iron cage.

"You don't have to be so mean. I was having fun." I sulked childishly, crossing my arms across my chest.

The movement did not escape Marco's attention, and his eyes caught there a moment.

Then a wicked idea came to my drunken mind.

He wants to call me a slut for dancing? Fine, I'll show him one...

The next song bled into the one before and just as the new rhythm flooded the speakers, I turned in his arms and rolled my ass firmly into his crotch. I reached up my arm and clutched the back of his head in one hand, threading my fingers through his hair before I began moving as sensually as I could against him.

"Ada."

I heard the warning in his voice but chose to ignore it,

preferring to slut drop in front of him instead to give him a good view of my ass.

My blatant boldness stemmed mainly from the alcohol, but I would have been lying if I'd said it had nothing to do with the women in the booth as well. The moment I stood back up his arms wound around me even tighter, holding me still. I could feel his breath tickle against my neck.

"Stop. It." His voice was tight as he spoke against my ear.

"Why? You don't like my dancing, Marco?" I asked innocently, turning my face into his neck, leaving only millimeters of air between us.

The muscle in his jaw flicked but he remained silent.

I was getting to him, and it made me feel powerful and giddy all at once.

"My bet is that you do... Maybe even *too* much." I brushed the words over his skin, teasing him.

"Let me remind you, Ada. This little game you're playing only has one winner—me. I can do anything I want with you, and no one would dare to stop me. Remember that." A shrill of excitement shot through my system at the brutal edge in his words.

"In your dreams." I smirked and the muscle ticked in his jaw again.

He released me then and swiftly made a motion with his hand.

Jesse cut through the crowd with a goofy smile playing on his lips not a moment after.

"Stay with her." Marco's glare didn't waver from my face as he continued speaking, switching over to Italian.

Jesse nodded a few moments later, agreeing to something somberly with all traces of his earlier playfulness eroded. With Jesse's confirmation, Marco stalked back through the packed dance floor toward the general direction of the meeting.

When I turned to face Jesse, his good mood had once again recovered, and he bobbed his head to the beat.

I decided not to push my luck any further as I danced with him, only imitating grinding as opposed to *actually* grinding against him.

After a couple more songs I was beginning to overheat and in desperate need of another spritzer. When we approached the bar, my drink and a beer for Jesse were placed before us without even the need to ask.

"So, what the fuck is his problem?" I asked after a few glugs of my delicious cocktail.

"Oh, nothing really." He shrugged dismissively, tipping back his beer.

"It didn't seem like nothing. I was just dancing with some guy and then suddenly he's getting dragged away." I argued.

"Dancing!" Jesse scoffed.

"And? I can't have a sexuality too?" I demanded. "You guys sit up there groping whatever girl you like and call it 'business'. Yet when I do the same, I'm a slut. That's double fucking standards."

"Good point well made." He laughed and clinked his beer against my glass. "But this is the Cosa Nostra and most of the men in it wouldn't agree with you, Bandit."

"You don't say." I rolled my eyes at him but knew better than to argue. He was right and whether I liked it or not, it didn't matter.

With another few drinks in my system, I pulled Jesse back onto the dance floor.

The alcohol was making my head spin, and I latched onto him as we danced a second time. Unlike my previous partner, Jesse's hands never strayed from my waist...no matter *how much* I rolled my hips. I was starting to think he never took a day off.

A few songs later, the buzz I was on started to morph into exhaustion and Jesse led the way through the mass of people to a pin-protected door off to the side. Alonso and the others were not far behind us, and when we emerged on the other side, I was surprised to find myself inside a sophisticated hotel lobby.

"Let me guess, Marco owns this building too." I rolled my eyes as we stood in the elevator, going up.

"Yes, Ma'am," Alonso answered.

When the bell pinged, announcing our floor, we exited into a short hallway housing a single double door. Once inside, an expansive and expensive penthouse suite greeted us. It was decorated in the same deep grey hues, abstract art, and masculine furniture as my room at the mansion and it didn't take a genius to work out who had commissioned it.

A sunken seating area faced floor-to-ceiling windows on the far side of the room, revealing the dazzling city lights and darkness of Lake Michigan beyond. To my right was a sleek white counter that appeared to double as a bar and a black marble dining table sat off to the left.

"Your room." Jesse gestured to the door beyond the table. "Your bags are already in there and you have your own bathroom." He gestured to the various doors.

"Okay. Goodnight, Jess." I yawned and waved as I disappeared behind the door he'd indicated.

I flicked on the light, and as promised, my duffle bag and all its contents had been neatly laid out on the bed. I snatched up my makeup remover and went into the bathroom to scrub the makeup from my face. I brushed my teeth and stripped down to my panties, throwing my camisole nightdress on and flicked out the lamp before crawling into bed.

I let out a sigh as I settled for the night.

————

I'D BEEN asleep for less than an hour when noises tore me from sleep.

I pulled the covers away from my head and sat up in confusion, unsure of the sound.

A second ticked past and then a loud groan filtered through the walls.

Why now? I'm shit tired!

I buried my head under the duvet and smothered myself with a pillow. Unfortunately, it did little to dampen the sounds that were growing louder as the minutes ticked by, and I crushed the pillows closer until all I could hear was the thudding of my own heartbeat.

Eventually, I gave up trying to dampen the sounds, knowing there was little chance of falling asleep suffocated as I was under the heavy pillows.

Right that fucking does it!

I lunged out of bed and threw open my door in frustration, half expecting the sounds to be coming from the living room area, they were so graphic and loud. Thankfully they weren't. The noises were coming from the room adjacent to mine and the only room Jesse hadn't pointed to earlier...which meant it could only belong to one person.

Fantastic.

Anger fueled by alcohol had me marching over to the door and pounding violently against the wood.

"Tell your motherfucking donkey to shut the hell up, Marco! Some of us are trying to fucking sleep!" I yelled.

Probably shouldn't have said that.

Immediately, I heard heavy footsteps heading toward where I stood, and I braced myself against the inevitable onslaught.

The door flung open forcefully, revealing a very angry... and very *naked*, Marco. My eyes involuntarily wandered over his body, and I tried unsuccessfully to force my gaze away from his sizeable length standing to attention through his boxers.

It was only then that I realized that he was literally *covered* in tattoos. Two full sleeves and a huge chest piece that stretched down one side of his rib cage camouflaged his skin in large swirls of rich black images. His long-sleeved shirts certainly hid more than perfectly chiseled abs, that was for sure.

Fucking hell.

I audibly gulped and arrogance glistened in his eyes.

"What did you say?"

I crossed my arms, trying to regain my composure, "I said, 'tell your motherfucking donkey to shut the hell up, some of us are trying to sleep.'" I recanted, meeting his eyes in unquestionable challenge while keeping my voice sickly sweet.

"Hey bitch, fu—" a woman's voice started to say behind him.

"Quiet." Marco barked over his shoulder.

The woman's mouth snapped shut and a smug smile lined my face as his attention focused squarely on me.

I suddenly felt hot and keenly aware of the *lack* of clothes we were both wearing.

Shit.

"Go back to your room."

Surprisingly, it was exasperation that lilted his voice instead of the familiar anger I was expecting. Marco stepped back and slammed the door in my face not a second later, the lock clicking into place on the other side.

I stared angrily at the wood for a second longer than was entirely necessary before stomping away.

The moaning started up again the second my door closed, only this time louder than before. *His* groans were more audible than hers now and I found my cheeks smoldering at the sound. Something akin to excitement pooled in my belly with each of his loud grunts and I couldn't help but imagine the actions that went along with those intoxicating sounds...

Lord help me.

CHAPTER
SEVEN

MARCO

It was a respect thing—or at least that was what I told the others when I had gone back to the booth with my hand dripping with an imbecile's blood earlier that evening.

I had decked that stupid little twerp with the shitty tattoos and God-awful spikey hair not because of his blatant disrespect toward Adalyn—like I had told everyone else was the case—but because I had merely *wanted* to. And fucking hell had it felt good.

Just not as good as what had come *after* I'd punched him.

Ada's sweet ass bent over in front of me and her lips brushing my skin had me stiff as a blade and wound up so tightly that I needed to either fight or fuck to calm down. This time I had chosen the latter, picking up one of the girls that had swarmed around me and my men all evening like goddamn buzzards.

It was an easy fuck until Ada came storming to the door dressed in nothing but a scrap of black silk and lace. I had to force myself to slam the door in her face, her audacious confidence a second away from snapping any self-restraint I had left.

I wanted to fuck her so bad in that moment I could barely think straight.

But instead of giving into the screaming urge to take her, I had forced myself to turn my attention to the female that had still been wrapped up in my bedsheets. I gave into my carnal need for release by pounding into her. Imagining sleek blonde hair and wide doe-like eyes staring up at me while fucking the mousey looking woman I never truly wanted.

When we had finished, I promptly booted her ass out and took a hot shower. I worked my neck and shoulders under the steam, needing to ease the tension that a quick fuck had done nothing to sate, but it was no use.

I'm losing my goddamn mind.

I sighed and pressed my forehead against the cool tiles, adjusting the water until it ran cold.

———

ADALYN

"Get your grumpy ass up! Breakfast is here."

Jesse's familiar voice rang out across the room, rousing me from sleep. He had flung open the door and was waiting impatiently just inside it, bathing the room in bright light.

"Get lost, Jesse!" I groaned, turning and burying my head back into the pillows.

"It's ten thirty! If your grouchy ass isn't in here in the next ten minutes, then I'll drag you out myself." He threatened and shut the door behind him.

I sighed and unwillingly pulled myself out of bed, finally lured by the smell of breakfast and coffee that wafted into the room. I shuffled into some black leggings and threw on the oversized shirt I'd packed, pulling my hair into a bun and dabbing a bit of concealer under my puffy eyes before giving myself a once over in the mirror.

Yup... still look hung over.

I shrugged it off, giving up on making myself look half decent for the sake of my growling stomach.

I heaved my way out of the door and almost balked.

I had grown so used to eating alone with Jesse that it hadn't occurred to me that Marco would join us for breakfast. Yet there he was, seated at the head of the table in front of a plate of pancakes and bacon.

Thankfully, he hadn't noticed my entrance yet, as he tapped away on his phone.

"You look like shit." Jesse chuckled around a bite of sausage meat.

"Gee, thanks Jess." I smiled back sarcastically, plating some pancakes for myself and downing a few painkillers.

"Have fun last night?" Jesse mocked.

"It was...alright. Though I remember dancing with an uncoordinated twit most of the evening so that was a bit of a dampener." I taunted and he gave me the male equivalent of a resting bitch face.

"I'll have you know I am a great dancer." He argued, pointing a fork in my direction.

"Hmm... I've been with better."

"Wow, Bandit, just wow." I couldn't help but giggle at him, earning me a wink.

"Bandit?" Marco frowned, directing his question to the man on his right.

"It's just a nickname, Marco." I answered instead, rolling my eyes. "I guess we don't need to ask whether *you* had a good night seeing as the whole of the city could hear it."

His frown turned into a glare as he gave me a look, and Jesse burst into laughter across the table.

"She sounded like...quite...*something*?" Jesse winced at his own word choice and I hid a chuckle behind my hand.

"Hee-Haw. Hee-Haw." I did my best donkey imitation, causing both Jesse and I to erupt into peals of laughter.

Marco, on the other hand, did not look amused.

"Oh, lighten up. It's a joke." I said once I'd managed to get a hold of myself.

"That was that Amanda girl, right?" Jesse suddenly asked, intrigued.

I bit into my pancake and pretended to look interested at the label on the back of the ketchup bottle. *Yes, this is ketchup. Ke-t-chup.*

"Yes." Marco sighed. "At least I think that was her name. No mentioning it to Lexi."

Who's Lexi? I fought the scowl forming on my brow.

"Gottcha."

"The last thing I need is her getting an excuse to keep coming over." Irritation seeped into his voice.

"Agreed. That woman is like a human moth." Jesse snickered.

"You're both pigs." I grumbled.

———

By EARLY AFTERNOON, Jesse and I had driven back to the mansion. The moment the tires rolled to a stop outside the familiar sandy stone walls, I had traipsed inside and collapsed on my bed, desperate to catch up on last night's lost sleep.

I slept peacefully for a few hours, waking up shortly before four and throwing on a couple of mindless shows to keep myself busy. Jesse had found me a couple of hours later, informing me that I was invited to a formal dinner with Marco, which was surprising. I didn't think a young Don like himself would be in the habit of having a formal dinner every evening...but apparently, he did. It was just this time I was also invited.

With only an hour to get ready, I jumped into the shower, blow-dried my hair and put on a fresh layer of barely-there makeup. Not knowing quite how formal this 'formal dinner' was, I settled on a floral mid-length camisole style dress and paired it with wedge sandals.

At precisely eight o'clock, I walked into the extravagant dining hall I had only been in once before when on my tour with Lucia. When I entered, a butler in a white-tailed coat approached, escorting me to one end of the colossal table at the room's center. It could quite easily have seated sixteen people, but tonight only two places had been laid out at opposite ends.

A tall glass of champagne accompanied me shortly after I had taken my seat.

"Good evening, Adalyn." Marco greeted.

The coldness in his tone now, as opposed to how it had been just the previous night at the club, was like night and day. How he could switch between the two personas within himself so easily, I had no clue. I could barely keep up with it myself.

"What's all this about?" I waved at the room and four waiters standing silently nearby.

"Dinner." He shrugged, pulling his tie loose from around his neck and settling back into his chair.

"I meant why am *I* here?" His sullen eyes met mine across the expanse. Before he could answer, the doors opened, and two more waiters approached with a steaming bowl of soup and freshly baked bread.

It was only once they had left again that he set about answering my question.

"I thought I owed you the truth."

The truth?

That was surprising. I had long since given up with the idea that Mafia men cared about the truth.

"The truth about your ransom." He continued, picking up his spoon simultaneously.

A few seconds of silence passed while he seemed to consider his next words.

"My men made contact with your father, Alberto, and commenced discussions about your ransom before my jet even landed at O'Hare International. Your capture had been planned for months, Ada. I was just waiting for the right time to take you." He spoke measuredly as if he were unsure of my reaction.

He had hinted when I'd first arrived here that his men had been watching me for a while, but months? All the while my family were oblivious to the silent threat lurking amongst the shadows...

"My turning up at The Venetian Prince that night was your doing then, I take it." I guessed, thinking back to the VIP passes we had scored for the night and how my friends and I could not believe our luck.

"I see why you would think that, but no. It was merely a coincidence that you ended up at my club that night." He said nonchalant.

"Your club? *In Las Vegas*?" I wasn't sure I had heard him right.

Las Vegas was Mannino and Romano territory.

The city was divided right down the almost-middle, with my family owning the majority. The Romano's were a small family with less manpower, less ruthlessness, and less history in the city than ours. Our agreement over territory had been in effect for many years and left no room for anyone else. Or so we'd thought.

Did my family even know that the La Torre's had moved right into their backyard? I doubted it, from the smug smile on his face.

Marco really hadn't been lying when he said he wasn't

afraid of starting a war.

He shot me a knowing look.

"Initial talks did not go as well as anticipated. Abducting you did not seem to be enough motive to force Alberto's hand, so I had my men deliver a package to your home in Boulder City as well. It contained images of your family going about their various daily routines. Your Mamma sleeping with the handyman at her shop. Your father meeting with his men at one of his restaurants, you driving around in your Hellcat and so on and so forth. We thought that it might give him the... *nudge* he needed to submit to our demands." He chuckled darkly. "It seems we were wrong once again."

The safety of his family were on the line...and that wasn't enough?

I was so lost in the thought that I scarcely registered a new plate of food being set before me.

"Your family promptly abandoned their residences and cut off all forms of communication. I believe their argument for not financing your release was that you are not an heir to your family's empire nor have any useful information that they would want to keep out of my hands."

The truth of his words cut deep.

I had long since resigned myself to the knowledge that I wasn't worth a lot to my family. It had been a truth I had tucked away for most of my adult life...but it didn't make it any less painful when confronted by it.

No! I was his daughter. That had to count for something!

"My fa—"

"Your father is as abhorrent as he ever has been." His words cut like ice. "If you think he cares about you Ada, you are wrong."

"You would say that though, wouldn't you?" I argued.

He signed and pulled out a small silver device, laying it atop the table.

It crackled for a second before two familiar voices rang out from the speaker, and my heart sank.

"Do you really think your pictures would intimidate me, boy?" My father's distinctive voice scoffed through the recorder. *"It will take much more than that, I assure you!"*

"I am merely demonstrating that your days of hiding are over. You are the one who instigated conflict between our families and ran like a coward when the fighting started. Well, now you know I can find you wherever you are." Marco's voice was venomous, making him sound every bit the powerful Don he was.

"I am not the coward who kidnaps young women to extort for money! As if that would mean anything in a man's game!" The words were biting, and I flinched.

"Your own daughter really means so little?" I could hear Marco chuckle through the recording, but it didn't contain an ounce of humor. *"One hundred million for her release and I will end this conflict."*

"And why would I pay you that? No one is worth such a high price. She is of no use to me or this family." His dark, maniacal laugh bled through the speaker. *"Keep her."*

My father was just about to speak again when Marco stopped the recording.

Tears lined my eyes, and I was suddenly grateful he'd stopped it before I could hear anymore. I patted at my tears with my fingertips as if I were able to wipe away the hurt overwhelming me.

Rejection and hopelessness crushed my chest painfully until I had to will myself to breathe through it.

I didn't realize how worthless I was to my family.

"I'm sorry you had to hear that, but I felt you deserved the truth." I could feel him watching me.

I replied with a weak 'Yup' before gulping back the remainder of my champagne.

"Are you alright?" Concern resonated in Marco's voice, his

gaze still grazing my skin, but I refused to meet it. *Couldn't* meet it.

"It's not every day you find out how...*worthless* you are. Even to your own family." I just shook my head sadly, unable to formulate the words without feeling my heart breaking all over again.

The room fell into a tormented silence as I looked at my hands numbly.

"I want to give you a chance to start over, Ada. Here in Chicago."

Of all the things I was expecting to come out of his mouth, I wasn't expecting *that*. It took my brain a full minute to catch up.

"Through marriage?" I guessed, fully aware of what '*fresh starts*' often meant in our society.

Marco didn't respond right away, instead waving at the waiters who moved in unison to remove our plates and placing before us a warm chocolate dessert. Only once he had picked up his spoon and had taken a bite did he deign to continue.

"It's something I am considering."

I nodded, powerless to stop it even if I had wanted to...but I didn't. It was the best I could hope for given my situation, and it was more than I could have expected. I doubted that any other Don would have considered it, given that I was the daughter of his enemy.

If I were married off to one of Marco's men, it would mean that I'd be cared for financially and given a home. I could learn to care for my husband in time, perhaps even come to love him. If not, then at least I still had my children to live for and a home to run... It was my best chance at happiness.

"Until I can come to some kind of *arrangement* with that, you will live here. You are no longer confined to the estate, but you will take security with you when you leave and return here every evening. Other than that, you can go about your life just as every other female in my family does."

A small spark of hope lit in my chest.

"Can I go shopping?" I asked tentatively.

"That constitutes going out, doesn't it?" He responded dryly, wolfing down another mouthful.

"Can I get a job?"

Marco looked slightly insulted by my question, pausing mid-chew and meeting me with a curious expression on his face. "Do you want a job?"

I guess it wasn't common for women in the Cosa Nostra to want to work, with many perceiving it as a blight on the male she was attached to. Indeed, my Mamma certainly never had to lift a finger before the 'Parker Family' ruse and even then, exactly what she did at her store couldn't be considered *work* in the traditional sense. She had staff for *that*.

It just wasn't the way in our society and while the rest of modern women have marched on with the times, most of us were happy enough with our traditions to not wish for more.

I contemplated my answer a moment. "Maybe. I will need some way of financing my *wonderful* new life in Chicago after all." I finished sardonically.

"If that is your only reason for working, then you need not bother."

Marco reached into his jacket and pulled out something small and black between his fingers. He then rose from his seat and slowly walked the distance to my end of the room, much like a Lion casually stalks its prey.

He came to a stop mere feet away and slid a shiny card across the table beside me.

"Abuse it and you will lose it."

I stared cautiously at the onyx card while he retook his seat, feeling a swell of gratitude for the Don who was seemingly less of a monster with every day that passed.

I glanced over at him and met his gaze. A glass tumbler of whiskey already swirled in his hand.

"Thank you."

CHAPTER
EIGHT

ADALYN

The next morning, I woke up with a killer headache and puffy eyes that no amount of makeup was going to fix, but despite that, I was feeling better. The sadness I felt about my family was now carefully caged away to deal with on a later date...or never. I hadn't decided yet, but I was done crying about it either way. It wouldn't change anything.

I threw myself out of bed and took a quick shower, plastered on a thick layer of foundation and grabbed a cute one piece from my dressing room. I pulled my badly grown-out blonde hair into a high ponytail.

"You seem chirpy." Jesse commented as I skipped into the garden room that morning. He was in his usual place at the round table, dressed in his ever-present black suit and shirt which looked almost identical to the ones Marco wore.

"I've decided to make the most of my situation." I drawled around a mouthful of food. "Besides, if I don't have a home anymore how can I miss it?"

I could see Jesse's eyes cloud over as he looked at me and I waved it away.

"Oh, don't look at me like that. I'm fine." I said as convincingly as I could. "Anyway, I know what I am going to do today."

"Hmm and what is that exactly?" He asked intrigued.

"I'm going to get my hair done!" I did a small clap in excitement. "So...could you arrange that for me? Pleeasseeeee." I exaggerated, trying to coerce him into helping.

I flashed him my best innocent smile.

"Fine." He huffed. "Alonso will take you. When do you want to go?"

"Sometime this morning." I suggested.

He quickly dove a hand into his blazer pocket and left the room while bringing the phone to his ear. I poured us both a coffee in his absence.

He resumed his seat a few minutes later, "It's sorted. Alonso will be out front in thirty minutes."

Jesse then proceeded to shove a rasher of bacon in his mouth like a pig.

"Thank you. And be careful—you're going to get grease all over your suit." I threw him a paper towel.

"Greasy is how I like it." His grin was met with my chorus of 'eww'.

"So, what exactly are *you* doing today?"

"Oh, you know...this and that." He said, clearly dodging.

"Are you choosing not to tell me or have you been told not to?" I scowled at him over my steaming mug.

"That is the million-dollar question isn't it, my dear old Bandit."

I can't be trusted by this family either, I thought angrily. Though, I couldn't exactly blame them for it.

"Are you sure I can't get you to come with me to the salon? I'll treat you to a fancy pamper day!" I teased.

"Umm no. I'm not sure I could fulfill my role as big scary

Mafia guy if I had a French manicure, so thank you but no thank you."

"Very well then," I said, getting to my feet. "Thank you for helping me, Jess. You know with...e-everything." I finished awkwardly.

Jesse was fast becoming my only friend in this 'new life' of mine and I wanted him to know that I appreciated it. At times, he was the only thing keeping me sane.

"You are...welcome." He coughed into his fist, equally as awkward.

———

NOT TWENTY MINUTES LATER, I met Alonso and Tom on the drive out front. My shiny black credit card and brand-new phone were carefully tucked away in my handbag, and I was feeling more normal than I had in weeks.

As we drove into town, it seemed like Marco's mansion was in one of the more exclusive suburbs of Chicago as opposed to the city center itself. It took a little over ten minutes for us to reach what I assumed to be a local high street, with a clustering of various up-market shops and restaurants.

We pulled up outside a sophisticated salon, which looked somewhat out of place against the plainness of the other stores. Alonso and Tom traipsed behind me as I stepped inside, and I wasn't sure whether they were debating following me or not. It wasn't exactly their *scene*.

Cool air conditioning hit my skin and a bubbly woman at the front desk greeted me. Her eyes immediately darted to the two men stood behind me and her mouth slackened in surprise.

Guess it's not every day that two meat-head security details wander into a hair salon, I mused.

Four hours later, my radical new look was complete.

My severely grown-out, shit-bright blonde was finally gone, replaced with a color that more closely resembled my natural raven hair. I finally looked like *me* again.

Not the Adalyn Parker me, but the *me* I was before everything changed seven years ago. I was officially giddy with satisfaction.

With one swipe of my new credit card, I was done and heading back to the car with Alonso. Tom reappeared from wherever he had disappeared off to for the last few hours and reclaimed the driver's seat.

"Where to now, Ma'am?" Alonso questioned once we were all inside.

"Hmm." I contemplated for a moment.

I was feeling good. The best I had felt in weeks in fact, and I didn't want to go back just yet. I had only just begun to taste freedom after all...so I quickly devised a plan.

"Shopping. Is there a shopping center or something around here?" I questioned.

"Absolutely, Ma'am." Alonso nodded and Tom started the car, peeling out into the road as we continued on our journey.

The drive this time took just under an hour as we made our way along countless busy streets, driving further and further toward central Chicago. We didn't stop until we hit the infamous Michigan Avenue, which, as predicted, was heaving with crowds of people.

Tom somehow managed to pull the car to a stop as close to the shopping center as possible. Car horns immediately sounded behind us, but neither man seemed to care. Alonso got out with me and walked us inside Water Tower Place while Tom drove around to find parking.

Countless floors circled above us as we entered, each holding a seemingly endless warren of shops, well-known brands and restaurants. Endless opportunities to use my credit card awaited, and I certainly didn't blanch at the chance to use it.

For the rest of the afternoon, I managed to drag the impassive Alonso from shop to shop, only stopping once for a quick bite to eat. Somewhere along the way, Tom joined us, and he too followed my every move.

To my amusement, both men refused to accompany me when I insisted on going into 'Victoria's Secret', preferring to stand outside like doormen to a nightclub instead. I went a bit wild without their presence reigning me in and racked up an almost one-thousand-dollar bill in the process.

Marco's gonna feel that.

Then a devilish idea popped into my head.

With my evil plan quickly coming together, I passed my white and pink bags over to the men and headed off in search of the more luxury brands I truly adored. After five minutes and the help of Google maps, I found my way inside Bloomingdales and the place of dreams.

Michael Kors? *Not a problem.*

Gucci? *Don't mind if I do!*

Another two hours later and at least $5,000 lighter, I was exhausted but fully satisfied with myself.

Was it mature of me to spend a shit load of money in retribution for a few weeks being kept as a hostage? Probably not. But, did it make me feel better about it? Hell yeah, it did!

Once all the bags and boxes had been loaded into the vehicle, we weaved through the traffic heading back in the general direction of the mansion.

I pulled out my phone and realized I had received a few unread messages from Jesse while I was out.

Jesse: Wat is taking so long?

Jesse: HELLO?

Just then my phone buzzed again, and a new message popped up.

Jesse: Bandit! Marco wants you 2 join 4 dinner 2night. Serving @8pm

I fought against the urge to gulp at the invitation. Last night hadn't exactly been pleasant and I didn't think I could take any more bad news so soon.

Me: On way back now. Wont b long.

Me: Nothing bad happened while I was out, did it?

I couldn't help but type the last message. Anxiety starting to eat away at my good mood.

Jesse: No

Jesse: Wait why?

Relief quickly stopped my pessimism in its tracks.

Me: No reason

Forty minutes later the car rolled to a stop outside the front of the familiar house. In the daylight, the perfectly maintained structure bore more resemblance to a modern castle than it did a mansion, what with the sandy stone walls, sizable ornate windows, and decorative fountain out front. There were definitely worse houses to call home.

Once everything had been toted up to my room, I began unpacking and sorting through the various items. I carefully paired some of the new outfit combinations together and stored them away with a little too much enthusiasm.

It helped keep the permanent sense of abandonment at bay when my hands were busy.

There was a gentle knock on the door behind me. "You have ten minutes, Bandit."

"Thank you." I smiled. "Is he going to be mad?"

Jesse just laughed, knowing immediately what I was referring to.

In some sick, twisted way, I really hoped he would be. I wanted to get under Marco's skin and make him realize what he'd been asking for when he'd said I didn't suit '*weak*' or '*simpering*'. And if it pushed him into a decision about marrying me off quicker… Well, it was worth the risk.

"I think the Boss just wants you to have fun. That card he gave you is pretty much bottomless."

"Bottomless?" He had to be joking.

"Pretty much. Now, you have eight minutes." Jesse smirked and quickly left the way he'd come.

I hurriedly straightened my clothes, spritzed some of my perfume and dabbed on some more powder under my eyes before I left for the dining room. With Jesse's previous reassurances in the back of my head, I was actually looking forward to the meal tonight.

The room was dressed the same as the night before. Two places laid out at either end of the table, while four waiters were stationed attentively at the far sides of the room. As soon as I entered, one of them came forward to hold out my chair and another began pouring some wine.

It was an ostentatious display of wealth having so many staff complete such minor tasks, but then again, the La Torre's didn't seem like the kind of people to prefer the understated.

Marco arrived shortly after I got settled. Unusually, his short hair was slightly disheveled, and he looked somewhat exhausted as he took his seat opposite me. I watched as a waiter served him a rich amber liquor instead of wine.

A starter of deep fried mozzarella was served as soon as we'd settled, and unable to bare the uncomfortable silence for longer than the five minutes that had already elapsed, I decided I would attempt a conversation.

"Rough day?" I asked without looking up from my food, trying to avoid the eyes I could feel like a caress against my skin the moment I spoke.

"Something like that." His deep voice sounded surprisingly weary, and I glanced at him.

"Want to talk about it?" I asked.

"No."

Silence descended again and I toyed with the salad on my plate.

"Well, I had a lovely day." I remarked.

"I heard."

He'd heard about my day, huh? His dark eyes finally met mine, but he didn't look mad like I had expected.

"The dark hair suits you." The unexpected compliment had my heart spluttering, and he quickly looked away. "Did Chicago meet your expectations?"

I got a handle on my heart and my voice after another moment. "It is now my favorite thing about living here." I paused, cautiously. "You aren't mad at me?"

"Why would I be mad at you, Ada?" *Ada*...I decided I liked his nickname for me.

"Because of all the money I spent," I hinted, confused.

The waiters came and removed my plate at that point, replacing it with the most incredible smelling steak. Marco took several bites of his.

"That was the reason I gave you the card," he said simply as if his answer were obvious.

You have got to be kidding me. I must have spent over ten thousand dollars and yet he looked as indifferent as he usually did.

I scowled.

It wasn't the reaction I was expecting and it thoroughly pissed me off. Another one of my plans now totally derailed, we lapsed back into a deafening silence. But at least it wasn't as uncomfortable this time.

I turned my attention to the beautifully tender meat before me, popping a sliver into my mouth and almost groaned at the taste. I quickly downed the rest of the dish, foregoing any further attempt at conversation until I was well into eating my Crème Brulé.

What was the point of asking me to dinner to sit in total silence? The long swaths of quiet between us were starting to eat at my nerves.

"Do you always eat in such stoney silence?" I questioned, allowing myself to stare at him from across the table.

He laughed once, but it was devoid of humor. "Sometimes."

"Then why invite me for dinner? What is the point to all this?" Irritated, I gestured to the ridiculously ostentatious set up of the room just as I had the day before.

"I eat like this every night. You are invited because you live here." His expression was condescending and cold.

Clearly, he didn't like having to explain himself.

"Can Jesse join us?" I asked, suddenly hopeful that having another person at the table might relieve some of the tension between us.

"No." His eyes flashed and the muscle in his jaw twitched as it frequently did when he was angry.

Rattled by his reaction, I leaned back in my chair to scowl at him contemptuously, not understanding where his sudden hostility had come from.

I opened my mouth to ask him about it, when one of the doors to the room swung open and Layton stepped into the hall. Marco looked just as surprised to see him as I did.

"Apologies for the interruption, Boss. Lexi has arrived as requested," He announced, keeping his eyes respectfully trained to the floor and away from my curious gaze.

Lexi? *Who the fuck is Lexi?*

The name rang a distant bell and after a moment, I remembered it was the person Jesse referred to as a 'buzzard' yesterday morning after the club. You didn't have to be a genius to work out exactly what *Lexi* was buzzing around Marco for.

I took an instant dislike to her.

"Tell her to wait in the living room." Marco waved dismissively, resuming his eating.

"No need, Layton." I spoke up. "I was just leaving this *riveting* conversation anyway. You can send his lapdog in." I added acridly, throwing my napkin on the table and rising to my feet.

A glance toward the Don told me he was quite obviously trying to contain his temper. I didn't bother acknowledging it though, briskly walking back out the way I had arrived and slamming the door behind me.

CHAPTER

NINE

ADALYN

"Just to confirm, Miss Mannino. Are you happy with the vehicle's specifications before I process the order?"

"Yes, I am. As long as it will have the wide body kit and red calipers we talked about, then I'm happy." I smiled brightly.

It was the following afternoon, and the second day of my disastrous plan to rile my captor. Was it a wise plan? No, it wasn't. But was I going to stop behaving like an ass and leave it alone? Also, no.

I was currently in the middle of purchasing an exact replica of my Dodge Hellcat from back in Las Vegas. Only this time, I opted for every single optional extra and of course bought it from new. The idea had come to me in the shower that morning, and while it was a potentially dangerous idea, I was excited to have something I could call my own... *Well, kind of.*

I quickly signed the papers and handed them back before making the payment. I was almost certain it would be declined, figuring that the odds of the Don giving me an account with

$90,000 sitting in it were slim to none. But it was at least worth a shot.

To my complete and utter surprise, the payment went through instantly.

Once we were back in the familiar SUV and hurtling down the street, I directed Alonso to take us to the nearest fast-food franchise and pulled out my phone to call Jesse.

"Yo. Guess what?" I squealed as soon as he picked up.

"Oh god. What now?"

"I bought a car!"

"You did *what*?" I could hear his shock.

"I bought a car! And not just any car, Jesse. MY car!"

"Dear God..." I heard him mutter. "What kind of car is it?"

"Why a Dodge Challenger Hellcat of course," I teased, and he groaned.

"When do you get it?"

"Two weeks. Do you think Marco will be mad?" I asked somewhat hopefully.

He just laughed into the receiver. "Doubt it. He won't even get a notification unless a transaction goes over 150k."

My jaw dropped.

"So, you're telling me I have more than $150,000 on this card?" I asked cautiously.

What. The. Fuck.

"I would guess you have a lot more than that on there. I told you—it's practically bottomless." He chuckled.

"Fuck."

"Yup."

"Alright. I'll let you know when I'm on my way back."

We ended the call, and fifteen minutes later, we pulled into the parking lot of a restaurant that clearly served anything but the fast food I had asked for. I shot the guys my best despairing look but otherwise didn't protest as they escorted me inside.

I was seated at a private booth by myself, while the men sat in another behind me.

I internally sighed and got up to sit next to them.

They both looked somewhat perplexed at my sudden appearance at their table, but didn't protest as I took a seat. I suppose it wasn't every day that their ward chose to have lunch with them.

I turned to scowl at Alonso. "Didn't I say a fast-food place?"

"Sorry, Ma'am. Boss ordered no fast-food." Came his gruff response.

Who the hell does that asshole think he is!

I fought the sudden urge to text Marco that he was an ass for trying to control my new life and flipped open my menu instead.

"Well then, fill your boots boys. The bills on Marco."

———

THE GARAGE WAS a car enthusiast's dream.

Limited editions and top spec vehicles lined the expansive forecourt culminating in only the most iconic supercars on full display in the showroom. The whole place reeked of money.

It was perfect. My plan, just a hint of an idea at the restaurant, now coming into flourishing fruition.

An enthusiastic man greeted us as we entered and quickly directed us to a private desk area, despite having no appointment. Apparently having two gigantic bodyguards in-toe didn't seem to faze the older man as he quickly got to discussing the reason for my visit and showing me their catalogue on an iPad not half an hour later.

"What did I miss?"

The sudden sound of Jesse's voice startled me, and I swiveled in my chair to find him strolling into the office.

"What are you doing here?" I questioned as he collapsed into the other chair.

"Helping you car shop." He offered good naturedly, making no attempt to stop me in my quest.

He took the tablet out of my hands and began flicking through the listings, questioning the salesman on some of the vehicles while making grunts of disgust at others.

We then took a tour of the lot, opening the various cars that piqued my interest. There was a lovely white Porsche 911 GT3 with a custom interior which was kind of cute, but ultimately didn't scream 'badass' enough so I kept looking. There were a couple of Bentleys I had a look around, but decided I didn't like and a steel grey McLaren that was stunning. I jokingly pouted at Jesse as I walked up to the purple mirrored Lamborghini Aventador, but was met with a resounding 'no' so I didn't linger long.

Ultimately, I decided on one I had seen in the catalogue earlier—a Brabus C63 AMG Coupe. Otherwise known as *the car of dreams.*

If it were a man, I'd have married it on the spot and climbed it like a tree.

It was *gorgeous* with an obsidian black exterior, privacy windows and plush rich leather interior. The car pushed over 800 brake-horsepower. My mouth was practically watering. It made my Hellcat look like a kitten.

The salesperson printed off all the paperwork and went through it with me while Jesse observed patiently. Once all the documents had been organized and it was time for payment I suddenly became very nervous. Fully expecting Jesse to laugh at me as my card was declined.

You shouldn't be doing this...This isn't even your money! A voice in my head scolded as I pulled out the card.

But the reason I was here was *because* of Marco. He was the reason my family had turned their backs on me, and I was alone. He had taken me from my family, my friends, my home and held me ransom. Only now with the ransom left unpaid I was in limbo...and facing the very real possibility of being married off to someone that hated my guts because I was a Mannino. *If* he could get someone to even agree to marry me in the first place...

Fuck him and fuck his money. I swiped the card.

One second. Two...

"That has all gone through, Miss Mannino. Here is your receipt and delivery is confirmed for one month's ti—" My phone started ringing, cutting him off.

I pulled it out and smiled when I saw the caller ID.

Right on time.

"Hello?"

"What the fuck are you doing?" Marco's voice was unmistakably furious.

"You are going to have to be more specific." I toyed.

I could practically hear his jaw muscle clenching and unclenching, "What the *fuck* did you just spend $240,000 on?" *Oh yeah, he's definitely pissed.*

"Oh, *that*!" I said airily. "Well...you were saying about how I should build myself a life here... so I bought myself a car." I drawled.

He didn't say anything for a few moments, and I pulled the phone away to check the connection.

"I thought you'd be happy!" I prompted when he still didn't speak.

I heard him exhale heavily, "What kind of car is it?" His voice was still annoyed, but I thought I could detect a trace of humor to it.

Which was something I was *not* expecting.

"A Brabus C63 AMG Coupe. It is the new love of my life."

Another sigh bled through the receiver, then a dry chuckle. "Good choice. Fine, you can keep the car."

"YAY!" I all but screamed into the phone.

"I'll see you for dinner." He started to finish, going to cut the call.

"No wait!"

"What, Ada?" I could definitely hear humor in his voice now.

"I need to show you something."

I pressed a few buttons on the phone, requesting a video call as I exited the office. The moment his face popped up on screen I could see he was sitting in his study back at the mansion.

Even on a six-inch screen he was intimidating.

I walked over to the Lamborghini Aventador I had seen earlier, carefully showing it to the camera before staring at him pointedly.

"What?" He asked cautiously.

"Pleeasseeeee." I whined, putting on my best adorable face.

"No." He scowled, and I could see his temper begin to flare.

I wasn't expecting him to say yes. I just wanted to see how many more buttons I could push, knowing I was already dangerously close to the edge. Part of me was curious to see what would happen if I did finally push him over it... I didn't think it was death that awaited me on the other side.

"Oh, come on! I'll be a good little housemate and do whatever you want..." I hinted and added in a suggestive wink for good measure.

For a split second a strange expression crossed his face, but it slipped behind his familiar mask of indifference before I could make it out. "No."

I scowled at him.

"You are forgetting that I did just buy you a *car*, Ada." He was clearly running out of patience, judging by the frown etching itself into his skin.

"Actually, you bought me two." I smiled sweetly.

I heard an audible sigh and watched as he shut his eyes, pinching the bridge of his nose between his fingers.

"Pass me to Jesse." He demanded.

I headed back to the office and shot Jesse a pleased smile as I handed the phone to him. The salesperson had notably made himself absent. Clearly the man knew how to handle himself around mobsters.

Marco and Jesse continued their conversation in Italian, exchanging sentences I didn't understand, but from the Don's tone sounded like orders being fired at Jesse.

Once they had ended the call, Jesse turned and handed me the phone with a smirk.

"Are you trying to get yourself killed?"

I grinned, but unease quickly started to swirl in my stomach despite it, "Something like that."

A half hour later and we were on the way back home. This time I rode with Jesse while Alonso and Tom followed behind us in their SUV.

The journey back passed a lot quicker than I was hoping for and by the time we had pulled to a stop outside the front of the mansion all my earlier bravado had worn off.

I was freaking out.

"Boss wants you in his study." Jesse notified me as we walked into the foyer.

My stomach flip-flopped nervously.

"Of course he does." I muttered, resigned to my fate.

I walked as slowly as I dared, trying to regain my composure before our little showdown. Another guard—Wyatt—greeted me as I approached and immediately held the door open for me as I entered.

Marco was seated behind his desk as stoic as ever, a glass of amber liquor in hand. His dark eyes settled on me the same moment I entered, and I did my best to avoid his glare. I forced myself to stare at his chest instead...which also turned out to be a mistake. Hard muscle stretched beneath the fabric and nervous flutters combined with something else erupted in my stomach.

I quickly looked away, staring at *literally anything* else in the room.

"Do you realize how much money you have spent in the last two days?" He demanded, condescendingly. "You've spent almost $400,000."

I fought the urge to gulp. There was not a chance I was getting out of this unscathed.

Well, I'm truly up shit creek now, might as well enjoy it.

So, I laughed.

"You think this is funny?" He asked, his knuckles turning white around the crystal in his hand.

"Oh, give me a break. You really don't have $400,000 lying around?"

"Let me be clear, $400,000 is nothing to me. *Nothing*," he emphasized. "What I'm pissed off about is that you've abused all the luxuries I've given you." He downed the remainder of his glass before getting up and replenishing it. His bicep flexed unmistakably as he reached for the decanter and a burn that wasn't entirely unpleasant leaked into my stomach.

Damn. I didn't have a response to that.

He's right... I shoved aside the voice in my head that told me to shut up and apologize, but I was too far down the rabbit hole to turn around now.

"For your information, *you* gave *me* the card, so excuse me if you cannot handle two days of shopping!" His brow tensed in anger.

I don't know why I did it. *A death wish? A lack of self-control?* I didn't know...but once again, I found myself prodding at the tiger I knew lived beneath his cool exterior, if only to prove to him that I wasn't the *weak* and *simpering* girl in his office only a few days ago.

"I didn't realize you were so strapped for cash, Marco. Guess you are not used to the same lifestyle as the Ma—"

That did it.

His right arm moved so violently I didn't see the glass as he launched it into the wall. It shattered and splintered into thousands of sparkling pieces on impact. The speed he moved temporarily shocking me into silence.

I quickly recovered though, shoving aside the fear that had my heart racing.

"Don't you dare mention that fucking name in my house!" He yelled, making me fight a flinch.

Before I could even blink, my back was pushed firmly into the study's wall, and I had no recollection of how I'd got there, the motion too fast for me to process. A strong hand clenched around my waist while another caged me in. Marco's black eyes were now only an inch above mine. A shiver of heat raced up my spine as his familiar spicy sent hit my nose.

"If you don't want to hear that name then maybe you shouldn't be living with one," I breathed.

Another second ticked by before Marco released his grip on my waist, only to plant both hands on the wall either side of my head instead.

"Do you really think I want a Mannino living in my house?" He wore a look of contempt on his face but leaned closer, until only a sliver of air remained between us. "That I keep you here and take responsibility for you because I have nothing better to do?"

His words cut like a razor and extinguished the intoxicating heat that had started to bubble and swell.

"Then marry me off already!" I shoved against his chest as hard as I could, but it did nothing to create space between us.

He let me continue struggling until he finally grasped my forearms and pinned them to the wall either side of my head.

"That's your plan, isn't it? You think that you can provoke me into marrying you off quickly."

Shit.

Clearly, I had not been as cunning as I had thought. I looked away guiltily.

He shook his head, letting out a quiet chuckle.

"You're going to have to come up with something better than that." An amused smile played on his lips as he straightened up finally, leaning away from me and freeing my arms.

Now I'm pissed.

I followed him, closing the distance between us once more. Close enough now that I was standing between his legs. I stood on my tiptoes and moved as close to him as I dared.

I tried to ignore how his warm breath brushed against my skin as our faces neared.

"Fuck. You." I said venomously. "Fuck you for taking me. Fuck you for keeping me here, and fuck you for ruining my life."

I turned to walk away, but once again found myself shoved firmly against the wall. His forearm pressed along the front of my chest and the contact between our skin temporarily dampened my anger.

"I *will* have respect." His voice took on a brutal edge as his eyes commanded mine.

"Then you're *really* talking to the wrong person."

For fucks sake, shut up Adalyn!

His freehand immediately slammed against the wall beside my head, the thud so loud it made my earache.

"You're playing with fire."

His words were dark, but his eyes were alight with something else I couldn't place, and I panicked, thinking I had pushed him too far...until his gaze dropped to my lips.

My unease was contorted into something else entirely when I felt his hand slide down the wall behind me. His warm skin coming to rest on the small of my back. The heat of it radiated to other, more *sinful* parts of my body and I tried to ignore the confusing feelings he was eliciting.

It was no use. His fingertip began tracing against the exposed sliver of skin above my pants, and I surprisingly didn't flinch away from his touch like I normally would have. Like I always did when a man touched my naked skin. This time instead of trying to get away from his touch, I found myself leaning into it.

The heat rising in my stomach immediately ached and pooled. My body urging me to close the distance between us and I sunk my teeth into my lip trying to thwart the sudden desire that rose within me. His eyes snagged on the motion, and his jaw twitched in response, as if he too were trying to restrain himself.

But just as my body started to give in to the irresistible pull between us and his finger dipped beneath the material at my hip, the study door swung open, and Benny waltzed into the room.

He paused mid-step when he noticed our precarious position against the wall.

"Excuse me, Boss. It's urgent." The older man said gruffly, diverting his gaze.

Marco didn't move, as if contemplating whether there was an option that didn't involve dealing with Benny's interruption.

One second. Two... Eventually he released me, turning back toward his desk. I shook my head slightly and took the opportunity to leave, promptly heading in the direction of the study door while Marco's back remained turned toward me.

I didn't dare look at Benny as I passed him, and I didn't dare stop until I was halfway down the hall, hidden behind a section of wall.

My heartbeat thundered in my ears.

Well that definitely wasn't part of the plan.

CHAPTER
TEN

ADALYN

For the next week, I was banned from leaving the house. My credit card was thankfully still in my purse, but my relative freedom and happiness were well and truly down the drain. I had lounged by the pool, practiced my cooking, read books and worked out in the gym...never once coming into contact with Marco.

By the eighth day of house arrest, I was going stir-crazy and just about ready to trash the place in frustration.

Luckily, Jesse brought me some good news that morning.

"We are going out tonight." He announced after he had swallowed a mouthful of orange juice.

"We are?" I exclaimed with unprecedented excitement.

"Yup. We have business at one of our clubs in Milwaukee. It's an overnighter so don't forget to pack a bag."

"Alright. What kinda dress code are we talking?"

"You know, the norm. High heels, lots of makeup, slutty dresses." He winked and I laughed.

"You won't have to abandon me the whole night, will you? I hate dancing by myself."

"Naa, just some of it." He grinned. "We are there for business after all."

The rest of the day was spent on cloud nine, excited for the evening and getting back some relative 'freedom'. I had packed my bag for the night and spent the next few hours planning my outfit.

I had decided on a very short black dress with long tight sleeves and a high neckline. The dress clung to my curves in a sexy but sophisticated way, showing off my best features. I finished off the look with a Yves Saint Laurent clutch and over-the-knee leather boots that accentuated the tops of my thighs. I dabbed on an intoxicatingly red shade of lipstick and paired it with dramatic smoky eyeshadow.

By the time I came downstairs it was six o'clock and Jesse's G-Wagon was waiting out front for me. I could see two other armored SUV's already heading down the driveway as we left the house and presumed that Marco was inside one of them. I was suddenly grateful I wasn't expected to ride with him.

Nothing like postponing the inevitable.

My stomach flip-flopped violently, though whether it was from anxiety or something else I didn't know.

The drive to the club took just under two hours and by the time we arrived in the underground garage it was close to eight. My stomach grumbled with hunger as we made it to the elevator and proceeded to ascend the numerous floors.

When we came to a stop, we weren't in a club as I had expected, but a very classy restaurant complete with a live pianist and waiters in white-tailed coats.

A friendly hostess immediately approached and greeted us, making sure to pay extra attention to the man at my side.

She swiftly walked us to a glass corridor which seemed to

boast multiple private-function rooms, and she gestured for me to continue as we turned the corner. Layton and Wyatt stood outside the last remaining door and they both nodded to me as I passed.

Unsurprisingly, Marco sat at the head of a modern glass table as I entered. He was typing away on his phone, looking very much like sin incarnate as I took my seat across from him. Once I'd settled, he placed the phone to the side and fixed me with his gaze for the first time in over a week.

My stomach somersaulted.

He smiled. "You loo—"

"Save it," I dismissed.

I didn't want to hear it.

Not when there had been such a dangerous moment between us before. I needed to keep him at a distance. The lines were beginning to haze and blur between us, and I couldn't afford for that to happen.

He scowled at my rudeness.

"I'm a bit surprised you brought me here," I said, inspecting the room. "I thought you would be too ashamed to be seen with a *Mannino*," I jeered.

He smiled half-heartedly and shook his head. "As it turns out, not very many people know who you are around here."

I pursed my lips at his backhanded comment.

Before I could respond, two waitresses entered carrying plates of food and poured us both some wine. I didn't miss the flirty smile one of them flashed Marco as she filled his glass, or how she pivoted her hips to show off her cleavage. He shot her a charming smile in return.

I bristled at the sight but couldn't exactly place why it had annoyed me so much.

I bit back the crappy comment I had on the tip of my tongue the moment they left and focused on eating the creamy pasta dish instead. It tasted absolutely divine and was a welcome distraction from the awkward tension in the room.

After a few minutes, I decided to break the silence. There was something I did, *in fact,* want to talk to him about.

"I've actually been thinking about that. I think it's probably best for me to change my name now that I'm, well...not part of my family anymore." I couldn't deny the pain I still felt saying the words aloud. "I thought it might be safer."

While the decision made sense, it didn't take the pain away from my suggestion.

He looked at me quietly a moment. "I agree. I'll have someone come by the house in the next couple of days to help with the paperwork."

"I don't know what I'm changing it to yet." I admitted.

"Does it matter?" His dark eyes burned into mine.

"Of course, it matters. It's going to be a fresh start." I fidgeted nervously, looking down at my food to break his unflinching gaze.

"In which case, I would suggest you change it to La Torre." He suggested.

I immediately began choking on the food in my mouth.

"W-what kind of suggestion is that?" I asked incredulously, clearing my throat with a gulp of wine. "You can't be serious."

My stomach knotted both from anxiety and something else —something that felt oddly like anticipation, but primarily like fear.

He shrugged and lounged back in his seat. "The name La Torre is respected and more importantly, it is *feared*. It would provide you simultaneously with opportunity as well as protection by way of association."

I opened and closed my mouth a few times, trying to piece together my argument despite his sound rationale.

"Or it could put an even *bigger* target on my back," I pointed out. "First of all, your family are not going to take kindly to a *Mannino* using their name. Secondly, changing it to a rival family's would only give my *real* family more reason to hate me."

"What I say goes in my family, whether they like it or not. I'm it's head and they obey me. End of story. As to your second point—your family abandoned you. If you want to join another family, then that's on them." He took another swig of his glass. "At least my family protects its own," He added quietly.

I sighed, "The answer is no, Marco."

His fist clenched, and I could tell he was unhappy with my rejection.

The silence resumed to a painful degree, and I could feel his anger lingering in the air up until the waitresses flittered back into the room, collecting our plates. A decedent cheesecake left in their place.

"How long have you been a Don for anyway?" I grappled to say something. *Anything* to stifle the discomfort in the room.

"Seven years."

Around the same time my family went into hiding. It was a strange coincidence.

"And no, it's not a coincidence," He answered my internal thought, completely freaking me out.

"What do you mean it's not a coincidence?" I asked, confused.

He seemed to contemplate answering my question for a few moments.

When he did finally speak, his voice remained slow and measured. "Seven years ago, my family was in negotiations with the Manninos over a narcotics deal. It would have united our families logistically speaking and established a new country-wide line guaranteeing an expansion of profits. Your father decided that instead of honoring that deal, he was going to make another deal...a deal with the DEA." Marco's face remained cold and calculated. Unfeeling.

I knew Marco was telling the truth.

I could remember the two DEA agents coming to our mansion in Las Vegas before we disappeared and became the

'Parkers'. I remembered the numerous meetings my family had hosted with them, the numerous times their cars were on the driveway... I hadn't known what it was about at the time. It was like a puzzle piece finally falling into place.

"He set us up. It was practically an extermination of my family, and my father died in the process. I had no choice but to become the head of this family when I was twenty-two. I've been seeking revenge ever since," he finished simply. He slid his empty tumbler across the table and rubbed at his chin, as if he could rub away the hint of emotion etched across his skin.

"That's why you took me. To take someone he loves away from him... You were going to kill me," I said, finally understanding everything.

"It did cross my mind to kill you, but it turns out that I'm not as ruthless as I thought. So, I held you hostage instead," he said, looking away somewhat shamefully after admitting his weakness. His humility.

"My intention was to get back the money my family had lost and make him suffer in the process. But your father is even more abhorrent than I could have anticipated. He didn't hesitate to turn his back on his own."

The sentence hung there for a minute, weighing heavily against the silence. Against me.

My family were rats... A disgrace to everything our society valued about honor.

"I'm sorry you lost your father so young... And I am truly sorry for what my family has done to yours. It is unforgivable," I said after a quiet moment. "I now understand why you hate me so much. I don't even blame you," I said, meeting his eyes so he could see my sincerity.

"I don't hate you, Ada." His deep voice took on a rough edge, raw with his own honesty. "None of what happened was your fault. I will not punish you for the crimes of your father."

Our eyes fell into a kind of deadlock across the table, and I felt something shift in the air between us. I couldn't be sure, but I swore I could see the darkness in his eyes simmer into something softer.

Something I was certain he would have seen echoed in mine.

He wasn't the cruel, calculated Don I had convinced myself existed. He was a man who had lost his father and tried to enact revenge in the only way he knew how. Only he wasn't cruel enough or twisted enough to go through with it, so he changed tact and demanded a ransom instead. He wasn't the merciless killer he needed to be or thought that he was.

He was a square peg forced into a round hole—just like me.

Something like recognition flickered between us.

Thankfully, the door slamming open and Jesse waltzing into the room broke through the trance that had ensnared us, stopping Marco from uttering the next words poised on his lips.

Jesse immediately informed Marco that the men they were meeting with had begun to arrive and a flurry of activity ensued. The three of us accompanied by our collective bodyguards made our way down to the main club in preparation.

When the elevators opened this time, it revealed a private seating arrangement on its own mezzanine floor above the rest of the room. It was both intimate and classy, featuring its own solid oak bar and two waitresses ready with decanters full of whiskey. The guards took their positions by the exits, and I took that as my queue to leave, heading down the stairs to the floor below just as three leery middle-aged men approached.

At the bar, I ordered myself a drink and took one of the open seats, swiveling around so I could look up at the balcony. I was intrigued by what the meeting was about and who the unfamiliar men were that I had passed on the steps.

The first thing I noted was Jesse standing against the rails observing me and I did a little wave at him. He smiled before taking a seat with the other people. I say people... The men had apparently been joined with six or so other women. All scantily clad and all extremely beautiful. *Hookers.*

My lips pursed, and I turned my chair back to the bar, not wanting to watch any longer.

————

AFTER AN HOUR of crowd watching and drinking, I became restless and bored. I had downed my drink and, feeling gutsy, decided I would go in search of Jesse.

Alonso was at the foot of the stairs now alongside Tom. I greeted them both before making my way up to the raucous laughter and undeniable smell of sickly-sweet perfume.

Jesse was the first to notice me, grinning as if he was genuinely happy to see me. I began to smile back but stopped the moment I saw the full scene in front of me.

The three men I had passed earlier were sat with Jesse and Marco on a luscious red sofa. Women were scattered between them, languishing suggestively over the men and serving something on a platter. As I came closer, I realized the white trails on the silver surface were, in fact, cocaine.

It didn't bother me that drugs were present in the booth—as much as I despised drugs, I had half expected it—what bothered me was that Marco was shooting a line while a stunning brunette sucked on his neck and groped at his crotch.

The moment he pulled away our eyes met, and I felt inexplicably...*hurt.*

The closeness and care I had felt toward him earlier all but vanished in an instant.

They were all the same—Mafia men. Whatever I thought was happening between us earlier, I had been wrong.

I turned on my heel and escaped back to the bar, fully intending to drown my stupidity and hurt into oblivion.

I ordered three shots of vodka and downed them one after the other.

When that didn't dispel my unease, I ordered another round and drank until the buzz of alcohol overtook everything else. Until all that I cared about was enjoying the music.

"Hey, Girl. What's your name?"

I looked over my shoulder to see a muscular blond guy leaning against the counter beside me. He was clearly the athletic type with heavy-set shoulders and the most dazzling blue eyes.

I flashed him my flirtiest smile and stuck out my hand.

"Adalyn. And you are?"

"Brandon." He smiled handsomely at me and shook my hand. "Can I get you a drink?"

"No, no it's on me." *Well Marco...*

I gestured to the bartender, and he quickly got me my signature lime spritzer (don't ask me how he knew what I drank) and a beer for my companion.

"I don't think I've seen you around here before, are you from Milwaukee?"

Ha! If only you knew.

"No, I'm Chicago!" I lied, yelling over the music. "And you?"

"I'm Milwaukee born and raised. I thought you weren't local... I'd remember a girl like you." He winked.

"Oh, really?" I leaned in closer, resting my hand on the back of his neck. "Now tell me...does that pickup line ever work?"

"Like seventy percent of the time," he admitted sheepishly, and I threw my head back with laughter.

"I admire your honesty," I said, shooting him a flirty smile.

His hand gently came to rest on my thigh, and my smile faltered for just a second as I fought the inevitable flinch. The physical touch making my mind flash away from the club and to a distant point in my past. The unpleasant memory rattled in the back of my mind, and I shoved against it, blocking it out. Unable and unwilling to think back to *then*. To *him*.

I regained my composure and leaned in closer to the handsome jock before me.

"You really are beautiful you know..." He trailed off as I stared squarely at his lips, effectively giving him the green light.

I wasn't usually so forward, but with everything going on lately I was craving some kind of escapism. No matter what it looked like.

He took the bait, planting a hand on the side of my face and pressing his lips to mine. I opened my mouth to deepen the kiss and then...

Then he was gone.

A second later something wet splattered across my face and I tore open my eyes in shock. Brandon was on the floor bleeding profusely from his nose.

I whipped my head around and found a murderous looking Marco standing over him, fist still clenched and smeared in blood.

"What the fuck are you doing?" I screeched at him, bending over to help Brandon up from the floor.

The man was already on his feet and squaring up to his attacker challengingly, pushing me out of the way in the process.

"What the hell is your problem, dude?" Brandon demanded.

But before the question was fully out of his mouth, Marco had a Glock pressed harshly beneath his jaw.

"*You* are my fucking problem," he spat through clenched teeth, the veins protruding from his forehead as searing rage contorted his features.

Jesse and Layton quickly emerged, descending on us and looking to diffuse the situation. But Marco was already too far gone for that, his finger dangerously close to pulling the trigger.

"Stop it!" I yelled, but he either ignored me or didn't hear.

I knew there was a chance I would get hurt, but I wasn't going to let a man get shot over one drunken kiss.

I lurched forward and forced myself between the two men.

"Marco!" I shouted up at him.

Nothing.

"Marco, enough!" I grabbed either side of his face with my hands and forced him to look at me.

His black eyes sliced to mine, full of nothing but violence and I flinched at the brutality I saw within him. A brutality I had never seen before.

"Please don't do this." When the words didn't seem to be enough, I caressed the side of his face gently.

His breathing remained heavy, but I could see the turmoil on his face as he weighed up whether or not to listen.

He eventually gave me a slight nod and relief flushed my skin.

"Jesse! Get him out of here!" I immediately yelled over my shoulder.

I felt, rather than saw, the man be shoved away.

Marco retracted the Glock and stored it back behind his waistband, never taking his eyes off me.

I waited until I was sure Jesse and the other man had left the area, before I let my hands drop back to my sides. "What the fuck was that?" I demanded, stepping away from him.

He smirked and shrugged as if nothing had happened. "What was what?"

This man's personality was like a tornado, and I was starting to grow fucking tired of it.

Anger and frustration engulfed me in an instant.

I downed the rest of my drink and grabbed my bag off the chair. "I'm leaving."

I shoved past the asshole and after spotting Jesse in the crowd I walked toward him. One look at my face and he immediately took me to the elevators, calling one for us and letting me in first when it arrived. But just as the doors started to close, a hand swung in, and they jerked open with a whine.

My scowl of annoyance quickly turned into a growl.

Marco barked something I didn't understand at Jesse as he stepped into the confined space, and it quickly sent Jesse flying back out the open doors. He shot me an apologetic look from the hallway, leaving me alone with the Don as the doors slid shut.

I seethed quietly in the corner as the elevator began moving, descending the floors and heading for the underground parking garage.

I couldn't hold back my irritation any longer. "You're a fucking asshole, d'you know that?"

Marco let out a boyish laugh and my blood boiled.

When the doors dinged open for our floor, I immediately sprung out of the elevator and marched over to Jesse's SUV. I pulled at the handle, but unfortunately for me, it was locked and there was no sign of Jesse. I mentally smacked my head against a brick wall.

"Why are you so mad? You don't even know the guy." Marco leaned against the car casually, as if he hadn't been holding a gun to someone's head less than five minutes before.

"Why do you think?" I yelled. "You can't just scare off everyone that approaches me and threaten to shoot them! Who do you think you are?"

I could see his light-hearted expression turn irritated at my question.

"*I'm* the guy that owns your ass. I do what the fuck I want. When I want. If I don't want another man touching you, then he isn't fucking touching you!" He shouted right back at me, storming closer as he spoke.

"This isn't the middle-ages. I can do whatever I want. Get over yourself!"

"I can't decide if you're brave or stupid speaking to me like that," he spat, now less than a foot away.

"Guess it's easy to be brave when you have nothing to lose." I glared. "It also doesn't help when your captor's a total piece of shit."

Probably shouldn't have said that.

Within a second, I was cornered against the car door.

It was then that I felt his other hand.

I expected to flinch like I had earlier with Brandon, like I always did when a man touched my skin...but it never came. The warmth of Marco's hand felt nothing like the one that frequented my nightmares.

My breathing faltered as I became keenly aware of Marco's touch, feeling him trace along the outside of my thigh, skimming upward along my hip. His hand slowly reaching my waist, then grazed against the side of my ribs. I fought a shiver as it rolled down my spine. His eyes traced his touch, following the path upward across my dress until I felt his warmth settle over my breasts.

Heat instantly pooled between my legs and my breathing hitched in response.

"You might *think* you are in control, Ada, but you are not." His words brushed against my neck. "I can do whatever I want with you...or to you."

His words washed over me like a bucket of ice.

"What's your point? That you can touch me and no one else can?" I spat.

I'll show him who's in control.

I called his bluff and grabbed his wrist, leading his hand back down my body and under my mini skirt. When his hand rested on the outside of my lace panties, I stilled. His eyes darkened with lust and his head sprung up to look at me, arousal and confusion clouding his features as his eyes swam in and out of focus.

"What about here?" My voice came out breathier than I intended it, but I was getting to him and couldn't stop now.

With my other hand, I caressed his face like I had earlier, and he leaned in, closing the distance between us.

I waited until the last second before turning my head away, brushing my lips to his ear.

Don't do it. Don't do it... DO. NOT. DO. IT.

"You're not the first, Marco. Many men already have. You wouldn't be anything special." I let disgust drip into my voice, and he growled, roughly moving every inch of his hard body against me. Trapping me against the side of the car.

His hand roughly fisted the material of my panties while his other hand simultaneously wound around my neck. The muscle in his jaw twitched uncontrollably.

"You'll see how *special* I am when my dick is so deep inside you, you can't fucking breathe."

My mouth slackened in total and complete shock. His brutal words sinking beneath my skin, causing my stomach to flood and pool with something that felt entirely too much like arousal.

He grinned devilishly at the sight of desire clouding my features, very much enjoying the show.

I was both irked and relieved when a booming voice rang out against the silence of the garage. "What's going on here, then?" Jesse's voice echoed across the cement, but I could detect his usual lilt of humor.

Marco released me and shoved himself away two seconds later than I expected, turning toward the other man as Jesse crossed the lot. They both exchanged a few sentences again that I didn't understand, deliberately omitting me from the conversation judging by the glances they both occasionally threw in my direction. Marco ran a hand through his hair, muttering another sentence in Italian before storming back in the direction of the elevators without so much as a backwards glance in my direction.

Part of me breathed a sigh of relief when his form disappeared. The only problem was that a larger part of me was frustrated he'd walked away before we could see where our little game was taking us.

"What was all that about?" I asked, turning to Jesse incredulously. Not sure what the two had talked about and what had subsequently caused Marco to storm off back into the club.

"I was about to ask you the same question," he responded, eyeballing me and opening the passenger side door. "Now get your ass in before you give the CCTV guy another heart attack."

I immediately glanced around to check for cameras and flushed bright red when I spotted several. I threw myself into the SUV and leaned my head against the cool leather.

What the hell are you playing at? I didn't even know. *The whole world's gone bat shit crazy.*

———

MARCO

I had to stop attacking the clientele—it was becoming bad for business.

I slammed my palm against the buttons on the elevator panel, the metal thudding dully as the light flickered on for the floor I wanted.

You wouldn't be anything special.

Anger bubbled under my skin and, unable to stem the tide of rage burning within me, I threw my fist straight into the mirror at my side. The shards fractured and bowed under the force of my knuckles, microscopic pieces quickly embedding themselves into my skin. *Good.* The stinging helped clear my head.

I gripped the handrail, glaring at my crooked reflection as the lift slowly ascended the floors.

I couldn't unhear the disgust in Ada's words or unsee the hatred in her eyes as she had said them.

I had more power and money than 99.9% of the fucking planet—it wasn't often I felt *unwanted.*

And yet, she had kissed that blonde fucker—*a fucking nobody.*

My teeth snapped together as my muscles clenched, anger once again churning beneath the surface.

How could she do that?

I could have sworn that something had shifted between us at dinner. We had found common ground, talked about difficult and *personal* things...things I didn't freely discuss with just anyone.

Then she ran off and made out with some randomer at my bar, like it all meant nothing.

The doors slid open, and I promptly crossed the hall toward the main room. It was hot and heavy as I entered. Alcohol tinging the air with a stale, sweet smell that mingled inelegantly with tacky perfume. The bass of the speakers were cranked as high as they could go, almost cancelling out the squelching of spilled beverages underfoot.

I really need to raise the entry fee, I thought disdainfully. This type of clientele was not to my usual standard.

The private seating area was still littered with people as I retook my seat. Integrating myself back into their drunken discussions and deftly batting away an insolent woman that tried to mount me the second my ass hit the cushion.

I grabbed my drink and downed the double shot of bourbon in one, gesturing for a refill.

"That bloody Mannino is more hassle than she is worth,

Cousin." Roberto slapped me on the shoulder, taking the now vacant seat beside me. "You should just kill her already," he said, finishing off the remainder of his beer.

"If I wanted your advice, I would have asked for it," I muttered, sipping my own drink.

"Even *you* must see that she is bad for business."

I swiped my hand across my face, trying to quell my temper as it slowly began building once again.

"We could say it was an accident," he offered, grinning like it was his greatest idea yet, and perhaps it was. Roberto had always been as thick as shit. "If you don't want to pull the trigger, Cuz, I can always do it for you. I'll even do it for free if you let me fuck her first."

I didn't even try to control my response.

I grabbed him by the back of his neck and slammed his face against the edge of the table with a sickening crack. Blood sprayed up my leg and screams from the women dotted amongst us rang out, but I hardly even noticed.

I bent over him. My head inches away from Roberto's ear, as his face leaked all over the floor and onto my leather Tom Ford's. *Goddamn it, these were new.* His pleas and apologies quickly cut off the moment my hand tightened against his scalp.

"You're *done*." I spat. "Get the fuck out of my club and disappear or I will kill you myself."

I released the miserable excuse of a man and shoved him away. I had been trying to get rid of him for years anyway.

He quickly scrambled to his feet and without so much as a glance back, ran for the exit.

"Let that be a lesson to you all."

CHAPTER
ELEVEN

ADALYN

First thing Monday morning I called the Dodge dealership to arrange collecting my car and got Alonso to take me to the store to purchase a laptop. I spent the rest of the day muddling through a CV and applying to various jobs in the local area. Whether it was common or not amongst women in the Cosa Nostra, I decided that a job was likely the only way I'd stay sane in this new life I was given. Marco was just going to have to deal with it.

On Tuesday, a solicitor came to the house to help me complete paperwork for my change of name and by Wednesday I was officially Adalyn *Rossi*. I had gone to collect my beautiful Hellcat that Thursday and Jesse took me out for a track day afterwards so we could both take turns driving it around the Chicagoland Speedway. As it turned out, Jesse was a pretty talented driver, and we had an adrenaline-filled after-noon, which was the most fun I'd had in as long as I could remember.

On Friday, I had decided that if I was to make a real go of it in Chicago, then I needed to have a space that felt like home. The only way to do that: redecorate my room.

In order to gather inspiration for my project, I decided to take a tour of some of the other guest bedrooms in the house. There were six in total, excluding my room, Jesse's room and Marco's wing. As far as I could tell, the other members of security and house staff either lived over the expansive garage or in a separate building on the property. Even Jesse hadn't lived in the main house until I arrived.

Much to my dismay, the other guest bedrooms had all been designed similarly to mine, though none were quite as superior. I was met with dark charcoals, mahogany furniture and muted shades of grey dispersed with colorful artwork on the walls of each one. After I had closed the door to the final guest room, I found myself overcome with curiosity.

Thankfully, Marco had been away for the entire week, and with no risk of bumping into the devil himself... I crept over to the double doors leading to his wing of the house.

I cracked open the door and slid inside once the coast was clear. I was immediately met with a hallway containing four additional doors and I tiptoed my way through the largest of them.

I didn't know what I had expected his room to look like, but it definitely wasn't what I saw.

The room was enormous. Two story high windows stretched along the furthest wall, entrapping the bed at the room's center in light. A grand walnut balcony clung to the edges of the room, accessible by matching brass spiral staircases in the corners and housing bespoke shelving above. Contrary to the other rooms of the house, this room's design was much more elegant and timeless. Deep caramels and nudes bathed the room, a calming contradiction to the rich polished wood.

I quietly wandered around, noting the relatively uninhabited nature of its decoration. No pictures were hung on the walls or placed on the bedside tables, nor were there any possessions in sight. It was strangely impersonal.

I didn't linger in the room long, figuring I had pushed my luck enough for one day. I abandoned his wing of the house without exploring any further and went back to my room to start compiling ideas. I wanted something that not only reflected my personality, but complimented the rest of the home's décor as well, which was proving to be no small feat.

By late afternoon, I had chosen my color scheme and some of the key furniture changes I wanted to include.

I picked up my phone to call Jesse.

"What's up?" He answered after the second ring.

"Where's a printer 'round here? I got stuff I gotta print off." I asked, finishing up on my laptop.

"You can use the one in my office."

"You have an office?"

He did tend to disappear all day, but it hadn't occurred to me that it was because he had an office to go to.

"Yes, Bandit." He sighed in mock exasperation. "It's in the annex, first door on the left."

I hung up the phone, slipped my sneakers on, and collected my laptop before making my way down the imperial stairs and out onto the drive. I walked around toward the right side of the house and followed the drive until an enormous garage and an entirely separate building emerged. I hadn't been to this part of the property before, so when I saw one of the four garage doors open, I couldn't help but peek inside as curiously as a cat.

My mouth slacked when I did.

Firstly, the garage was far larger than it appeared from the front, going back five car lengths in fact. Secondly, the number of valuable cars it housed was staggering. Lamborghinis, Bentleys and even a Pagani were parked along its length—and those were only the ones I could see. There appeared to be one or two more hidden under satin cloths that I didn't dare approach.

Most men would have sold their soul to the devil just for a chance to own a collection like his... Or willingly become a gangster.

Opposite the eye-watering collection were three armored security vehicles, including Jesse's own Mercedes. Only two seemed to be absent from the fleet, their spaces ominously vacant.

After doing my fair share of rubbernecking, I decided it was time to locate Jesse's office. His office was at the front of the annex building and wasn't all that difficult to find. Though, *office* wasn't exactly the term I would have used for it, given that it more closely resembled a control room than an actual work-space. TV screens ran the length of the wall behind his desk and six computer monitors sat below them. They seemed to be broadcasting various CCTV camera feeds from around the house as well as some other rooms I didn't recognize.

"I always knew you were a pervert." I greeted, throwing myself down into the chair opposite his desk.

He let out a chuckle and leaned away from his computer, relaxing further into his chair.

"What are all those?" I asked, mesmerized by all the pictures I was seeing.

"CCTV cameras." He swizzled around to look behind him. "It's pretty cool. I can switch to show some of the feeds from our businesses in Chicago as well." He picked up a remote and suddenly a casino lobby came into view on one.

"That's awesome," I said, coming around the desk to take a closer look.

"Not bad, hey?" He said with obvious pride.

"That's how you knew I had left the first night," I realized, and he laughed.

"Oh yes, the night of the great robbery," he mocked.

"Shut up."

He flicked the remote again and suddenly the TV was back to displaying various feeds from the house. Movement in the top right of one caught my attention and I watched as two cars pulled into the portico out front.

I saw Layton quickly get out of the first car and hold open the rear door, allowing a tall blonde woman to step out. She was dressed in high waist blue jeans and a white bandeau top that did little to hide her fake tits. Marco emerged behind her and as soon as his feet met the pavement, the woman wrapped her arms around his neck and all but threw herself at him.

I scowled at the scene, my teeth snapping together with a click.

"That's Lexi." Jesse said noting my gaze.

I had taken an instant dislike to the woman when I had first heard her name, but my dislike was now growing rapidly into contempt.

"Marco's girlfriend." I guessed, trying to hide the irritation from my voice.

"Oh god no. Don't let him hear you say that." He laughed. "I think it is more similar to your *Jason* situation."

I turned to him in shock. My cheeks heated in embarrassment.

Marco must have shown him the messages on my phone.

"Smokinnn." He mocked, and it was all the confirmation I needed.

"Shut up. You're both perverts." I scowled and he grinned mischievously.

"So, that's where he's been all week?" I tried my best to hide my interest.

"No. I think she just turned up at the airport to greet him." He eyed the screen where they had moved to sucking face in the foyer.

"Sounds like a girlfriend thing to do to me."

I turned away from the screen, resuming my seat, not wanting to see the display. Being bothered about it meant I cared, and I was *not* going to allow myself to do that.

I popped my laptop on the desk opposite Jesse and with his help, managed to get printed all the things I needed for my mood board. After digging around in a supply cupboard nearby, he also managed to find me an old corkboard that I could use to piece together my ideas. I didn't go back to the house to work, preferring the floor of Jesse's office instead. I immersed myself completely in my task, trying my best to keep my mind from wandering back to the house and what Marco was doing.

I refused to allow my disappointment to settle as it sunk beneath my skin.

———

THE NEXT EVENING, I sat at a bar on my second drink and completely bored out of my mind. Déjà vu was kicking in, and I didn't fucking care for it.

Isn't there more to being a gangster than going to clubs? I sat, speculating bitterly.

As one hour morphed into two, I decided the only way I wasn't going to kill myself out of disinterest was to get fabulously drunk. I ordered a couple of shots of tequila and sunk them back until I felt the warm buzz of alcohol.

"Alonsooo!"

I moved closer to the mountain of a man who was situated at one end of the bar monitoring the room, stoic as usual.

"Yes, Ma'am?" He asked, a small smile contorting his rugged features.

"You are doing some shots with me!" I commanded.

"I'm sorry Ma'am, I can't join in with you tonight." He said apologetically.

"Oh come on, Alonsooooo," I whined, refusing to allow him out of it. "I'm so bored, pretty please? I need a drinking buddy."

"I'm sorry, Ma'am." He said resolutely, but I could hear the humor in his voice. Unfortunately for him, I wasn't going to quit that easily.

"Right then!" I announced, turning to the barman who was only too eager to help me. "Hey handsome, I would like six more shots of tequila for me and my boring friend."

"Of course, beautiful." The bartender grinned and poured out six shots, lining them up for us.

"Now, here is the deal, Alonso. Every shot you don't drink means I must drink it. And I don't think I can drink six more shots without passing out...so you had better help a girl out, okay?" I said to him expectantly.

He eyed me suspiciously but didn't say anything in response.

"One, two, three!" I tipped back the first one and looked at him expectantly. When he didn't move, I grabbed his shot and downed it as well.

"One, two, three!" I called again, tipping back another before turning to him.

"Alright, alright. Hold on a second." He put a hand to his ear and started speaking into his wrist, apparently asking someone for permission.

I bet it's Jesse.

"Jesse! *Please* let Alonso drink with me! I'm fucking bored!" I yelled at his wrist.

After a few more seconds of quiet mutterings and nod of the head, Alonso grabbed his shot and downed it.

"Yes, my man!" I screamed, doing a little drum roll on his chest. "Another!" We both did the last one together and I applauded him playfully. Earning me a grin.

"Now seriously, Ma'am, I can't drink anymore with you." I started to pout but his face turned stern and serious.

I was about to call over Tom, hoping to convince him to play along too, but as I turned a swarm of black suits came into the room. It took me a minute to realize that what I was actually seeing was about fifteen of Marco's men. They moved as one as they crossed the room, descending on a group of tables to the side.

I shrank behind Alonso as best I could, not wanting to draw any attention from the man I really didn't want to see tonight. I had even begged Jesse to leave me at home for the evening...

I should be so goddamn lucky.

Marco stopped directly in front of us and Alonso stood to attention, inclining his head respectfully.

"You're drunk." Marco observed, addressing me with his familiar dark eyes.

"And all you ever seem to do is tell me off." I fired back, crossing my arms challengingly.

"If you just behaved, I wouldn't have to."

"If you let me stay at home then you wouldn't have to. Or, even better, let me *go*—then you wouldn't have to." I smiled sweetly.

"Watch it." He stepped closer, invading my space as his eyes narrowed. "Do you need me to remind you of what happened the last time?" Immediately images of him threatening the man with a gun flashed across my mind.

His breath brushed along my skin, and he went to move away, but I stuck a hand out and grabbed his collar before I could even register what I was doing.

I feigned correcting his tie as I spoke. His eyes darkening as they bore into me. "If I want to fool around with someone, Marco, then I will. Threat or no threat." I promised, releasing him and turning.

He was quicker though, catching me by the elbow and spinning me back around. His face mere millimeters away. "I will shoot any man that touches you." I could see the possessiveness in his fierce expression and didn't doubt he meant it.

"Why?" I found myself asking.

My stomach did a flip in anticipation.

Anticipation? Ugh what is wrong with me.

A second ticked by, then another. I could see his expression closing down, reverting back into his familiar indifference and I knew he wasn't going to answer me.

I yanked my arm free from his grip and trotted off toward the dance floor, joining the gyrating bodies instead. I moved to the upbeat rhythm suggestively, getting lost in the music for a while as the alcohol buzzed and made my mind numb to much else other than the pounding in my ears.

It didn't take long for my moves to attract some attention, and after a few songs, I felt someone grinding up behind me. I changed my tempo to match whoever had joined, but the moment I spun around to see who it was they disappeared. I brushed it off as a passer-by and continued dancing until I felt another man's hands on my waist. I once again moved to see the person, when the hands suddenly disappeared. This time, there was a small space in the crowd where the person *should* have been.

Growing suspicious, I kept my wits about me as I started dancing with another person. When it happened again, I spun around just in time to catch Tom dragging the man through the crowd and away.

What the fuck?

I marched unsteadily over to Alonso who stood nearby with a smirk on his face.

"What the hell is going on?" I demanded.

"Apologies, Ma'am. Boss's orders."

I growled in frustration and ploughed through the crowd to the table where Don Dickhead sat.

Alcohol still simmered in my veins, completely drowning out the voice in my head that told me this was not just a horrible idea, but a suicidal one.

My anger only increased when I saw a blonde woman who looked suspiciously like the bimbo from the CCTV, perched on Marco's lap. The other men around the table were in similar positions with an array of different women. Scantily clad legs and sky-high heels littered the scene.

Unfortunately, their presence did little to stem my boiling rage.

"What the *fuck* is your problem?" I yelled, coming to a stop at the foot of the table and glowering at Marco.

Everyone froze and mouths fell agape as they all turned to stare at me. Marco's face flared with unmistakable fury, and I swallowed, regret and fear making my mouth dry as sand as I realized the extent of my actions.

To question the Don, much less *shout* at him in front of other family members was the equivalent to using an electrical cord as bungee rope when jumping off a bridge. I never would have dared the same behavior with my own family back in Las Vegas—but then again, I had a family that wanted me *simpering* and *weak* back then.

Well... I hope I have a nice funeral.

I kept my face immovable as I stared at him, unwilling to show my apprehension and instant regret.

The muscle in Marco's jaw worked overtime as he shoved Lexi away carelessly, ignoring her sounds of indignation. He rose from the seat and stormed over to me. His vice-like hand circling my upper arm as he pulled me away from the group, not stopping until we were through a small side door marked for staff use only.

I didn't resist as the wall pressed into my back. Just as I didn't flinch as his large hands gripped my arms.

Well done, you've finally made him snap. Are you happy now?

Fuck. No, I wasn't. Fear prickled at my skin.

"Who the *fuck* do you think you are talking to?" He questioned, voice steady as ice and as sharp as a razor.

I stayed silent.

"If you speak to me like that aga-"

"You'll what?" I interrupted, sounding surprisingly unaffected.

For the love of God, shut up Adalyn!

He didn't answer, his black eyes clashing against mine.

"Do not confuse my not killing you for weakness, Ada. If I wanted you dead, you would *be* dead." One hand moved to my throat and squeezed as if to emphasize his point. "I am the Don of this family; the sooner you learn that the better."

"You are forgetting something." I breathed, struggling to suck in a proper breath. He loosened his hand a little in response. "You may be the Don to this family, but this is not *my* family. To me, you are just another asshole with a Rolex." I smiled as his expression darkened. "You don't scare me." I lied.

Why don't I just douse myself in gasoline and light myself on fire?

His palm slammed against the wall two inches from my head, making me jump and sobering me up. His grip once again tightened at my throat and I fought off the rattling of another, less pleasant memory, as it threatened to resurface. I could see his teeth clench as violence shone in his eyes.

In that moment, I truly did fear him. I had no doubt that most people never lived to see him so enraged.

I gulped, trying to clear the lump forming in my throat.

Inexplicably, my obvious fear seemed to clear some of the brutality in his eyes and after a minute passed, his hand loosened from around my neck.

He took a step away, looking anywhere but at me.

I could see the anger burning inside him slowly recede as he worked to bring himself back under control. His carefully crafted coldness slowly returned to his handsome face after a handful of seconds ticked by. He muttered something quietly that I didn't understand as the last of his turmoil drifted away.

"Why are you getting Alonso to forcibly remove every person that dances with me?" I questioned cautiously, not forgetting the reason I marched over to him in the first place.

He gripped his hips and shot me a condescending look. "I already told you. If I don't want another man touching you, then he isn't fucking touching you."

"I don't get you. You think you can dictate my life and who I can hook up with just because you're keeping me at your house? That's fucked up."

He just looked at me with a strange expression, refusing to offer an explanation. My frustration swelled again.

Nothing to say? Great! I have tons.

"Let me make something clear to you, Marco. You've told me to start a life here because you won't kill me or cart me away, but you don't get to dictate what kind of life I choose. If I want to sleep with someone, I will. If I want to dance with someone, I will. Hell, if I want to get my nips out and dance on the fucking bar out there, then I will! I am a living *person,* and I can do what I want!" I heaved, mimicking his stance and planting my hands on my hips.

"Is that what this is about?" He asked, shocking me by flashing a boyish smile that held no trace of insincerity. "You want to get *laid*?"

I stumbled. "I, uh—" *Oh, come on pull it together!* "I ha...I have needs you know!" I blurted, avoiding his gaze.

"Oh, really? That's not very Catholic of you now, is it?" He mocked, his face growing stern.

"You of all people don't get to judge me. You're a total man slut and you know it." He scowled at that, but I could see a spark of humor lurking in his eyes.

Marco seemed to contemplate something for a few moments before speaking again.

He leaned toward me, placing his hands on the wall behind me and caging me in.

"My earlier statement still stands...I will kill any man that touches you. If you want attention you come to me."

What. The. Fuck. Did he just say...

I looked up at him in complete shock, convinced he was joking.

I swallowed back the flutter in my chest when I found no trace of humor in his calm expression. Just steely indifference. I didn't know what to say. I couldn't even string two words together. I was certain he couldn't even stand to be around me but...this?

What the hell is happening right now?

"So...do you want attention?" He asked seductively, his eyes clearly roaming over my chest and southwards.

I tried not to visibly tremble under the intensity of his gaze and roughness of his voice. This version of Marco...*fuck,* it was lethal.

I want attention! My body screamed and for a split second I felt myself lean toward him, surrendering to him.

A hand drifted down from the wall behind me, coming to rest on my waist as his head tipped toward me in response to my unspoken words.

But the second my body almost gave in to it, to him, a flash of red lipstick on his neck caught my gaze.

Just like that, any and all traces of desire vanished.

"No. Not from you. Go back to fucking your whore."

I couldn't keep the disgust from my voice as I ducked under his arm and scurried out the door, entering back into the throng of the crowd.

———

WHEN I GOT BACK to the mansion that evening, the stone palace was desolate and silent with most of the normal mafioso still at the club with Marco. Jesse included.

I sat on my bed in contemptuous silence, contemplating the events of the evening and the fact that I had very nearly given in to Marco, despite everything he had done.

I was angry, frustrated, and confused. But more than all of that, I was fuming. As soon as I escaped out of that small room, I had seen the Don go straight back over to the table and pull that blonde woman—Lexi— back onto his lap. Like what had almost happened between us had meant *nothing*. As if *I* meant nothing to him.

Perhaps that was true for him, but it wasn't the same for me and I hated it.

I sat contemplating my next move and an idea sparked to life, spurring me into action before my window of opportunity disintegrated.

I dashed out of my room and across the landing to Marco's wing. Tentatively, I opened the door and crept inside, retracing my steps from earlier in the week. I ended up in his colossal bedroom now bathed in stunning moonlight and strolled to the bed. I flicked on the lampshade and then began rifling through one of the bedside drawers.

Bingo!

I pulled out the large blue box of condoms and grinned. Just to be sure I hadn't missed anything, I hunted through the remainder of the drawer and pulled out any loose ones I could find.

Once I was certain there were none left in any of the other drawers either, I promptly turned off the lampshade and ran back to my room. I emptied the box into my bathroom bin and covered them with toilet paper and makeup wipes just in case anyone came looking.

I burst into maniacal laughter as I slunk out of my dress and put on my pajamas, clicking off the light as I climbed into bed. I placed my night mask over my eyes in an attempt to feign sleep and waited.

I wasn't sure how long I tossed and turned in anticipation, but after an hour or so I heard the distant sound of cars pulling up to the house and voices in the foyer. After a few minutes more the voices went quiet, and I heard the distinct sound of Jesse's door shutting in the hallway outside. Ten minutes went past and... nothing.

Maybe Lexi didn't come back with them after all.

After another few minutes ticked by, I started to get irritated that my plan had failed miserably.

The sudden bang of my bedroom door being flung open had me jerking upright before I had even realized why.

"What have you done with them?" Marco's rough voice rang out.

"With what?" I exclaimed in mock innocence, tearing off my eye mask.

When my eyes focused, Marco was standing inside the doorframe with his hands balled at his sides. My stomach knotted when I realized he was wearing nothing but black boxers... which were barely concealing his aroused manhood. *Oh. Fuck.* I tried to redirect my gaze, but it was no good. I was transfixed by it. My body was reacting without my permission like it had done the last time.

This isn't part of the plan, Adalyn!

"Where are they?" His voice was quieter this time, but I could hear the fury behind it.

"I don't know what you mean." I looked up at him innocently, uncontrollably flicking my eyes southward and back up again.

"Don't fucking play dumb." He marched to the bed, leaning down so our faces were only inches apart. "Tell me where they are. Now!"

My eyes dropped to his lips, and I felt a tingle in the pit of my stomach. I heard his breath deepen and his expression darkened in response to my gaze, but not with anger this time.

"You don't want me sleeping with other women, is that it?" He said softly, slowly putting the pieces together.

My retort never made it off my tongue as an ugly high pitch squeal filled the room.

Marco flinched very slightly at the sound and my eyes immediately found a disheveled looking Lexi stood in my doorframe. Her long hair had begun to mat on one side, and she had clearly thrown her dress back on in a hurry.

Her eyes kept moving between Marco and me, clearly not happy with the lack of distance between us.

"What is going on?" She whined like a child. "Did you find them?"

"Get the fuck out of my room." I spat. Hatred for the woman coursing through my veins.

"Excuse me, bitch! Are you going to let her talk to me like that?" She huffed pointedly at Marco, crossing her arms.

"Don't talk to him!" I answered instead, catching her off guard. "*I'm* fucking talking to you—now get out of my room and take your idiot man toy with you."

Her face contorted into an ugly scowl, but before she had a chance to act on her rage, Marco retreated and slammed the door directly in her face.

A smile pulled at my lips as Marco stalked back to my place on the bed. He leaned down, pinning me against the sheets as he climbed over me. His strong body now flush with mine. His skin branding and hot against my own.

I didn't resist. No part of me was sane enough in that moment to push him away. His familiar spicy smell filled my senses, making my insides clench in anticipation.

"You play a very dangerous game." Marco's hard voice had turned ragged.

"Wouldn't have it any other way." I smiled mischievously, my hips tilting toward him of their own accord. The contact made his nostrils flare, and his eyes smoldered above me.

"I will *have* you, Ada." His lips pressed against my neck, and I desperately stifled the moan in my throat. "And when I do... I'll fuck that vicious mouth of yours too." His tongue flicked against my skin.

"Doubt it," I breathed, trying to maintain some air of dignity, even if my self-control was now fully out the window and floating along the surface of Lake Michigan.

He rolled his hips into me, pushing his hard length against my sensitive spot, eliciting a loud moan from my throat.

"It's just a matter of time...and I'm in no rush. But let's get something clear: you are *mine*. Only mine. That has been your fate from the moment I took you."

To anyone else, his words may have been stimulating, but desire froze in my veins and ripped me out of my hazy state.

He took you, remember?

He was the reason I had no family. No home.

To add fuel to that fire, images of his mouth sucking on Lexi's neck not five minutes ago flashed across my eyes and suddenly his touch was shallow. Meaningless.

Having me wouldn't mean anything to him.

But, it *would* mean something to me. My past and the memories I tried so desperately to suppress meant it would always mean something *more* to me.

"Get the fuck off." I freed my hands and tried pushing him away.

His black eyes dipped out of my view as he placed another, duplicitous kiss against my neck. I could feel how much he wanted me, and it took all my will power to resist his touch.

I brought my fists to his chest and pounded against him, my body tensing and anxiety making my hands shake. He stilled, his eyes slicing to mine and searching my face. Whatever he saw there made him retreat instantly.

He kneeled on the bed, gazing down at me a moment longer. Conflict etched across his features. "This isn't over."

He then shoved himself the rest of the way off the bed and out the door, slamming it shut behind him.

CHAPTER
TWELVE

ADALYN

At breakfast that morning, I learned from Jesse that Lexi didn't stay the night and although I felt somewhat satisfied by that information, I didn't exactly know why.

In the days that followed, Marco continued to play the part of Dr Jekyll and Mr. Hyde, but whereas before I was annoyed by not knowing which character he'd play for the day, I now found myself intrigued by it.

Using my newly acquired car, I spent a few days visiting various up-scale furniture shops, galleries, and textile stores to gather inspiration for my room. I had done little more than purchase a lamp by the end of the week, yet I still felt a sense of progress. It may have only been a lamp, but to me it represented acceptance of my life in Chicago.

My other car was scheduled to arrive over the weekend, and I could hardly contain my excitement. As the week wore on, not only did I find myself accepting my new life, but I was also starting to *enjoy* it.

Despite having been brought to the pale, stone walls of

Marco's mansion as a captive, it was starting to feel...more like home.

"I HAVE A JOB OFFER FOR YOU."

Marco and I sat in the formal dining room on Friday evening just as we had the rest of the week. At first, I'd found our new routine odd and uneasy but as time wore on, I was starting to look forward to our evening conversations.

"I thought you didn't like the idea of me working," I answered, recalling what he'd said the previous day when I had first brought it up.

I was growing increasingly weary of sitting by the pool and given the number of staff he had around the place, it wasn't like I could make myself busy by being useful. I needed something to do with my time, regardless of whether it was conventional in our world or not.

I had even offered to volunteer at Marco's church, which he had vehemently prohibited, and it made me question whether he had even been attending recently. They were certainly unlikely to be happy with our particular *arrangement*...

"I changed my mind." Marco responded simply, his eyes coasting to me across the table.

I grimaced, "No, I am not being one of your cocaine girls."

A half-smile pulled at his lips.

"I wasn't thinking *that*." He rubbed a hand absentmindedly across his jaw. "I have an opening at one of my casinos. It is an assistant general manager role."

My mouth gaped and my fork clattered noisily to my plate.

"Wh-I am *not* qualified enough for a job like that." I tripped over the words, completely overwhelmed.

"You are organized and astute, those two things cannot be taught. The rest you will pick up through training and experience. The venue is twenty minutes from here. Your hours will be flexible, and the pay is good too. You should take it."

There was no possible way I could agree to the offer.

"What's the catch?" I asked, skeptical for obvious reasons. There was always a catch with the Cosa Nostra.

"There's no catch, Ada."

I turned it over in my mind as I finished my bite of food. "Can I think about it?"

"Of course."

I turned my attention back to eating and speared another piece of spaghetti, popping it into my mouth.

"I hear your new car is being delivered tomorrow." Marco offered after a few minutes.

I grinned, "I cannot wait!"

My beautiful Brabus C63 was scheduled to arrive tomorrow around lunch time, and I was damned near counting down the minutes until its arrival. I was feeling truly excited, and I couldn't keep the happiness off my face.

"Then it was worth the $241,320 it cost me," He drawled sarcastically.

"Woops. Guess you won't be able to afford another hostage anytime soon then," I mocked.

"Unfortunately," He lamented and I giggled, my good mood making me more jovial than normal.

A smile pulled at the corner of his lips, flashing his perfect white teeth in a way that caused my heart to sputter in my chest.

"I was thinking..." I began, half to distract myself from it. "I know my Hellcat isn't allowed in your fancy pants garage, but is there space for my Brabus?"

He chewed his food slowly, as if contemplating the question in great length. I could tell that rushing him was unlikely to get me the answer I wanted, so I focused on pushing my food about the plate rather than the fact that I wanted to tear my hair out with impatience.

"Potentially... but you're not allowed to drive it inside. You can leave it out front and one of the others will move it."

Well, it wasn't a flat no. "Don't trust me around your expensive cars?" I concluded.

"Something like that."

I huffed but eventually agreed.

———

AFTER A TERRIBLE NIGHT'S sleep and a restless morning, I decided to give up trying. I crawled out of bed and into the shower at a little after six. I straightened my hair, threw on some jeans and a loose fitted blouse, then headed downstairs in search of some coffee to help wake up.

As I approached the kitchen, Marco and Jesse's familiar Italian filtered down the hall. I hovered outside the door a moment trying to understand what they were saying, but it was useless.

I silently cursed my father for his failure to provide an Italian tutor when I was growing up.

I decided now was as good a time as any to make my presence known.

"Morning." I muttered, strolling over to the coffee maker on the side and collecting the ground coffee.

"Not a morning person, hey?" Jesse mocked, and I promptly flipped him the bird.

"I would have slept fine if it wasn't for your irritating voice booming across the halls." I retorted, watching the coffee as it brewed.

"Seconded." The unfamiliar humor in Marco's voice compelled me to look over at him.

I wish I hadn't.

It was the first time I hadn't seen him in a suit...or almost naked.

This morning he was dressed in casual shorts and a tank top, accentuating each of his heavily tattooed, muscular arms. His dark hair wasn't its usual pristine self, tousled in different directions as if he had just run his hands through it. A thin sheen of sweat coating his forehead. He looked like he had just finished up in the gym...or a serious sex session.

With that lingering thought, I forced myself to look anywhere other than at the glorious man as he stood leaning casually against the counter.

It was the first time I noticed Jesse dressed in similar attire too.

"Why are you both so sweaty?" I questioned, looking more at Jesse than the God of darkness beside him.

He was the kind of man that women happily sold their souls to the devil for, and judging by his air of cool confidence, he knew it.

"Gym. You should try it once in a while." Came Jesse's sarcastic response.

"Oh, ouch. If you were *actually* attractive, then that might have hurt." I lilted, turning back to my task and pouring the steaming coffee into a mug.

"Can I get one, please."

I jolted in surprise as Marco materialized beside me soundlessly, a mug already in hand.

"S-Sure."

I recovered and took the mug, placing it beside mine and filling it. I went over to the fridge to retrieve the cream and milk, collecting some sugar along the way. I poured a little of the cream, a little of the milk and two scoops of sugar before swirling and tasting. *Damn that's good.*

I placed it back down on the counter and within a blink of

an eye a hand snaked out and took it. Marco took a big swig from the cup before setting it back down on the counter.

I looked at him, dumbfounded.

Where has all this come from?

"I was skeptical." He shrugged, answering my unspoken question. "But it's good. Can you make mine like that? Please."

I had never heard him so much as utter the word please before and now he was saying it twice in a five-minute window... It was like hell had finally frozen over.

I sighed and shook my head in disbelief and got back to work repeating the process.

Jesse muttered something I couldn't understand and started laughing as Marco retook his earlier position against the counter. The latter just smiled charmingly, flashing his perfect white teeth, completely unaffected.

I finished up making his coffee and slid it over to him.

"What about breakfast then, Bandit?"

I rolled my eyes at him. "I have more important things to do this morning!" I half-sung happily as I made my way across the tiled floor.

"Like what? Rearranging your sock drawer?"

"Aw sweetie, did some girl give you that excuse at a club? That's really sad." I mock-soothed him, rubbing him on the back like a child. "But no, I have to prepare for the love of my life...who is arriving any minute!"

Jesse's face looked at me confused until Marco clarified for him. "She means her new car."

"Well, I am off to rearrange my sock drawer. Bye, boys!"

―――――

A SOUND of a reversing truck echoed from the other side of the mansion, and I jumped to my feet, screeching with excitement.

I had been sitting on the terrace online shopping for furniture all morning, unable to sit still in anticipation for my new car's arrival.

It's here! It's here!

I all but ran out to the driveway as a covered transporter came to a stop on the driveway.

"Mrs. La Torre, it is good to see you. You look well." The salesperson greeted.

Mrs. La Torre?

He must have said it by mistake.

I didn't raise it though. "I am well, thank you."

The doors to the transporter were pulled open by the driver and a few minutes later my car was descending slowly onto the driveway. The sleek onyx paintjob gleamed against the sunshine, and a smile so big it hurt, plastered itself across my face. It was goddamn beautiful.

"So, what do you think?" He asked, gesturing to the vehicle that was more akin to something out of a *Batman* movie.

"I think it looks too fast for her to handle." Came Jesse's mocking voice as he approached us.

The men laughed at my expense, and we proceeded to walk around the car, examining it intently.

"As you can see, the armoring company have fitted extra thick ballistic glass and ballistic steel, culminating in high grade run-flat tires and armored wheel wells."

Armoring company? That was news to me.

I shot Jesse a pointed look that said 'we'll talk about this later', and he shrugged sheepishly.

We took our seats in the front, and I was talked through each of the various functions available. The thing resembled a spaceship more closely than it did a car, and I was blown away by all its features. There was an array of different screens, control panels and buttons adorning the console...none of which I had the faintest idea how to use.

I stayed out in the car the rest of the afternoon, too busy

reading the driver's manual to contemplate going in for lunch. I only took it for a drive once, too invested in learning everything about my new car before properly taking it out. I played around with all the features and learned how to use the navigation system and entertainment center in more detail. I also figured out the car had a distress beacon... which quickly led to two of the security guards legging it out the side of the building toward me. *Oops!*

I made a mental note not to touch that particular button again.

After they went back inside and the afternoon had drifted into evening, I set about adjusting the interior lighting until the cockpit glowed a deep shade of red.

A gentle knock on my window brought me back to reality, and I rolled down the glass, unable to make out who was on the other side in the darkness.

"It looks good, Ada." I heard his voice before I saw his face. "Do you mind if I join you?" He gestured his illuminated chin to the passenger side and my chest sputtered.

I nodded, and the passenger door promptly opened. I tried not to watch as Marco's muscular body came to rest gracefully in the leather bucket seat beside me.

The car filled with his spicy scent and his presence immediately warmed the air, brushing against my skin. He didn't seem to notice the sudden heaviness between us, focusing on adjusting his seat and looking over the car's interior.

Lord have mercy.

"It's alright, isn't it," he remarked looking about the inside. I couldn't help a stupid laugh from escaping my lips.

"Marco, you are sitting in a $240,000 car, and all you can say is 'it's alright'? You're such a snob."

"I prefer 'vehicle enthusiast'," he corrected with a smirk, earning him an eye roll.

"So…" He began growing nervous, which was odd for him. "Are we going to take it for a spin?"

"Yes, *I* am. And you are most welcome to come along for the ride."

He scowled and muttered an irritated, "Fine."

I handed him the driver's manual I was still reading, and after a few seconds of staring at me like I had just escaped from a zoo, he stored it away in the glove compartment. I then readjusted my seat, checked my mirrors, and strapped myself in, ready for my first evening drive.

Anxiety quickly made me rethink my decision however… Not because it was the most expensive car I had ever driven at night, but because I had Don Marco La Torre, one of the most powerful men in the continental United States, as my passenger.

One look at Marco's face told me that that particular fact hadn't escaped his knowledge either.

This is ridiculous. Start the car! I commanded myself.

I pressed the ignition button, and the car purred to life. Growing to a growl as I gunned it down the driveway and out into the street. I turned up my music and relaxed back into the plush leather, enjoying the sense of calm I could only achieve through tires on the road.

"Christ! Would you slow down?" Marco's voice interrupted my pleasant train of thought.

I immediately looked at the speedometer and scowled. *What the hell was he talking about?*

"Quit your shit, I'm hardly above the speed limit." I dismissed.

"You're going forty in a thirty." He retorted.

"Well, it's my car. My rules."

"That I paid for." He observed.

I chose to ignore him, turning my full attention to the road.

After ten minutes or so, my stomach growled loudly, and I

was reminded that I'd skipped lunch and dinner earlier. Looking at the clock now, it was fast approaching half nine and eating was becoming a necessity rather than optional. I did a quick U-turn and headed back down the high street we had just come from, pulling into the McDonald's we passed earlier and joining the back of the drive-through queue.

"What the hell are you doing?" Marco demanded, staring about in disgust.

"Getting fast food. I'm starving."

I pulled the car forward with the traffic and studied the menu board now visible before us.

"Hmm... I'm fancying a quarter pounder with bacon. What are you gonna get?" I looked over to him as he stared, clearly annoyed, out the window.

"I don't eat fast-food crap."

Didn't realize I had a food connoisseur in the car.

I sighed derisively and a few minutes later pulled up to the microphone to place our order.

Marco had fallen into a stoney silence beside me, and after a few minutes passed, I sighed. "Oh, would you stop sulking? This is fun!" I enthused, tapping my hand impatiently against the steering wheel while we waited to pull up to the serving window.

"Yes, eating a questionable burger in a brand-new car, what could go wrong?"

"Shhh. Shut it." I exaggerated, pulling the car up the next window.

The young man behind the glass did a double take at the car, whistling lowly. He carefully handed over the brown sacks of piping hot food and drink, which I passed to Marco for holding. I quickly paid and pulled out of the drive-through, parking the car in a quieter part of the lot.

I took the bags and unceremoniously handed him back a

Big Mac meal with chicken nuggets, before taking the rest and getting out of the car.

Our security detail had not gone unnoticed by me, so I made my way over to the familiar black SUV a few spots down and passed both Wyatt and Layton a meal each through the window. They looked just as confused as Marco had, and I couldn't help but smile all the way back to my car.

"That was nice of you." Marco murmured as I retook my seat behind the wheel.

I shrugged, uncomfortable with his unexpected praise.

When I looked over at him, I was surprised to see half of his burger had already been demolished.

Doesn't eat fast-food my ass.

But I knew better than to call him out on it.

I tucked into my bacon filled burger of heaven and we settled into comfortable silence for a moment. Although we had eaten dinner together many times before, we had never been completely alone. This time the quiet felt much more *intimate* and my stomach grew nervous.

"So, your aversion to fast food… is it a life you chose or did the life choose you?" I questioned, trying to disperse some of my internal tension.

I thought I heard a snort of muted laughter. "I guess it's more of a habit than a life choice," he mused. "I played varsity football in college and it just kind of stayed with me."

Of course, he had been the typical high-school jock…popular, handsome, and good with the ladies. That much I had expected…but varsity football? That was surprising.

"Really? Where for?"

"The University of Michigan." He shrugged.

"You're joking." My jaw slackened as I stared at him.

"Nope. I was a running back, number thirty." He said around a mouthful of chicken nugget.

"That's incredible. I bet it was awesome to play in a stadium that big."

"Yeah, it was." He sighed and stared out the window. "But it didn't last. I was halfway through my final year when my father died in the raid, and I had to step up to lead the family."

My heart filled with genuine empathy for him, seeing the weight of emotions now lining his face. It wasn't easy for him to talk about this, I realized.

"It was good though... I remember those days fondly."

"Let me guess, that's where you picked up your girlfriend Lexi?" I rolled my eyes at him, trying to lighten the mood.

Lexi was the typical cheerleader type—leggy blonde with an abundance of confidence.

"God no." He laughed darkly. "She waitressed at one of my clubs... and is definitely *not* my girlfriend." He shook his head as if in disgust.

Interesting... I took satisfaction from that particular piece of information.

"What about you? Did you ever go to college?" he asked, though I am pretty sure he already knew the answer to that question.

"I wanted to. Even applied to schools and everything, but my father refused to let me go." I shook my head sadly at the memory.

I had barged into his office one afternoon with not one but *two* acceptance letters in my hand. I was desperate for him to congratulate me. Tell me he was proud of me... Instead, he became enraged and declared me selfish. My 'insistence on following a hare-brained dream would blow the safety of our whole family', as he so lovingly put it.

"What would your major have been?" He questioned, breaking the silence that had enveloped the car.

"Business." We both shared a look and simultaneously broke into laughter.

A thrill of excitement swirled in my stomach at the sound of his laugh. It was incredibly deep and attractive, warming me in places I *really* didn't want to think about with him less than a meter away.

"That's original," he remarked, and I grinned. "Did you ever use to cheer at school?"

"When I was Adalyn Mannino... no. I would rather die than cheer. But when we went into hiding and I assumed my Adalyn Parker role... I was forced into try-outs by my parents and made the squad because my father paid off the coach. I was the worst on the team." Marco began shaking his head disbelievingly. "What? I kicked the mascot in the head once in the middle of a sequence. It was really bad." He had looked away, but I thought I heard him chuckling quietly.

"You wouldn't have made varsity then," he pointed out.

"No, probably not." I breathed out around a laugh.

"So, if you didn't cheer in school and you didn't go to college, what did you actually do?" he questioned, finishing up with his fries while I took another bite of my burger.

"I was captain of the volleyball team throughout high school, so you could say I did that...but overall, I just threw a lot of parties that served a lot of alcohol. It's pretty funny how much popularity you can attain with those two things alone."

He chuckled and shook his head, watching me as I continued eating my food.

"How about this," he suggested. "I've finished eating the crap you've put in front of me, and you haven't, so why don't I drive us home?"

I eyed him suspiciously and he flashed a boyish smile that was so devastating it caused my heart to skid to a stop, knocking me into a kind of daze.

That kind of smile was dangerous. *Very* dangerous.

"Not to mention I did pay for the damn thing." He added when I still hadn't said anything.

My heart restarted and I frowned. One look at his expression and I knew there wasn't going to be an easy way out of this one.

"Fine," I grumbled, collecting my food and heaving myself out of the driver's side door.

I met him halfway around the car and stopped in front of him. "You so much as ding an alloy, run over a moth, or wrap us around a tree, and I will rip your dick off. Am I clear?" I barked, thoroughly hating relinquishing control to someone I had never even observed driving.

He rolled his eyes but muttered, "crystal" as we both rounded the car and retook our seats.

He immediately sank the driver's seat flat to the floor and repositioned himself to get comfortable. His long limbs hit the ignition button, and the car purred to life beneath his strong, capable hands.

Fuck.

Seeing him handle the car expertly was making my core smolder with heat.

I tried to ignore the sudden aching between my thighs as he pulled the car out of the parking lot and headed back down main street.

Realizing I was getting overwhelmed and was now blatantly staring, I turned my attention to my fries and looking out the window. Trying to distract myself from the part of my brain that wanted to mount him like a bike, whether he was a big scary Don or not.

It was then that I realized something.

"What the fuck is this?" I blurted, looking over at the screen in front of him. "Why are you driving so slow?"

Marco scowled for a minute without answering...or driving any faster.

"I'm driving sensibly."

"You're driving like an old man," I observed.

"It's a limit, not a target," he retorted.

"I thought you Mafia men were supposed to be hardcore. You know: don't give a crap about speed limits and all that?" I mocked. "I think I've been short changed."

The internal lighting illuminated the familiar ticking of his jaw muscle... I was getting to him.

"My Grandmother drives faster and she's dead," I prodded.

Nothing.

"Or is it you're just a bad driver?" I asked, feigning innocence.

"That's it!" He growled.

Bingo!

Without warning, he violently threw the car to the right and stepped on the gas. I started panicking until I realized, he had pulled us into a mostly abandoned carpark outside of Target.

He brutally turned the wheel, and we started drifting across the empty expanse, tires screeching against the tarmac. I squealed with the initial shock but began cheering as adrenaline kicked in. It spurred him on, and after initially righting us, the car sunk into a large doughnut that left black tire marks streaking across the floor and smoke lingering in the air.

"I take it back! I take it back!" I laughed as we came to an abrupt halt. Marco was smiling as well, flashing me a perfect, toothy grin that made me feel...*things*.

"Again!" I demanded, and he immediately repeated the process.

This time he held the doughnut until we spun out and my head felt dizzy. Skid marks littered the parking lot, and I couldn't contain the grin of contentment adorning my face.

It was then that I noticed a police car pull up slowly just outside the entrance behind us.

"Shit! Marco, the cops!" I exclaimed, touching his shoulder to get his attention and trying to ignore the jolt of static the contact sent up my arm.

He just laughed. "Then let's give them a show."

He reversed fiercely, the speedometer hitting almost thirty before he jerked the steering wheel, throwing us to the side. We came to a violent standstill, facing at the squad car as he revved the engine thunderously in challenge.

"Are you crazy?" I yelled.

It appeared my fears had been short lived however, as the cop car lingered for only another second before slowly peeling away and disappearing down the road.

"What the hell?" I asked in confusion.

I mean we paid off the cops in Las Vegas don't get me wrong... but they didn't know us by our vehicles or anything. Not to mention I'd had the car for less than 12 hours.

"It's the number plate. It tells them to fuck off."

How powerful is this family? I gulped.

"I told you. The name La Torre comes with a lot of perks," he said, reading my expression.

Instead of continuing our stunts around the parking lot, Marco pulled off into the now quiet streets and headed back to the house at his previous languid pace. The once alien surroundings were fast becoming familiar, and I couldn't deny the sense of comfort I felt as we pulled into the perfectly manicured driveway of the mansion.

Marco didn't park the car outside the garage as agreed, instead preferring to pull up out front. He then handed our garbage over to Layton and Wyatt, who materialized behind us, and after triple checking the car was locked properly, I joined him inside.

The house was quiet and dark as we entered, and I couldn't catch sight of Lucia or Jesse, which indicated it was probably much later than I'd thought.

"I think everyone's gone to bed," Marco said. His muted voice resonated in the silence.

I turned on my heel and found him standing close behind

me. I met his gaze and felt a familiar heat vibrate through my body. He looked ridiculously hot, still dressed in civilian clothes similar to those he wore this morning.

His hand reached out and caught a stray hair from the side of my face, gently tucking it behind my ear.

I held my breath, shocked by the tingles that danced across my skin at the contact.

Slowly and cautiously, he leaned in toward me and I stilled as his lips brushed my cheek gently.

"Goodnight."

He pulled away and looked down at me with a half-smile playing on his face.

It took me two seconds too long to process the gesture before my legs started working, "Goodnight, Marco," I said as I turned to the stairs, beginning my ascent.

"Ada?" I turned around to look back down at him.

"Do you still think I'm a bad driver?" His charming boyish grin was back.

Damn I could climb that like a tree... No! Stop it!

"Jesse's better." I shrugged and his arrogant smile turned into a frown. I laughed. *Got him again...*

"Just kidding, Boss," I mocked and continued up the stairs.

His deep chuckle followed me as I went.

It felt like I was seeing a different side to him...again.

Again, the lines between ruthless Mafia boss and twenty-nine-year-old relatable and extremely attractive guy were becoming blurred and I didn't know how to stop it.

CHAPTER
THIRTEEN

ADALYN

The moment I stepped out of Jesse's G-wagon at Diamond City Casino, I regretted leaping at Marco's job offer. I had accepted it over the course of the weekend. I finally summoned up the courage to say yes to the management role he had offered, despite being horribly under-qualified for it. I had felt up to the challenge at the time...but staring up at the enormous sleek structure that Monday morning had me feeling nothing short of a nervous wreck, with a side of imposter-syndrome to boot.

I was about to duck and run when Jesse, sensing my unease, grabbed my arm and heaved me inside.

My anxiety was somewhat eased when we were greeted by the bright and cheerful smile of my new personal assistant, Keeley. She enthusiastically gave Jesse and I the grand tour, introducing us to staff along the way and babbling about the latest renditions to the hotel. She showed us through the various casino floors, restaurants and showed us some of the more luxurious hotel rooms too.

My office was on the same floor as the general manager's, Jon, and although not as grand in design it was unnecessarily ginormous. Ceiling-high windows ran the entire length of one room, allowing me a view of the city beyond from the comfort of my desk. It was quiet, comfortable, and definitely *me*.

I was just getting myself settled and logged into the work system when the phone on my desk rang, scaring me half to death.

"Hello?" I asked hesitantly.

"Miss Rossi, I have Don La Torre on line one for you. May I patch him through?" Keeley's now familiar voice bled from the speaker.

My brain took an extra moment to catch up before an anxious thrill ran up my spine.

Why the hell is Marco calling me?

"Yes please, Keeley."

I waited for the quiet click before speaking again. "You're through to Miss Rossi, how can I help?" I toyed.

"Hello Miss Rossi, Don Marco La Torre calling. But you can call me Sir for short." His familiar voice echoed down the phone, a lilt of humor coloring his tone.

I couldn't help but smile.

"Is that so? How very informal of you. What can I help you with, Sir?"

I was met with a heavy silence and looked back at the screen to check we were still connected.

"I'm just checking in to see how the new job is," Marco eventually said, though his voice sounded rougher than before.

"It's awesome. My office is huge, my personal assistant is lovely, and I think I'm in the manager's good books," I enthused. "Although, the owner is a bit of an asshole I hear." I bit back a laugh.

"Oh, is that so?" He questioned. "That's a shame. If only

there was some way to bribe yourself into his good graces..." He trailed off suggestively.

That was an interesting thought, I mused.

"Keep dreaming, sweetheart." I quipped.

"Did you just call me sweetheart?" His voice was so incredulous, and I couldn't stop my giggle.

Eww what am I, twelve?

"I'm glad you're settled and enjoying the job."

"I really am. Thank you... Don La Torre." I said softly, all traces of my earlier humor gone replaced by genuine sincerity. I never would have got a job like this without him.

Again, his voice came later than expected.

"You're welcome. I'll see you at home, Ada."

He disconnected the call, and I couldn't help the moronic smile plastered on my face as I turned back to my work.

Things between us were changing again, and I didn't know what to make of it.

This fun, jovial side of Marco was something I had never expected and the other night in my car had shown me that perhaps there was more to like about the Don than I could have possibly imagined. Something that went further than just sexual attraction and this game of cat and mouse we were playing.

That part of myself desperately fought to keep my heart locked tight, knowing all too well what it would mean to give it to someone within the Cosa Nostra. Hurt, disappointment, betrayal and potentially even death awaited on the other side of that mountain, and I had no intention of finding out which were in store for me.

Or at least, that was what I was telling myself.

———

THE REMAINDER of the afternoon I spent leafing through the training manual and handbook, getting to grips with my main responsibilities and tasks. Keeley would periodically visit with a coffee in toe to see how I was doing, and we ended our day with a meeting discussing the rest of the week's schedule.

"Was your first day a success?" Jesse questioned, throwing himself down in one of the chairs opposite my desk as the clock turned five. He had disappeared for most of the day to update the casino's security systems apparently.

"It's been awesome." I said in my sing-song voice.

"Well then, let's go celebrate!" He announced, getting himself back up.

"What did you have in mind?" I questioned, unsure what he was planning but certain I needed to be in bed by nine.

"How about dinner at the restaurant downstairs? You get like a forty percent discount, you know."

"Wow. Now I see why you've been hovering around me all day." I clutched my chest in mock hurt.

"Obviously."

We exited the room and headed over to the elevator bank, but before the doors had even chimed open, Jesse's phone began to ring. He gestured with his hand for me to wait with him as he took the call.

Within a heartbeat his expression changed from his usual playful self to dark and stormy, culminating in fury.

Whatever he was being told wasn't good.

He hung up the phone and immediately called for the elevator again. "We're heading back now."

"Jesse, what's happened?" Instead of answering, he smacked the button again impatiently.

I had never seen him angry before, and it was starting to make me panic.

"Jesse, tell me what's going on!" I shouted.

The doors opened and he swiftly took my arm, all but dragging me inside. He pressed the button for 'underground'.

"Je—" I began again.

"I can't tell you, alright? But we need to get back." He sighed.

"Did someone get hurt, Jesse? Is it Marco? Is Marco okay?" I demanded, pulling at his arm.

His eyes snapped to me then, shooting me a strange look.

"It was no one you know." he said slowly.

Despite his tone, his answer provided me with some degree of unease and comfort at the same time.

"Are they going to be alright?" I questioned, but one look at his face told me he was done answering my questions...and I could probably guess the answer.

When our elevator reached the underground parking garage, we briskly marched over to his SUV and climbed in without saying a word. The tense silence continued during the twenty-minute ride back to the house.

I kept steeling glances at him from the corner of my eye, but his expression never changed. I had never seen Jesse bothered by anything before and it was putting me on edge.

As soon as we pulled up to the house, I could see a whole squadron of armored vehicles out front, most of which I didn't recognize. When we entered through the door, Jesse excused himself to Marco's office and the dining room, where the rest of the men seemed to have started gathering, judging from the voices I heard echo down the hallway. I could easily spot at least twenty people present with more arriving every minute.

I didn't see Jesse, Marco or anyone apart from Lucia for the rest of that evening, their meeting dragging on until the early hours of the following morning.

———

THE DAYS that followed were less than normal.

Jesse and Marco seemed to have disappeared off the face of the Earth, and the house was filled with more men than an all-you-can-eat strip club. Security was clearly to the max with faces I didn't recognize stationed across the property. Even my Brabus was off-limits, and apart from going to work, I was once again under house arrest.

To top it all off—I still hadn't a clue what was going on.

So, like a good little hostage, I went to work and pretended I wasn't bothered by all the new meat-heads at home.

On the plus side, by the end of my first week, I was much more settled at work and had had meetings with most of the department heads. Keeley and I had developed a good under-standing of one another too, and her endless kindness toward me only made my transition that much easier. Jon, my new manager, seemed to like me as well, often inviting me to his office to impart some worldly knowledge or sometimes just for a chat.

I was starting to really love my new job.

The weekend rolled around quickly, and I spent it by myself.

I was exhausted after a long working week and both Marco and Jesse were still nowhere to be found. My earlier unease at their absence had quickly turned into panic as the weekend passed, still without any sign of them reappearing.

I texted Jesse on Tuesday evening out of frustration, but he never responded.

I wasn't sure whether they were still in Chicago anymore and everyone I asked wouldn't confirm nor deny my theory.

Thankfully, the security nightmare began to die down, and by the middle of the week I was allowed to drive myself to work again. Though the more substantial entourage of Mafioso that followed me persevered, much to my dismay. Two would station themselves at the main entrance of Diamond City, two more in the underground parking garage, and Alonso and Tom would never stray far from the entrance of my office.

By Friday, I still hadn't heard from Jesse or Marco and pure desperation had set in. I was clean out of ideas.

I checked my phone for the thousandth time that day and as usual, there were no new messages.

Me: Jesse if you don't start telling me wtf is goin on ima start screaming

I texted him for the tenth time in twenty-four hours.

Nothing.

After five minutes passed, I ground my teeth in irritation. Jesse always responded to my messages. Always.

Desperate times call for desperate measures.

I tapped on Marco's name and pressed 'call' before I could chicken out of it. It rang twice before someone picked up. I sighed in relief.

"Marco?" I called down the phone.

"What's wrong?" Marco's bored voice filtered through the connection.

I was instantly enraged by his flippancy.

"What the hell do you mean, 'what's wrong'? Where is everyone? What the *fuck* is going on?" I yelled down the phone at him.

"Nothing is going on. Jesse and I have been away on business, but it's sorted now." His voice sounded guarded. Clearly there was more to it than he was willing to let on.

"That's it? That's all I get?" When I was met with nothing but steely silence on the other end, I continued. "Care to explain why my entourage has tripled?"

"Not really."

"You're pissing me off. Goodbye." I seethed, moving to terminate the call.

"Wait!" I heard him shout down the receiver.

I hesitated and brought the phone back to my ear.

"What?" I asked coldly.

"Can you come to my club after work?"

That meant he was back in Chicago then and confirmed my earlier theories that he and Jesse had in fact left the city without saying anything. Potentially even the state.

"Why?" I sighed.

"Why not? Live a little." I could hear the humor in his voice. He sounded almost... *playful*.

I contemplated his offer for a minute.

On the one hand I was furious I had been left in the dark and completely abandoned for over a week. On the other, I knew the nature of the family 'business' and knew it was often best to be left out of the particulars...

"Fine. Which club?" I answered reluctantly.

"Bellator." He confirmed. "See you soon."

I hung up the phone and although irritated by his impertinence, felt considerably better knowing that whatever danger there had been had passed.

Everything is okay... He and Jesse are okay...

———

Four hours later, I was in my Brabus heading across town to Bellator.

It seemed to be a smaller club than the others I had been to and had a much more exclusive feel to it.

I pulled into the underground garage, followed by my security detail in two further vehicles. I parked and was promptly escorted by Alonso and Tom over to the elevators, taking them up to the third floor.

When the doors opened, they revealed a large onyx room with a smoky mirrored ceiling. Golden furniture and artwork complimented the darkness, giving the space both an edgy and sophisticated atmosphere simultaneously. A recessed LED dance floor and DJ booth were placed at the room's center, illuminated only by multiple thick black chandeliers that hung from the ceiling. It was stunning and definitely more to my taste than any of the other clubs I had visited.

I spotted Wyatt and Layton standing by one of the larger booths at the side of the room and I waved to them in greeting before passing by the intimidating men. They smiled in unison.

They were beginning to warm up to me and that knowledge gave me an inexplicable sense of happiness.

The first person I saw as I approached was Jesse. He was sitting off to the side with a beer in his hand. A broad smile erupted on his face the moment he spotted me, and I started walking toward him—only to stop dead in my tracks.

Marco was there—locked in a passionate kiss with none other than *Lexi*.

His tongue firmly lodged down her throat, while her hands were pressing against his crotch seductively.

My heart sank in complete deflation. My stomach hit the floor.

Déjà fucking vu... Something which felt a lot like hope extinguished in my chest.

"Hey, Bandit! How was work?" Jesse called out, clearly oblivious to the scene beside him and sounding intoxicated.

At Jesse's words, Marco rapidly pushed Lexi away and our eyes met mercilessly for a second.

Then I left.

I tore away from the gut-wrenching scene in front of me, unable to contain my hurt.

I mentally kicked myself for being such a bloody stupid fool. I had allowed myself to think that something was changing between us. Obviously I had been wrong.

The feeling wasn't mutual, and it hurt.

I didn't bother waiting for the elevator to arrive, aiming straight for the stairs and taking the steps as quickly as I could.

My Louboutin's clicked angrily against the tile with each step I descended. Once I was down the first two flights, I could hear the distinctive thuds of someone following me, so I quickened my pace.

I needed to be alone.

The moment my foot hit solid ground I sprinted out the stairwell and across the garage to my car. I wasn't six feet from it before I was yanked back by the arm.

"Where the hell are you going?" Marco's cold voice reverberated in the silent garage.

Shit.

I looked anywhere but at his face, refusing to give him the satisfaction of seeing the disappointment in my eyes.

"Away from you, you selfish prick!"

I tried shoving away his touch, but it was no use. His grip held firm like a vice.

We struggled for a moment before he walked me to the car and trapped me against it. The chill of metal was bitingly cold through the thin material of my blouse.

"Ada—" he began, but I didn't want to hear it.

"Is that where you've been all week?" I demanded. "Fucking that whore?"

I glared up at him, anger pulling my face taut.

"Of course not!" He frowned, as if the thought disturbed him. "It was business."

"Some business! I didn't realize there was enough space for a board meeting between her legs!"

His dark, clouded eyes penetrated me with a look that I couldn't possibly decipher.

"I was in New York until this morning," he said measuredly. "I didn't know she would be here. She means nothing to me."

"I don't give a shit what she means to you." I lied. "I was worried sick about you both the whole week. You left me in the dark and I was scared. I didn't know what was going on! Now I know you've been screwing that *bimbo*—."

"I have not." Marco said viciously. "And even if I had, why does that bother you so much, hey?"

My mind swirled, "I-I..." I stumbled over the words, knowing that once they were spoken, they could never be clawed back.

His eyes darkened, but he waited patiently for me to continue.

"I thought there was—"

I didn't get to finish my sentence as a rage-inducing voice cut me off.

Lexi.

"What's going on, babe? Just ignore that brat, she's always making a fucking scene." Lexi's sultry voice rang out.

Is it possible to hate someone without ever speaking more than a sentence to them?

Right now, my answer was yes.

Behind her neon pink slip of a dress and fake tits, the entire security team had also emerged.

Frustrated, Marco moved away to bark orders at the approaching men and address the desperate mess heading straight for us.

I didn't hang around long enough to listen.

The moment he moved far enough away, I flung open the driver's side door and launched myself into the car. Locking the doors behind me. Marco pounded on the window shouting something unintelligible on the other side.

I ignored him and punched the ignition, throwing the car into drive, and hitting the gas pedal simultaneously.

The car sprung forward and I sped out of the garage at full speed, leaving them all dumbstruck in my rearview mirror. I pulled sharply out onto the street and drove as fast as I dared across town, following the roads home. I threw the car into park the moment I pulled up outside the mansion and fled to my room, refusing to stop until my door slammed and locked behind me.

I fell against the duvet and allowed the tears welling in my eyes during the drive to escape.

I was a fool.

A complete and utter fool to think that anything had changed between us. That he was anything *other* than the typical Cosa Nostra Don that only cared about money, sex and power.

Cosa Nostra men were all the same—heartless and selfish. All they knew was violence, and all they cared about was sex and money. They didn't care what they had to do, who they had to hurt or who they had to stand on so long as they got what they wanted. And I didn't want any part in that. To be *used* like that—utilized for pleasure and then discarded like trash.

I had been so desperate to not feel alone that I had fooled myself into thinking that Marco and I had anything in common. That perhaps we weren't so different. That something had shifted between us.

How easily I had been swept up in the realm of make-believe and fiction.

No. I couldn't allow myself to shed tears for someone like him. He didn't deserve them.

I still had an amazing job, my dream car and now lived in a beautiful mansion. That was enough, wasn't it? Every day the chains of being a hostage were slipping away...which was exactly the problem. I had allowed myself to believe that I had *chosen* my life here. When that couldn't have been further from the truth.

I rubbed the streaks of mascara from my face and climbed into the shower, hoping to soothe the seemingly permanent tension in my shoulders.

Knowing I wasn't likely to get a minute of sleep with my

thoughts swirling at full force, I decided I needed something warm and comforting. I listened at the door for a few minutes and heard nothing but silence.

I wasn't sure whether the others had come back from the club yet, but the absence of movement in the halls told me there was a good chance they hadn't.

I padded down the stairs and through the entry way to the kitchen.

I flicked on the kettle, pulled out the cocoa powder and a mug, and opened the fridge to retrieve the milk. As I shut the door, movement on the other side of it caught my eye and I jolted in surprise.

"Marco! For fucks sake, you scared the shit out of me." I screeched, narrowly missing dropping some milk. I clasped a hand to my chest, trying to regain my breath.

He smirked.

Idiot.

Hurt lapped at my chest once I met his familiar raven eyes. I deliberately turned my back to him, unable to keep the grimace off my face.

"I need to say something." His deep voice filled the heavy silence. All traces of his earlier humor gone.

"I don't want to hea—"

"Tough," he interrupted forcefully.

I sighed and faced him again, leaning against the counter in an outward display of annoyance.

"There is something I need to say, so just listen." His voice was serious as he walked toward me, stopping only a few feet away.

He let out a heavy breath before he spoke.

"Lexi means nothing to me. I hadn't seen her since that night when you threw away the condoms and I kicked her out. She invited herself to the club tonight and kissed me before you walked in. I should have pushed her away immediately, and I didn't... I *know* I should have, but I was feeling the alcohol and I fucked up, alright? I don't want her—I want *you*."

Before my brain was able to even consider his meaning, Marco closed the distance between us and pressed his lips to mine in a kiss that felt like fire.

The soft and eager touch of his lips consumed my thoughts and knocked me into delirium.

It took two seconds for my body to respond, but when it did, my lips met his with equal parts desperation and *need*. My arms wound their way around his neck and our bodies collided. His hands finding my ass as mine threaded in his hair, pulling each other closer. Marco's tongue found mine and I moaned at his taste, my stomach pooling with desire as his familiar, spicy taste hit my tongue.

I could feel him, and he was *everywhere*.

Without breaking our kiss, Marco lifted me onto the edge of the counter. My bare legs hung either side of his thighs, and his hands moved slowly along my skin. The material of my nightdress bunched as his hands coasted upward, exposing me to the evening air. He kissed my lips savagely when his fingers met the elastic of my panties, like an addict being handed his vice. I pulled away to suck in a breath, and his lips fell to my neck in response.

His nipped against the sensitive skin, eliciting goosebumps down my spine.

I pulled at his hair, bringing his face back up to meet mine as our lips crashed together once more. Feeling emboldened and desperate to feel more of him, I sucked on his lip, and he grunted, his hands dipping below the elastic at my hips.

Just when I thought he was going to pull the material down my thighs, a buzzing erupted.

"Marco..." I sighed, struggling to formulate words. "Your phone."

"Ignore it," he muttered immediately against my throat, lips pressing against my collarbone as the phone fell silent.

The quiet didn't last long as his phone began vibrating once again. This time more relentless than before.

"Fuck," he said angrily, moving back from me enough to retrieve the phone from his pocket.

He didn't look at the screen as he answered. "This better be fucking good," he spat. His features immediately morphed into a scowl as he listened to whatever was being said on the other end.

It was enough to sober me up from my intoxicating arousal and it slowly sunk in what we had just done.

My brain *finally* catching back up.

Shit.

It didn't matter that he said he wanted me. This was just a game to him. He wanted me *now*, but what about next week? What about tomorrow? I was just a pawn in an elaborate game that Cosa Nostra men liked to play. A game of cat and mouse, of sex and vanity. A *challenge* for a man bored by the easy girls that flocked to his side.

My earlier thoughts echoed through my mind, and I felt nothing but disdain.

How could I let this happen?

It was enough to spur me into action.

I pushed Marco back another step and jumped down from the counter without sparing even a second glance at him. I sped out of the kitchen and up to my room locking myself in for the second time that evening.

What have I just done?

CHAPTER
FOURTEEN

ADALYN

There comes a time in everyone's life where the need for self-preservation outweighs everything else. Now was one of those times.

Over the next few days I scarcely left the confines of my room and decided that avoidance was my best strategy. I wouldn't allow myself to be in the same situation again. I couldn't. Not if I wanted to survive and have a chance at being happy in Chicago.

It didn't matter that he wanted me. It didn't matter that I wanted him. If I gave in to whatever feelings I had for the Don, there was a decent chance my heart would get broken in the process...and I couldn't give everything I had to a man for it to mean *nothing*.

It would always mean *something* to me because of my past and what another man did.

I was already fractured by it, so to risk myself for someone who I could scarcely trust...it had the potential to shatter me irrevocably. And I didn't know if I could survive it.

Instead, over the course of the weekend I focused on locking away whatever feelings I had for Marco until they were inaccessible to me. Until self-preservation, distrust, and fear shrouded our kiss in a heavy fog and deterred me from lingering on my feelings any longer.

My phone buzzed where it lay on the desk beside me.

I glanced at the screen and immediately scowled, turning back to my computer. I tried to concentrate on the email I was in the process of writing.

Less than ten seconds later my work phone rang.

"Miss Rossi, I have Don La Torre on line one. Would you like me to patch him through?" Keeley's now familiar voice called through the handset after I picked up.

"No, thank you Keeley. Please tell him I'm in a meeting."

I put the phone down and sighed. I had managed to avoid him the entire weekend, and while I knew it was only a matter of time before I had to speak to him, I wasn't done being a coward yet.

Later, I decided.

I collected myself and got back to the email.

Not two seconds after I began typing, my work phone rang again.

I was fast becoming frustrated with the constant inter-ruptions.

"Keeley, I still don't want to speak to him. If he wants, he can leave a mes—"

"I don't want to leave a message," came a blunt and all too familiar voice.

My heart spluttered in my chest anxiously.

"I'm busy Marco," I said flatly. "How did you even get this number?" Noticing that the screen showed it as a direct call.

"You forget who I am. Why are you avoiding me?" He demanded.

"Work's been busy." I lied.

"It's because of Friday."

I swallowed back the lump forming in my throat. "What? No!" Even I could detect nervousness in my voice.

"Don't lie to me, Ada. It wasn—"

"Look, I can't talk about this right now." I cut him off, *really* not prepared for this conversation. "I have a deadline at five and a shitload of work to do..."

"Fine." Marco snapped, clearly annoyed at my tone. "Another time."

With that he hung up the line and I breathed a sigh of relief.

———

THANKFULLY, 'ANOTHER TIME' didn't come up during the next two days as Marco was apparently not at home.

Jesse kept me company instead, and the topic of mine and Marco's kiss stayed surreptitiously *out* of our conversations. Whether that was because he wasn't aware it had happened or because he didn't know what to say, I couldn't tell. Either way I was grateful.

It was now Thursday morning, and I was standing in the kitchen throwing back the last of my warm caramel coffee before heading into work. I collected my handbag from the bar stool and made my way to the entrance hall, just like every other morning since starting at Diamond City Casino.

"Adalyn!"

Jesse's voice shouted from somewhere in the house just as I started opening the front door.

Anxiety immediately swirled in my stomach at his tone, and I turned on my heel to see him jogging down one of the side corridors, concern lighting his face.

"What's wrong, Jesse?"

"You're not going to work today." He paused, as if measuring his next words as he came to a stop before me. "Something's happened. I can't give you the specifics, all right? But it wasn't good. Everyone will be here soon. Do not leave this house."

"Jesse I will be fin—" I began.

"No!" He barked, his face darkening at the thought. "Until I can guarantee your safety you aren't stepping one foot out that fucking door."

His voice was unwavering, devoid of all humor and light-heartedness.

I nodded immediately in agreement.

Clearly something else had happened and whatever that was, it was serious. The last time he'd only been angry or enraged by whatever had happened. This time it was different.

He was...*rattled*.

———

I CALLED Jon to say I wouldn't be in that day or the next, stating there had been a 'family emergency'. Jon seemed to understand exactly what I meant by that, making me question whether my *actual* boss had links himself to the La Torre syndicate. Though at times like this, that didn't seem like such a bad thing.

Not long after I got off the phone with Jon, numerous vehicles began pulling up to the house and a slow stream of La Torre men came filtering through the front entrance. I hovered around the doors to the kitchen, unsure what to do with myself until I saw a few of the men shoot hateful glares in my direction.

It didn't take a genius to guess that whatever had happened, it had something to do with my family. Their usual hate had now morphed into a violence that clouded their eyes.

"Jesse!" I whispered loudly across the hall to him.

He was standing beside the front door nodding at some of the men as they entered. Seeing me waving for his attention, he immediately left his position and came over.

"What, Bandit?" His voice was stern, but at least my nickname was back.

"Does this have something to do with me?" I asked gesturing to the men and scene before us.

"No." He answered without hesitation.

I sighed and tried again, "Is *my* family to blame for this?"

His darting gaze immediately fixed to me for a second, his eyes softening. "Yes."

———

I HAD RETREATED to my room before more men could arrive. I couldn't help the guilt I felt, sensing that I was somehow the reason another incident had occurred in only a handful of weeks.

What if he's had enough of the violence and sends me back?

Agitation clawed at my throat and a wave of uneasiness swept over me.

Weeks ago I would have done anything to go home, but now... even if Marco sent me back to my family would I *want* to go back?

No.

A knock on my bedroom door interrupted my brooding.

Jesse's head poked through, "Boss needs to see you."

I slowly rose to my feet, stiff from sitting for so long, and followed Jesse to Marco's study.

I was surprised to find that only Marco and Benny were present in the room, the rest of the men having either crowded into a nearby lounge or the dining hall. The air in the study felt warm and heavy as I entered, but the unmistakable spice of Marco's cologne still clung to the space.

My heart stuttered as I met the gaze of the man I had been avoiding for the last four days. Tingles pooling in my stomach as my brain involuntarily darted back to our kiss in the kitchen.

I smacked the mental image away with a figurative baseball bat in the hopes of suppressing it.

Today Marco wore his usual black dress shirt and trouser combination, though his sleeves were bunched at the elbows. It was seemingly the only outward indication of a stressful day as his expression was as unaffected as usual.

His eyes fell from my face, skimming down my neck and to the collar of my work blouse I hadn't yet changed out of. I quickly diverted my gaze, feeling a blush spread under my skin and hating the way one look from him could make me feel unsteady.

My emotional barriers were disintegrating into ash.

I took the remaining chair next to Benny before the desk, careful to avoid looking at Marco any more than was absolutely necessary.

"There have been several attacks during the night." Marco began, also settling down into his chair. "Attacks we believe were orchestrated by your family."

"What happened?" I asked hesitantly, not entirely convinced he would answer me.

My father never had.

Marco ran his hand across his chin, pulling at the skin. "They hit two of our narcotics labs. The laboratories were in the basements of businesses I had in New York. One was a dive bar, the other a motel. They annihilated everyone on site."

Marco pressed a button on the black remote that was laying on the desk beside him. A television news broadcast filled the room, and I swung around to watch the news headline as it trailed across the screen behind me.

"Twenty-one people confirmed dead in a deadly mass shooting in downtown New York. The incident, now being termed the 'Deadly

Dive Bar Shooting' coincided with an equally deadly motel shootout in the early hours of this morning. Twelve are thought to be dead and sixteen more seriously injured after gunfire was heard on the property. A police investigation is currently underway."

Body bags being heaved into ambulances flashed across the screen and people were seen on their knees in various states of despair. Flowers being laid in respect of the dead.

The newscaster's voice cut off abruptly and the study fell back into a harsh silence.

Tears leaked from my eyes, and I quickly swiped them away with my sleeve.

"Your family's representatives took responsibility for both attacks this morning." It was Benny who spoke this time, his gravelly voice somewhat calming.

I shook my head, words escaping me.

This went much further than raiding drugs and money... This was the indiscriminate killing of over thirty innocent people. *How could they do this?* I felt sick knowing that the same blood that went through those murderous veins, pumped through my own.

I swallowed thickly, feeling my coffee from earlier trying to resurface.

"As grisly as the attacks are, the good thing about this situation is we now know your father's hand. It is clear the Mannino's think we are limited to our territory in New York and is oblivious to our stronghold here in Chicago," Benny said.

"It is of some consolation," Marco agreed mutedly.

I met his gaze as it brushed against my skin. "Ada, you should know I have every intention of striking back."

His expression was lethal but somewhere in the swirling darkness of his irises I thought I saw regret.

I looked down at my hands, clutched tightly on my lap.

I didn't want my father or anyone in my family to get hurt...

but doing nothing would mean permitting the slaying of innocent people. And these attacks were only the beginning.

"I need your help."

That caught my attention.

I shook my head, meeting his gaze. "They never told me anything."

"Perhaps you may have overheard something? Any business trips he frequently made?" Benny questioned gently.

It would mean betraying my family if I relinquished what little information I had.

At the same time, hadn't they already betrayed me?

"I know they own a casino on the Las Vegas strip called Paradise Place."

It was a bit of information I had learned while snooping in my father's study one day. He had mistakenly left the door unlocked, the paperwork with deeds to the casino sitting openly on his desk. It was the very casino I had kept asking him for a job at.

"That confirms our intel." Marco said, looking at Benny who nodded slightly.

I cast my mind back to Las Vegas, to Boulder, to anything that could be useful to Marco. Sifting through my memories now made me feel nothing short of shame. Back then, I had thought that all families within the Cosa Nostra were just as depraved as each other, with no one's hands being clean. But now, I couldn't help feeling like my family were at the top of that ever-shifting list with more than just their hands coated in innocent blood.

Perhaps that was why I decided to surrender the last piece of information I had.

"There's... something else," I said quietly.

After working for almost four years at Pretty Penny Loans it was clear that the business had a few...*misgivings*. Aside from the obvious money laundering that is.

Although the company was considered only a small business with five members of staff to its name, there was a custom fit vault in the basement that cost more than my Brabus. I didn't know for sure...but I was going to hazard a guess and say there was more than just a pretty penny stored inside.

"My old work. There's a vault in the basement."

"At Pretty Penny Loans?" Marco questioned, and I nodded.

"Not uncommon for a loan company." Benny shrugged.

"Maybe not, but I'm pretty sure a dual-combination vault that's double the size of this room is something to write home about," I offered. "Not to mention the reinforced concrete walls and armored guards."

That caught their attention. The men shared a look.

"Interesting. Very interesting," Benny muttered, while Marco appeared deep in thought.

"We need to conduct covert surveillance of the site. I want to know everything that goes on in that building and why it's so heavily guarded." Marco said authoritatively, directing his words over my head to Jesse, who I didn't realize was still present in the room.

"Yes, Boss." Jesse nodded once and promptly left, leaving Benny, Marco and myself.

"Food for thought. Thank you, Miss Rossi." Benny got up to leave as well, smiling down at me good-naturedly. "I will begin preparations."

He nodded respectfully to Marco and departed the study.

Desperation clawed at my throat.

Had I just sentenced more innocent lives to the same fate as the thirty-three already dead?

"Promise me you will not harm them," I blurted the moment the door closed behind Benny.

"Who?" Marco asked, rising from his seat and going over to the side of the room to pour a finger of whiskey.

"The employees. I am begging you not to do the same as my father. Let them live. *Please*, Marco," I begged.

Desperation was causing my chest to constrict. If I had consigned those people to the same fate, then I was no better than my father. Bile rose in my throat.

My raw panic must have reflected in my voice as Marco immediately turned to look at me, surprise coloring his features.

He didn't respond for a moment, sipping on his drink before placing it onto the table. "You have my word."

Trouble was, I didn't trust his word.

"Your word is not good enough."

He bristled, immediately perturbed by my insult. Clearly, it wasn't often people didn't trust his word.

"I'll make you a deal," He offered, coming to lean against the desk, so close his legs were nearly brushing mine. "If any one of those people get hurt during our raid, even so much as bleed...I'll set you free." He gave me a dark look. "But. If they remain unharmed then you must do something for me."

My stomach clenched with anxiety knowing he had the upper hand and could literally ask anything from me, and I would have to agree to it.

Anything to avoid death.

Anything to avoid becoming my father.

I hesitated but continued anyway. "Do what?"

"Come to Sicily with me."

I didn't exactly know what to expect but it certainly wasn't that.

"Deal," I said without a second's hesitation.

He reached for his drink again, tipping it back with his dark eyes studying me. "I know that must have been hard for you earlier, telling us that information. I want you to know that I appreciate it."

"It's nothing."

The emotions I had been so desperately trying to stifle over the last couple of weeks threatened to resurface and I looked away, staring at anything other than the man that made me believe he cared.

He sighed, clearly irritated with my flippancy and placed his glass on the wood with a loud thud, "Care to explain why you've been avoiding me all weekend?"

"Not really," I dead panned.

I still wasn't ready for *that* conversation. Especially not after everything else that had been going on.

"It's because of the other night." He observed flatly, crossing his arms across his chest.

His gaze brushed my skin like a physical touch and the pull to look at him was fast becoming overwhelming. "It was a mistake. It should never have happened."

"A mistake? I told you I *wanted* you." His flat voice morphed into frustration.

"You don't want me, Marco. You want to *fuck* me. They are two very different things." I glared, giving into the urge to look up at him. "I am not another Lexi who you can just fuck and toss away whenever you feel like it. I'm not some game."

"I never said that you were."

"I'm not stupid Marco, I know how this works. It shouldn't have happened, and I'm done talking about it."

He didn't stop me as I half ran out the study door.

I tried to keep my face impassive as I passed the crowds of men still lingering amongst the walls as I went straight to my room.

I felt guilty.

Telling Marco about Pretty Penny Loans and Paradise Place meant choosing to betray my family. Something they would soon learn of the moment Pretty Penny Loans was attacked. They were going to hate me for it, and despite everything that had happened, that still bothered me.

Even though I knew I would never go back to my family, the idea of being completely alone in the world was troubling.

On the other hand, allowing them to continue to massacre innocent people without retribution or restitution was downright disgusting, and I couldn't just sit by and allow that to happen either.

Marco was out for blood, and for the first time in my life, I understood why.

CHAPTER
FIFTEEN

ADALYN

"Oh, for the love of all that's Holy!" I screeched, clutching my towel closer to my chest.

It had been just over a week since the discussion in Marco's office and I had yet to return to work. The mansion still hadn't got back some semblance of normality with papers, plans, and meatheads scattered across the marble in every direction.

I had once again found myself languishing my time and distracting myself with trivialities to get through the day. House arrest was not just annoying but downright depressing.

Nevertheless, it still didn't explain Marco's sudden presence in my bathroom.

He looked about the room as if he had never even seen this part of the mansion before and part of me wondered if he ever had.

I spun away from the mirror, narrowing my gaze on him. I didn't miss how his irises darkened or how his eyes trailed down to my black painted toenails before bouncing back up.

Just like how I didn't miss that his suit trousers clung perfectly below his waist or how his white shirt did little to hide the extensive tattoo's that laid underneath.

"What the hell is your problem? Weren't you ever taught to knock?" I huffed, feeling *very* naked and all kinds of tingles that my mental bat was not doing a good job at smacking away.

His eyes were cold as they met mine. "You have two hours before guests start arriving."

"What guests?" I spluttered.

"Today has been cause for celebration." When my blank expression didn't change, he continued, "Pretty Penny Loans has been dealt with," He said smoothly.

My shock must have registered on my face.

Only a week had elapsed since I'd told them about the vault, and now I was finding out they had already carried out an attack. The amount of power the La Torre's—Marco—possessed was sobering.

I swallowed heavily as I thought of the people that worked there and the deal I had made for him to spare them.

"The staff, did you kill them?" I demanded, blood draining from my face, part of me too afraid to hear the answer.

He appeared irked at my obvious concern and remained silent as he observed my reaction.

Overcome with the desperate need to know the truth and whether I had been the executioner of innocents, I rushed over to him and gripped his shirt between my hands.

"Please tell me you didn't. Please tell me you are not like my father. *Please*," I begged. Some of my carefully locked away emotions clawed their way back to the surface in my desperation, making my voice waver, something inside me threatening to snap.

I could see the hint of a scowl forming between his brows. "I told you I wouldn't, didn't I?" His voice was firm.

It rung with truth.

A weight I didn't realize I had been holding lifted from my shoulders and I sagged against his chest in relief. My forehead resting against the soft material of his shirt while his familiar spicy cologne enveloped me like a comforting embrace.

Before I could move myself away or rationality could rush back in, a heavy set of arms wound around my waist. He pulled me into the hard plains of his chest, and I felt Marco's lightly stubbled chin come to rest against my head.

"Guess that means you're coming with me to Sicily." He observed quietly, an edge of humor creeping into his voice.

My voice was muffled. "Thank you."

"Tell me you were wrong about me. That I'm not the monster you thought I was." His voice was rough, smoldering with an intensity I couldn't place.

I pulled away and stared up into his familiar eyes, seeing a storm hidden beneath their surface.

"I was wrong. You are not the monster I thought you were."

With that statement hanging in the air I realized my feelings toward the man had inevitably resurfaced, impossible to fight off.

I was drawn to him.

The power, the control, and the fact he let me push buttons no one else alive was allowed to press, had culminated into an attraction that burrowed beneath my skin and crawled unrelentingly in my veins.

The fact that I was still alive was testament to the fact that he *was* different, and despite everything, he had listened to me when I'd asked him to spare the lives of people I had once known. That was something that no other man in his position would have done. No other Don would have cared for the wishes of a traitor's daughter.

The feelings I had desperately tried to lock away in favor of self-preservation, were now escaping the cage I had so artlessly created. The irresistible pull I felt toward Marco weakened any remaining threads of self-restraint I had left, and it was only a matter of time before the cage would give way completely.

It didn't matter what this man wanted from me anymore or what the damage would be to my soul—it was inevitable I would give myself to him.

Just as the mafioso becomes compelled by the irresistible pull of the trigger—it was too late for me to find another way.

———

To say I was being glared at by seventy percent of the guests in attendance would have been an understatement.

The La Torre family were unmistakable amongst the swathing crowd gathered in the grand entrance hall, leaking out toward the terrace. All of them had raven colored hair and similarly darkened irises. All were beautiful, handsome, or at the very least *attractive*. I felt horribly out of place surrounded by such glamorous and wealthy people. Though that was hardly surprising given the steady stream of disdainful glances I was getting.

It made the Mannino family gatherings look like child's play. Like uncivilized desperation and new-money ignorance. I couldn't help but feel stupid. I had no idea what true wealth really looked like until I came here.

I stood awkwardly off the side of the main hall which was alight with chatter and the occasional raucous laugh. Jesse stood with me chatting animatedly to someone I assumed to be either his good friend or distant relative—Enzo. He didn't look like a La Torre in his appearance, but something about the way he held himself made me certain there was some distant association in his family tree.

The apple never did fall far amongst the Cosa Nostra, after all.

Enzo was a handsome man of a similar age to me but was smaller than the usual six foot La Torre clan. Having said that, he didn't miss it by much. Unlike a lot of the other men in the room, Enzo wasn't wearing a plain black or white collar shirt but a bright green floral one. Though it seemed like a testament to his light-hearted character as opposed to a keen sense of style.

My awkwardness morphed into irritation the moment one particular bimbo walked her way through the ornate double doors.

Lexi was once again wearing an overly small bit of fabric I would liken only to a nightdress. The pink material barely restrained her fake boobs and left little—more like *absolutely nothing*—to the imagination.

It was in stark contrast to the sophisticated black satin maxi dress I had selected for the night.

"Excuse me a moment." Jesse said, interrupting his conversation with Enzo and heading into the crowd in Lexi's general direction.

"Uh oh. I see trouble on the horizon." Enzo joked, filling the space Jesse had left by my side.

I made a noise in agreement, distracted by watching Jesse talk to Lexi. She was pouting at something he had said, and all his earlier joking had frozen into ice in her presence. *There's no love lost there,* I realized.

"The Boss isn't going to be happy about her being here." Enzo observed, bringing his beer bottle to his lips and taking a sip.

As if on cue, Marco appeared from one of the double doors to the side of the room, leading out onto the back terrace. He did a quick scan of the sea of faces and for a second his eyes fell on where Jesse and Lexi were standing. His expression darkened infinitesimally, but his gaze didn't linger there long. Flicking to me only a moment later as if he could feel me watching him.

Our eyes locked and the rest of the room seemed to fall away, muted by his mere presence for a moment. I almost didn't notice the woman approaching him until her neon pink nails had wrapped their way around his neck.

Jealousy and contempt swirled in my chest, but it quickly morphed into smug satisfaction as Marco extricated himself from the woman and shot her a look that was sharper than freshly cut steel. Her expression soured with his rejection, and I fought the urge to smile.

"Seems like he isn't the only one whose unhappy Lexi is around." Enzo observed beside me, giving me a knowing look.

There was something oddly familiar about that look. "How do you know Jesse?" I questioned, certain there was a family connection somewhere between the two men.

"He's my brother." Enzo smiled sheepishly.

"Half-brother," Jesse tagged on, re-joining the conversation. "On our father's side."

I nodded, now understanding why Enzo seemed so familiar to me. It wasn't that he looked like Jesse, in fact in facial appearances, the men were not the slightest bit alike. It was in their mannerisms. Their light-heartedness and easy-going temperament were what marked them as family.

"What happened with Lexi?" I asked Jesse.

I had lost sight of her and Marco amongst the swathe of people.

"Sent home, Bandit. Boss doesn't want her here and no one else does either." He took a beer from one of the waiters' trays as they flittered past.

The men had begun talking again for a few minutes when I spotted Marco amongst the crowd. This time he was talking to a balding man with a pot belly. A fabulously attractive girl stood off to his side, stroking the older man's shoulders while simultaneously shooting flirty glances at the Don he was speaking too. My lips pursed in irritation.

I didn't know why it was bothering me, but seeing numerous women fawn over Marco reminded me of exactly why I had decided to cage my feelings away in the first place. Not that it very much mattered now. Hadn't I decided I wasn't strong enough to resist him any longer? *Fool.*

"Bandit?" Enzo asked, bringing my attention back to the two men I was standing with.

Jesse laughed around his drink. "This one," he said, pointing to me. "She's the Bandit. Nearly cleaned out all the expensive purses in the house."

My cheeks flamed as he launched into the embarrassing story of my 'great escape' as he so articulately described it. Including how I fell into the bush and crawled my way underneath an open gate.

I couldn't help but join in with their laughter though. Looking back at the attempt, it had been wholly ridiculous. I doubted I would ever live it down.

As time ebbed on, Jesse and Enzo got swept away by other family members, and I was left to my own devices. There were a few interested glances thrown my way by various men in attendance as well as some more vicious ones from the women. When two in particular started whispering in each other's ears while looking in my direction, I went searching for a drink.

I cut a path through the crowd to the kitchen island, which had been set up as a bar and was littered with everything you could possibly want or need to make a decent cocktail.

Initially, I made myself something with a passion fruit I found, but upon glancing around the room and seeing Tom and Alonso stationed toward the back walls looking suitably bored, I decided to make a couple of virgin mojitos as well. Once I had shaken the concoction and poured it out into the two sugar rimmed glasses I had prepped, I took them over to the men on a tray.

They both inclined their heads and smiled down at me as I approached. It seemed that I was fast becoming friends with Marco's security personnel, and surprisingly, I was happy about that.

"These are to say thank you for being the best security guards a girl could wish for," I said sweetly, presenting them with the tray of drinks.

They looked at the drinks and then each other. I rolled my eyes, seeing where this was going.

"Would you both relax! It's alcohol free." I smiled triumphantly at them.

After a second of deliberating, they both reached for the glasses. "Thank you, Ma'am," Tom said, and Alonso chimed in with the same.

"Jesus Christ, it's Addie, okay? Or Adalyn. I'm not *seventy*," I scolded around a laugh. Alonso chuckled and Tom shot me a bemused look.

"Have a good night boys," I said, turning round on my heel and heading back to the makeshift cocktail bar.

Unsure of what to make next, I perused the little menu card with recipes listed on it. I wasn't a very experienced cocktail maker, so chose to chiefly examine the recipes marked as 'beginner cocktails'. After only a few minutes of looking at the instructions, I huffed in confusion and gave up, preferring to go with the flow and throwing a bit of everything I liked into the mix instead.

"What are you making?" A familiar deep voice questioned, coming up behind me, amusement lifting his tone.

"I am making..." I began but hesitated. "I don't really know what I'm making," I admitted, my usually quick tongue failing to come up with its normal sarcastic response.

Marco ran a hand over his mouth absentmindedly, taking in the cacophony of ingredients scattered across the work surface.

"I figured that if I just put in everything I like then it would come out okay." I shrugged, picking up the metal shaker and sloshing the mixture together.

He nodded slowly but didn't look too convinced. The boyish smile I adored but rarely saw tugged at the corner of his lips as I poured the mixture into a glass.

Well, that looks fucking rank.

White and yellow lumpy pieces of God-knows-what sank to the bottom of the glass and the liquid appeared to be curdling.

I pursed my lips at the mess and looked over to Marco. To my surprise he was shaking with quiet laughter. His perfect white teeth flashed as a smile contorted his face and his eyes sparkled with amusement. His laugh was infectious, and I couldn't help giggling as I observed the clumping cocktail.

"What the fuck is that?"

"I don't even know," I said around a laugh. "I'd better get rid of it before it poisons someone."

I went to move the drink away, but Marco was faster. Removing it from my grip, he brought the glass to his lips before I had a chance to intervene.

"Marco!" I shouted and tugged on his arm to try and stop him. A few curious gazes turned in our direction, but I ignored them. "Are you crazy?" I half-laughed, half-shrieked.

After two big swigs he brought the now empty glass down onto the counter and pulled his face into a grimace, making me laugh even harder.

I eventually got out, "I'm not being held responsible for your death."

"Noted." He said in agreement. "It was probably the worst thing you've ever made. I'd stick with brownies." He grinned, flashing his perfect white teeth and my heart fluttered in response.

"Gee, thanks," I muttered derisively as he leaned against the counter.

"La Torre!" A man suddenly interrupted us, breaking into our conversation to pull Marco into a flinchingly hard hug.

"Ronaldo." Marco greeted with a pat on the back. Familiarity making his confident voice smooth as silk.

He got quickly drafted into the small group of men that subsequently descended on us and I took that as my cue to leave.

Deciding it was probably best to keep away from the cocktails, I grabbed a bottle of Pinot Grigio and made my way outside to sit by the pool.

My shadows, Tom and Alonso followed behind me as I settled into one of the comfortable seating areas. I poured a glass of wine and sat back, watching the party from a distance. Periodically a few glances were shot my way. Most curious, some somewhat angry, and others a bit leery, so I turned my attention upward to try and locate any of the star constellations I was familiar with.

"YOU!"

A vaguely familiar female voice rang out across the patio, and I glanced down in time to see a furious looking Lexi marching through the group of people loitering nearby. It took me a moment to figure out that it was in fact *me* that she was storming toward and shouting at.

"You fucking slut!" She screeched again and people began turning in our direction.

I could see she was unsteady on her feet even from this distance. Her sky-high neon heels glinting in the candlelight as she continued on an apparent warpath toward me.

Alonso intercepted her about fifteen feet away from the table, bringing her to a halt. She immediately took a swing at him, but he blocked as if swatting a fly and she growled in frustration.

I didn't know what the hell her problem was, but I had a feeling I was going to find out whether I cared for it or not.

"You're a little bitch, you know that? I don't know who the fuck you think you are—"

"I think you've said enough Lexi." I cut her off, my voice cold and biting. "Take your trashy ass home where it belongs." I picked up my glass and took a sip, dismissing her.

"*Me* trashy? I hear you sleep with anything wearing an Armani suit, you gold digging skank!" she screamed.

Ah, I see where this is going.

"Cesare Attolini actually," I corrected mockingly.

"I bet you begged your daddy to leave you here just so you could whore your way through a new family." My teeth snapped together with that, anger beginning to bubble in my veins. "I don't blame him for not paying your ransom. No bitch is worth that kind of money."

My temper flared, and I put the glass down on the table, fearing it would snap if left in my hand. My fingers twitched to be let loose on Lexi's face as I walked to where Alonso stood restraining her.

"Say that again. I *fucking* dare you." I stopped less than six feet away as the blonde struggled to get closer to me, her acrylics biting into Alonso's trunk of an arm.

"I think too much dick has made you stupid, Adalyn. What I said was: no *bitch* is worth paying that kind of money for. Or any kind of money, actually." She spat acerbically.

"Alonso. Please move."

Lexi's face contorted into a bloodthirsty smile at my words.

"Ma'am—" he begun to protest.

"*Now*, Alonso."

Hesitantly, Alonso removed his hand from Lexi's arm.

Predictably, she sprang at the opportunity and threw herself in my direction. Her uncoordinated legs flailing as she ploughed across the mere feet that now separated us.

Her hands went for my face, and I blocked her arms with ease having already anticipated her move. Her sharp nails sailing through the air only inches away from my face.

I used the opportunity to swing one of my legs round the back of her knee, knocking her off balance as she grabbed a fistful of my hair. My head jerked, and soon enough I was tumbling with her, thankfully landing on top of the skank rather than under her.

Once I got my bearings, I slapped her clean across the face until her grip in my hair loosened. She shrieked and clawed my arms instead, drawing thin red tendrils across the skin. I smacked her again, but this time harder than before, the adrenaline fueling my violence. The crack against her cheek was sickening, but it was scarcely more than a sting to my hand.

Her eyes glossed over in a daze, and I staggered away from her, walking back to the table. I tried my best to ignore the crowd of onlookers that had begun to descend on us.

"Do you really think he wants you?" She laughed, crooning behind me.

God's, this girl just doesn't know when to shut up.

"How better to stick it to your family than to screw its only heir?" She rose to her feet, a cruel smile lining her lips. "Don't you see? By fucking you he's fucking over the enemy. It's *pathetic* really."

A quiet gasp went through the crowd, but I barely heard it.

I saw red.

Bright *fucking* red.

I yelled and hurled myself at her.

The second we collided, I started clawing at whatever I could get my hands on and she did the same. Skin, clothing, hair. It didn't matter. The aim was to inflict pain—it didn't matter how. Lost in our thirst for each other's blood we toppled to the floor as we both started grappling for the upper hand.

Lexi shrieked as I struck her in the jaw, and I smirked in

satisfaction. She clawed at my arms once again, but another hit to her jaw sent her flying off me. *I'm winning this fight,* I realized.

However, the satisfaction was short lived.

Lexi grabbed a fistful of my hair and threw her weight to the side, sending us both crashing into the swimming pool. Our scrap continued for a second or two underwater, until our need for oxygen outweighed our need for blood—though in my case it wasn't by much.

A symphony of shouting, laughing and exclamations shattered the temporary silence of the water.

When I looked about me, the first thing I noticed was Marco standing at the pools edge. His expression was one of pure fury and I instinctually shrunk away. It took a second for me to realize that his fury wasn't directed at me for once, but at the half-drowned Barbie off to my left.

"Get the *fuck* out of the water! NOW!"

"She started it!" Lexi's whining response shouted back.

Humiliation over the entire situation heated my face despite the mildness of the water.

Too ashamed to stand my ground in front of the hoard of people who already hated my guts and now believed me to be nothing but a naïve slut, I swam to the furthest edge of the pool. Keeping my eyes trained on my hands, I lifted myself onto the edge and pulled off my heels before finding my feet. Soundlessly, I dived toward the path leading down the far side of the mansion and away from the scene behind me.

———

MARCO

"Get her out of here. I swear to God if she gets into this complex again, I will cut your fucking dick off." I hissed viciously into Jesse's ear after Ada had fled.

Part of me wanted to follow her, but I knew I couldn't.

I hadn't seen all of the fight, but I had seen enough of it to know the damage Lexi's words would have caused.

Despite what most people knew of the Mannino daughter, she wasn't as assured or as fearless as her smart mouth made her out to be. Underneath it all there was a.... A softness that was rare to come across amongst the Cosa Nostra, having been quashed in our early years by a propensity for violence. It was a softness that seemed to make devotees out of anyone that she dined to show it to. My staff, Jesse, and my fucking self included.

My self-restraint pulled dangerously taut as her figure, soaked in pool water, disappeared down the side of the house.

God, she was beautiful. The things I could do to that woman...

Now really isn't the fucking time!

I shook my head to clear the thought.

Unfortunately for me, Lexi was fast approaching with a manufactured sadness in her eyes and a bullshit apology on her lips. She looked closer to a drowned thrift store doll than the classy hooker she often tried to imitate.

I didn't feel an ounce of remorse when I nodded at Layton to dump her gold-digging ass off my property. I turned my back to her, ignoring her protests as she was dragged away in what I was hoping would be the last time I would ever see her.

Truth be told, I didn't know why I had fucked about with Lexi for so long. She was an easy lay and a guy had to eat, I guess. It was also a way of releasing all the extra energy one *particular* hostage kept manufacturing....

I turned to the spectators that had gathered in the garden.

I could see the accusations Lexi made about Ada had made an impact, marring their view on the Mannino descendent that had done nothing to earn their disgust. We weren't even sleeping together. *Yet.*

"Adalyn Rossi has done nothing to earn the accusations made here tonight." I addressed the mixture of friends and family milling about my yard, immediately silencing them.

The men looked back at me with a combination of reverence or fear, while the woman looked at me with either reservation or barely restrained attraction. Even some of the older ones.

"She is part of this family now. She is a La Torre. If anyone has a problem with that then your family will have your body back in a box. Am I clear?" I swear I could have heard a moth shit it was so quiet.

I turned and stalked back inside.

I needed a plan to show Ada Lexi's words weren't true.

I needed proof. *Evidence.*

I needed a fucking drink.

ADALYN

I wasn't sure how long I'd sat under the steady stream of water, but it was long enough that the marble white slabs no longer felt cold, and my hands had turned wrinkled, like an old, weathered hag's. So, I assumed it had been a while.

The constant babbling of guests had long since fallen silent when I turned the faucet off and wrapped myself in a towel, so I was pretty certain the party had ended.

Much as I hated to admit it, Lexi's words had gotten to me.

Once again, I was doubting the invisible tie I felt to Marco. He'd told me he wasn't a monster right from the beginning and up until the party I had believed him.

But sometimes monsters hide deep.

Could this all be part of an elaborate game? One where he

ended up fucking me just to stick it to my father and simultaneously break my heart in the process?

I scowled at my reflection and grabbed a nearby cotton pad
from the vanity to begin wiping my face of any remnants of the
evening. Movement in the mirror made me pause a moment.

A familiar presence warmed the room, but I refused to
acknowledge it. Keeping my gaze trained to my hand as I
continued scrubbing the lingering foundation off my face.

Marco leaned against the bathroom wall; hands tucked into
both pockets.

I need to hide my heart from this man.

Caring for him would mean death to my peace of mind.

"What?" I demanded icily, unable to bear the loaded silence
any longer.

"Are you ok?" His usually cold voice held a tinge of concern,
but it was most probably a figment of my imagination.

I looked at the scratches on my arms but eventually
nodded.

"Lexi got to you didn't she."

It wasn't a question, so I didn't answer.

I grabbed my hairbrush from the counter and started
racking it through my dark tangles of hair. He remained silent,
but he looked to be contemplating something. His brows
furrowed in thought.

"You agreed earlier that I am not a monster." He eventually
said, pushing himself up from the wall.

"Yes, but you are still a *Don*." I snapped, slamming my hairbrush down. "Known for ruthlessness, violence, and manipulation. There is no place for caring or love in the heart of a Don.
Just power. And while I believe you to be different, I would be
naïve to think that fucking me as a power move hasn't ever
crossed your mind."

I finally met his watching eyes in the mirror.

His voice was cold. "It hasn't."

"Do you really expect me to believe you? Just take your word for it and skip through my days with my head in the clouds?" *Did he really think I was so ignorant?*

A scowl creased his brow, and he took a measured step in my direction. "I guess you will have to trust me."

I spun around to face him angrily.

"Trust you!" I scoffed.

"Fine. Then I'll make you another deal," he said flippantly, and I crossed my arms in response, tired of the games.

"Seems like a lot of work just for someone to sleep with. You're better off leaving me alone," I said airily. Tauntingly.

Surprisingly he didn't bite—he just smiled.

"You give me your trust." I opened my mouth to immediately protest, but he quickly cut me off. "You give me your trust, and if I so much as break it once, I will set you free. You can keep your car, the clothes and all the money you could ever need, but you would be free to disappear. You'd never have to see me again."

I sucked in a breath, "How do I know you'll hold up your end of the bargain?"

"How do I know you will hold up yours? Proof."

He reached into his back pocket and pulled out a wad of paper. Slowly his large hands unraveled its contents, revealing a dark blue passport and some other documents. He gestured for me to take them.

For a second, I stared at the paperwork in my hands.

They were all the documents I would need to start over. A passport with my picture and my name, Adalyn Rossi. A new social security, bank accounts, identification documents, health card, and educational diplomas. All the documents that could get me wherever I wanted to be.

He wasn't lying about the bargain. This was the proof.

He had done all this to get me to trust him and to trust the fact that Lexi's words were just as fake as her personality. Something akin to hope burned through my chest as unease circled in my stomach.

He pulled the paper from my frozen fingers and carefully tucked it away. His eyes coasted over my body, a storm slowly brewing beneath their surface.

"Trust me now when I say that being with you is not a power move. That you are not part of some game, and you are not a tool for retribution." His voice was so deep I felt it in my chest.

The documents, the care he'd shown, how he listened about the employees of *Pretty Penny Loans*... I nodded. I *could* trust him.

"Prove to me that you believe me. That you *do* trust me."

My brain slowly caught up and I faltered, fresh out of ideas on how exactly to prove it.

He took a slow step forward, his hand rubbing across his lips as a dark smile tugged at their edges. It did nothing to ease the thundering in my ears or the tingle in my stomach.

"I have an idea." His voice took on a rough edge, but he offered no further explanation.

He edged closer to me. His muscled form dwarfing mine as heat pulsed from him in waves. The back of one of his large hands came to rest on my cheek, a finger gently brushing my bottom lip. My breath hitched and butterflies pooled in the pit of my stomach, while his other hand weaved its way into my wet hair, and he pulled softly. Maneuvering my head to an angle where he'd have access to my neck.

His face lowered and my heart rate drummed in nervous anticipation as warm breath traced along my skin.

His lips came to rest at my ear, "Tell me something."

"What do you want to know?" I asked breathlessly, completely absorbed by his touch.

"Something no one else does. Something you would only

tell someone you trust." His lips pressed against the hollow of my ear, making it difficult for me to focus on the words.

"I don't... I can't think of anything."

"I need proof, Ada." He scolded darkly. Teasingly.

Fuck I can't think straight.

"I-I um... I watch porn sometimes."

Marco pulled back and let out a quiet laugh, his shoulders shaking.

I instantly smoldered, having let out *that* embarrassing morsel of information.

He shot me my favorite boyish smile before descending back onto my neck.

"I was thinking of something else..." He hinted, but at what exactly I wasn't sure. I could barely see past the shiver stretching down my spine from where his lips met my skin. "How many men have you been with?"

That brought me somewhat out of my blissful reverie, and I gulped.

Sex outside of marriage, especially for women, was frowned upon in our society.

Ruled by the Catholic church, the age-old principles on purity, the body, and marriage were ingrained in the Cosa Nostra's very core. For a woman to have had sex outside of marriage or without a contract drawn up by her father was not just scandalous—it marred the family name. Not that it *didn't* happen from time to time.

While it was no secret to Marco that I seemed...more *promiscuous* than most in my position. He didn't know to what extent—if any. Telling him that *extent*, however, had the potential to ruin me... which was exactly why he'd asked me that question. He knew that by giving him my answer, I had to trust him implicitly.

"T-t-two." I stuttered out.

Surprisingly, he didn't seem bothered by the information.

His lips continuing to press against me languidly, just below my jaw.

"Where are they now?"

"One is...at the bottom of Lake Mead." I sighed, bringing a hand up to thread into his disheveled hair.

"The other?" His voice was scarcely audible despite the proximity.

"I don't know." I answered honestly.

Truth was, I didn't *want* to know where he was.

Marco slowly moved back an inch to watch me with lidded eyes. My hand fell to his large chest as a sliver of air now separated us and I missed the hardness of his body instantly. My unease evaporated when his hand moved from my hair to my shoulder, gliding downwards to rest on my waist.

His head tilted to the side in a silent question, his eyes tender.

I didn't answer but nodded my head, knowing exactly what he was asking.

His hands moved slowly to my chest, and he pulled the material knotted there loose, with a flick of his wrist. The towel fell with a soft thud to the floor, leaving me standing completely bare before him.

I had never been so acutely aware of my nakedness.

My pulsing anticipation only intensified as his face darkened with need, coiling between my legs and sending tingles dancing along my skin. I watched as his impenetrable gaze trailed over my body, eventually coming to rest on my lips.

With snake like speed, he reached out, pulling me flush to his chest. His lips crashed into mine with unwavering ferocity as restraint fractured within him.

I met his kiss feverishly, sucking on his lips and pushing mine wider, inviting him to taste my mouth. Instinctually, my hands wound around his broad shoulders. He groaned the moment his hands skimmed my waist and landed on my naked ass.

I sighed as he sucked and nipped a trail across the plains of my chest and captured a hardened nipple with his tongue. He played with it, biting down on my taught skin with surprising gentleness, licking the sting of pain away before moving to the other nipple. I hissed in ecstasy.

But the moment I felt him drop to his knee in front of me I froze.

Was I ready for this?

I didn't know what *this* even meant to Marco, but I had a pretty good idea.

He had told me he wanted me...but sex was sex to men like him. It was a commodity. A transaction. The moment I gave in to the irresistible attraction there was between us, there would be nothing left for me to give him.

Once he had *had* me, everything would change.

How could I possibly live in his home as he brought back countless other women? Watch him as he eventually married and settled down, while my feelings for him remained unchanged?

I didn't fit into his future.

To me, whatever *this* was, it was more than just sex. It meant something not only because of my past...but because despite *everything,* I had caught feelings for the man now kneeling before me.

If I gave in to him now...I risked feeling the pain of it forever.

"Marco."

I could feel him pause a moment, his breath swirling against my stomach. Then his lips sucked at the skin beneath my belly button and his strong hands started trailing the backs of my calves.

"Marco. I can't do this."

His hands stilled against my skin as the words hung in the air.

A handful of seconds passed before he turned his head away from me, a sound of discontent resonating deep within in his throat. Slowly, he rose to his feet and turned his back toward me, letting out a heavy sigh.

I caught a glimpse of his expression in the mirror. Arousal mixed with frustration shadowed his eyes and creased his brow as he looked down at the floor.

He didn't make another sound as he walked out, leaving me weak and trembling in his wake.

CHAPTER
SIXTEEN

ADALYN

It was fair to say flying on private jets was nothing new for me. So, when Jesse insisted I didn't know what I was "in for" for our journey, I brushed him off.

It wasn't until the moment the SUV's pulled to a stop alongside a humongous, sleek white airliner that I realized why he was so smug. The plane was probably double the size of any private jet I had even seen, let alone been on.

Jesse had been right—I really had no idea.

When I asked what kind of plane it was, he wore a rather proud expression as he informed me it was a Bombardier 7500. Though he might as well have been speaking in Klingon for all that meant to me.

The plane was split into three distinct seating areas excluding a bedroom, bathroom, and fully fitted kitchen. Cream colored leathers and highly polished dark wood finished the interior, and I couldn't help but graze my fingers over the perfect, shiny surfaces as we boarded.

Unfortunately, despite the cabin's pleasing appearance, the twelve-hour trip from O'Hare International to Catania airport was anything but pleasant.

Marco wore a permanent scowl on his face and his tumbler was continuously filled with whiskey by the flight attendant. I was starting to think the man had a drinking problem.

His piss-poor mood kept the air tense the duration of the flight and it didn't escape anyone's notice that I was seemingly the cause of it.

By the time we had landed at Catania, the silence was stifling, and I breathed a sigh of relief when Jesse and I travelled separately to Marco's villa that evening.

Despite the late hour, the grandeur of the nineteenth century castle was not completely lost to the darkness. Lights shone up the walls, emphasizing two square turrets and a fifteen-foot portico made of elaborately entwined arches. The property was equally as grand on the inside. White and black veined marble decorated almost every surface, interspersed with ornately carved wood and hand painted ceilings. It was breathtaking.

Unlike the rest of the mansion, my room was relatively modern. Remodeled to include pure white walls, remote control shutters, and glass double doors that led out to a large balcony. Attached was a spacious dressing room and a pristine black-accented bathroom.

I tossed my duffle bag onto the white polished vanity and threw myself on the bed.

I'm actually in Sicily.

I was far, far away from my family and the life I had always known up until several months ago and yet...I didn't miss it. I didn't even feel like I had left anything behind.

The thought was as freeing as it was unnerving.

———

THE NEXT MORNING I had breakfast on one of the most beautiful terraces I had ever been on. It overlooked the property's extensive grounds in a tranquil stillness, the turquoise sea glistening off in the near distance. It was a peaceful morning with bright sunshine and a cloudless blue sky. The perfect weather for sunbathing.

I hadn't seen Marco since he walked in the opposite direction to me when we arrived last night. Presumably he was locked away in a study somewhere attending to business. My assumption was only strengthened when I saw various groups of men filter in and out the castle halls that morning, all heading in the direction of what I assumed was his study.

Not that his disappearing act bothered me—I needed as much space from him as I could get after what had happened between us. I had no idea what it all meant or what the consequences might be. We were dangerously walking along a tight rope at this point, and I had no intention of falling off, for fear of what lay beneath it.

Hurt, I imagined.

Thankfully, Jesse's presence wasn't needed by Marco for the day and so his only job was ensuring I didn't get lost amongst the many corridors and doors. With both our schedules wide open and the weather as beautiful as Sicily got, we decided to make use of the villa's private beach. It was just a stone's throw away and accessible through an elaborate topiary garden to the east.

Finding three sets of white canopy beds lining the sweeping shore, I settled on the closest while flipping through a magazine. Jesse parked off on the other one nearby and passed out within thirty seconds of laying down, clearly feeling the effects of jet lag and snoring loud enough to scare away the local wildlife.

At just after three that afternoon, Jesse groaned at the

sound of a gull squawking overhead and after a few moments of looking about himself disorientated, suddenly sprung to his feet.

He shouted something in Italian and run off frantically to the far side of the beach with a huge smile on his face.

I rolled my eyes and watched as he made his way onto a small dock that was jutting out into the water. From this distance, I could only see one or two smaller boats tied to its edge.

I turned back to the tasteless magazine I was reading, rather regretting not bringing along a book or something more interesting to read.

The quiet purr of an engine soon interrupted my train of thought and suddenly Jesse reappeared, flying across the water like a mad man. The black jet ski he was straddling kicked up water in his wake and sent ripples across the water's surface, stretching out into a large V.

It didn't take much encouragement before I started rummaging around in the storage box myself in search of another life jacket. I got onto the identical jet ski still tied to the dock and Jesse talked me through the various controls, knotting the ignition key around my arm.

I eased the throttle and was suddenly flying along the water too. I screeched at the top of my lungs. It was damn right exhilarating and, not that I would ever admit it, a little bit terrifying.

Jesse and I spent the next few hours speeding across the water, racing each other and playing chicken. He was evidently more skilled than me, and I had fallen rather ungracefully on several occasions, earning myself a mouth of sea water in the process.

"We should go over and explore those caves tomorrow," he shouted across to me as we came to a relative still. He pointed to an alcove of rock out toward the furthest edge of the secluded beach. "I think there's a beach inside one of them."

"Sure. That sounds like fun." I nodded in agreement.

As I was looking back across the water, I noticed movement on the dock.

"I think Marco wants you." I shouted over to Jesse, whose back was still to shore.

He turned the jet ski in a circle, looking back across to the beach. He muttered something under his breath before gunning the throttle and zipping through the water. With a reluctant sigh I followed, navigating the waves behind him.

I could hear Marco's angry voice was raised before I could even make out what he was saying. *The piss-poor mood continues then.*

"Why isn't your phone on you? I've been trying to get hold of you for the past hour!" He was shouting across the water to Jesse.

Despite the humidity, he was wearing his usual slacks and black long-sleeve shirt. Though his top button was undone, and his sleeves were rolled back enough to show the tattoos on his arms.

Unquestioningly, it was his best look.

"What's wrong?" Jesse asked. "Did something happen?"

"Nothing happened!" Marco shouted. "But it *could* have, and you are nowhere to be seen." Marco's hands slapped his thighs before he grabbed his hips.

"Give him a break, Marco. He's keeping me from drowning, and aren't you supposed to be safe here? This is *your* territory, in *your* province." I argued.

Marco's glare sliced to me for a second then away, treating me as if I were invisible to him. "You will stay alert and have your phone on you at *all* times. On duty, off duty I don't give a shit." He continued. Clearly angry by more than just the phone.

Marco slammed the device against the dock so hard that for a second I thought it might shatter.

Jesse muttered a "Yes, Boss," while I shouted a rather undignified, "Oh for Christ's sake."

Once again, it was as if I hadn't spoken.

"You don't have to be such an asshole all the time," I said antagonistically, getting thoroughly annoyed by the silent treatment. The muscle in his jaw ticked just as I'd hoped it would.

"Put the jet skis away. Our meeting is in an hour." Marco ordered.

"No! What the hell Marco!" I protested, but Jesse was already reaching for the rope to secure himself along the dock.

Marco finally turned to acknowledge me for the first time in over twenty-four hours. A signature scowl marred his handsome face, and he looked nothing short of the sinister Don of Sicily he was. Not an ounce of boyish charm hidden amongst his carefully schooled features.

"I need my security team *working,* Ada. Now get out of the fucking water."

I was sick of his attitude. All because I'd told him *no* the other night. It wasn't fair, and he wasn't the only person that could throw a tantrum or act like an ass.

"Not until you say *please.*" I smiled sweetly. Tauntingly.

I knew that he wouldn't. I'd only ever heard the word come out of his mouth twice in the whole time I'd known him...and judging by the sharp snap of his clenched teeth I was pretty confident I was unlikely to hear it again.

"Get out the water now or *your* pleas will be next."

A thrill went down my spine at his insinuation, settling into a warm pool in my stomach.

Damn. I don't have a good response to that.

Part of me wanted to stay in the water to see what he would do to make good on his promise, but my nervousness won out and I relented after another second.

Irritated, I swung the jet ski closer, and Jesse grabbed the handles, securing the vessel to the docking post. With the help of his hand for balance, I planted my feet firmly back onto the solid wooden slats.

I tried to ignore the embodiment of sex and sin itself as it stood glaring at me less than a few feet away.

Doing my best to appear unaffected by his presence, I undid the life jacket buckles around my waist and unzipped the nylon fabric with deliberate slowness. My strappy black bikini fell into view, and I felt his gaze flick to my chest, which was barely restrained by the fabric.

Before I could talk myself out of it, I crossed the space between us and slapped the sopping wet life jacket against his chest. "Ass," I muttered, turning away from him with a glare and walking back down the dock in the direction of the house.

———

By the time sunset came, I had changed into a khaki bandeau maxi dress ready for dinner. I had finished my hair and was just putting the finishing touches to my outfit when voices and footsteps from outside distracted me. I drifted toward the balcony and peered out over the stone ledge, curious as to what was going on.

A cobblestone pathway that spanned the entire side of the villa ran beneath my feet, leading off to several smaller buildings on the property. Some I presumed were staff residences, while another I was pretty certain was a gym.

Standing along the path just below me was Marco, Jesse, and Benny, as well as the normal security personnel and family members. They were engaged in some kind of jovial conversation, but about what I couldn't be certain.

I really need to learn Italian, I thought bitterly. Another silent curse sent squarely in the direction of my father, wherever he was right now.

After a few minutes of chatter between the men, I heard

Marco mutter "Scusa" and the men drift in the direction of the front entrance, their footsteps falling away to the silent evening air.

"I was wondering when you would call." Marco spoke after a few moments.

I was surprised to hear he was still there, and I couldn't see or hear anyone else with him.

"I've been...busy," he said in a bored tone to whatever the person on the other end of the phone was saying.

Five seconds passed again before he then murmured, "Oh, is that so?"

I bristled.

He no longer sounded bored and irritated, but his voice took on a lustful edge that told me what I was hearing was anything but a business call—it was a booty call.

"And what are you wearing now?" *Are you for fucking real!*

This only cemented how right I'd been to stop the other night when I did. Before we had crossed that line.

God knows where I would be right now if I hadn't.

When I told Marco that I had been with only two men, I hadn't been lying. I just omitted a few details... Like how I'd only had sex twice in my whole life and how only *one* of those times had been consensual. The sad thing was that the man who'd asked my consent was the one that had found himself with a bullet in the head. The other? He was allowed to live because of *who* he was.

That was why I had stopped it, because it could never be *just sex* to someone like me.

It was the reason anger and hurt coiled under my skin now, hearing him talk to someone else like nothing happened between us.

I shook my head refusing to think about it any further.

"Fine. Give me an hour." Marco said and cut the call.

I couldn't see him from my position hidden behind the stone, but I could hear a heavy sigh and curses leave his lips. Then the distinct sound of his footsteps trailing away toward the house.

Any desire to give in to the irresistible pull of Marco La Torre was now exiled to the furthest recesses of my mind... again. Regardless of whether it was from jealousy, hurt or just plain sexual frustration, I wasn't going to take his disrespect lightly. I was going to punish him for it.

This isn't a game? Well, let's see who's playing now.

———

THE NEXT MORNING, I had watched from my window as countless expensive cars had begun to arrive. I had never seen so many tailor-made suits, golden Rolex's or Gucci loafers in one place before. The money made my head spin.

Judging by the raucous laughter and dark complexions, I guessed the majority of them were La Torre's but there were some outliers in the mix as well. Enzo was notably one of them.

Springing into motion, I tore through my dressing room in search of the perfect outfit for my plan.

The maids had already unpacked all my things, and soon enough I came across the shorts and neon pink sports bra I had in mind. I pulled on the stretchy black shorts, satisfied when the material sat a quarter inch higher than the crease of my butt cheeks. The sports bra I had chosen was almost backless with skimpy straps falling in a zigzag at its base. The ensemble left little to the imagination. *Perfect.*

Grabbing my headphones and a yoga mat I took from the gym yesterday evening, I made my way outside and down the stone steps to the lawned area of the garden. The area was recessed and elegantly sculptured into the landscape. It made the already high walls of the mansion look even more imposing as they loomed high above.

The sounds of chatter and debate were unmistakable as I walked toward the gardens. The men had moved to gather on the patio overlooking the area I had marked as my target.

I knew it was ballsy, and I knew it was obvious. But I didn't care.

I was no longer ruled by sanity or reason but by pure frustration and sexual angst.

I wanted to punish him for thinking he could lead me on and play away. For thinking I was some game, or worse—*Lexi*.

I rolled the mat out on the grass, grateful for my sunglasses as I saw a few heads turn in in my general direction. Tactless curiosity staining their features.

Picking up my phone, I selected one of my playlists and the music started trickling through my air pods.

I had taken a few yoga classes some months back in Las Vegas, but had grown bored of the tameness of it all. Nonetheless, I had remained somewhat flexible and remembered some of the moves well.

I wasn't entirely surprised by the wolf whistles sounding off behind me as I stretched, but I ignored them.

I moved as gracefully as possible into the cobra, stretching my back out. After thirty seconds, I moved into a variation of child's pose to relieve some of the added pressure, before lifting with the balls of my feet into downward-facing dog. It took everything in me to keep the smug smirk off my face as my ass lifted high in the air. *My ass looks fire in these shorts...*and judging by some of the hoots I was hearing, apparently I wasn't the only one that thought so. I did the circuit a few more times until my back grew more supple.

It's time to take it up a notch.

I sunk into the cow pose, with my back arched as far as I dared. Moving onto my knees I sunk backwards, keeping my arms straight above my head and pushing my boobs into the ground.

"What the fuck are you doing?" Came the six words I was waiting to hear.

I didn't bother looking up at the shadow looming over me.

I moved back into the cow pose before I answered. "Yoga."

"I can see that," he gritted.

I turned and sat back to face him as I took out one of my earbuds.

I noticed over his shoulder that quite a few of the men were watching us, Jesse and Enzo included.

"Is there a reason you're parading around my men with hardly any clothes on?" I swallowed hard but didn't answer. "I think I know why," he muttered after a few seconds of silence.

He took a step toward me, his crotch almost in line with my face only a foot away. I didn't miss the way his eyes flashed at the sudden proximity and something like anticipation wove itself into my veins.

"I've said it before, and I'll say it again." An electric heat pulsed between us at his words. "If you want *attention*, you come to me."

"In your dreams."

"It sure didn't feel like a dream." He smirked arrogantly.

"That's funny, I didn't think you got to *feel* anything." I snapped and his features grew tense, the muscle in his jaw ticking.

Feeling a combination of bravery and daring, I scooted closer to him, running my hands up the front of his knees and onto his muscular thighs. I raised myself up, still on my knees but his crotch now completely in line with my face.

"You want to fuck me." It wasn't a guess. He'd already told me as much numerous times already. The heat of his gaze didn't waver as my hands continued their slow caress of his thighs. The heat between us caused me to shiver, but I ignored it. "Only you. No one else."

"No one else," he agreed.

I smiled softly at the confirmation.

Don't say it. Don't say it. DO NOT SAY IT.

"But did it ever occur to you that *I* don't want to fuck *you*?" My voice may have been gentle, but it provoked a harsh response.

Before I knew it, he had dragged me to my feet, hooking his hands behind my elbow and lifting me like I weighed no more than a sack of potatoes. Our bodies pressed together tightly. Inescapably.

"You're a fucking liar." His lips pressed to my ear. "I don't know what game you're playing, but I told you I wasn't playing games anymore."

"Is that why you fucked someone else last night?" I bit back.

Surprise made him falter a second before an angry noise resonated in his chest. Realization dawned on his face.

I pulled away. "I won't be treated like an option. Not even by you."

———

MARCO

I let my arms fall to my sides as she scooped up the mat and her phone from the floor. She shuffled past me without a second glance, and I couldn't help the flex in my jaw as I burned in frustration.

How could she think I was treating her like an option? I couldn't even if I'd wanted to.

I hadn't slept with anyone since Ada threw my domes out and that was well over a month ago. I might have slipped up a few times, what with Lexi kissing me at the club and last night...but *fuck* I was doing my best.

Last night hadn't amounted to anything anyway.

One of my regulars from before, Sofia, called me up as she heard I was back for my cousin's wedding and asked to meet up. My balls were so blue they were almost fucking *black*, so I went. She was a sure thing. She always was.

What I hadn't banked on though, was the shiver of disgust that trilled through me when her lips were on me. I couldn't get out of my head Ada's watery blue eyes. The way they always looked so innocent or the way her mouth tasted when I'd explored it. I couldn't go through with Sofia because it wasn't *her*.

I was starting to think Ada had tainted every other woman for me, but what was perhaps more unnerving was that I didn't think that stain would ever come back out.

I sighed and turned, taking the steps back up to the terrace two at a time.

I hadn't missed the watchful eyes of my men as I'd approached Ada, but I couldn't let her continue making a spectacle of herself. Flashing her tight ass around like a bunch of hypersexual men weren't within a hundred-yard radius...if I had let it continue, I'd have shot about ten of them dead by now.

The look of approval that greeted me back on the terrace made me realize just *what* it had looked like to them. Not that I could blame them for assuming she had sucked me off.

She had been on her knees and her face only inches away from my dick.

The mental image of her big, bright eyes looking up at me so close to my crotch made me want to sack off this bullshit meeting, track her down and fuck her in that vicious little mouth of hers. Not that she would let me.

I would be so fucking lucky.

Instead, I focused on pouring out a large whiskey and took a swig. After a few moments, Jesse came up beside me with a smirk.

"Looking a little rough there, Brother," he said, running a hand across his face to hide his amusement.

"Shut the fuck up." He laughed but the edge in my voice kept him from saying anything else.

I was more frustrated than I ever remembered being, and the sole reason for that frustration was upstairs probably easing out of her hotpants, freeing the mounds of her bubble butt... My dick twitched. *Fuck me.*

"Marco, my man!" Carlos, one of my distant cousins, drawled. "Fucking that old bastard Alberto's daughter; sly move Cuz. Well played."

Without a second of hesitation, I spun around to face the steroid injecting moron that was lucky enough to share a sliver of my DNA and smashed the tumbler over his head.

Fucker didn't even feel it.

Carlos just smiled as the lacerations quickly started to bleed. Bright red blood trailing down the side of his face and onto his shirt. I barely felt stinging in my own hand as a wetness dripped down my fingers.

"Damn it, Marco. This shirt was new," was all he said, looking at the blood.

The chatting in the room hadn't even stuttered at the disruption, such were the ways of my family, but I thought I saw Jesse shake his head infinitesimally.

"Speak of her again and I will cut your fucking tongue out." I spat, gripping him by his tie.

"Understood Cuz, understood." He held his hands up placatingly.

Thoroughly pissed off and ready for this meeting to be over despite it not having even started yet, I took to my seat at the head of the table and the men quickly followed.

"Now." My voice commanded the attention of all in attendance. "Who wants to explain what happened with my goddamn weapons shipment?" I demanded, removing my gun from my trousers and placing it on the table.

All the men either looked away, gulped or took an unsteady slug of their drink.

Good.

They should be fucking scared.

CHAPTER
SEVENTEEN

ADALYN

In typical Chicago fashion, I was given only an hour's warning before the car pulled up at the front entrance to take me to Marco's cousin's club in town.

It wasn't quite as grand as some of the venues I'd been to in Chicago, but something about the white fixtures and furnishings gave it an ambience unto its own. The blue strobe lights reflected off polished white surfaces, giving the whole place a more ethereal quality than any other bar or club I had been in.

Marco had done his usual disappearing act after the meeting earlier had finished. Not that I minded or cared. I needed to focus on re-building my walls if I stood any chance of surviving in this new life. I certainly couldn't do that if I was pining over a man that *would* never, *could* never want me the way I wanted him.

I sat at the bar with my usual shadow, Alonso, by my side. I had already tried taunting him into being my drinking buddy for the night, but I was met with his usual gruff smile and shake of the head. To make things worse. I couldn't understand anything anyone around me was saying either.

I ordered myself a glass of white wine and just as I took a sip of the cool liquid, the familiar swarm of designer black suits filtered in. The crowded floor of people parted around them immediately. Clearly, the sudden presence of mobsters was anything but unusual for this club, though I was hardly surprised. Displays of reverence, awe or just plain fear washed over some of their faces. Others wore a lustful expression that made my blood smolder and I turned my back to them, downing the rest of my glass in two.

Predictably, Marco and his men went to occupy the club's restricted area. Raised on a platform, they overlooked the single-story building, more akin to the devil and his demons in hell than the God's the crowd below clearly believed them to be. I wanted to roll my eyes.

After I emptied another glass of wine, the boredom had started to subside and the urge to dance took over. The floor was packed with warm bodies, all moving to the heavy base and upbeat tempo of the music mixed live by a DJ. I ingratiated myself effortlessly with the crowd and swayed to the music.

It wasn't long until I felt a familiar sensation brush against my skin.

Following it, I found Marco watching me from across the floor. His chiseled jaw was tilted to the side as if in contemplation, his thighs slightly parted and in his hand was his usual tumbler full of liquor. The picture of ease and power.

And right now his focus was solely on me.

A more provocative track bled into the one before and I began moving to it instinctually, never breaking his gaze. His eyes flicked to my hand as I let it trail between my breasts, swaying my hips in a figure eight before bringing it down to graze my crotch.

His jaw clenched at the motion.

Feeling emboldened, I turned to my side and bent forwards. Flicking my hair behind me in one swift motion that he certainly would have *something* to say about.

I glanced back over to the booth but felt my heart fall to the floor when I found his seat empty. The glass he had been holding abandoned on the table beside it.

Annoyed, I carried on dancing to the music anyway. I let my body take over, and mid-way through a body roll felt someone press up behind me, their hands coming to rest lowly on either side of my hips.

"I wouldn't do that if I were you. That big guy over there will beat your ass for touching me," I yelled over my shoulder to the person, not forgetting Marco's 'rule'.

They didn't listen, pressing their hips into me with an unrelenting firmness. I felt them lean in toward my ear. "I'd like to see him try."

My heart stuttered and it took me a second to realize who the voice belonged to. Part of me wanted to revoke his touch, shove him away and promise him he would never touch me again just to prove to him I wasn't an option.

But another, more potent part of me knew I was fighting a losing battle. That I wasn't strong enough to resist the overpowering attraction that clouded my mind and tossed away all rational thought. To resist *him*.

So I didn't.

Heat burned through my veins as the length of Marco's body claimed me, engulfed me. I began moving again, lifting a hand to wind around his neck and through his hair. One of his hands strayed from my waist in response, coming up to rest just under the edge of my bra. I threaded my fingers through it, moving it leisurely down my flat stomach, so low it almost pressed against my sweet spot. He hissed in my ear, and I could feel his hardness digging into my back. I let his hand and hips trap me against him for a split second more before moving it back to my waist.

"You're so fucking hot right now." His voice grated low in my stomach.

I looked down at his other hand as it began easing its way between the cut-outs of my dress, tracing my bare skin. Once again, his touch didn't evoke the flinch I was expecting.

It was only then that I noticed the fresh wounds criss-crossing his palm.

"What happened to your hand?" I asked, turning so I could just see him over my shoulder.

He turned his head into my hair as if he were smelling me, "I got mad."

"Does it hurt?" I asked, finally meeting his blackened eyes when he looked up.

He shook his head in answer, but unconvinced, I lifted his hand and brought it to my face so I could inspect the injuries.

His breath was at my ear once again. "Do you want to make it feel better?" His voice was husky and, *my god,* the sexiest thing I had ever heard.

A haze of lust washed through me. Curiosity and alcohol were making me forget why I was fighting my feelings for him in the first place.

He lifted his hand, bringing it to the side of my face and stroked my cheek gently. The second his index finger skimmed my bottom lip I knew what he was asking.

His finger slipped between my lips as his grip on my hip tightened and I felt rather than heard his groan. I swirled my tongue around his finger before sucking, pushing my ass into him at the same time.

"Fuck. Ada." He gritted out.

He quickly pulled his hand free and encircled my wrist, pulling me through the crowd of people dancing and to a side door hidden amongst the shadows. To my surprise it led to a vacant office at the back of the building.

He closed the door behind us with an audible bang and my nerves kicked in instantaneously. I felt him come up behind me. A wave of heat rolling off of him like he was his very own kind of sun.

"Marco," I started, turning around to look at him.

"Shh," he soothed, placing a hand on my cheek in a display of gentleness that left me breathless. "Do you trust me?"

I nodded without hesitation, realizing that despite everything, I did trust him.

It was the inevitable afterwards that I didn't trust...

Before I could protest, his lips sealed around mine in a kiss that stole my breath and erased any semblance of rationality I had left.

It consumed me.

I met his kiss with equal ferocity, forgoing my reservations and ignoring the voice in my head that screamed this would only hurt me more down the line.

Taking his bottom lip between my own, I sucked it like it was the sweetest thing I had ever tasted. He groaned into my mouth, and I sighed as his tongue pushed between my lips, teasing and swirling against my own. Struggling to catch my breath, I pulled away a fraction, and his kisses descended to my neck without hesitation. His teeth nipping at my skin before sucking the pain away.

My fingers involuntarily threaded through his hair, again coming to rest on the back of his neck as his lips trailed just above the neckline of my dress. His hand drifted across my waist, coming to grip my ass consumingly. *Possessively.* It sent hot tingles up my spine and my insides melting.

One of his hands snaked up to my back, unzipping my dress and pulling at the material until it fell like a puddle of water around my feet.

He pulled away to rake his eyes over my body as I stood before him in nothing but a strappy black thong and my favorite Louboutin stilettos. He growled out a "fuck" before slamming himself into me once more.

Capturing my lips roughly with his, one hand gripping my breast, a 'mmm' noise escaped his throat as his fingers pulled at my nipple and I let out a quiet moan when his fingers were replaced with his tongue.

His hands skimming the backs of my thighs was the only warning I got before I was lifted onto the couch that ran along the side of the office, the scarlet material soft and smooth against my heated skin.

Marco kneeled at the very edge of the sofa and gripped my thighs, jerking me toward him until he was situated directly between my legs. Anxiety kicked in as his gaze fell *there*. I could tell by the tension in his features that he could see just how turned on I was. That he could see just how *wet* his touch made me.

I would have been embarrassed by my vulnerability if I wasn't so insanely turned on.

Marco descended on me, sucking on my skin just a millimeter above the line of my thong. His fingers slipped under the thin straps at my hips and he swiftly pulled the material down my legs. A jolt went through me as cool air caressed my newly exposed skin.

Anticipation thundered in my ears as his arms wound their way around the backs of my thighs, holding me in place with absolution. A moan tore from my throat the moment his tongue swirled against my sensitive skin for the first time.

A sound of satisfaction reverberated deep in his chest as he began lapping at my throbbing bud and licking me in places I ached to feel his touch. A violent shudder of pleasure trickled down my spine and my hips rolled of their own accord. His grip on my thighs held fast though, trapping my skin against him.

Marco's eyes met mine erotically as his tongue circled my entrance teasingly.

When his tongue plunged inside an embarrassingly loud moan escaped my gritted teeth.

He pulled away an inch, his raspy voice breaking through my heavy breathing as he muttered, "You taste so fucking sweet."

Pleasure and embarrassment consumed me in equal parts a moment, before his face descended again, and his tongue pushed back inside. Shoving away the remainder of my unease.

After a few moments I felt a gratifying burn as a finger replaced his tongue. His attention turning to my bud once again, sucking on it gently while his finger pumped in and out in a slow but intoxicating rhythm. After a few more pumps he slipped another finger inside and I suddenly felt full of him.

"Yes." I sighed and he groaned, picking up the pace.

"You're so tight, Ada." He bit down lightly on my thigh. His other arm cupped my breast and squeezed.

The release was so close now I could feel it burning, begging for release inside me. The pressure in the bottom of my stomach became unbearable, the heat driving me to the brink of insanity with Marco as my only antidote.

I couldn't stand it any longer.

"Please," I begged, my voice coming out breathy and weak.

"Please, what Ada?" I felt his breath against my skin as he spoke.

"*Please* make me come, Marco."

With that, his fingers dove into me harder and faster. His tongue lapping at my slit relentlessly and I screamed as a wave of pulsating ecstasy washed over me.

My thighs trembled and darkness temporarily clouded my vision.

My body flushed and then cooled as his fingers moved

languidly, drawing out the climax until my body eventually calmed and stilled.

I sighed, enjoying the come down.

The first time any man had made me orgasm and Marco had been the one to do it. But the moment his fingers left me, my euphoria was quickly replaced with piercing uncertainty.

He rose to his feet. His half-lidded eyes slicing to mine with a carnal arousal burning in his irises. Without breaking eye contact, he brought his moistened fingers to his lips and sucked them into his mouth to taste me.

My cheeks burned with embarrassment, the salaciousness of the act catching me off-guard.

With a wicked grin adorning his face, he offered his hands out to me help me sit up. The bulge in his trousers was as unmistakable as the scent of sex that clung to the air.

My eyes flicked between him and his bulging crotch. I bit my lip, not exactly sure what to do. *Do I just grab it?*

He let out a dark chuckle and pulled me to my feet.

I was keenly aware of my nakedness, especially given that he was still fully clothed. His suit trousers and long sleeve shirt barely disheveled while I sat in nothing but a pair of stilettos.

I didn't know what Marco was going to do next...but I certainly didn't expect for him to drop my hands and back away from me completely.

He reached down to pick up my discarded panties from the floor and stored them in his trouser pocket. Shooting me my favorite boyish smile, he opened the door and disappeared back out to the club.

What the fuck?

I shook my head and let my thoughts catch up with me a moment.

I didn't know why I had done it.

I wasn't strong enough. It was inevitable. It would be worth the hurt.

They were the only excuses I had, but the truth was that the excuses didn't matter. The damage was done now. It was irredeemable. Inescapable. I couldn't deny my feelings for Marco any longer. I *was* going to give myself to the man and it wasn't a matter of if but *when*.

Giving in tonight had proven how impossible to ignore my feelings had become. It also meant I would rather risk a future full of heartache than resist him any longer.

Being with him was too intoxicating, too exciting. He brought out a side of me that no one else had.

A side where I was strong and free.

Then again, when Eve took a bite of the apple in the garden of Eden, she probably thought she was free too.

———

MARCO

She was so fucking submissive in the sack.

It was like someone had infiltrated my thoughts and created a woman just for me, based on all the features that were guaranteed to fuck with my senses.

I hadn't intended to watch her dancing at the club. Just like I hadn't intended on going over there, putting my finger in her mouth, pulling her into my cousin's office and fucking her with my fingers on his couch.

Not exactly how I had envisioned it happening.

When she had begged me for her release it had turned me on so much my vision went hazy and my dick so hard, I thought it would shatter. I had to force myself to leave.

If I had given in to the wild desires stirring in me, I was sure as shit not going to be gentle. I was going to fuck her. *Hard.*

And I wasn't going to do that in my fucking cousin's office.

She was different from everyone else...which was exactly why I couldn't do her on that couch as if she was *anyone* else.

She'd told me before that there had been two men in her past, but judging on the way she responded to me tonight with those dick-stirring moans and heavy sighs at the slightest touch...I had a feeling she had never truly been touched before. Not to mention how *tight* she was.

Her body was driving me to the brink of absolute fucking distraction.

Knowing that nothing short of sex was going to truly help with my hard-on, but with everyone else on the shitting planet out the window—my only option was the shower.

The second the SUV pulled up to the door I made a beeline for it and the moment the water hit my shoulders, I gripped my dick in my hand and started pumping like a teenage chump. It was pathetic, but entirely necessary.

Thoughts of her laying out before me, her sighs and *please*s... her face when she climaxed hard around my fingers.

I came undone beneath my own hand, letting out a quiet groan as a small sense of release washed over me. Unfortunately, it did little to still the beast that still prowled inside.

She's driving me goddamn insane.

CHAPTER

EIGHTEEN

ADALYN

Restless from the events of the previous night, the next day I found a quiet spot on the terrace and logged in to my laptop to catch up on some work from the casino.

My emails were a complete mess, so I'd spent the better half of the morning responding to colleagues and sorting out the most important admin bits I hadn't managed to get around to before leaving for Sicily.

Thankfully, Jesse had joined me for lunch, but his mood was more serious than normal, and he was vague when I asked what was bothering him. He mentioned something evasive about a deal falling through, which they were currently trying to 'handle' and said that he didn't know if he'd be around for dinner. He didn't sit with me long after that.

Trying my best to ignore the knot in my stomach that had formed since last night, I threw myself back into my work with renewed vigor. I checked through the interdepartmental dockets and finalized some of the blueprints for a newly re-developed second floor.

I was sifting through the company expenses when a loud BANG echoed through the halls and jolted me from my work.

But it wasn't a bang at all—it was a gunshot.

A wave of sheer horror hit me like a ton of bricks.

I was on my feet and running before I even realized I was out of my chair.

I sprinted through the halls, my sandals slapping against the marble as I took turn after turn toward the sound. As I got closer, another bang blasted through the halls.

No, no, no. NO! This cannot be happening.

Panicking, I picked up the pace and ran as fast as I could down the final hallway.

Without a thought for what I was getting myself into, I crashed through the double doors into Marco's study. The moment I did, I noticed two things simultaneously.

The first: The heads of Jesse, Benny and the security team all swinging around in shock at my entrance.

The second, and perhaps the most unmistakable: Marco with a gun in his hand, looking down at two lifeless bodies.

The Don's expression wasn't one of anger, frustration or even remorse. He simply looked bored. Like the life he'd extinguished and blood pooling on the floor meant nothing to him. And while that menacing coldness should have repelled me, the only thought that registered in my head was: *He's okay.*

Then the room dropped to black.

———

WHEN I CAME AROUND, I was in my room and lying in the center of the bed. I tried to remember how I had got there, given the sunlight still shining through the open windows, but my mind just drew a blank.

I pulled myself upright and was surprised when my head started throbbing with pain.

The second my hand touched the sore spot on my scalp, the memory of two men lying unconscious flashed across my eyes.

Marco had killed them. I had fainted.

"Move slowly. You hit your head pretty bad." My head swung around to the occupied seat in the corner of the room. Marco's hooded eyes met mine instantly. "The doctor said you'll be fine. No concussion."

I studied him as he rose to his feet, taking a few slow steps toward me. Just like one might do when walking toward a wild animal.

He thinks I'm afraid of him, I realized. *Was I afraid of him?*

I was more afraid of myself when I found that the only answer I had was *no*.

"You can stop that. I'm not scared of you." I threw myself back on the bed and he let out a dark chuckle.

"Are you sure? You did just see two dead men in my study." He asked sternly, though there was an edge of humor to his voice that I didn't miss.

"Big deal. My father shot the boy I was seeing in my bed. I've seen worse." I blanched at myself.

Why the hell did I just tell him that?

I'd never told anyone that before.

He let out a low whistle, "Intense." I could feel his weight compress the bed as he took a seat beside me. "What happened to the other?"

"The other what?" I asked not understanding.

"The other man you were seeing."

I choked on my own breath. Fear suddenly constricting my throat and anxiety crippling my tongue.

"Surely it can't be that bad." He prompted after a moment, misinterpreting my silence for something else.

"Last I checked Jason was very much alive and kicking... though I'm still contemplating rectifying that." He added the last bit with an amused chuckle, but I was too lost in thought to respond.

I sat upright and turned my back to him. "I wasn't seeing Jason or anyone else," I muttered.

"You told me there were two men you'd been with."

I shook my head not knowing where to start...or if I *could* even start.

"Ada." Marco reached across the bed and touched my hand gently. "What's going on?"

"I-I don't... I don't want to talk about *him*." I got up and walked to the window, anxiety making my feet feel unstable and my head pounding with each step.

I felt his warm presence against my back after a moment, an arm wrapping protectively around my waist.

"What are you not telling me?" He asked, his cheek resting gently against the side of my head.

"Can we just drop it? My head hurts."

He agreed to drop it for now, but something in my mind told me it wouldn't be long before he started digging for information again.

Marco was not a man to let things go.

He'll find out eventually.

God knows what would happen when he did.

I WAS INVITED to attend dinner on the terrace with Marco that evening. It was our first formal meal together since arriving in Sicily, and for some reason, it sent a wave of shyness through me.

After everything that had transpired in the last seventy-two hours...I wasn't exactly sure what to expect from the evening.

When I exited the patio, I was convinced my concussion

was worse than the doctor had diagnosed, and I was seeing double. The table Marco was seated at was overflowing with an assortment of bruschetta, arancini, lasagna, risotto and everything in between, his usual wait staff notably absent.

"What the hell?" I asked, not understanding the scene before me as I took a seat.

Even on a nearby side table, I could see cannelloni, gelato, and what looked to be tiramisu.

There was enough food to feed maybe fifteen or twenty people.

"I didn't know what you'd like." His hand grazed his mouth to hide a smile.

"And you thought this..." I gestured to the freshly boiled lobster before me, complete with a mini chef hat, apron, and small bunch of rosemary wedged in its claw. "Was what I'd like?"

Our eyes met over the table, and I couldn't help but break into a laugh at the intricate absurdity of the lobster.

Marco released a deep chuckle and the charming boyish smile I'd come to love resurfaced.

"Just for the record, I'm a risotto kind of girl. And you?" I asked, realizing that I didn't even know what his favorite food was.

"If we're talking Italian, then I'd have to say ossobuco. Back home though, it's steak."

"How surprising," I drawled and he smiled. I helped myself to some white wine.

"Did you come to Italy a lot when you were younger?" He asked, serving himself a bit of everything.

"We visited Rome a few times because we have family there, but only every few years," I answered around a mouthful of spinach and mushroom risotto. "Did you come to Sicily a lot?"

"Yeah. My Nonni were always out here so we would stay

with them for three months every year." I recognized the Italian word for Grandparents.

"Must have been lovely growing up and coming home so much," I murmured, popping another piece of food into my mouth.

"It was alright." I heard the reservation in his tone though. "When my father died my mother came home for good. She lives in her childhood home now with my aunt."

"Do you come to visit her often?" I asked, wanting to pull him away from the darkening expression coating his face.

"Not as often as I would like." He took a swig from his tumbler and looked away.

"Well, we should make a habit of coming here, then," I said with an enthusiastic smile that faltered the second I realized what I'd said. I blushed and looked away.

In my periphery I could see Marco's expression fall from humor to unreadable in a flash. Whatever he was thinking, he seemed to recover after another moment.

A smile pulling at the edges of his lips. "You'll see her at the wedding tomorrow. She's excited to meet you."

I stopped mid chew and felt my brows raise.

She must hate my guts.

The sad thing was I didn't blame her. What my father had done to her husband went against everything that the Cosa Nostra stood for.

"What's wrong, Ada?" Marco immediately asked, picking up the shift in my mood.

"Nothing. I just...You'd tell me if she was going to kill me, right?"

The belly laugh that erupted from him made me jolt in surprise.

"I'm glad my imminent death amuses you so much," I muttered, scowling at his reaction having asked the question without an ounce of humor.

He sobered up quickly with that. "On the contrary. I find it amusing that you believe my mother capable of killing you."

I rolled my eyes. "I can't say I blame her for hating me."

I also hated myself for having Mannino blood in my veins. Even if that wasn't exactly something I could control.

"My mother does not hate you." His words were confident and final. *Truthful.* "She is...curious about you actually."

"Curious?" I asked. *What the hell is there to be curious about?*

"I'm sure she'll tell you about it tomorrow." He said dismissively, grabbing a lobster tail and pulling the steaming meat out from its shell.

I had no idea what he meant, but I suddenly felt nervous at what tomorrow might hold. We ate in silence for a few minutes before he spoke again.

"How are you enjoying Diamond City?"

"I'm loving it." A genuine smile pulled at my lips. "There's still loads for me to learn, but I think I'm getting there. I get on with all my colleagues, and Keeley, my assistant, is great."

"I'm glad you're enjoying it. I've heard nothing but good things about you." That took me by surprise a bit.

I smiled at the compliment and finished the last bite of my food.

Seeing I was finished, Marco got up and approached the side table laden with different desserts. He looked somewhat uncomfortable as he clapped his hands together and turned to face me.

"What would you like?"

Hell had officially frozen over and turned into a cotton candy flavored snow cone.

When he picked up a plate and a spatula my mouth fell ungracefully agape.

Was he going to...serve me?

I didn't think Marco was the type of man that served *anybody.*

His attempt to be gentlemanly released a swarm of butter-flies in my stomach and my heart stuttered momentarily.

"Marco...you're fucking freaking me out. Are you having some kind of stroke?" My words came out a little harsher than I intended them.

His jaw twitched. "I was getting you dessert," He said, instantly angered, tossing the spatula back on the table before turning to lean against it. "But now that you're being difficult, *you* can serve *me*."

I gave him a look that said *you've got to be joking,* but he only held the plate in my general direction. He then nodded very obviously between it and the platter of desserts.

This man!

I wanted to laugh at his audaciousness, but after a few seconds of silent stand-off, I relented.

Heaving out a sigh, I got to my feet. *If he wants me to humor him, fine, I'll humor him.*

I took the plate from his outstretched hand but leaned in close to look up at him through my lashes.

"What would you like, Marco?" I asked, making myself sound intentionally breathless.

"Tiramisu." He answered like the oversized stroppy teenager he was.

I bit back a laugh and fought against the smile threatening to pull at my lips.

Moving to the table I bent over, unnecessarily arching my back and ass high in the air to retrieve a portion of the deca-dent smelling dessert. I could feel my dress rise, giving him a flash of my lacey black panties and I smirked in satisfaction.

He stirred beside me, and I knew his restraint would be wavering by this point. After another second, I straightened and turned on my heel to lay the plate back down on the table by his seat. I then served myself some cannelloni and sat back down.

Marco stayed standing another few seconds and then, with a small laugh of disbelief, he meandered back to his seat.

"You're a pain in the ass you know." He muttered.

"You're not exactly sunshine and butterflies either."

But you goddamn love it, don't you Ada?

He smirked, looking every bit as charming as the devil himself.

After a few moments, comfortable silence lapsed between us and something I had been meaning to ask for some time came to mind. It probably wasn't the best time to bring up the topic, but I needed to know for my own sanity the answer.

"So, what happens now?" I asked, looking anywhere but at the eyes I knew were scrutinizing my face.

"What do you mean?"

"I mean when we get back to Chicago." I picked up my glass, refusing to meet his gaze. "You can't really intend for me to live in your house forever, Marco. What's the plan?"

"Is there something wrong with my house?" His voice sounded irritated. I dared to glance up and wished I hadn't.

Yup, definitely irritated.

"Of course not. I just... I can't be your *ward* for the rest of my life. I might not be a part of my own family anymore because of all this." I waved my hand vaguely in the air before looking down at my lap. "But that's not your fault and it certainly isn't your responsibility to take care of me. You've set me up with this amazing job, bought me a car. Maybe in the next few months we should look at finding someone to marry me off to." I looked over at him, but he was already looking into the distance. His jaw clenched.

"Is that what you want?" His quiet voice was filled with something I couldn't place.

At first, I thought it was anger, but it felt like something softer.

Is it what I *wanted*? No.

Was it the best I could hope for? *Yes.*

The longer I stayed at the mansion, the more I was surrendering myself to torment, especially if I gave into him like I knew eventually I would. I would be forced to watch as his life marched on irrevocably without me. I'd have to watch as he brought home whatever woman he wanted each night. Watch as he fell in love. Got married. Became a father. Grew old. All of it both with and without me.

My only options were to move out or be married off, and frankly marriage was my best option. At least that way I could have a house of my own, a family...

"It's not about what *I* want. *You're* not going to want me around forever and if you marry me off then you know I can't go back. My presence in your home is only going to make your life harder."

He remained silent a moment, swiping a hand across his face. "So let it. The answer is no."

A flash of disappointment stirred within me, though it was eclipsed entirely by the spark of hope that I let ignite in my chest. Did that mean he wanted to keep me around?

Either way it didn't matter—not really.

"Your future wife isn't going to be happy with another female being in the house. Especially one you've done *stuff* with and have refused to marry off." I reluctantly pointed out, pushing the matter further.

"Do you really think I give a shit about what anyone else thinks? The answer is no." His words were biting, resilient and immutable. "Why are you so insistent on removing yourself from my house, Ada?"

"Why are you so insistent on keeping me *in* your house, Marco? You think I am not good enough to marry into your family, don't you?" I shouted, my temper flaring in response to his.

Not that I wanted to marry just *anyone* in his family if given

247

the choice. Deep down I knew that the man I found myself wanting to marry *would* never and *could* never want me the same way. I was the daughter of his sworn enemy. His ward. His hostage.

He slammed a palm down on the table, "Answer my fucking question, Ada."

"Not until you answer any of mine." I threw my napkin down on the table too, pissed off with the turn our conversation had taken.

He lent back in his chair, holding his glass tightly in one hand. Silence hung between us as the minutes ebbed away.

"I will not marry you off."

"Then I'll move out and find somew—"

"No!" He refused. "Now answer my fucking question." A frown contorted his features, etching deeper with every passing second.

"What question?" I played dumb.

As planned, it only aggravated him more. His teeth snapping together with an audible click.

"Why do you want to leave, Ada?" His eyes were vigilant, scanning to see my reaction. I looked away.

"I can't be your *hostage* fore—"

"You're a terrible liar."

I pursed my lips, not sure on how to answer without sacrificing my heart in the process.

"Truth, Ada. Now."

Maybe it was the demanding tone to his voice or the roughness of his words, but I suddenly didn't care if it made my feelings obvious—I wanted to tell him the reason. Maybe then he would finally understand and agree with me that an arranged marriage was the best outcome. That it wasn't a case of me running away from the La Torre's, it was a case of me running away from the heartache that would inevitably follow having found myself infatuated with their Don.

"I don't want to see it," I said softly, voice barely above a whisper.

Confusion lined his face, "See what?"

I let out a heavy breath.

Let the chips fall where they may.

"I don't want to see you bring someone else home. I don't want to see you meet someone, fall in love and get married. To see your life move on without me. I don't want to watch it happening right in front of me and know that there is nothing I can do to change it. Wishing every day of my goddamn, shitty little life, that we stood a chance under different circumstances. Wishing even just for a *moment* that I could ever be enough for someone like you." My fingers trembled and my heart leapt into my throat, unsure how he was going to take what I'd said.

I stared at my lap, unable to meet the gaze I felt burning into me, setting me on fire.

My chest smoldered with embarrassment as he remained silent for a solid minute, and then another. The blush that had started at my chest, swept up to my face as humiliation and regret hit me. I couldn't bare it any longer.

I leapt to my feet and half-walked, half-ran through the halls to the safety of my room, throwing open the door and pulling it shut roughly.

I swung back around again when the door slammed open behind me.

I only had a second to process what was happening before Marco tore across the space, grabbing my face in his hands as his lips crushed mine with a ferocity that made my heart splutter.

My tense shoulders instantly molded against him and my stomach pooled with arousal. My mouth opening against his as his tongue swept inside. Sweeping away the last of my humiliation into pure bliss with a moan.

One of his hands immediately tangled in the hair at the

nape of my neck as the other simultaneously found my waist. He walked me backward across the room until the bedframe hit my knees.

The second I stopped, his hands found the tops of my arms and spun me away from him. I felt the material of my dress fall as he made quick work of the zip, not missing how his fingers lingered on the bare skin of my spine. Less than a second after his touch disappeared, I was pulled back around to face him and once again our lips collided in a mess of wetness, skin, and teeth. Desire and need flooded through me, engulfing me in an aching heat that seared and begged for more.

Gone were all my reservations, doubts and fears about what could come next. It didn't matter.

I wanted this. *Needed* this.

I moved backward onto the bed and kicked my heels off with Marco following me, never breaking our kiss. His strong knees rested on the outside of my thighs as he leaned upright, pulling at his tie and discarding it. His head descended to my neck, and I felt the warmth of his tongue as he lapped at my skin. My hands trailed around his shoulders, coming to rest at the buttons of his shirt.

I managed to undo a few of them before he grew impatient and pulled the dark material up over his head instead, with a growl. As if he couldn't stand it being between us any longer.

When his muscled chest pressed against my bare skin, a satisfied sigh escaped my lips. It quickly turned into a moan when his kisses trailed across my collarbone and chest, settling on my nipple as my hands threaded into his hair. He sucked one of the firm peaks into his mouth, rubbing the other between his fingers. His tongue swirled against the tight bud over and over, before he moved to the other. Nipping and sucking until I was breathless and disorientated.

My insides ached for more and the emptiness became so much I started panting.

When his mouth didn't move, I yanked on his hair until his lips sealed to mine once again. My hips rolled against the firmness between his thighs desperately.

I felt a rumble emanate from deep in his chest and it spurred me on.

My hands ran down his sides until I found the waistband of his suit trousers. I didn't hesitate as I pulled at the buckle of his belt and undid the button beneath. I could feel his hard bulge scarcely trapped behind the fabric as my hands skimmed along the edge of the material. He moaned and took over, pulling the trousers over his toned thighs and throwing them to the floor with the rest of our discarded clothes. His erection stood proud against his boxers, and my body responded with a carnal shiver, moisture leaking into my panties.

Marco's hands traced the outside of my thighs until they found the thin strip of material either side of my hip. He slipped my panties off in one go and tossed them to the floor before he shifted and his mouth descended on my wet slit.

When his tongue touched my sensitive spot, I let out a whimper. My hands immediately weaved back through his soft hair, pulling him closer. His hands gripped my ass and suddenly he tilted my hips up, allowing his tongue to reach places I'd never been touched before by a man. He groaned.

An eruption of tingles raced along my spine and a flush ran straight to my cheeks. It was so obscene, so *erotic*. A deep moan resonated from my throat as I danced scarily close to the edge. Tingles dancing on every nerve.

"So fucking sweet," he commented, his tongue tauntingly tracing the path over and over.

It was too much.

I screamed as I came. *Hard.*

My head flew back against the sheets, and my vision faded to darkness as euphoria and bliss descended like night onto day. My hips rolled and jerked, my body instantly flushing with the climax.

Marco's licks became gentler and slower as my body started to cool, and the tremors died away.

The release didn't last long though, with the warmth of him still pressed to my sensitive slit. My body was aching even more than before, desperate to feel his length inside me.

His tongue moved to tracing my entrance, lapping at my wetness and an animalistic rumble echoed from his chest. "Fuck."

A second later a finger pushed inside, and I gasped suddenly at the fulness. Another finger joined the first and my hips rocked in response, desperate to feel more of him.

He moved languidly, rubbing against my sensitive inner walls in a way that had my breathy moans filling the room all over again.

"You're ready for me, aren't you baby?" I could hear the roughness in his voice, and it made me even wetter.

His mouth found mine and I slipped my tongue between his lips, grinding against his fingers. He groaned but moved away, and I scowled impatiently as he got off the bed to retrieve something from his discarded trousers. He came back a moment later, slipping off his boxers and emptying the small square packet into his hand.

"Have you ever had sex without one?" I asked inquisitively, watching him put the condom on expertly.

"No." He pulled his face in a half-smile when he saw me watching.

Two seconds later, Marco reappeared above me and positioned himself back between my thighs.

"Look at me," Marco rasped.

I obeyed him immediately, looking up into his warm eyes.

When our gaze locked, he pushed himself inside me with a deliberate slowness.

My eyes fluttered shut and I tensed. I could feel my body burning as it stretched to accommodate his large length. He stopped halfway, allowing me to adjust for a second as my breath caught in my throat. When my eyes re-opened and met his once more, he pressed himself in all the way until I was so full I could barely breathe.

His face flushed and his eyes glazed above me in the most erotic display of arousal I had ever seen. A groan escaped him, and I felt myself clench around his cock in response. My own arousal becoming too much, just at the sight and feel of him.

"Your so fucking tight, Ada." He gritted out.

He retreated slightly, only to drive his length back into me with increasing conviction a moment later. I whimpered and his lips came back to mine. His thrusts growing harder and faster as my body became increasingly pliable to his immense strength.

"Good girl," he muttered when my insides relaxed, allowing him to thrust deeper.

The fact that Marco was a talker in bed was turning me on so much I couldn't think straight.

My hips began meeting his, thrust for thrust as we moved in agonizing synchronicity. I moaned into his neck, gripped his hair and kissed whatever skin I could get to.

With that, his movements became rougher, his hips rushing into me with a force that had my insides trembling. I could feel the scorching, irresistible burn of orgasm starting to smolder at my nerves, and I ran my hands to his ass, pulling him into me even harder.

Just when I thought I was going to be engulfed by the fire, Marco retreated, flipping me onto my front and pulling me up onto all fours before slamming back into me. I choked on the fullness. His length filling me deeper than ever before.

Pleasure and pain consumed me, and my eyes rolled with

the sensation. The scorching bliss of orgasm drew so close I was no longer in control of my body.

"Come for me, I want to feel it," Marco demanded.

The possessiveness in his voice had me flying over the edge and I screamed as pleasure seared every nerve. I pulsed against him as my climax took over. My legs trembled. My body flushed violently.

I heard him suck in a breath and then a powerful growl erupted from him as he too reached his release.

We collapsed on the bed in a heap.

Our panting was the only noise filling the otherwise silent room.

I stared soundlessly at the heavy-lidded and exhausted man beside me as he laid on his back. His fingers trailing along my skin, drawing lazy patterns.

When he noticed me watching, a heavily tattooed arm encircled me gently and he pulled me against his chest. Holding me with surprising intimacy.

I didn't resist and laid my cheek against his bare skin, hearing his heart beating steadily beneath me.

I wish I could stay in this moment forever.

We stayed like that for what seemed like hours. Until his breaths had grown even and deep.

I lifted my chin to look up at the peaceful expression on his now sleeping face. He looked more boyish in his sleep, happy even.

Even if it's just for now.

With that thought, a cool sense of dread and premeditated rejection sunk beneath my skin, permeating my bones.

I was in too deep—cared too much.

Whether it felt right or not, it was a path that would inevitably lead to pain.

Yet, I couldn't quite bring myself to regret the choices I had made that led me to this moment. I knew that the odds of escaping this situation with my heart intact were slim to none —I just didn't care anymore.

I pressed my lips to his chest and closed my eyes, trying to dispel the impending sense of helplessness consuming me. I refused to fall asleep, trying to live the moment with everything I had.

I knew that one day I would most likely give anything in the world to have it back.

CHAPTER
NINETEEN

ADALYN

I woke the next morning tangled amongst the bedsheets with my muscles aching and sore. Marco was notably absent from the bed, but his smell still clung to me and saturated the morning air.

Tendrils of rejection slivered in my chest looking at his now empty space and I tried my best to push them away. I had expected this. Now I had to live with the consequences.

The clock on the nightstand showed the time was still early, but knowing any attempt at sleep would be futile, I decided to face the day.

Despite the morning sun, heat wafted through the balcony doors, so I took a quick shower and threw on a bikini determined to spend the day by the pool.

I tugged on a sheer kimono and some sandals before padding out to the gardens and relaxing into one of the loungers. I wasn't there long before one of the staff came over with some orange juice and a selection of foods. I declined the food but accepted the drink, too uneasy to have much of an appetite.

I didn't know how the day was going to play out, especially not when I was expected to meet Marco's mother at the wedding reception later.

I slipped on my shades and tried to ignore the unease that still lingered in my stomach.

When the sun's rays beat down with an increased ferocity, I took off my kimono and undid the knot of my bikini top. Letting them fall to the floor beside me.

The last thing I need is tan lines.

With my earbuds in and my favorite band blasting away, I dove in and out of consciousness, feeling the effects of last night's lack of sleep and uhm... *exertions.*

I wasn't sure how long I had been drifting in and out for when I felt a shadow stretch across me. The lack of sun cooling my skin instantly.

When I glanced up, I was met with Marco's narrowed eyes, and I could see his mouth moving.

I pulled my headphones out of my ears. "What?"

In a clear display of frustration, he gripped his hip in one hand and rubbed an angry hand across his face simultaneously with the other.

I couldn't help it as my eyes flicked to his crotch and a flutter of anticipation erupted in my stomach remembering what he had felt like last night. What he had murmured into my ear as he thrusted into me. *Oh, shit.*

I bit my lip and forced myself to look away, immediately grateful for my sunglasses.

"Why are you naked?" He demanded, gesturing with his hand toward my exposed breasts.

"I'm sunbathing," I said simply, not understanding his tone.

He sighed in exasperation, "There are people everywhere

and your fucking tits are out. Put your top back on. Now!" He reached down to grab my bikini top and threw it at me.

Irritated that *he* was irritated, I gathered the material and got to my feet. I walked the few steps from the lounger to the pool and dropped it into the water.

"I can't. It's all wet." I smiled sweetly.

I didn't miss how his eyes trailed along my body and came to rest on my chest.

"I don't give a fuck. I'm leaving in one hour and I'm not leaving you naked by my pool with staff nearby to watch." He argued, stalking in the direction of the pool.

He knelt down just before he reached me, planting one hand on the pools edge while he went to retrieve the floating top.

A wicked idea skidded into my thoughts.

Don't do it! DO NOT DO IT! DO. NOT. DO. I-

I gave him a quick shove on the shoulder and sent him straight into the pool, suit and all.

When his furious and drenched face emerged from the water, I doubled over in fits of laughter

"ADA!" He shouted furiously, but it only made me laugh harder.

Lightning fast, he sprung to the side and grabbed me by the legs, dragging me into the water with him.

I immediately shrieked at the sudden movement and felt the cold envelop me like glass as I toppled. When I broke the water's surface, a mischievous smile contorted Marco's face. My sunglasses floating along the surface between us.

"You asshole!" I tried my best to sound angry, but I couldn't hide my smile long enough for it to be convincing.

I slapped my hand against the water, spraying him across the face. He scowled and immediately moved to come after me. I screamed and did my best to swim away from him, but he was too fast. He grabbed me by the waist, lifting me up out of the water and threw me back in a few feet away. I giggled as I caught my breath, and he drifted back over to me.

"Not funny," Marco muttered, his hands coming to rest on my hips.

My legs encircled his waist instinctually.

"It was very funny, and you know it." I laughed, my arms coming to rest across his shoulders as a boyish smile pulled at his lips.

Our faces were only a few inches apart and I could feel the heat from his hands despite the water. The air shifted noticeably between us and his expression darkened as if he were just as aware of my closeness as I was his. The urge to close the distance between us and push myself against him was unbearable.

I wanted to ride him right there in the fucking pool.

Not trusting myself or my fragile self-restraint, I swam back a few paces. The further away from his heat I got, the easier it was to think straight.

"You know you're being ridiculous right? We're in Europe! The motherland of boobs-out sunbathing. No one cares!" I rolled my eyes and turned my back to him.

I focused on threading my fingers through the water for a moment until I felt it shift behind me. The material of his suit brushed against my back and his inescapable arms locked around my waist. I felt his head dip toward my neck, his breath sending goosebumps across my skin. My heart raced.

Lips against my ear he murmured, "I don't want people looking at what's mine."

My breath caught and arousal swirled between my thighs, but it was met in equal measure with a cold uneasiness.

"Yours?" I asked breathlessly.

"Mine," He confirmed, his lips pressed against my skin.

I couldn't help but add, "Until you're bored of me."

My voice was barely above a whisper and while I hadn't

fully intended for him to hear it, from the way his body tensed I knew he had.

He started turning me to face him, "Wha—"

The sudden sound of footsteps approaching the pool cut him off and he looked behind me in the direction of their owner.

I turned to see Layton walking the length of the pool toward us, stopping as he reached the edge.

"Excuse me, Boss. We have to leave in the next thirty minutes to make the ceremony in time," His gruff voice announced.

Marco nodded once in acknowledgment before Layton retreated, walking back the way he came. His eyes never once looked over at me—smart move.

"I have to go," Marco muttered, seemingly annoyed.

He stood to his full height in the water and leaned forward, brushing his lips against my forehead before making his way to the side and lifting himself out. His clothes clung to his skin, dripping onto the warm stone beneath him as he stood.

He looked like a fucking Italian God even wet and disheveled.

"Now you see what I meant about wet clothes," I said sarcastically, trying to diffuse the tension building inside me.

He turned around, meeting my gaze with an unexpectedly playful smile.

"Nonetheless, put your top back on," he ordered, but I could hear humor in it. "I'll see you at the reception later."

He shoved his hands in his pockets and walked slowly back to the house.

Regrettably, I did as he said and grabbed my bikini top, strapping it back on. Then I leaned back in the water. Allowing myself to float effortlessly on the surface while my head whirled.

What was he going to say just now?

I didn't know.

———

I HAD BEEN SHOCKED LATER that afternoon when I'd found a hair stylist and makeup artist set up in my dressing room, but it quickly turned into appreciation. Marco had organized it all as a surprise for me, apparently.

I had been even more surprised when I wandered into the bathroom to find a black sequin ballgown hanging on a golden hook. The dress was absolutely stunning, and judging by the designer label I found when putting it on...was the most expensive dress I'd ever worn. It was backless except from the thin spaghetti straps that crossed once in the center of my shoulders. The material clung to my skin in a way that perfectly accentuated my hips before fanning out at the knee and pooling on the floor. It was sexy and stylish. The embodiment of midnight and sin.

I barely recognized the reflection as my own when I stood in front of the mirror some hours later. I was beautiful.

"Fucking hell, Bandit." Jesse gave a low whistle as I walked down the monolithic stairs to the front doors.

"Nice dress, huh?" I asked, not missing how his eyes looked slightly more coal-like than usual.

He shot me a grin, "It's alright."

I rolled my eyes and passed him my overnight bag before following him to the car. He drove us across to the other side of Catania, not stopping until we pulled up in front of a breathtaking 18th century villa. When we stopped beside a set of tiered stone steps, beautiful orchestral music drifted through the open windows of the car as well as the distant chatter of hundreds of people.

Jesse came around the car and offered me his arm as he threw his keys to a nearby valet.

"Stay near me and Enzo tonight," he said in a hushed voice, greeting people up ahead with a nod or a small smile. "And don't talk to anyone you don't know unless we are around."

"Most people here hate my guts and want me dead." Uneasiness settled in my stomach as I said the words. "I know that, Jesse. I'll keep my head down." I promised.

"No one here wants you dead. And even if they did, nothing will happen to you." His voice was earnest as he looked at me, but it did little to stifle my anxiety.

I didn't miss the curious gazes that looked our way as we crossed the threshold into the ornate hall. Hundreds of people were crowded inside, gathering around tables or splintered off into smaller groups standing about the hall. Drinks were being passed around on silver platters by butlers in black tailcoats with white gloves, as they moved effortlessly through the masses of lavishly dressed people. Large round tables littered the room, each overflowing with beautiful, white flowers and large pillar candles. Beyond them, the orchestra was situated on a golden filigree balcony and looked to consist of over twenty people.

It was extravagant.

It made the weddings I had attended growing up look like village festivals and I couldn't help feeling deficient in some way. *It's no wonder they hate my father so much...* I mused. To them, Manninos were the proletariat while they were the immutable bourgeoise.

Jesse and I wandered over to one of the tables near the back of the room. Enzo was already seated as we approached, wearing his usual flamboyant shirt and talking animatedly to another man I didn't recognize. Jesse greeted them both with a smack on the back, while Enzo gave me a kiss on both cheeks and the other man nodded in my direction. The men immediately lapsed into animated Italian and I internally sighed, knowing that I was unlikely to understand anything all night.

A butler approached with a flute of champagne and as the minutes ebbed away, more and more people began taking their seats.

I eagerly scanned the room looking for Marco, but I couldn't see him amongst the hordes of ostentatious gowns and hand-stitched designer suits before the meal was served. Four courses were served, each seemingly dragging out longer than the last.

Jesse was still engaged in discussions with Enzo and the other man, 'Carlos', leaving me to my own devices. The two other people at our table, a man and a woman, also interjected now and again in discussions, but otherwise kept to themselves. They looked to be newlyweds, and I often found myself looking away from their intense displays of affection.

"Going to the restroom," I announced to Jesse once the music started morphing into a more modern piece and the food courses finally stopped coming.

My legs were stiff as I got up from the table and made my way through one of the white corridors that fed off the main hall. My heels audibly clicked against the hard stone as the music grew quieter.

I wasn't surprised when I heard the shuffle of feet behind me and saw Alonso following me down the hall.

"I'm just going to the restroom. You don't need to follow me." I called gently to him.

He smirked but continued following, "I have orders, Ma'am."

"How many times with the 'Ma'am', Alonso?" I muttered and I heard him chuckle gruffly behind me.

I heaved open the door to the toilet, but stopped when I saw Alonso also move in the direction of the door. "Don't you fucking dare. You are not hearing me pee!"

He held his arms up innocently, "I'm just standing guard, Miss Adalyn."

I sent him a look anyway and turned to face the elaborate marble room.

What is with these people and marble? I sighed, locking the door behind me.

I quickly went to the loo and flushed, but just as I was pulling my dress skirts back into place, the doorknob to the room turned and opened.

I shrieked in surprise about to yell at whoever had entered, but I faltered when I saw Marco slip through the door.

I thought I locked that!

"What the hell are you doing here?" I demanded, clutching a hand to my chest and trying to breathe normally. "I was peeing!"

It was like he didn't even hear me. He leaned against the wall and allowed his eyes to rake over my body with an agonizing slowness that left me feeling all kinds of aching. I pushed away the feelings he was stirring, turning my back to him and walking to the sink. I lathered up my hands with the jasmine soap on the side and rinsed off the suds.

"You look gorgeous, Ada." His voice came out thick and deep.

I observed his reflection in the mirror, trailing my eyes over his choice of outfit for the evening. He wore his trademark designer black suit, but his usual dark shirt had been replaced with a white cotton one which he wore buttoned up to the collar. A matching bowtie was around his neck and the glint of a gold Rolex hinted underneath the sleeve of his jacket.

Lord give me strength.

"And you look straight out of The Godfather," I observed, causing him to chuckle. I retrieved a lipstick from my clutch and traced my lips with the vivid red stick, feeling his eyes watching me as seconds ticked away. "Are you having a nice time?"

"It's alright." Came his gruff answer.

"Not very talkative this evening, are you?" I observed, turning to face him. He smiled.

"Talking isn't really what I want to do with you right now," he remarked, pushing himself off the wall and stalking toward me with a slowness that felt equal parts dangerous and exciting.

A shiver ran up my spine.

He didn't stop until he was a foot away, and he caressed my cheek with the back of his fingers, sending tingles racing along my skin. My gaze fluttered to his and I could see the longing I felt mirrored within them.

"That's a shame because talking is all you're gonna get from me right now."

He smirked and lifted his head away from me dramatically.

"Fine." He sighed, seeing the sternness of my expression. "Are you having a nice time tonight?"

"It's alright." I copied his earlier words, failing to find my own. "I don't understand a word anyone is saying, but I'm pretty sure I don't wanna know anyway."

He laughed, flashing me that boyish smile I had come to love. "Smart girl."

"Am I in danger tonight or something?" I asked, having started connecting the dots from Jesse's warning and Alonso's constant presence in my head. There shouldn't have been a need for either of them tonight.

He snorted derisively. "You know who I am, right?"

"Then why is Alonso playing the role of bathroom attendant?"

His smile deepened, "There are just *some* people here...I'd rather you didn't meet tonight."

Which people? Just as I opened my mouth to ask my question aloud, he cut me off.

"We'd better get back before people start to miss us."

"Miss *you*, you mean," I corrected.

"That's not what I said," he answered cryptically.

With surprising tenderness, Marco leaned forward and placed a kiss to my forehead the same way he had earlier. He then took my hand in his and pulled me with him out of the bathroom door.

Alonso, Wyatt and Layton were now gathered in the hallway outside, and I blushed. *God knows what they think we were doing in there!* Though judging by the cool expression now adorning the Don's face, I was apparently the only one that cared.

As we approached the end of the hall, the chatter of the guests became louder, and the beat of music grew heavier. When we finally stepped into the bustling room, I was certain Marco would let go of my hand at any minute but surprisingly his grip only became tighter. Satisfaction pulled at my lips as the minutes ticked away with my hand still in his, and I stood up a little straighter, proud to be on his arm.

However fleeting it may be.

People nodded or stared as we walked past. Only the bravest among them dared to approach the Don and even fewer said more than a word or two.

After a few minutes talking to a fat older man with a sufficiently artificial looking wife, Marco pulled us to a smaller gathering of people. I didn't recognize any of the faces before me, but their expressions nearly all held a sense of familiarity that made me second guess myself.

Marco leaned in to kiss one of the older women on the cheek, resting a hand on her back affectionately.

"Ada, this is my mother, Eliyana La Torre. Mother, this is Adalyn Rossi," Marco introduced us.

There was a striking resemblance between Eliyana La Torre and her son.

Not only was there familiarity in the curve of their smiles, but it was also there in their unusually large chocolate eyes and raven black hair. Unlike her son, however, Eliyana had a gentle face that looked as if it only knew kindness. She had an elegant softness about her. A kind of softness that any other woman in the Cosa Nostra would have given their entire inheritance to possess.

I could see now why he had laughed when I suggested she wanted to kill me. Eliyana La Torre was no killer.

Eliyana turned and extended her hand toward me, which I immediately took. A smile that I recognized as one of Marco's lighting her face.

"It is a pleasure to meet you Mrs. La Torre."

She smiled. "I assure you the pleasure is all mine Adalyn. I have heard a great deal about you. I do hope that Sicily has been to your liking so far," she said affably, her tone motherly and warm.

"Yes, very much so," I answered with an appreciative smile.

"Ada, this is my uncle Leonardo Moretti and my aunt Catarina," Marco introduced me to the remaining two people in the small circle.

They both smiled kindly in greeting and murmured their 'hellos' in turn.

With the introductions out of the way, the five of us fell into relaxed conversations about the newly married couple and how beautiful the church ceremony had been. Despite my not knowing the couple in question well enough to comment on many aspects of the subject, they were gracious enough to continue speaking in English to allow me to at least follow the conversation.

After a few minutes, Eliyana asked about my job at Diamond City and after a while the discussion moved on to Marco's poor gambling skills.

"If I told you that Marco here lost €50,000 on a roulette wheel in one hour, you might rethink working at one of his casinos!" Marco's uncle Leonardo chortled, smacking the younger man on the back affectionately.

"The damned wheel was rigged!" Marco insisted, immediately going on the defensive.

"It was at *my* casino," His uncle responded good-naturedly, causing us all to laugh.

"Then it was definitely rigged." Marco smirked.

———

AFTER ABOUT AN HOUR or so of casual conversation, Layton approached us and spoke to Marco quietly a moment. Marco nodded in acknowledgement at the man and after a second, politely excused us from the group. He led me quickly back through the throngs of people until I found myself once again seated at the same table as earlier.

Jesse and Enzo were still sitting with Carlos, but the newlyweds were now notably absent. Two younger women had taken their place and were chatting enthusiastically to the men instead.

The table promptly lapsed into silence at our sudden arrival.

The men muttered respectful greetings and nodded to the Don, while the women keenly observed him with lascivious eyes.

"Wait here. I have some business to take care of." Marco declared as we came to a halt.

The unfamiliar women flicked their gaze to our still entwined hands and disappointment turned their pretty features into bitter scowls. Marco curtly said a few words in Italian before dropping my hand and stalking off with his security detail a step behind him.

Trying my hardest to not look disappointed, I re-took my seat at the table and resigned myself to people watching. With sipping on champagne my only source of entertainment for the evening, time passed even slower than before. What with the obvious attempts of flirtation and ridiculously childlike voices of the women before me. Even without understanding what they were saying, the tell-tale signs of desperation clung to them as they attempted to compete for the mens' attentions.

*Looks like Miss Italian Gold-digger one and Mafia Mrs.-Wannabe two have entered the chat...*I rolled my eyes and downed the rest of my drink.

CHAPTER
TWENTY

ADALYN

One hour passed by. Then another with no end conceivably in sight.

I had even gone to the bathroom three times just to give myself something to do. *Is it too childish to play a game on my phone?* I was seriously contemplating pulling it out when the familiar head of disheveled raven hair and black suit caught my attention from across the room.

Marco had re-emerged off to the side of the dance floor.

However, my relief at seeing him didn't last long. Quickly becoming tinged with irritation when I noticed a beautiful brunette at his side. She leaned forward to speak to him, a hand resting on his shoulder too close to his neck to be friendly. Her dress was the color of rain with a plunging neckline and slit up to the very top of her thigh. She all but screamed Jessica Rabbit, complete with hourglass hips and $10,000 boob job.

I hated how my irritation simmered into something more closely resembling insecurity.

I didn't miss the way she seductively pressed her body

against his as they continued talking. Or the way her other hand crept up to caress the other side of his neck.

The same side of his neck that I had moaned into last night.

"Jess." I prodded the tipsy man next to me to get his attention. "Who is that woman talking to Marco?" I asked once I successfully got his attention.

His eyes followed my gaze across the room, landing on the woman as she smiled affectionately up at the Don, batting her eyelashes.

"That's Sofia," He answered with a shrug and tossed back some of his beer. "They used to have a thing."

"*Used* to have a thing or *still* have a thing?" I questioned, irritation making my voice dryer than intended.

"Uh... I can't be sure to tell you the truth." He scratched his chin awkwardly and coughed into his fist. "But you have nothing to worry about there, Bandit," he said patting my arm condescendingly, as if he knew something I didn't.

"And why is that?" I asked doubtfully.

"It's worth more than my inheritance to tell you *that* piece of information." He shrugged and laughed as my eyes narrowed at him.

Without permission, my attention drifted back over to the two figures across the hall. To my instant outrage, Sofia's hand was now threaded between one of Marcos while the other toyed lightly with his hair.

Something that felt like crushing rejection sunk into my chest.

I can't fucking watch this.

I got to my feet and immediately left the table, exiting out one of the nearby doors that lead onto a veranda. Alonso was hot on my heels, and I shot him a warning look that made him halt just inside the door. I didn't stop until I reached the far end of the stone balustrade, overlooking the expansive gardens that surrounded the villa.

The view was so beautiful, it made it hard to remember the heartbreak that I had left inside.

I heaved in a deep, calming breath and looked up at the stars.

I knew that Marco would grow bored and move on to someone else. I had already made my peace knowing that my time with him would be fleeting, and that soon enough I would be relegated to the sidelines. I just hadn't anticipated that it would be *so soon... Could he be sleeping with us both?*

The question weighed in my stomach like a rock.

"I thought I might find you out here." The gentle words reached my ears at the same time as I heard footsteps approaching.

I was surprised to hear that the voice belonged to Eliyana La Torre. I turned and gave her a small smile as she approached.

She stopped beside me, resting her forearms on the stone and looking out across the gardens as I did. A small shawl was wrapped around her petite shoulders, shielding her from the slight chill in the air.

"It is a beautiful venue," I offered, trying my best to keep my voice light.

"It is indeed." She leaned in a little closer to me and then lowered her voice as if disclosing a secret. "Though it is a little ostentatious for my liking."

I grinned. "I think I would have to agree with you on that one." Her gentle laugh was as musical as her son's.

A few moments ticked by before I spoke again.

There was something I needed to say to this kind woman, but I was struggling to find the right words.

"I owe you an apology, Mrs. La Torre-"

"Eliyana." She insisted.

I smiled before continuing. "Eliyana. In fact...I owe you a great deal more than an apology." I couldn't keep my voice from trembling as I continued. "What my family did to yours was unforgivable and disgusting. I am truly, truly sorry." I couldn't help it as tears lined my eyes, remorse weakening the walls I so frequently built up.

Delicately, she took my hand and squeezed it affectionately. I was surprised to find her gaze held not an ounce of judgment or resentment.

"You are not to blame, cara mia. Your father must shoulder that responsibility alone." She patted my hand comfortingly.

"Marco is very much like his father." She continued after a thoughtful moment. "He is just as strong-willed and as practical as Manuel ever was. Loyal almost to a fault." She gave a sad chuckle. "When my Husband died, part of Marco and myself died with him. It destroyed us and Marco wasn't ready to become the Don to this family. Back then, all he wanted to do was play football and race around in his cars." She smiled at the thought.

"But he didn't have the luxury of time or choice. Today, he is one of the most feared Dons Sicily has ever known, hardened and ruthless like no other because he has had to be. But underneath that *tenacious* exterior...my son still exists. And I think you have seen him too."

Images of us eating McDonalds in my car flashed across my mind. Him doing donuts around the parking lot, just because I told him he couldn't. Play fighting in the pool this morning because I'd pushed him in... The boy within Marco didn't come out very often, but beneath all his cold indifference, that boy was there. I *had* seen him.

"You care for my son, don't you?" Her question was more rhetorical, but I nodded anyway.

It was strange for me to feel so trusting of someone I had only just met, and yet not one part of me felt ashamed to admit my feelings to her. In fact, it was freeing.

"He cares for you too, you know."

273

W-wait, what?

She laughed at the surprise on my face, "I know my son well enough to know the signs, cara mia. Did you know that he extricated some of his cousins for believing you should be killed when your father refused your ransom? It caused quite the stir." She clucked her tongue disapprovingly. "That's when I knew you were something special."

My brain refused to process the words she was saying, and I shook my head in disbelief. My thoughts flashed to the brunette inside and I internally compared myself to the other women he must have available in his life. There wasn't even a comparison.

She chuckled gently, understanding my skepticism, "My son has had many *friends* in his time, but he has never defended and fought with his family over one before. Only you."

I couldn't quite believe what I was hearing.

But what if she was wrong?

The consequences would have been too painful to bare if she was... but *could* she be? She was Marco's mother and knew him better than anyone else, or at least knew how to *read him* better than anyone else did.

"That may be true for now but... I-he- I am just one person. I'm not *enough* for someone like him. The money, the power... he can have anyone he wants. It is just a matter of time before he grows tired of me." My voice quivered as I let out my deepest insecurities to her.

"It's a possibility," She conceded, her tone gentle, "but love is never guaranteed forever, Cosa Nostra, Mafia or not. My son has played the role of an impervious Don for a long time now... but it isn't a role one wants to play forever. Adalyn, you will either be the worst thing for my son or the best."

A spark of hope lit in my chest as her words finally sunk in.

I let out a heavy breath, tension I didn't know I was hiding lifting from my shoulders.

"Now let's go have a dance!" She suggested, dispelling the tangle of emotions that lingered in the air.

Our conversation had been a lot to process, so in a daze of disbelief I let her lead me back to the hall and onto the dance floor. Aunt Catarina and Uncle Leonardo also joined us after the first song had passed. It was PG-13 dancing for sure, but nonetheless I laughed and moved to the music beside them. My heart was full of happiness with Eliyana's words still ringing in my ears and amusement lined my lips as she waved her hands wildly out of sync with the music.

After the third song melted into a fourth, I met a few glances as I looked about the room, my eyes eventually finding the only person I wanted to see.

Marco sat in my seat next to Jesse with the boyish smile I had come to love gracing his features. His attention focused entirely on me.

For the first time in a long time, I felt true happiness.

For the first time in a long time, I felt *free*.

———

THE PARTY STARTED to die down at around two in the morning. The music descended into background noise and only small groups of people still milled about as the tables slowly grew vacant.

After saying goodnight to Eliyana and Marco's Aunt and Uncle, I found Jesse as Marco had once again vanished. I asked him for help with finding my room, completely lost in the sheer size of the place and without a hope in hell of figuring out which room was supposed to be mine.

Jesse thankfully led the way upstairs and we weaved through various corridors until he stopped at one of the ornate polished doors. He swiftly pushed it open and gestured dramatically for me to go inside.

The suite was just as grand as the décor downstairs, decorated in creams and golds. A beautiful bathroom, living area, and exterior veranda made up the lavish space. Thankfully, my bags were partially unpacked in the corner and my personal effects were lined neatly to one side of the vacant room.

Jesse did a quick, albeit unsteady, check of the room before stepping back into the corridor. "I'm right across the hall if you need anything. But please try *not* to need anything; Eloisa might be stopping by..." He grinned, shooting me a wink.

I recognized the name of one of the girls at the table earlier and rolled my eyes at him.

"Ew. Just don't catch anything." I muttered.

"Sure thing, Bandit." He chuckled and left, closing the door behind him.

I sighed and unhooked my heels, pulling them off and dropping them to the floor.

I undid my dress in front of the vanity in the bathroom, pulling the heavy material away and laying it over a nearby chair. I pulled on my nightdress, just as I saw movement in my periphery.

I relaxed when I felt a familiar, warming gaze.

Marco leaned against the doorjamb to the living room, watching me silently as I approached the vanity and started scrubbing the makeup from my face.

I ignored him for as long as I could, but the silence was quickly becoming unbearable as numerous questions weighed on me.

"Who was that woman you were talking to earlier?" I asked, trying to keep my voice casual and uncaring.

"No one important."

"Didn't look that way," I muttered, allowing a little bit of my annoyance to seep through.

"Jealous, are we?"

"*Should* I be jealous?" I asked, swiping away the red stain of my lipstick.

Eliyana's belief that Marco cared for me was unignorable. If she was right, then the brunette—*Sofia*—was just as attention seeking as the rest of the women that often flocked to him and Marco held no real feelings for her.

But was she right?

When he didn't answer I sighed and turned to face him. His suit jacket and bow tie were now notably absent, his white shirt partially open at the top while his hands remained hidden in his pockets.

"No," he said the moment my eyes flashed to his.

With one little word, the spark of hope Eliyana had lit earlier turned into a flame in my chest. A tingle ran down my spine.

"I spoke with your mother."

He looked unsurprised by my words and waited for me to continue.

"She told me that you care about me. Is she right?"

His face remained pensive, and I thought he wouldn't answer...but then he nodded his head slightly.

My heart thundered in my ears and my breathing shallowed.

He cares.

I gave my head a gentle shake, trying to process it all. He had called me *his* numerous times since he took me hostage, but I always assumed he'd meant it in a sexual or perhaps proprietary way...not in a way that coexisted with *caring.*

It suddenly felt like my whole body was on fire.

Marco crossed the tiled floor to me, slowly coming to a stop and cupping my face between his hands.

"Did you really fight with your family over me?" I asked,

looking up into his eyes. The ice within them slowly melting away.

"Yes," he said quietly, bringing his head down to place a kiss in the crook of my neck. I sighed in contentment.

As light as a feather, I felt his hands trail up my sides, bunching my night dress up and slowly pulling it off in one swift motion. He allowed it to drop to the floor between us.

Once again, I found myself completely naked before him, while he remained fully dressed.

With deliberate slowness, he palmed one of my breasts before bringing it into his mouth, his tongue tracing the sensitive skin. I groaned and arched myself toward him. His other hand trailed down my stomach, reaching to cup the sensitive skin between my thighs.

I let out a breathy "ahh" as his finger found its way inside me, making me ache for him even more. I unbuttoned the material of his shirt and pushed it from his shoulders, suddenly desperate to feel his skin against me.

He relinquished his touch on me to momentarily discard it, before pulling me back to him, crushing my lips to his in a bruising kiss that left me breathless. His tongue pushed between my lips at the same time he thumbed my nipple, and I moaned into his mouth. Marco's responding growl was enough to elicit an ache deep in my stomach.

His hands skimmed the backs of my thighs for a moment before lifting me onto the dresser. The wood was cool against my flushed skin, and I yelped in surprise.

Before I had time to recover though, Marco was sucking on the inside of my thigh. He ran his tongue, teeth and lips dangerously close to my sensitive spot, and my hips rolled involuntarily, desperate for his touch. His shoulders shrugged beneath my legs as he lifted his eyes to mine, his expression was as dark as his soul.

It was so salacious I blushed.

"Tell me you're mine," Marco gritted out.

My insides melted as his breath fanned against me *there*.

"You know I am," I said, hips rolling once again.

"Say it," He demanded. His hands gripped my skin as if he was struggling to restrain himself while he waited for my answer.

"I'm yours." I sighed, leaning backwards onto my hands.

"Who fucks you?" He pressed, his eyes lethal.

"You fuck me." Desperation colored my voice and my body trembled with a need only he could sate.

He seemed satisfied with my answer, pressing his face between my legs and his tongue lapped from my entrance to my clit. I moaned so loudly it should have made me blush with embarrassment.

Instead, I burned and tugged his face closer.

He immediately complied. His tongue sweeping more forcefully than before and trailing around my entrance before plunging inside. He let out a guttural noise that made me shiver, before gripping my ass and tilting my hips up toward his face. His warm tongue languidly strayed to the sensitive skin between my cheeks and my body flushed immediately as he turned his attention to an entirely new area of my skin.

"Marco..." I gasped, fear and reservation constricting my lungs.

He pulled away slightly, "Don't fear me." He continued playing with the spot. "We'll get there, but not tonight," he said after a moment more, then proceeded to lick me from my ass to my clit.

A shudder ran through my body and a rumble sounded from his chest.

A second later, Marco got to his feet, lifted me by the back of the legs and walked us the short distance to the bed.

He dropped me in its center, looking down at me and I watched as he unbuckled his belt and stepped out of his shoes.

The second his trousers hit the floor, I could see his hard-on beneath his boxers. My body ached with longing, muscles growing rigid as his gaze coasted over me.

The waiting was driving me to madness, and without thinking, I raised my arms above my head, spreading my legs wider. Showing him both my submission and my need. His muscles tensed at the sight, and he yanked down his boxers as if the material irritated him, climbing onto the bed the moment his erection was free.

He came to rest above me, the hard plains of his chest and stomach meeting my skin in a motion that released butterflies in my belly. My hips rolled against him in response and he hissed. Retreating slightly.

I felt him reach toward the nightstand and I heard a crinkling noise somewhere near my ear, but I didn't want to wait. My hips grinding dangerously against him.

"Need a condom. Wait." He growled.

I didn't.

Fueled by my burning, *aching* need for him, my hips moved against him again of their own accord. This time the force was enough that his tip slipped inside.

I stilled and he simultaneously went rigid.

A second later he let out a groan so loud I felt it vibrate against my chest.

I moved again, sinking a bit more of him inside and let out a whimper of relief as the empty ache turned into a blissful burn. My insides stretching to welcome him.

"I haven't got one on." Marco growled. Unmoving and tense inside me.

"It doesn't matter," I murmured, sucking on his neck.

I didn't fully understand why I did it, but I knew it wasn't just on impulse.

In the back of my mind, I knew it was because I wanted to be *different* to him. Different from Sofia, from Lexi and every other female he had ever been with. I wanted to share something with him that he hadn't with anyone else.

I'd had sex before, that much was true, but Marco was the only man to have ever *touched* me. He had explored, tasted and kissed every taboo part of my body... and whether it made me reckless or not, I wanted to mean something to him as well.

Marco remained still above me, his eyes scrunched closed, jaw taut. Spurred on by the arousal I saw on his features I moved against him again, pushing in more of his length.

"God, you feel... you're so fucking soft." He spat, racking in an unsteady breath. "I gotta stop, I got to—" His eyes met mine, conflict swirling amongst the darkness.

"No, you don't. I'm on the pill," I whispered, meeting his gaze so he could see I wasn't lying. A small piece of indecision still marred his features, so I added, "I haven't done it without one either."

His eyes burned into me for a couple more seconds before his uncertainty dissipated.

"Ask me to fuck you," he said, voice ragged as he leaned down and begun trailing kisses down the side of my neck.

My hands tangled in his hair. "Please fuck me, Marco." And just because I was more turned on than I had ever been before, I murmured against his ear. "I want to feel you come inside me."

Any remnants of restraint died away as pure hunger took over him.

With a half growl he thrust the rest of his length into me. A whimper tore from my throat as a familiar fullness made my body flush. He hovered there a second, allowing me to adjust before pulling almost entirely out. I cried out as he rocked into me again, my back arching to meet his hips.

"Fuck." He pressed his lips to mine, his tongue delving into my mouth, and I sucked on it gently. His hips picked up their pace.

Our kiss was wet and rough, leaving me breathless and disorientated. He tasted like the whiskey he always drank, and his spicey smell drove me wild while the friction of his skin burned deep into my stomach. I ran my nails down his back, gripping his toned ass.

"Harder," I moaned, feeling myself at the precipice of an orgasm and wanting so desperately to fall off the edge.

He ignored me and kept his rhythm the same. I huffed in frustration. "Ask me nicely."

"Please," I said breathlessly.

"Please what, Ada?" he ordered roughly.

"Please fuck me harder." I sighed as the dirty words left my lips.

He immediately complied, rolling his hips with more force than before and rubbing himself against me. The friction burned across my most sensitive area, driving me to the brink of madness.

I let out a breathy moan and resorted to begging, feeling dangerously close. Just *two* more. *One* more.

My orgasm was fierce. The intense release of pressure and tension made my body violently shudder.

Marco made a soft sound in his throat as my body contracted around him. He had stilled, concentrating on the feeling and watching me as I orgasmed, waiting patiently for my body to settle.

The moment it did, he began moving again. This time his strokes were much more intimate, reaching deeper inside me with an excruciating slowness.

He leaned his forehead against me. "I'm going to come inside you now."

I nodded, watching as his own pleasure enveloped him and contorted his features, knocking him into a half-lidded daze.

Marco on the brink of release was the most erotic thing I had ever seen, and it sent a shiver skating across my skin.

His grunts turned into a moan as he came, echoing so loudly in my ear that my stomach pooled with arousal and my hips arched into him, pushing him deeper. He stilled, trembling for a moment as warmth spread between my thighs.

He collapsed on top of me, chest to chest with one arm supporting his weight. I felt the gentle pressure of his lips brush against my forehead.

"Well, that was a first." He breathed and I flashed him a triumphant smile.

"A good first?" I asked. A pang of nervousness hitting me as I waited for his answer. My hands rubbing his back aimlessly.

"Put it this way..." I felt his lips trail across my hairline. "I'll never be the same."

My breath caught as he pulled out of me, falling to his back. I felt his familiar warm gaze rest on my skin, and I looked over to him, feeling about as happy as I ever had. The boyish smile I had come to love lit up his face.

Then I realized something.

It wasn't just the boyish smile I loved—I loved *him*.

CHAPTER
TWENTY-ONE

MARCO

Jesus Christ.

She had to be the best lay of my whole goddamn life, but tonight...*tonight* took that to a whole other level. I didn't just feel satisfied after our session or blissed out on cloud nine. I felt like a fucking King.

Sex felt different with Ada anyway, but without a condom? Man, it was my undoing. It took everything in me not to nut in the first thirty seconds, like I was some fucking fifteen-year-old virgin all over again. I shook my head in disbelief.

She really is driving me insane.

She had felt so goddamn good. Just like last time but better. Softer. *Wetter.* The feeling was indescribable. I climaxed harder and longer than I had even thought possible. God the things I wanted to do to this woman.

She was sleeping soundlessly beside me now, completely oblivious to the beast she had awakened within me.

All men in the Cosa Nostra had a vice, and while I had

always thought whiskey was mine, I realized now that I had been wrong. It was her.

She was damn close to perfect, utterly beautiful and all kinds of sexy. Smart-mouthed but intelligent. Not like most of the airheads that bartered for my attention. She didn't treat me like everyone else did, and while her insubordination had pissed me off at the beginning, I had come to find it oddly refreshing...and now that I knew she was submissive in the sack? Well, she really was my perfect woman.

Tonight had been a first for me but it had apparently been a first for her too. Something I couldn't help but feel smug about.

Despite that knowledge though, a large part of me still wanted to know what her experience was and who the men were she'd been with before me. One of them she'd said was at the bottom of Lake Mead, but the other? I had no idea where he was...and judging by Ada's behavior when I broached the subject, I guessed that she wanted to keep it that way.

When I had touched her the first time, I could see it was new to her. I could see the surprise—apprehension even— burning behind those delicate blue irises. Not only that, but she was so *fucking tight,* and her hands explored my body with a distinct timidness. A complete juxtaposition to the way she danced and the air of sexual confidence she so frequently projected.

Whatever men she'd been with before it couldn't have been for much longer than a one-night stand, I'd decided.

Just the idea of other men being with her in that way, even just once, was enough to make my jaw clench in anger and a red haze tint the edges of my vision.

The fucking bastard took what's mine.

I didn't know which of the two had been the one to have done it, to have taken her *virtue,* but if I found out he was the one still alive... the fucker's body would be unrecognizable soon enough.

A searing hot hatred poured through my blood stream.

Ada suddenly turned in her sleep in response to my tension. The sheets around her falling away, exposing her entire back and ass to the air.

God she is beautiful.

She sighed in her sleep and the sound went straight to my dick, causing it to harden instantly. With her tight ass right there and her midnight hair curled across the pillow, I burned no longer with anger but with *need.* I *needed* to be inside her again.

I shifted over to her, pushing myself against her small frame as my free hand trailed across her stomach. She stirred slightly and I sucked on her neck, beckoning her awake. My restraint paper thin as I pressed my hips to her ass. My dick throbbed.

Fuck.

She turned slightly, rousing a little to mumble, "What, Marco?"

"I want you," I said without hesitation, rolling my hips into her again to prove my point.

"Ask me nicely," she breathed.

I smiled into her neck as she used the same words I had earlier.

Normally, I didn't ask for fucking anything. I was Don Marco La Torre, and under normal circumstances, I would have discarded any woman that told me to *ask her nicely* to fuck her. But *man, oh man* these were not normal circumstances. This woman was my fucking drug and if I didn't get my fix, I didn't know what I was capable of.

So I did something I'd never done before.

I asked *nicely.*

"Please, Ada." I whispered against her ear.

My hand came up to palm her breast and her nipples hardened in response to my warmth.

She was taking too damn long to answer.

"I need to be inside you, Ada. *Please.*" The desperation in my voice made it almost unrecognizable, even to my own ears. "Fuck!" I gritted my teeth, growling the profanity as she pressed her ass firmly against me, my cock pushing into the crevice between her cheeks.

"Be gentle Marco, I'm a little sore." Her voice was less sleepy than before, and she glanced over her shoulder to look at me with those perfect, doe-like eyes.

I nodded and readjusted my position, sinking downwards until I lined up with her entrance. She sighed as I rocked into her as gently as I could.

I moaned in relief, the warmth of being inside her hitting me instantly. She whimpered in my arms as my full length slid into her.

"Are you okay, baby?" I breathed.

She nodded, "Just go slowly."

Our fingers threaded together on the pillow as I fucked her as slowly and as gently as I could.

The whole world fell into oblivion around us, until there was just Ada and me.

———

ADALYN

A vibrating sound buzzed somewhere near my head, and I groaned in irritation.

Something warm shifted beneath me and I became vaguely aware that the source of that warmth was in fact a rock-solid human chest. It took me another half a minute to remember where I was, and more importantly *who* I was with... My pulse accelerated as the realization hit.

I felt an arm lift from the bed and the buzzing grew louder for a moment.

"What?" Marco's gravelly, sleepy voice demanded. He paused before sighing, "Fine, we're coming."

I heard him end the call and felt it as he looked down at me. I cracked open an eye.

He smiled, and my heart stuttered. "Hi."

"Hi."

I felt like I was suddenly in some parallel fucking universe.

"We gotta get up." I could hear the reluctance in his voice.

I nodded and sat upright slowly. "Do I have time to shower?"

"Yeah. Just make it quick."

I nodded and got up.

I padded to the shower, turning on the water and standing under the stream, carefully washing away the remnants of last night from my body. Fifteen minutes later, I threw on a blue bandeau dress and met Marco at the door.

He was wearing his usual black suit trousers, but this morning he had chosen a snug fitting black polo instead of his normal shirt, showing off his thick arms and intricate black tattoos. He took my hand and flashed my favorite boyish smile that sent a tingle all the way down to my toes.

Our entourage of bodyguards were outside as we exited, and they escorted us through the halls of the villa, now lit with a stream of gentle, warm sunshine. The noise of quiet chatter and laughter reached my ears as we came through the reception area toward the hall for breakfast.

Just as we began to enter the room, Marco's phone started ringing again, and he gestured for me to go in without him.

It didn't take long for me to spot Jesse and Enzo at one of the tables and I was relieved to see that the bimbo twins from last night were notably absent.

"Where's your girlfriend, Jess?" I mocked, taking a seat at the table.

He scowled around a bite of bacon. "Not my girlfriend and I

do *not* care." He said, irritated by something but obviously unwilling to discuss it.

I shared a look with Enzo that clearly said *do not ask*.

Heeding his warning, I dropped it and ordered some orange juice, helping myself to a few pastries from the table.

"What is it with girls and commitment?" Jesse eventually voiced with a sigh. "You sleep with someone *one whole time* and they suddenly want your number, email address, and fucking social security."

I rolled my eyes, "One, you're in Italy not America, so I know she didn't *actually* ask you for your social. Two, you hooked up with a girl at a *wedding*. Weddings can make us women go cray cray. It's not our fault though, blame Hollywood and all their rom coms." Jesse's eyes widened as if I was speaking in pig Latin.

"Really? Jesus, what else don't we know?" Enzo cut in, the astonishment in his voice also mirrored on his face.

It was like I was fucking Albert Einstein to these two.

"I'm gonna go ahead and say a lot," I said, smirking at the riveted men before me. "Weddings are definitely a no go. On or around her birthday...and valentine's day, I would say they are all bad choices for a casual fling. You don't want to give the wrong impression."

I could see their heads practically exploding with the information and I couldn't help but laugh.

Suddenly I felt a warm, familiar presence.

Jesse and Enzo nodded in greeting to the man I knew I'd find behind me.

"What's so funny?" Marco asked, pulling up a seat.

"I'm just filing them in on a secret about women." I answered, smiling in greeting at him.

"And what is this secret?" He asked.

"If a girl hooks up with you at a wedding it's because she wants more than just the D," Jesse answered coolly.

"She wants commitment," Enzo chimed in, cringing in a way that usually would have had me chuckling if I wasn't too busy panicking.

I tensed, knowing how that would sound to Marco...after having hooked up with me *right after* a wedding.

He'd think that I wanted more from him than sex, and while that was in fact *true*, I didn't exactly want him knowing that piece of information right now. It threatened to damage the fragile understanding that currently existed between us and had the potential to throw everything into total chaos, whether he cared for me or not.

Shit.

"Who the fuck knew that?" Jesse finished.

"I was speaking generally Jesse. It isn't true of all women," I said, forcing nonchalance into my voice.

"That's not what you just said," Jesse argued irritatingly, and I glared at him.

"Is it true for you?" Marco asked turning toward me.

Yes. "No," I answered but my tone was slightly off and I internally cringed.

I swiftly turned away, flipping my hair over my shoulder and acting like I hadn't seen the knowing smile forming on his lips.

"I think it is." He chuckled darkly, making two pairs of eyes flicker between us quizzically.

"It really *isn't*," I answered refusing to meet his gaze. "What are everyone's plans for today?" I rather unsubtly tried to change the subject.

A tattooed arm came to rest on the back of my chair, and I pretended to ignore the flutters up my spine.

"What kind of commitment do you want from me now then, Ada? A heartfelt poem? Those three important words?" Marco's tone was jovial. No outward signs of running away and screaming like I had anticipated.

Trouble was, my satisfaction at his reaction was overshadowed entirely by Jesse and Enzo's faces...which were now lit up with sudden understanding.

Crap.

"HOLY SHIT!" Jesse exclaimed, smacking the table with his palm. "You slept together?" he spluttered, gesturing between us with a zeppole.

I all but died from embarrassment while Marco shot him an arrogant grin.

"Three times." Marco added, smiling broadly as he brought *my* juice to his lips and took a swig.

I didn't bother pointing out that those three times were in fact over *two* days and not just last night as he had implied. *Men.*

Enzo muttered a 'wow' while I sent a silent prayer up to whatever deity could bloody well hear me, before hiding my face in my hands.

"Niceee." Jesse approved.

"I'm right here, you know! You are *such* an asshole." I rounded on Marco so he could see my glare.

He smirked but was otherwise unaffected. "So, what is it that you want?" He insisted, going back to the original subject. "For us to buy a house together? Maybe a diamond ring?"

I pretended to contemplate his words for a moment, "I'm not really here for your sparkling personality or fantastic sense of humor. I'll just take the sex for now," I responded acerbically.

Enzo and Jesse howled with laughter and Marco's expression burned with an intensity that set my insides ablaze.

"Are you sure that's all you want? I've heard I'm quite the catch," He continued tauntingly, raising a brow.

"Hm, that's not what I've heard. Besides...the more time I spend around you the less likely I am to want anything else," His smile met mine as I challenged him.

"On the contrary, falling in love with me is inevitable." The confidence in his voice was unmistakable, despite the humor. *This man!*

I snorted derisively. "How deluded you are, my dear Don La Torre," I said, patting his cheek condescendingly and he flashed me my favorite smile.

Enzo and Jesse watched our little exchange with knowing amusement before we all lapsed into a comfortable silence.

Marco ordered us two more drinks while I focused on pulling a croissant off the platter. I halved it and lathered one side in butter until it got whipped from my plate without warning. Marco already had half of it in his mouth by the time I'd manage to scowl at him, so like the dutiful fuckbuddy I usually *wasn't*, I coated the other in butter and placed it in front of him as well.

I didn't think much of it until Marco caught me off guard with a smoldering look that made all my insides feel exposed.

Toward the end of breakfast, Eliyana had come over to invite us to a family gathering she was hosting later that evening in town. We graciously accepted the invitation, and I thought I saw a trace of satisfaction light her features as she took in the proximity between her son and me. His arm was still slung on the back of my chair, his thigh pressed up against my own under the table.

Thinking that I had somehow won her approval sent a pang of happiness straight through my chest, and my heart ached.

It's all temporary, I tried to remind myself.

But it was growing harder for me to remember that fact as time wore on...my heart was already irrevocably lost to him.

————

WE LEFT the breakfast and headed back to the house not long after eleven. Marco had done his usual disappearing act shortly after our return, and I busied myself by catching up on work from the casino for the rest of the afternoon.

By the time five o'clock rolled around, I started getting ready for the restaurant. I picked out an emerald-green dress with a cowl neckline. It had a slit that ran halfway up my thigh and clung to my body in all the right places, making it both a classy and sexy choice.

The car ride to town had felt more cramped than usual that evening, though that probably had a lot to do with the fact that I was riding in Marco's SUV with Wyatt and Layton. Jesse, Alonso and Tom followed in the car behind us.

The restaurant screamed wealth and exclusivity as we entered, painted stone walls and decedent smelling candles littering every square inch of available surface. Large arched windows overlooked the Ionian Sea, combined with gentle music being played on a pianoforte. It gave the space a distinctively formal and intimate feel.

Thirty or so family members had already arrived when we entered and were milling about the space, engaged in excited chatter. With one hand resting on my back, Marco led us through the crowd, greeting those in attendance until his mother came into view.

"My darlings, I am so happy to see you both." She smiled adoringly at us.

I was quickly realizing that Eliyana was everything that my mother was not. Where my mother was as cold as ice and as sharp as a razor, Eliyana's warmth radiated like sunshine. Her love for her son unmatched by any other mother I had ever seen. Even the fondness she seemed to extend to me after only a short period of knowing her was enough to make my heart swell.

"It has only been a few hours, Mama." Marco admonished gently.

"Oh hush, child. Adalyn you are looking beautiful," She enthused, giving me a kiss on both cheeks.

"Thank you, Eliyana."

"Ada, stay with my mother while I speak to some of the other guests," Marco all but commanded. He pulled me toward him and swiftly placed a kiss on my forehead before walking away.

A knowing smile crept onto Eliyana's face as Marco's form drifted out of sight.

"Come, Adalyn, let me introduce you to some key family members."

With that, she took my hand and led me over to the nearest group of people.

———

FIFTEEN.

That was how many 'key' La Torres I had met leading up to and during the course of dinner. Eliyana had introduced me to them all with so much affection and warmth, that by the time our dessert plates were cleared away, I was starting to feel less like an unwelcomed guest and more like a part of the family. Eliyana and her sister Catarina seemed to have that effect on people, I noted.

Even when some of Marco's cousins began heatedly arguing over a boxing match coming up, they managed to deescalate the dispute within seconds. They were balm to the boiling hot tempers of La Torre men and who, ultimately, seemed to keep the family as strong as it was.

A little while later and toward the end of a conversation with Eliyana's cousin Francesca about her flourishing new garden, I excused myself in search of a drink. I wandered over to the bar and placed my order: coconut lime spritzer. The last time I'd had one was back in Chicago at one of Marco's clubs. I smiled at the memories that came with it.

"So, you're Adalyn Mannino." An unfamiliar female voice said, coming up beside me.

Unfortunately, her face wasn't as unfamiliar as I would have liked.

Sofia.

"It's Rossi." I corrected. "And you are?" Though I knew all too well her goddamn name.

"Sofia." She had a smile on her face, but her tone was anything but sweet. "I'm a *friend* of Marco's," she hinted suggestively.

I knew I shouldn't feel jealous of this woman. That her hint of being *friends* with Marco didn't mean a whole lot—at least not according to him. Yet, I still found myself bothered by her insinuation and questioning Marco's truthfulness...which was, of course, exactly what she wanted.

Instead of showing that she had struck a nerve of insecurity within me, I took a deep sip of my drink and did my best to look bored. "Good for you," I muttered.

"We've known each other for years. Practically grew up together," she continued, while I put on my best show of ignoring her.

That was until she took a step in my direction.

"Consider this a warning, Adalyn." An edge creeped into her tone and her expression soured. "Someone like *him* doesn't want to fuck Mannino trash like you. Especially not when he has someone like me warming his bed at night."

I chuckled darkly. "I think you need to check your facts, Sofa. Since he already *did* fuck Mannino trash like me."

Her face contorted into rage, and she immediately flushed scarlet red.

I felt a familiar warmth hit my back.

"What's going on?" Marco's hard voice cut into the thick silence.

Sofia's face morphed into a sickly-sweet smile as she turned her attention from me to the Don.

"Nothing at all, Don La Torre. I was just giving Adalyn some advice." Her voice took on an almost childlike tone as she pressed herself against his side in a well-rehearsed maneuver.

Bitch.

"Indeed. She was telling me all about Mannino trash and how un-fuckable we all are," I said with an equally innocent smile.

Marco's indifference turned lethal, and he took a deliberate step away from the woman, wrapping an arm protectively around my waist. My smug smile of satisfaction only grew when I saw the outrage on hers.

"I would never!" She feigned hurt at the accusation. "You *know* me, Don La Torre. She is clearly very bitter about our *friendsh-*"

"There is no friendship." Marco cut her off. "We used to fuck, Sofia. You need to get over it already."

She made a small noise of indignation. Her face growing even redder than before at his blatant rejection.

"But we've known each other for years!" She insisted, clutching onto Marco's arm like it was a life raft. The desperation in her appeals to the Don were as obvious as they were fruitless.

"Give it a rest, Sofia." He sighed in exasperation and pulled his arm from her grip, leading me away.

He led me down one of the nearby corridors and didn't stop until we were in a secluded room away from the bustle of the restaurant. The door closed immediately behind us, and it took my eyes a second to adjust to the dimly lit function room he had brought us into. I walked toward the lone lamp that stood in the corner.

"Are you alright?" He asked after a moment.

"Yup," I answered quickly, popping the 'P'. I looked about the room, avoiding the heavy gaze I could feel settling on me.

"If there is something you want to ask, just ask it."

I hesitated a moment, not sure I wanted the answer to the question on my lips. "She was your booty call the other night, wasn't she?"

He let out a heavy breath, "Yes."

Pain twisted in my chest.

He had slept with *her* after we had kissed, the day after I told him I wasn't ready. Had he had gone to *her* because I wasn't giving him what he wanted? I shook my head in disbelief, my expression darkening with anger.

"I did go to hers that night," he admitted. "But nothing happened. I realized I didn't want to be there, and I left."

"Do you really expect me to believe that?" I demanded, then shook my head dejectedly and shrugged. "You know what, it doesn't even matter. You're a Don and can do whatever the fuck you want," I said, resigning myself to that knowledge and pretending it didn't hurt.

He scoffed. "Maybe once." He shook his head, stepping toward me. "Lately there's this annoying dark-haired, blue-eyed succubus that keeps popping up to ruin everything," he said with a small chuckle, winding his arms around me.

"Gee, thanks," I muttered sarcastically, but my heart stuttered at the meaning in his words.

He lowered his eyes to look at me, "I'm not lying to you, Ada. Nothing happened."

I could see the truth in his eyes and the furrow of his brow.

A half-smile pulled at my lips, telling him I believed him.

Marco's head dropped to my neck, and he began caressing my skin with his lips, sucking gently. I sighed, my hands knotting in his hair as my body pressed tightly against him. His lips moved to seal against mine and he gripped the back of my thighs, lifting me onto the nearby table. I captured one of his plush lips, giving it a small suck before allowing my tongue to explore his mouth. He stepped between my legs, pulling the material of the dress higher against my thighs.

"What is it with you and black fucking lace?" He breathed against my lips, yanking the material down.

"You don't like my panties?" I questioned, moving to suck on his throat.

"Yes, I fucking like your panties. I just like them more when they're on the floor."

He tossed the material over his shoulder before sinking to his knees in front of me.

Less than a second after his head dipped between my thighs, I felt his tongue against my sensitive skin. I groaned as warmth flooded through me, sending tingles dancing into my belly. I leaned back onto a forearm as I tangled my other hand into his hair, scraping my nails against his scalp as his tongue teased my entrance. He ran one of his large hands over the material of my dress and up over my chest, my neck, not stopping until two of his fingers pushed their way into my mouth.

I sucked on them and swirled my tongue.

"Good girl." He praised.

Then he thrust the newly wet fingers inside me in a swift, blissful motion.

I moaned and my back arched against the table, hips rolling into him. His tongue flicked once more, and my body flushed with heat as a welcomed tension started to swell and grow.

Then a knock sounded at the door.

Marco ignored whoever was on the other side, his mouth continuing its beautifully torturous path.

The knock sounded again, followed by Layton's voice. "Sorry Boss, it's urgent. Mr. Fanelli's here."

Marco froze. "Fuck," He cursed quietly.

To my instant disappointment, Marco rose to his feet and pulled my dress back into place.

He picked up my panties from the floor and tossed them in my direction, "I'm sorry, baby. I gotta take care of this."

He abruptly turned and left the room before I could respond.

Not knowing what the hell was going on or what Mr. Fanelli being at the restaurant even meant, I quickly slid the material back into place and followed behind him.

"You fucking dare to come here demanding payment, Fanelli?" Marco's voice boomed down the hall as I approached, angrier than I'd ever heard it before.

The whole room was packed with people that had fallen deathly still as Marco, Jesse, Enzo, and a few other male family members as well as security were standing, facing off with three middle-aged men I hadn't seen before. The man at the center was clearly the ringleader, judging by the amount of gold jewelry he was wearing. He didn't seem to be armed, but his two friends certainly were. The barrels of their guns squarely trained on Marco.

"Just because all of the shipment didn't get there, doesn't mean I shouldn't get paid for what did arrive." The man insisted, looking about the people in the room as if they were going to side with him.

Clearly not the sharpest tool in the shed.

"In order to get paid you actually have to do your fucking job." Marco spat back. "You deserve nothing."

"Well, La Torre, I ain't goddamn leaving until I get what I am owed. I'm nothing if not amiable, so it doesn't have to be in Euros. Any of the girls here would do just fine." His eyes coasted over the younger women in the room, myself included.

Marco shoved his hands in his pockets and meandered leisurely over to the man I presumed was named Fanelli. Marco was seemingly at ease with the guns pointed at his head and only stopped when he was less than a foot away from the men.

"Then you can leave here in a box." He said quietly. *Dangerously*. The muscle in his jaw clenching.

He turned his back to the man and instantaneously two shots rang out across the room. The men accompanying Fanelli fell to the floor with a sickening thud.

Jesse and Enzo's guns were drawn and pointed at the now empty spaces, having been the source of the noise.

Leaving Fanelli defenseless.

That's when Marco attacked.

He swung a nearby chair across the man's head, bringing him to his knees in the blink of an eye. He then took his handgun from the waistband of his trousers and struck Fanelli clean across the face with the butt of it. Blood flew out of the man's mouth from the impact, and he fell to the floor barely conscious and totally disorientated. The Don then sprung on the man, gripping him around the throat with both hands and choking him until his eyes began bulging, and his face began purpling.

Choking him with hands that had been all over *me* only a few minutes before.

Hands that could hurt.

Just like *another* man's hands once had.

Even when I had begged him to stop. Even as I couldn't breathe.

A wave of nausea swept through me, and I stumbled back until I found the door to the ladies restroom.

I locked myself into one of the stalls as tears flowed unrestrained.

Panic gripping me, constricting my throat and I tried concentrating on levelling out my breathing. *I can't allow myself to feel this right now. Breathe!* I commanded. I racked in a breath, held it. Another. In. Out. In. Out.

"Are you alright, Bandit?" Jesse's voice drifted through the now open door to the hall.

I slowly let out the breath I was holding.

"Yeah, I'm fine. Just needed to pee," I lied, trying to make my voice sound even and light. "Do you mind if we head home in a minute? I'm kinda tired." I prayed he wouldn't detect the change in my voice.

"Sure. I'm just out here when you're done." He answered simply, shutting the door quietly behind him.

I flushed the toilet and unlocked the door, walking over to the vanity to check my makeup. I dabbed at the loose charcoal gathering around my eyes, trying to rectify the mess.

I met my own gaze in the mirror.

God almighty, get it together, Ada.

———

I HAD ALMOST DRIFTED to sleep when a sliver of warm light sliced across my bedroom floor from the hallway. The door clicked shut and I felt the mattress decompress beside me as a familiar presence spread across my skin.

Marco.

His heavy arm came to rest across my waist as his chest pressed against my back under the covers. I shifted, nuzzling deeper into his comforting embrace.

"Why did you leave early tonight?" His voice, a deep velvet whisper against my ear broke the gentle thrumming of my heartbeat.

"I was tired," I lied.

It wasn't the real reason I had to leave the restaurant, but I couldn't tell him the truth.

I couldn't tell him about the panic attack or that his hands on Fanelli's throat had reminded me of how another man's hands once gripped my own. I couldn't tell him that what I saw tonight triggered memories of what had happened to me. Memories that I had tried to bury for the last seven years.

Sharp, cold tendrils of anxiety crept into my chest as my thoughts strayed dangerously close to the subject I wanted so desperately to avoid.

He stilled. I froze.

Shit. Could he know?

"Were you afraid?" His voice was stern despite its gentleness.

I hesitated "I wasn't afraid of what I saw." I answered, side stepping the real cause of my fear. "I just wanted to come home."

He nodded and pressed a kiss to my neck. It eased the tension coursing through me, steadying my heart rate.

"So, you're still not afraid of me?" I could detect a trace of humor seeping into his serious words.

"You are many things, Don La Torre, but scary isn't one of them." I lied tauntingly.

In actuality, the Don beside me *did* have his moments. But his ego was big enough without me telling him that.

"I should be insulted," he said, contrite.

"But you're not, are you?"

"Nope. Not even a little bit."

I chuckled at his tone.

He turned me on my back to face him. His dark eyes gleamed in the moonlight streaming through the open windows, casting shadows across the handsome features I now found myself looking for in every room. His hand came to rest on the side of my face, tracing a line from my cheekbone to my chin.

"We have to leave tomorrow." Marco's eyes told me he wasn't sure how I would take the news.

"For Chicago?" He nodded and I smiled gently.

I had been missing the familiar stone walls of the mansion. Strangely, it had started to feel like home.

He let out a sigh, "Fanelli is dealt with, but the mess he left behind needs fixing and I can't do that from Sicily."

I knew better than to ask for the details and responded simply with "Okay."

He moved to lay back on the pillows and pulled me against him, tucking me under his arm while my head rested against his chest.

In the comfort of his embrace, it was hard to believe that he was the same man I had seen earlier. That he was the ruthless Don La Torre that had families on either side of the globe trembling in fear.

Another side of him came out around me. A playful, boyish yet charming side. A side that very few got to see.

But it would be naïve to think that it made him less dangerous. A sinister internal voice was quick to remind me.

"Marco?" I asked gently, unsure whether he was still awake and not wanting to rouse him if he wasn't.

"Ada?" Came his sardonic response.

I hesitated, suddenly fearful of asking him the question burning on my lips.

"Would you ever hurt me?" I said into the darkness, my voice barely above a whisper.

"No, I wouldn't." He let out a heavy breath. "Now stop asking stupid questions and go to sleep." Humor colored his words and I smiled happily to myself at his answer, snuggling further into his chest.

In his arms, I fell into a deep and peaceful sleep.

CHAPTER
TWENTY-TWO

ADALYN

The next day was a tiring one.

We got up early that morning to take the jet back to Chicago, leaving Catania airport shortly before ten. The thirteen hours or so on the plane journey back had dragged, much like our flight to Sicily the week before. However, unlike before, Marco and I were now sitting next to each other, engaged in jovial conversation with Jesse. Even when we weren't talking amongst each other, Marco would hold my hand or give it the occasional squeeze.

It was striking how quickly things had changed between us in the space of one short week.

When we had pulled up to the familiar sandstone walls of home that evening, it was just past midnight.

The men disappeared and I headed to bed, collapsing in a heap with only an oversized t-shirt for pajamas. I passed out within minutes and scarcely registered it when a familiar presence enveloped me that night and stayed until the early hours of the morning.

Unsurprisingly, Marco was working in his study much of the following day. Suit after suit filtered through the house as an endless swarm of Cosa Nostra dealings and family meetings ensued. Clearly, there was a lot to catch up on from the week we had been away.

By the time the last of the men had left, it had gone nine o'clock in the evening and I was in the cinema room watching *Bridesmaids*, resigned to spending the evening alone. Not even Jesse was around for company.

"What are you watching?" Marco's voice echoed from behind me.

I squawked like a crow and jumped clean off my seat in fright.

Very attractive, I internally scolded.

"Jesus, Marco!" I clutched at my chest. Turning to scowl at him. "You scared me!"

"*Finally.*" A boyish, crooked smile pulled at his lips, but his eyes quickly drifted to the screen behind me to where all hell was breaking loose. "Shitting in a sink...what the hell is this?"

I chuckled and resumed my seat as he descended the steps.

"Bridesmaids. It's the best." I answered simply. "I didn't think you knew there was a cinema room in your house."

To be honest, I never really saw him doing anything that didn't include working. Let alone him sitting watching a *movie*.

He just smiled and took a seat beside me.

After a few minutes of watching the scene on screen unfold, he grew bored and picked up the nearby remote, hitting pause.

"Hey!" I protested.

His darkening smile was all the warning I got before he closed the short distance between us.

His lips trapped mine in a rough, consuming kiss and I fell backward with the force of his body as it tumbled into mine. His arms quickly found my waist and wrapped around me, picking me up from the recliner. I didn't know what he was doing until I felt the soft carpet press against my back and the hard plains of his chest moving in alignment with mine.

When our lips parted, his stormy eyes sent a wave of heat across my skin and a pulse straight to the sensitive bud between my legs. His head sunk to my neck, sucking on my skin as if it tasted as magnificent as his favorite bourbon. When his lips traipsed back to mine, all I could think about was how hungry I was for *more*.

He pulled my crop top up and over my head swiftly, and I hesitated.

"Wait," I said, breaking away, poorly trying to push him back a few inches. "Wait. I want to try something."

He sighed and relented, moving back and leaning on an arm to look down at me, his eyes suddenly alight with excitement and curiosity.

"What do you have in mind, Ada?" His voice was all sin and sex.

I didn't have the courage to voice what I had in mind. My own inexperience constricting my throat and immobilizing my tongue. Instead of saying the words, I pushed gently on his shoulder. Understanding my unspoken meaning, he rolled onto his back, allowing me to straddle his hips as our gaze locked with punishing intensity.

Feeling myself beginning to crumble under the scrutiny of his gaze and the nervousness of what I was about to do, I tucked my head into his neck and started trailing kisses down to his collar bone. My fingers worked to unbutton his black dress shirt, revealing a sliver of hard chest and defined stomach. My lips followed the path of my hands downward, until they ran out of skin and found his belt buckle instead.

Without allowing myself even a second to think about what I was doing, I pulled the leather loose and began working on the clasp of his trousers. I felt him tense beneath me, his muscles growing still.

My hands shook with uncertainty as I strained the material down to his thighs revealing his erection, thick and hard as it stretched against his grey boxers.

God, I want to please this man.

I licked my lips and rubbed against the fabric. I could feel his barely contained desire. The warmth of his arousal.

"Take it out." Marco ordered.

I didn't take it as a harsh command though, my body very much liking his roughness...It knew it meant he was struggling to stay in control of himself.

I pulled his briefs down and wrapped my hand around his length. Marco immediately hissed at the contact, and it spurred me on.

His skin was surprisingly soft, almost velvet like, yet hard and hot all at the same time.

My mouth watered, and I tentatively reached my tongue out and flicked it against the tip. Feeling him grow instantly harder in my hand, I guided my tongue over him. Licking him from the base to the tip.

I looked up at him and his half-lidded eyes told me he was enjoying it. Satisfied I was doing it right, I decided to take the next step.

Still meeting his eyes, I took as much of him into my mouth as I could and sucked. Hard.

"Fuck." He groaned, his eyes closing and his breath catching on his curse.

Seeing the pleasure erupt on his face, I pushed him in further and my eyes watered as his head hit the back of my throat. He still wasn't all the way in though, so I moved him out a few inches, only to push more of him in again. Once, twice. Over and over. His soft grunts grew into pants with each motion, his hand curling into my hair.

After a few more sucks, Marco pushed me away gently and pulled himself out.

"You got to stop." Marco growled.

Anxiety flooded my system. *Did I do something wrong?*

"Why?"

"Because I can't fuck you if I come right now," he said gruffly, meeting me with hazy, lust filled eyes.

"Oh." A tentative, triumphant smile stretched across my face.

He was going to come. That thought brought with it a wave of satisfaction.

I kissed my way back up his body and found his lips. The second I reached them his hands delved into my shorts, yanking down the black nylon and the panties I was wearing. I stood a moment to slide them off, while he pulled the rest of his clothes off simultaneously.

Free from the remainder of our clothes, I straddled his hips once again and ground down on him. I groaned when I felt him slide into me. He was so large and warm, filling me to the brim until I couldn't think anything or breathe anything but *Marco*. He let out a hiss as I began moving against him, controlling the rhythm and pushing him deeper with each languid roll of the hips.

One of his rough hands found their way to my breast, squeezing and palming at the skin while the other rubbed at the sensitive spot between my thighs. I sighed with pleasure, letting my head fall back as I became lost in his touch.

The second my sighs turned into whimpers, Marco's restraint seemed to snap.

Quicker than I thought possible, he rolled us so I was once again on my back beneath him. He slammed into me causing punishing pleasure to erupt in my lower stomach. He pumped into me *hard*. His torturous tempo turning the white-hot friction of our skin into sparks of sizzling fire.

"That's right. Come for me baby. I want to feel it." Marco commanded.

A moan erupted from deep in my chest and I came undone in his arms. My nails dug into his back as my body began writhing and flushing against him.

"Good girl." He praised.

His strokes grew slower and deeper as my body cooled. He was so deep now I could feel him in the pit of my belly.

"Now I want to see that ass of yours." He muttered.

He pulled out of me completely and spun me over, as if I weighed no more than a bag of flour, propping me up so I was on all fours.

If I wasn't still riding the languid high of my orgasm, I would have been embarrassed by how exposed I was to his gaze. Instead, I found myself docile and obedient, the last of my dignity having apparently packed itself up and shipped itself off. *Figures.*

He thrust his length back into me, resuming his agonizing pace and sending sparks dancing across my skin.

Just as I felt pressure inside me starting to build again, Marco began to caress a *different* area of my body. His fingers delicately exploring as his thrusts slowed and then stilled. His breathing suddenly turned ragged, and a shiver ran through him as the very tip of his finger slid tentatively inside me *there.*

"Marco," I gasped, becoming flustered and overwhelmed by the new sensation.

"Tell me to stop and I will," He muttered, his voice gravelly and hoarse.

I didn't.

His finger sunk deeper and I sucked in a small breath, feeling so full and overcome with the different sensation that I could hardly think to breathe. He was everywhere, all at once. It was so dirty, so possessive, so *Marco.*

"Your ass is so tight." He grunted, struggling to restrain himself.

His hips began moving again, slower and deeper than

before, allowing me to adjust to the feeling. It wasn't long before pleasure like I had never experienced began to build to an excruciating degree.

All-consuming euphoria pulsed and vibrated within me. My nails dug into the carpet as I screamed, falling into blissful oblivion. Marco's own groan of ecstasy came not a second later, his body trembling and tensing as he too found his release.

We collapsed to the floor in a mess of discarded clothing and shaky limbs. Our heavy pants and racing heartbeats the only noise amongst the silence.

"Good thing we are in a room with soundproof walls," I muttered, completely spent.

He chuckled softly. "A happy coincidence."

It took another few minutes or so before our breathing began to slow, my heart rate gradually returning to normal.

Marco's voice broke the silence.

"I have to leave in an hour."

I watched as he slowly sat up and reached for his trousers and I was suddenly grateful he had turned his back to me so he couldn't see the dejection or disappointment lining my face.

"How long will you be gone?" I asked sitting upright, pulling my clothes toward me.

"A few days maybe." He rose to his feet, pulling on the black material and doing up his belt.

I watched on as a pang of sadness hit me in the chest. We had grown so close over the last two weeks, would distance change everything that had happened between us?

He reached down to caress the side of my face with a hand, almost as if he could see the concern in my expression and he wanted to dispel it in some way.

"Don't worry. I'll be back soon, baby." He flashed me his dazzling boyish smile before planting a soft kiss to my lips.

———

OVER THE NEXT FEW DAYS, life in Chicago returned to its normal routine. I hated to admit it, but the city was really starting to grow on me, and now that I had finished buying decorations for my room, it had started to feel like home. I went back to work when Monday rolled around and was happy to see the familiar face of Keeley, my assistant, as I walked out of the elevator that morning. Apparently, there was a lot of office gossip I had missed in the week I was away.

On Tuesday evening, Jesse came and joined me for dinner as I sat in the kitchen and we ate Lucia's homemade ravioli, which was hands-down the best thing I had ever tasted.

"So, what's going on with you and Marco?" Jesse asked after a brief pause in the conversation.

I wasn't sure how to answer him, so I tried being as vague as possible, knowing that he most definitely knew more than he was letting on. He just wanted to hear it from me.

"We... Um, Well..."

"Fuck?" He offered and then scoffed. "Well clearly!"

I chuckled darkly. "Well, yes *that*." I let out a sigh. "But that's all it is Jess."

"I don't know about that." He said, shooting me a skeptical look. "You seem pretty cozy to me."

My heart fluttered. The idea that we looked like a couple to anyone on the outside made a small smile stretch across my face. I speared another piece of ravioli and popped it into my mouth to cover it up.

"Have you even talked about what's going on between you two?" He questioned, undeterred by my silence.

"No, we haven't." I sighed, "But I'm not sure I want to anyway. I'm enjoying whatever this is between us, and I don't want to ruin it."

"Why do you think it would ruin it?" Jesse asked and I rolled my eyes.

"Oh, come on Jess. I'm not naïve. I know that none of this

can last." I could see he was about to ask 'why?' so I continued, "He's a *Don*, Jess. And I am only one person... I'm not enough for someone like him. If you could have anyone in the continental US *and* Sicily, why settle for a Mannino like me?" I shrugged my shoulder, pretending like the words didn't pierce a hole straight through my chest.

He gave me a peculiar look for a few seconds. His dark eyes roaming my face as if trying to examine whether I really believed the words I'd spoken.

"Seriously?" He cocked a brow at me, taking a deep swig of his beer.

"I'm not stupid. I know that what we have is just temporary and I'm okay with that."

He shook his head in disbelief. His troubled eyes indicated there was more that he wanted to say, but he didn't elaborate any further and we didn't broach the subject again the rest of evening.

By the time Wednesday rolled around, I was becoming restless. I couldn't help but worry about where Marco was or whether he was safe. No news was good news, but it didn't help the unease and anticipation that compounded me as the days wore on.

My feelings toward the Don were burning stronger than ever despite the distance between us. It was exhilarating, unnerving and exciting. It was just like how I imagined falling would feel like.

The only problem was, inevitably, one day I was going to hit the bottom.

———

I CLOSED my office door and strolled down the hall toward the elevator bank, looking around in the hopes of finding Jesse loitering somewhere amongst the many rooms.

The clock had already hit five thirty, and yet my best friend was suspiciously absent from my office. He'd driven me to work that morning and disappeared soon after we arrived, informing me about some update meeting he needed to have with the casino's security. But that was *hours* ago now, and I hadn't seen him since.

Alonso and Tom straightened as I approached the foyer, walking straight toward their corner of the space. It didn't matter what I was doing or where I was going, these two men were like my silent shadows.

"Alonso, where's Jesse?" I asked, coming to a stop beside the men.

Alonso fought against a smile as he turned to face me. "I think he's somewhat *occupied* at the moment, Miss Adalyn."

"Occupied?" I raised my brow and Tom snickered. "Well, whatever he's doing tell him we should have left thirty minutes ago."

"I'd love to, Ma'am, but he's not answering his radio right now." Alonso smirked.

"Well, is he alright? If he's not answering his radio…"

"Oh, he's definitely alright." Tom grinned and both men shared a look.

"Then can you go and get him? I'm dead tired and—"

Alonso started laughing and Tom grimaced. "Ugh…polite pass."

Right, what is so damn funny?

I sighed, "What the fuck is going on, Boys?"

"Uh…" Alonso scratched his chin but otherwise didn't continue. Well, that was a fucking first.

"If one of you doesn't start telling me what's going on *right* no—"

"Okay, okay!" Tom interrupted, lifting his hands up placatingly before pressing a finger to his lips, silently telling me to keep my voice down.

He motioned for me to follow him down one of the hallways off the foyer, silently stopping before a bathroom door.

What in the—

"Oh, *fuck*. Yeah. Just like that."

I jolted back from the door, staring incredulously at the dark wood that did little to stifle the moaning and panting of its occupants. Tom was soundlessly laughing at my side, and I smacked him on the arm.

"Yes, yes, yes." A female chanted from the other side.

Oh, God...that was *Keeley*.

"Fuck, yes. That's it. That's i—"

"Jesse Alessio Mancini, get your fucking cock *out* of my assistant. It's home time!" I yelled through the door, pounding my fist against the wood.

Tom's laughter exploded out of him just as my own chuckle tumbled from my lips, unable to keep a straight face.

I heard Jesse curse quietly. "I'm a little *busy* right now, Bandit!"

"You're supposed to be my ride home." I pointed out, but my voice, sadly, wasn't as stern as I'd hoped.

"I'm giving someone else a *ride* at the moment. Find your own way home!"

Well, that's fucking gross.

"You're fucking sick, Jess!"

I heard him laugh, but then sounds I *really* didn't want to hear started floating back through the door. I quickly walked the distance back to the elevators with Tom lagging behind.

"You're both perverts." I scolded the men as we all stepped into the elevator, heading down to reception. "But I would appreciate a lift home, so I forgive you both."

They both snickered and led the way out of the building toward the lot out front. The armored SUV was more than a little ostentatious as it glinted in the sunlight. A blight against the relatively mundane landscape of cars that surrounded it.

Alonso held one of the rear doors open for me and I climbed in as both men took their seats with Tom taking the wheel.

I flicked open my purse and pulled out my phone from one of the interior pockets. I quickly typed off a message but hesitated a moment.

Just do it!

I took a heavy sigh and pressed 'send'.

Me: I miss you.

The car slowly started pulling out of the parking lot and I focused on the movement of the vehicle instead of my heart-rate as it thundered in my ears. Would he even respond to my message? Or would it make him run for the hills?

Panic had me suddenly second-guessing myself and I started furiously trying to figure out how to unsend the message.

Shit. Shit. Shit.

The phone dinged in my hand.

Marco: Miss you too. B home soon x

Relief so intense had me collapsing back into the seat.

He didn't run for the hills.

I smiled at the thought and settled in for the ride back home.

I glanced out the window as we stopped at an intersection, my eyes drifting over to homeless people that loitered on the corner. They were always there but...today there was a new face among them. *Jimmy.*

A pang of sadness hit me in the chest.

Jimmy was a regular at Diamond City. He was always playing the slot machine in the corner of the main floor with a small smile on his face. I'd spoken to him just yesterday on my way out of the staff room.

It's an addiction for him, I realized.

The traffic light ahead of us blinked green and the car

started moving again, pulling us away from the misfortune of those on the sidewalk.

"Excellent, then that's it for today. Thank you all." I dismissed, flipping my leather folder shut.

The monthly interdepartmental meeting always took up the better half of my morning, but I didn't mind it. I had considered it a great honor when Jon had entrusted me to start running them without his oversight. It felt like I had finally found my place in the world of business, and I was sure as shit not going to blow it now. Marco was the first person to have ever given me a role within the family business and I was determined he wasn't going to regret it.

Regret *me*.

I collected my mug and the few other items I had brought into the meeting room with me, smiling at each person as they steadily filtered out of the conference room doors.

"Miss Rossi, here are the numbers you requested." Derrek, the Culinary Director, said as he approached. He wore a nervous smile as he extended a manilla folder in my direction.

"Great work, thank you." I nodded, retrieving it as he continued out the door.

I flicked through the paperwork a moment, scanning my eyes over the casino's food waste output and reviewing all the numbers over the last quarter.

Perfect.

I didn't linger in the deserted conference room any longer, keen to start pulling apart the documents in my hand in the privacy of my own office. I tucked the folder under my arm and collected my mug and other items too as I headed out.

The elevator bank was quiet now, the last of the staff having drifted through the closing doors. I was grateful for it; talking for the better part of three whole hours had proven exhausting and another coffee was fast becoming necessary.

After another minute or so, the elevator doors slid open again and I stepped inside. Pulling out my phone, I fired off a quick message as I slowly started ascending the levels to my floor.

Me: When will you b back today?

Marco had called last night after I'd got back from work, and we'd spent an hour or so talking on the phone. He'd been in New York all week lining up deals and attending meetings, but he'd promised to be home today in time for the weekend... and I was more than a little impatient to see him.

The elevator dinged as the doors opened on my floor and I stepped out into the foyer, noting the familiar smell of sandalwood and wild Lilies that greeted me. Our in-house florist never ceased to amaze me with her ornate, decedent displays. I'd made a good choice in hiring her for the place.

Keeley's desk was empty as I rounded the corner, though that wasn't unusual given the time. She always popped out about midday to get us some lunch from the kitchen or a coffee. She was good like that...when she *wasn't* fucking my security guys.

Fresh out of hands, I used my butt to push open the door to my office...and all but screamed when I realized that I wasn't alone in the room.

"Ada."

He was as handsome as ever, sitting at my desk as if he owned the space...which I suppose he *technically* did.

Marco's coal dress shirt was rolled to the elbows, exaggerating the intricate black artwork that decorated each arm. His midnight hair was perfect, precisely shaven at the sides and worn in his customary way.

God he really is beautiful.

As if he could guess what I was thinking, his sensuous lips stretched into that boyish smile I loved so much.

Fighting a smile of my own, I languidly crossed the room to the desk, depositing my items. Marco's dark eyes tracked the movement and continued watching as I rounded the polished glass to stand beside him. He turned the chair around to face me, leaning back against the leather as if I was the most interesting show on earth.

We were close enough now that his spicy sent hit my nose and white-hot arousal dripped into my blood.

With deliberate slowness, I stepped between his parted knees and bent at the hip to place a gentle kiss on his lips.

His eyes smoldered as I pulled away, continuing to watch me as I straightened. I caressed the back of his neck with my fingers, my hand coming to rest against his chest.

"How was your flight?" I asked, distracted by looking over every inch of his handsome face, silently inspecting him for injuries.

"Long."

Marco's touch found its way to the backs of my thighs as he spoke. The heavy warmth of his hands seeping through the tight fabric of my skirt.

My gaze clashed with his, "I'm happy you're home."

He smiled sweetly. "Me too."

The hands that were resting against my thighs pulled me closer and I stumbled forwards, catching myself against his shoulders. My hands splaying against muscle. Our faces were now millimeters away from each other and he didn't hesitate in bridging the gap.

The kiss was consuming. Branding me as *his* right to my core.

I parted my lips and moaned as his tongue tasted me, swirling and searching for my own. I sucked on it, my hands twining in his hair and forcing his face impossibly closer. The limited contact between us was by no means enough after a week spent away.

Marco's hands slid to my ass and squeezed.

I groaned into him, sucking on his lip and matching his bruising kiss with one of my own. Our lips molded together, a tangle of teeth, tongue, and warmth as we both fought to gain the upper hand.

My tight skirt loosened, and my breath caught in my throat.

"Marco..." My objection was a mere whisper. "Someone could see."

He didn't stop though, swiftly tugging on the material until it hit the floor.

"Do you really think I would let anyone see what's mine?" His words were rough and grated somewhere low in my stomach.

I didn't get a chance to answer him, my breath sucked out of me the moment his tongue flicked against the sensitive skin below my ear. I sighed and my fingers trailed their way down his neck, finding the collar of his shirt and swiftly undoing the tie and buttons until I could trace my fingers across his bare chest. He shivered at the touch, discarding the shirt entirely before he mirrored the action with my own, my bra quickly following.

His warm breath fanned my neck. "Bend over the desk."

I didn't hesitate.

I stepped over the puddle of material on the floor and planted my hands on the desk before me, acutely aware that I was covered by no more than panties and heels.

He has a thing for heels...

I didn't linger on the thought long as I felt him rise behind me. The hard muscle of toned thighs pressing against me, pushing me further onto the desk until my chest and stomach were flat against the cold surface, my head lying to the side.

"Good girl." He praised.

Marco's hands quickly found the straps at my hips and slid my panties downwards. Cool air brushed my sensitive skin as I ached and burned for him.

"Marco—" I began.

A quick smack on my ass had whatever words I was about to say dying in my throat. Tingles erupted across my skin, dancing their way to areas of my body I had never anticipated I could welcome a rougher touch. Arousal pooled low in my stomach.

"Hmm...you like that, don't you?" Marco's voice was husky and *oh god*, sexy as fucking hell.

Another smack landed on my skin, and I moaned this time, the feeling indescribably intense. *Intoxicating.*

His hands latched onto my ass, spreading my cheeks wide and exposing *all* of me to his gaze. I flushed and quivered, feeling more exposed in that moment than I had ever felt in my life. I was vulnerable, and defenseless and insecure...

What if he doesn't—

"*Fuck.*" He cursed, kissing the crease where my thigh met my ass. "You're always beautiful, Ada, but seeing you like this... you're fucking captivating."

My whole body melted. His words suffocating the anxious voice in my head that told me I wasn't good enough. That I wasn't beautiful enough. Strong enough. *Capable* enough for someone like him. Without knowing it, Marco's words had soothed that part of myself that had always lingered in the shadows, dispersing it in an instant.

I could be exactly who I was with Marco. He wanted me exactly as I was. Physically, mentally. All of it. *All of me.*

His face descended on me, his tongue tracing my folds as his shoulders hooked the front of my legs allowing him to press closer. I sighed and moaned, my legs shaking with every new swirl of his tongue as he tasted me. When his tongue dove inside, I shuddered with unparalleled pleasure. The feeling growing and swelling with each touch of his skin, brush of his lips, and sigh from his throat.

It was over too soon, cold air brushing my skin as he retreated and came up to standing. I watched out the corner of my eye as his heavy-lidded gaze stayed locked on my body. The tattoos on his chest and arms rippled and pulsed as he wove a strip of black fabric expertly between his hands. *His tie.*

Watching his expression darken, I could already tell what his next move was going to be.

"Put your hands behind your back." Came his soft order.

I immediately complied, moving my hands until they rested lowly on my hips. He gathered them in one of his as smooth, soft material looped around each of my wrists. It tightened, but not enough to feel restrictive.

"Have you ever been tied up like this before?" Marco asked, and I could hear his breathing was heavier than normal.

"No." Came my simple reply.

"If you want me to stop, just tell me."

I nodded, my words failing me as I felt him press up against me once more.

It was all the warning I got before his thick length pushed inside with a hard thrust of his hips. I cried out, overcome by the fullness and struggling to breathe around the blissful burn of pleasure that set my body alight. He retreated slightly, only to drive into me harder. *Deeper.*

"That's right, baby. Relax. You can take more." He murmured, one hand stroking my butt while the other latched onto the tie at my wrists, holding me firm.

Shit, that still isn't all of him?

I forced myself to relax, to become pliable under his capable hands.

He wasn't going to hurt me or give me more than I could handle...hadn't eight months in his home already proven that?

The second I melted, surrendering to him completely, he

plunged into me again and I screamed. A tangle of the sweetest pain and ecstasy danced at my nerves until I was a writhing, panting mess beneath him. He set a brutal pace, slamming into me over and over until I couldn't help but tumble over the edge.

My climax was hard and fast.

Marco's curse rumbled deep in his chest as he felt me tighten around him. He slowed and one look at his face told me he was dangerously close to plummeting himself but was fighting it. A thin sheen of sweat lined his dark brow.

His eyes found mine then and he leaned down, placing a kiss to my back as he made quick work of untying me. My body was heavy and slow as he helped pull me upright and turn me around, planting a warm and consuming kiss to my lips the moment I faced him. Our tongues messily collided, and I sucked on him, *needing* him closer.

He understood my unspoken words and lifted me onto the desk, spreading my legs as he lined himself up with my entrance. He thrust back inside me with a deliberate and intox-icating slowness this time. A growl resonating from his throat as he pushed himself in, inch by delicious inch. His eyes half-closed as he fully seated himself.

Marco paused there a moment, allowing me to adjust to the new angle before he retreated. Pushing back in only a second later and pressing a hand gently to my stomach so I would lie back. My hands slipped and slid across the papers behind me, scattering them to the floor as I moved. His hand promptly hooked behind my knee, pushing it into the air and exposing me to his gaze.

Once again, I was exposed to him, but I didn't care in the slightest this time. Watching Marco's face contort in pleasure as he rocked into me relentlessly was the most electrifying feeling I could ever imagine. The way his eyes surveyed me like I was the most beautiful person on the planet, like I *was* enough for him, was so erotic. So, *mesmerizing*. I was fast becoming consumed by my feelings for the man, and I didn't care enough to stop it.

I wanted him. *Needed* him.

"Rub yourself for me," he ordered, his voice gravelly and hoarse.

I let my fingers trail down my body until they found sensitive flesh, slowly swirling around the bud at the apex of my thighs.

Marco's gaze flashed between tracking the movement and watching my expression, and I moaned. The feeling too intense. The fact that he was *watching* me as I played with myself...it was too hot. When his hand squeezed my breast, I came.

Hard.

I cried out as my body jerked violently. My core pulsed around him as my body flushed red hot. Marco's movements became less succinct in response, and I could tell that he was only moments away from finding his own release.

"Look at me," I whispered.

He did.

His dark, heavy eyes sliced to mine with an unrestrained desire that had my body instantly craving him again. He pumped once, twice... His groan was powerful, reverberating deep into the pit of my stomach as his eyes stayed locked to mine.

It was the most intense and arousing thing I had ever experienced. Changing me in ways I couldn't even fully comprehend in that moment.

He quivered and dropped my leg to the side, collapsing on top of me with a deep, satisfied sigh.

"I missed you," he murmured softly.

I fought to catch my breath. "I missed you, too."

CHAPTER
TWENTY-THREE

ADALYN

U nease swirled in my gut as I sat at the dinner table beside Marco the following Wednesday.

I had spent the majority of the weekend and early half of the week figuring out the logistics of an idea that had been weighing on my mind since I had witnessed the homeless people loitering last week. I had proposed the idea to my boss at work, who was on board with the idea providing I could get Marco's approval on it as well...

My heart rate spiked.

I had only one chance to sell him on the idea and to be frank...I was fucking horrible at sales pitches.

"What's wrong?" Marco's hand came to rest over mine against the table, gaining my attention.

Ever since we'd returned from Sicily, my seat at the ginormous dining table had changed. During our first dinner back in Chicago, without even thinking I had taken my usual seat at the other end of the table...only for Marco to walk over to me, throw me over his shoulder and deposit me in the chair directly beside his and it had become our unspoken seating arrange-ment ever since. Not that I minded one bit.

I sighed, pulling my thoughts back to the conversation.

It's now or never...

"I...wanted to speak with you about something actually," I admitted.

His eyes flashed to my face and then trailed across my body. I knew there was nothing sexual in the look he was giving me, but heat pooled in my stomach all the same.

I cleared my throat in an attempt to control myself. "I've been looking at the numbers from the restaurants at work and noticed a high volume of produce is consistently being discarded every day. Whether it's food that's not sold or stuff which is about to expire... It got me thinking. There are so many people that are struggling to feed themselves, wouldn't it be beneficial to everyone if we put that food to good use?"

Surprisingly, Marco didn't miss a beat. He nodded, "I agree. What did you have in mind?"

Damn, I love him so much.

I couldn't help the grin that pulled at my lips. "I've already reached out to a few of the food banks closest to the casino and discussed with them how we can best support them. Looking at the numbers over the last quarter, we have a consistent food surplus and so I don't think we would encounter any issues if we committed to supplying them daily."

He nodded. "Then we do it."

"A-are you sure? Don't you want to see the numbers your-self?" I questioned, keenly aware that this was a potentially important business decision that he was trusting me with.

"There's no need, I trust your judgment. Whatever resources you need for it to work, they're yours." He shrugged, picking up his crystal tumbler and taking a swig. "Have you thought about doing a fundraising ball or something as well?"

I toyed with the idea in my head a moment. "That's actually a great idea. I'll speak to Jon about it in the morning."

Marco smiled at the excitement lining my features. "Then I will leave the planning in your capable hands." He gracefully rose from his seat, stepping beside me and pressing his lips to the top of my head. "I have to get to a meeting, but I'll be back later," he promised as his fingertips skimming my cheek.

"Be careful," I breathed, meeting his dark gaze so he could see the concern lining my eyes.

His boyish smile flashed in response. "Always."

———

OVER THE NEXT FEW MONTHS, things settled into a new sense of normalcy and routine.

As time wore on, I had started to grow accustomed to the nuances of Marco's personality and found myself seeing the boy within him more often than ever before. We ate together, slept together, watched TV together, and went out for date nights. We even celebrated Christmas together with his family in Sicily.

I was quickly becoming obsessed with him. *Consumed* by him.

Marco had sunk beneath my skin, and I had absolutely no intention or desire to get him out.

When I wasn't with Marco, then the majority of my time was spent working at the casino, planning the fundraising ball Marco had approved or learning recipes with Lucia. Cooking had never been my strong suit, but I was adamant that it one day would be. Marco was nothing if not traditional and while I broke all other interpretations of the word, I wanted to prove to him that I could at least play the part when I wanted to. That I could be what he *needed* as well as what he *wanted*.

For the most part, I played my part well. Dutifully dropping off my signature triple chocolate brownies every Sunday morning after he got back from church and organizing coffee when the meetings ran late into the evening.

Having said that—I wasn't always the dutiful lover.

After all, where would be the fun in that?

In true Adalyn Rossi style, I would push his buttons every now and again just to keep him on his toes.

Acting provocatively in a skimpy bikini by the pool, while Marco and Jesse were having a meeting? *No problem.* Hoovering the carpet while he's working late again? *Don't mind if I do.* Stripping in the gym because he's working up a sweat? *Absolutely!*

It was invigorating, exhilarating, and completely addictive. Risk had never felt so absolutely like reward.

And beyond anything else, I was happy.

But just like all good things—they come to an end eventually.

CHAPTER
TWENTY-FOUR

ADALYN

The end of my delirious happiness came when six words left Marco's lips late one Wednesday afternoon.

"Your father has requested a meeting."

"What?" I asked, taking a seat in the armchair across from him. I was shocked and confused by the news.

Marco swirled the glass of amber liquid in his hand. The tension in his expression unmistakable as we sat together in the study.

"It's unprecedented," Marco muttered bringing my focus back to the room.

His jaw tightened, as if he were annoyed with himself that he hadn't anticipated my father's request.

"Why now?" Was all I could think to ask.

"He believes there is a way to resolve this war between our families." Expecting my next question he added, "He didn't say what."

"And do you believe him?" I asked, skeptical.

My father never was one to change his mind once it had been made.

"I don't know what to think." Marco tossed his tumbler onto the desk and wracked his hands down his face. "The meeting is in two days and you're coming with me."

I nodded, having every intention of coming even if he hadn't offered, "Where is it?"

"Las Vegas. The Venetian Prince." Despite his unease, a vague smile pulled at the corner of his lips.

I laughed once without humor. "Let me guess. You picked the venue."

He shrugged nonchalantly, his smile growing. "It has a certain symmetry to it."

I got to my feet and circled the desk, coming to stand by his side.

"What do you think he wants?" I asked quietly as he tugged me down onto his lap.

"I have an idea." He said, eyeing me pointedly. "Not that it matters. I'd burn him and his entire city to the ground before he'd ever get the chance."

Butterflies erupted in my stomach, and I had no doubt that he meant what he said. Not when his deep brown eyes sliced into mine with an intensity that made my insides burn.

Marco was no monster, but he was certainly no hero either. If it meant keeping me by his side, I had no doubt he would follow through on his words.

"You are mine and if that means war with the Mannino's for the rest of my existence then so be it." His voice took on a lethal edge that promised violence and I stifled a shudder.

I brought my fingers to his face, caressing his skin trying to placate his inner turmoil.

"It won't come to that," I breathed. "Besides, I'm not going anywhere without putting up a fight. I'm very deadly you know," I said sweetly and quirking an eyebrow, daring him to challenge me on it.

His deep chuckle made my heart swell, and my arms wound around his neck on instinct. Humor sparked in his eyes and a smirk pulled at his lips.

"Deadly." He agreed.

———

THE PLANE RIDE to Las Vegas that Friday was tense.

The men talked heatedly over strategy at the conference table while I stared aimlessly out the window trying not to bite off the inside of my cheek.

Knowing I would see my father for the first time in almost a year, made anxiety bubble in my chest. The father I thought I had for twenty-five years wasn't the same man I now knew him to be. Everything was different.

I was different.

Most of Marco's security had already been assembled at The Venetian Prince. He had brought over thirty extra bodies to facilitate the evening meeting and to ensure everything went as planned. Although, the specific details of that *plan* weren't shared with me, Marco had insisted that killing my father wasn't part of it. That his primary motivation was getting everyone on our side in and out safely. Especially me.

The club was just the same as I remembered.

The building itself towered over everything within a two-block radius—a hard feat given that it was on the Las Vegas strip. The building gleamed with the light of Friday evening traffic and reflected the neon signs of nearby venues like an ostentatious mirror. Queues of people dotted the sidewalk outside as we sped past in the SUV, turning into an underground parking garage beneath the club itself.

The lot was deathly silent as we exited. Flickering fluorescent lights were setting my teeth on edge as we crossed the cement to the bank of elevators. The seven of us piled into a marble-paneled box to ascend up the levels. Jesse and Layton were talking animatedly into their wrists as we went, liaising with the rest of the security team stationed at various points across the club's blueprint. I couldn't help but tremble as my adrenaline spiked the moment the elevator doors opened on the fiftieth floor.

Jesse led us down a short, unfamiliar hallway and through a set of double doors, revealing an enormous conference room. At its heart stood a rectangular wood table, polished to perfection and surrounded by twenty leather backed chairs. Two of the room's walls were entirely made of glass, overlooking the familiar twinkling lights of the Las Vegas city skyline, while the other two featured large abstract paintings. It was sleek, modern, and undeniably sophisticated.

In my periphery, I saw Marco walk over to the console on the right and heard the clinking of glass as he poured himself a drink. The other men huddled in muted discussion by the door. A few heavy minutes passed by before Jesse cleared his throat.

"They are here."

Marco seemed unconcerned by the news as he slowly turned to the men. "Once everyone is in position, send them up."

Jesse nodded, and the men sprang into action. Alonso and Tom moved to stand on either side of the doors we had just entered through, while Wyatt and Layton moved to stand on either side of what I presume would be Marco's seat at the head of the table. I counted three guns on each of them...and those were only the ones I could see. Benny also sat off to the side, face stern and a gun strapped to his hip.

Marco had reassured me on the drive over that no blood would be spilled tonight, but he clearly wasn't betting on it.

If I wasn't nervous before, I certainly was now.

Marco took to his seat, furthest from the doors and gestured for Wyatt to move another chair next to him.

"Ada," he ordered, looking from me to the chair.

I complied without hesitation, feeling not only out of my depth, but as if anxiety threatened to eat me alive. My heartbeat thundered in my ears and my throat turned to sandpaper.

"Don't be worried. Nothing bad is going to happen." The confidence in Marco's voice was unmistakable and it dampened my apprehension a little. "Well, not to us at least." He smirked, flashing his teeth.

Jesse waltzed back in with another three men, each moving to flank each side of the room in stern silence. Their faces set in a grim expression.

The second time the doors opened, my father, his under-boss Ron, my cousin Leon, and their own small security team filtered slowly into the room.

The cold gaze of my father found me immediately but lasted mere seconds as he turned his attention to the man on my left.

This isn't the first time they've met. I quickly realized.

Marco was coolly unaffected by my father's scrutinous gaze, reclining in his chair with a whiskey. He was power and control personified, and it clearly left a bitter taste in my father's mouth. His expression soured as he took a seat.

"Alberto Mannino." Marco's impervious voice rang out in greeting.

"Marco La Torre." My father's gruff voice returned. "Need I remind you that a woman has no place at a negotiation." He didn't even look at me when speaking, focusing his attention solely on Marco.

He hasn't seen me in almost a year and that's all he has to say?

My temper flared but I held my tongue. Just like I always had as a Mannino. Just as I always did until I had met Marco.

My cousin Leon was already looking at me when I met his gaze, his round face forming a bitter smile across the table.

"You can remind me all you like Mannino, but she is staying." Marco's words were cool and confident, leaving no room for debate.

He sank back a mouthful from his tumbler before sliding the glass across the table, "Now. You wanted a discussion about peace between our families, so I suggest you get on with it."

Hatred flashed in my father's eyes, but he hid it well. Reclining back into his seat and bringing a hand up to his mouth as he contemplated his next words.

"Both our families have suffered as a result of this war. The hit you orchestrated with the help of my daughter some months ago being a particularly big *inconvenience* to my family." The disgust marring his tone was aimed squarely at me and I fought the need to shrink away in response. "In addition to the gold and the money you stole from me, you stole $30 million worth of premium-class cocaine. That cocaine was being stored as part of a deal with an old family friend and a high-ranking member of the Mexican cartel."

"I already know about your dealings with Arturo Lopez. Now get to the point." Marco barked, clearly bored.

"Arturo was murdered recently in a deal gone bad at the border and another has since stepped in to fill his position. The problem is…he isn't bothered about getting the product back or the money. There is something else he wants to pay off the debt." When my father's eyes landed on me, my stomach rolled with nausea.

That's why they are here.

Of course, that was the reason.

They had no intention of bringing me back into the fold or what they would perceive as 'rescuing' me. There was an ulterior motive. There always was with my family, and I couldn't say

I was completely surprised. Nothing about my father was surprising to me anymore.

"So, I'm prepared to make you a deal, La Torre. I will pay the ransom you previously demanded *with* interest, and I will declare peace between our families. In exchange I want my daughter."

"Who is it that wants her?" Marco's voice was cold, but I could hear the anger weaving its way between his words.

"Ricardo Lopez."

The air in my lungs whooshed out of me with a gasp.

Ricardo Lopez.

It felt like a punch in the stomach.

Cool tendrils of fear and dread sliced into my veins, the room around me suddenly becoming unsteady. The pounding in my ears growing acutely painful and the lack of oxygen in my lungs burning as I struggled to catch my breath.

I looked down at my hands, trying to hide the tears clouding my vision.

That name.

That was *his* name.

But my father already knew that. He knew what that name meant to me. What that man *did* to me. My cousin knew it too, but judging by their expressions they either didn't care, or they had conveniently chosen to forget.

I sucked in a deep, unsteady breath forcing myself to calm down. To see past the fear, the terror, and the pain consuming me as thoughts swirled back to that night.

I counted to ten, over and over to myself but breathing didn't come any easier. It was only when a heavy hand came to rest on my thigh that I was able to bring myself away from the spiraling emotions and memories that felt like they were drowning me.

Marco squeezed me reassuringly, communicating silently to me *you are safe*. That he would protect me. I focused on the soothing weight of his hand and the inky swirls of black visible on his skin. Slowly, I blinked away the tears.

As the ringing in my ears subsided, I could hear that the conversation had moved on, blissfully unaware of my internal suffering.

"$100 million interest." It was my father's voice I heard first.

"That would be a total of $200 million and peace between our families, all in exchange for your daughter?"

"Yes. Do we have a deal?"

"No." Marco's voice was menacing, but I thought I heard a faint trace of humor in it as well.

"Then name your price, La Torre." My father's hands fisted on the table, frustration rolling off him in waves.

"I don't have a price. You can't have her."

My father smiled calculatingly. "A marriage contract has already been signed. She belongs to him now."

The smugness on his face told me he truly thought had had gained the upper hand and trapped Marco in a corner.

Fool.

Marco let out dark, dry chuckle. "Your contract is void, Mannino."

"And why the hell is that?" My father demanded, clearly irked at the insinuation.

"Because Adalyn Mannino no longer exists." I didn't have to look at Marco's face to know that I would see a ghost of a smile on his lips. I could hear it in his voice.

"What!" Leon exclaimed, slamming his hands on the table. "How could you betray us like that!" He shouts, focusing his anger squarely on me as his face grew blotchy and red.

"Leon," My father warned quietly.

"No, it's not right. You never turn your back on family!" He yelled. "*You* did this to her!"

My blood boiled.

After everything my family had done to me. After everything they had put me through and made me endure...only to turn their back on me the moment I was taken behind enemy lines.

It was *them* who had turned their back on family. Not the other way around.

A dark laugh resonated from my throat before I could bite it back, earning me a hateful glare from my deplorable cousin.

"Then what exactly do you think leaving me a prisoner was, Leon? A fucking tea party?" My voice was venom and sounded eerily like the man sitting beside me. "My *family* turned their back on me a long time ago. What was it father said?" I questioned to no one, pretending to try and recall the words that were now etched into my very soul. "*She is of no use to me or this family.*"

"Adalyn." My father warned.

The look of consternation on his face was almost humorous. I doubted he had ever heard me swear before, let alone defend myself to a room full of men.

Nonetheless, I fell silent at his warning. Snapping back into the role I was forced to play for all my life—the dutiful and docile daughter.

"Lies!" Leon screamed.

I knew it wasn't a lie. So did Marco. So did my father.

It had been exactly those words on Marco's recorder all those months ago and the look of contempt now clouding my father's eyes was further proof of that very fact.

"You've been fed a load of bullshit and are brainwashed. It's pathetic." Leon argued, but I was no longer listening as he continued spuing bile.

White hot fury simmered beneath my skin, boiling me in rage. Not just with the irritating droning of my cousin, but anger with myself for falling back in step as the pathetic and meek Mannino I was raised to be.

I wasn't that person anymore and it was time they realized it.

Without thinking and guided only by violence, my hand drifted from my lap and over to the man beside me, knowing what I would find tucked in the waistband of his trousers, I snaked my hand under Marco's jacket until I touched the cool steel.

He didn't move to stop me.

Apparently, I wasn't the only one reaching my limit with this conversation.

"You've only turned your back on us because he got you on yours. You're nothing but a—"

I slammed the handgun down on the table in front of me. The bang echoed around the room, cutting Leon off.

I let it rest against the table beside my hand. Clearly locked. Clearly loaded. The warning was unmistakable.

My father's eyes flashed with indignation, but I didn't care.

"I think it's time you shut up, Leon." I spat.

Unfortunately, my idiotic bastard of a cousin never did like following orders.

"You don't get to—" he began again.

"Speak to her again and I will cut your fucking tongue out." Marco's menacing voice interrupted.

Leon's Adam's apple bobbed as he gulped, and I bit back a smile at his palpable fear.

"Enough of all this," My father complained, gesturing with his hand dismissively and not paying any mind to the increasing tension in the room. "This marriage contract was signed three months ago. It still applies."

"Adalyn hasn't been a Mannino for over six months." Marco shook his head derisively. "And to pre-empt your next move, she's already engaged to someone else. A *legitimate* contract is already signed and in effect."

My father's face blanched with that information, as did mine. I had no idea what Marco was talking about.

"To who?" My father demanded, and I too, wanted to know.

Had he finally decided to marry me off?

My heart raced as the seconds ebbed away.

"Me."

My father spluttered loudly, but I hardly even noticed.

Marco turned his head slightly. The hard onyx of his irises softened as they met mine, showing me just for a second the emotions that hid under the surface. Emotions that few alive ever got to see.

"Disgraceful. You must have a father's consent for such things, and you certainly do not have mine!" My father argued, immediately enraged.

"That's where you are wrong again," Marco replied, turning his full attention back to the older man. "You know, it's funny really...what you can do when you have no respect for tradition."

My father seemed stunned by the comment, unsure how to respond. He decided to change tack instead.

"That may be true, La Torre, but you forget that by failing to hand her over you will create yet another enemy. Ricardo will kill you and your entire family if he doesn't get what he wants."

The name—*his* name—sent a chill racing down my spine and I flinched. Marco's grip on my thigh tightened in response.

He shrugged, unaffected. "So be it. He'll be dead within a week."

The room lapsed into rigid silence as both Don's glared at each other over the expanse of table.

My father had always been an inflexible man. Once his mind was set on something, it was rarely the case that it ever changed. However, he had clearly misjudged how unflinching immutable Marco was as his opponent. An impasse had been reached and there was no clear way forward for the discussion.

I gulped in apprehension.

Violence was just around the corner and every person in the room could feel it.

A few tense minutes fell away, before my father's face contorted into a bitter smile. "Is my daughter really worth all this?"

I didn't have to see Marco's face to know he wasn't very impressed by the question, his body tensing up was indication enough.

"It is sad is that your family means so little." Marco released me and rose from his seat, languidly wandering over to the wall of windows. He shoved his hands into his pockets as he turned his back toward my father and the rest of the room, preferring to gaze out across the city.

He was cool confidence and control personified. I didn't think it was possible to respect him anymore than I already did, but in that moment, he was not only the most powerful man in the room...he was commanding. Captivating.

"That is why you will never win this war and why your family will never be as powerful as mine, Alberto. Loyalty breeds loyalty." He turned back around to face my father, looking every bit as powerful as the devil himself. "And your family are as loyal as rats on a sinking ship. Now get the fuck out of my club."

A scowl etched itself on my father's face as he began rising from his chair, clearly displeased with the abrupt end to the conversation but knowing full well they were outnumbered and outgunned.

Leon's eyes darted about the room as if scared of a massacre at any moment and all but ran to get out the door. *Coward.*

"A word of advice, La Torre," My father said, stopping just before he reached the doors. "While we are both men of violence, we are that way because we must be. Ricardo is no such man. He is savage and cruel because he wants to be. Make no mistake: he will stop at nothing to get what he wants. And what he wants is my daughter."

Fear and panic bled through me again, knowing the truth behind his warning.

My hands trembled in my lap and my heart sped in my chest. Flashes of his sadistic smile. Memories of his brutal nature came screaming back and my stomach rolled with nausea.

"It's a good thing I'm better at protecting my family than you are, then."

My father's eyes coasted to mine for a moment and his scowl deepened in thought.

For a second, it looked like he was going to say something. *Anything.*

But I was wrong.

He turned and left the conference room. Ron, Leon, and the rest of them following in his wake, escorted by our security team to the rear.

I doubted I would see any of them ever again.

I let out an unsteady, faltering breath.

This wasn't over.

Ricardo was never going to stop.

———

MARCO

I hadn't anticipated finding mutual ground with Alberto Mannino, that much I was sure of, but at least I now understood his motives.

He didn't want peace; he was desperate. And I would bet my entire fortune that he was desperate because he was *afraid.* Afraid of the man that wanted Ada—*Ricardo Lopez.*

I didn't recognize the name.

High ranking Mexican drug lord my ass.

It enraged me that I had more questions than answers.

Like why would her father promise her hand to a member of the cartel in the first place? It was unconventional...abhorrent. Mexican drug lord or not, he was a nobody to major players like us. So, why did this *Ricardo* think he had any right to her at all? He sure as shit didn't.

And on top of that, why would a father hand his only daughter over to a man he deemed a brutal savage? It didn't make any goddamn sense.

The moment the door slammed shut behind the miserable scumbags, my gaze flicked to Ada. She looked exhausted and pale, slumped in her seat. She refused to meet my stare, preferring to look at her hands lying idly on her lap and even from this distance, I could tell she was trembling.

Something is wrong.

She wasn't just upset about the callousness of her father or the cutting tongue of her idiot cousin—there was something else. Something else was going on that I wasn't aware of...and it was putting me in a piss-poor mood.

There were too many damn questions and no fucking answers.

"Are you alright?" I asked her, hating myself for sounding so rough and cold. It wasn't easy for me to drop my mask of indifference so quickly.

She didn't answer, too lost in her own thoughts. I doubted she even heard me.

My jaw tightened in frustration as Benny approached, and I reached to pour myself a drink as Benny did the same.

"That went as well as could be expected," He murmured.

"He doesn't want peace. He wants her back," I muttered in reply.

"We assumed as much." The older man nodded. "Whoever this Lopez is has him running scared, which is...*interesting*."

It certainly was.

"I want to know who he is, and I want him fucking dead."

Benny nodded once before the doors flew open again, announcing Jesse's return. Meeting the familiar eyes of my oldest friend I could sense an unease stirring within him.

"They're gone." He shot a concerned look in Ada's direction. "And I might know something about this *Ricardo Lopez* he was talking about."

Ada flinched. *Again.*

In fact, she had flinched every time that prick's name has been mentioned. Her face morphed from white to pale green. There was definitely something going on that I was missing, and I had every intention of finding out what that was...but I had to speak with Jesse first to get some fucking answers.

"Alonso. Tom. Take Ada to the penthouse and get her something to eat," I ordered.

The men quickly moved toward her, Alonso offering his hand to help her from the chair. She looked at him somewhat dazed before taking it, allowing him to help support some of her weight as she left. She looked so weak and docile, my blood boiled. I had never seen her look so...*breakable.*

My fists clenched as I fought against the primal urge to throw her over my shoulder and rip out the throat of any man that came near her.

Jesse cleared his throat the second the doors clicked shut, drawing my attention back into the room.

"I didn't recognize the name at first, but then I remembered a story one of our smugglers was telling me, about this lunatic from a cartel in Tijuana. Lopez, he'd said his name was, but he's better known as *Thrasher*." Jesse looked troubled by the name.

Thrasher.

Deep in the recesses of my mind the name rang a hollow, disturbing bell. I knew that name, or rather I knew the reputation that followed it.

Thrasher was a strangler of men, beater of women and an enslaver of children. The only word I could associated with men like him was simply *evil*. A monster.

The son of a prolific Mexican drug lord whose territories spread all through Tijuana. They were the largest in the area and the most dangerous, with a reputation spanning the entirety of Mexico.

Not that I gave a shit about any of that.

What troubled me the most is why this *Thrasher* or *Lopez*— or whoever the fuck he was—thought he had any right to Adalyn.

To what was mine.

I remembered how she flinched with each reference to his name. How she went pale... *She knew him.* Or at the very least she knew *of* him.

Blinding rage knocked the breath from me, and the glass in my hand was dangerously close to shattering.

The thought of Adalyn occupying the same room as a man known to beat women and do a lot *worse* to them, made me feel nauseas. But more than anything else—it made me murderous.

Ricardo Lopez was a dead man walking on borrowed time. And so help me God, I was going to make the bastard suffer for going after what was mine.

————

ADALYN

The penthouse was extravagant and beautiful. Walls of towering glass stretched across two stories, revealing the expanse of Las Vegas, similarly to the conference room earlier. The neon lights and crowded streets of the city framing the room like living art.

On any other day it would have been beautiful, but now... I didn't even glance at it.

Too wrapped up in the haunting memories and crippling feelings that threatened to swallow me whole. I crumpled on the bed and rolled into a ball, unable to keep my sobs at bay. The familiar tendrils of pain swelled in my veins, obliterating everything but debilitating self-pity.

He isn't going to stop.

After all these years. Despite all this distance. He wasn't finished with me. He still wasn't done *ruining* me.

As if that wasn't enough, my own father, a man who knew what Ricardo was capable of, and who had done nothing when he found out what had happened to me, was willing to bind me to him for the sake of 'business'.

From what I'd heard, time had only served to make Ricardo a more efficient monster. He was a sadist who enjoyed inflicting pain, particularly on women... particularly on women who couldn't fight back.

Thrasher.

My stomach rolled violently, and I scarcely made it to the toilet before throwing up. I pressed my head to the cool tiles and focused on trying to level out my breathing, my throat burning with every breath.

A distant voice echoed at the edge of my consciousness, but it did little to rouse me from my torture.

I ignored the gentle shake on my arm. The pain was too—

"ADA!" Marco's voice thundered around the room, snapping me out of my agonizing delirium.

I was instantaneously flipped onto my back and met with familiar, albeit frantic, black eyes. Marco's handsome mouth was set in a grim line as he took in my appearance, concern marring his handsome features.

"I'm fine," I muttered weakly, sitting up.

The nausea was nearly gone now, though the aching in my chest remained.

He lifted me from the floor and took me back into the dimly lit bedroom, gently dropping me onto the expanse of bed and removing my shoes. After a moment of tucking the covers around me, he took a seat at its edge, looking at me with concern and...*fear*.

"What is going on with you, Ada?" His voice was tight, heavy with an emotion he was trying to suppress. "Talk to me."

I shook my head and swallowed, tears brimming my eyes.

A different kind of trepidation pounded in my chest. The kind that told me that if he knew the truth, the *real* truth, then he wouldn't want me anymore. That he would think me broken.

Ruined.

"Ada, please. *Please*, Baby." His hands cupped my face.

Hearing the helplessness in his voice and seeing the vulnerability in his eyes caused something deep within me to finally snap.

I racked in a heavy, unsteady breath.

It was time to tell him my secret.

CHAPTER
TWENTY-FIVE

SEVEN YEARS BEFORE

T he warm August breeze whipped against my face as the sound of crashing waves and heavy music wafted across the beach. The dusky evening air was peaceful, and above everything else, full of the promises of freedom. It was my eighteenth birthday, and I was officially an adult, able to do whatever it was I pleased—within reason of course.

Always within reason.

I proudly flashed the bartender my shiny all-American driving license and he got to work making my first *legal* coconut lime spritzer.

The small beachside bar was rammed full of bodies and somewhere amongst them was Leon as well as some of our other more distant cousins. I tried spotting their faces amongst the crowd but couldn't see them. Leon always did that— abandon me despite being ordered not to.

I paid for my drink and walked around the makeshift dance floor toward a vacant table sat overlooking the beach. *Leon can look for* me *instead,* I thought. Content to bring in my eighteenth birthday alone and watching the distant cresting of the waves.

Cancun was always one of my favorite places to visit growing up. Two weeks of every summer we would find ourselves vacationing along the white sandy shores, basking in the fierce sun and indulging ourselves on the local cuisine.

Over the years it had become easier to convince myself that our trip to Mexico was just that—a trip. I had stopped seeing the heavily scarred men coming and going from our penthouse suite in those years. Had long stopped hearing the word 'narcotics' around our dining table every night and had completely stopped caring that my mother was screwing the hotel's gardener every chance she got.

It was just easier that way.

"This seat taken?" A male voice broke my quiet train of thought.

A vaguely familiar man stood towering above me, gesturing to the seat opposite. He looked to be in his mid-twenties, judging by his still slightly rounded features. He was undeniably handsome, what with his slight russet-colored skin, inescapably sharp jaw and short, perfectly styled black hair. He was muscular too, bulging arms stretching underneath his white dress shirt as he wore it tucked into suit pants.

He was at the penthouse the other day, I realized. *Arturo Lopez's son. That's why he's familiar.*

I gave him a non-committal shoulder shrug, instantly wary of his presence despite my family's long history with the man's father.

He smirked and took the seat swiftly, folding his six-foot-something self into the chair and dwarfing it. I probably would have found it funny if I hadn't been so wary of him.

It was my number one rule: don't date Mafioso men. Or any of their associates for that matter.

I had been around their kind long enough to know it wasn't

something that I was interested in putting up with. Whether my father would let me marry outside the Cosa Nostra though...was a different matter entirely.

"You're Alberto's daughter Adalyn, right?" I didn't give him an answer because it wasn't really a question.

He knew that I was. He was just testing the waters to see if I was receptive to him.

Prick.

While I appreciated male attention, I didn't particularly want it from a *business connection*. Especially not when that connection was almost certainly hopped up on something that was *not* donut dust. The white flecks of which still clung, unceremoniously, to his nose.

Then again, my father would punish me for not being at least civil. It was 'bad for business' you see.

"And you are?" I asked.

"Ricardo Lopez. My father Arturo and your father have been...*friends* for many years." He smiled around his characterization of their relationship.

I nodded in recognition but let the silence hang in the air.

If he was smart, he would take the hint. The problem was, at least in my experience, most people had either brains or beauty but rarely both.

"Well, Adalyn. You look gorgeous this evening." *Just beauty then,* I stifled a sigh. "A little birdy told me it was your birthday today." By little birdy, he most definitely meant Leon.

Rat bastard.

Ricardo lifted his hand in the air and gestured off in the distance, presumably to the bar. Less than two minutes later, a bottle of cold Moët & Chandon champagne arrived in a bucket of ice and two crystal flutes. The waiter deposited them wordlessly before drifting back through the throng of people to the bar.

I looked between the bottle on the table and the man smiling charmingly down at me.

"Let me guess, Daddy owns the club?" I observed dauntlessly, rolling my eyes. "How original."

"*Damn.* That's usually my best move." He joked, feigning insult.

I gave him a small smile as he reached across the table for the flutes and poured out the bubbly beverage. It smelled delicious, subtle and fruity. He slid one over to me and I eyed it skeptically, unsure whether my acceptance of the drink would only encourage him into thinking I might accept *other* things.

"There you are, baby Cuz!" Leon's vivacious voice interrupted my internal dilemma as he came bounding over to the table. "And look who we have here!" Ricardo stood from his chair and the two shared a hard hug.

Ricardo resumed his seat, but Leon remained standing, or rather swaying, on the spot.

"What are you on, Leon?" I asked, unable to keep the distaste from my mouth.

He was a borderline alcoholic with a propensity for drugs, women, and gambling. And although he wasn't an evil man, there wasn't all that much to like about him, either. It was distressing knowing that he would one day become the head of our family.

"Oh, quit the nagging, Addie. Lighten up! It's supposed to be your birthday for fucks sake," he shouted, his eyes moving in and out of focus. "HAPPY BIRTHDAY TO YOUUUU—" he started singing at the top of his blasted lungs.

"Shut it!" I hissed as people began turning to look at the spectacle, yanking on his shirt in the process.

"HAPPY BIRTHDAY TO YOUUUU—"

This time there were enough people jumping onto the disastrous singing of my cousin for him to continue screaming the song at the top of his lungs. I buried my face in my hands, blushing a crimson red with absolute humiliation.

When the crowd erupted into applause, Leon grabbed my hand pulling me upwards and turning me around on the spot. I shrank back down into my chair as quickly as possible, furious and mortified, while he was doubled over laughing. He knew how much I hated a spectacle.

"And with that, my work here is done!" He announced, turning to Ricardo. "Don't be put off by her shitty temperament, Ricardo. She just needs to get laid. Then she'll be alright."

My mouth slackened in outrage. "Shut *up*, Leon."

The prick just laughed and smacked Ricardo once more on the back before heaving himself back into the stream of dancers nearby. I didn't think I would be relieved by his absence, not with the solid hulk of a man sat staring at me, but the moment he left I felt myself relax back into my chair.

"Sorry about him, he's a bit of a—"

"Loose cannon? Particularly when drunk?" Ricardo finished for me, and I smiled apologetically.

Another silence started drawing out between us.

"Do you...come to Cancun often?" I asked, more to be polite than out of interest.

"Fairly. Business and all." He smiled, reclining back in his chair and hooking his arm over the vacant one next to him. The picture of ease.

I just nodded.

"I think I might start coming here more often. Perhaps once every summer?" He shot me an arrogant smile and I chuckled at his audaciousness. He had balls, I'd give him that. "Anyway, here's to you on your birthday," he said, picking up his flute and gesturing for me to do the same.

I pinched the crystal between my fingers, and he brought his glass against mine with a clink.

"Happy birthday, Adalyn."

————

THE FIRST THING I realized when my eyes opened was that I had no idea where I was.

My head spun and my heartbeat thrummed loudly in my ears.

I was lying on something, no not something—sand.

I could feel my fingers half submerged in it. Could smell the seaweed that accompanied it and the tang of salt on my tongue. I wasn't at the club anymore, the heavy beat of it off in the distance somewhere.

Where am I?

I blinked furiously, trying to regain my senses. *Beach.* The familiar shoreline of the beach meandered off to my left as far I could see. I struggled to comprehend it. My mind felt heavy like...like I'd been *drugged*.

That's when I felt it. A tugging sensation.

I froze, not sure what the source of the tugging was. I quickly cast my eyes downward, and adrenaline crashed into my system, ripping me away from what I saw: Ricardo.

Ricardo was on top of me.

No.

I screamed.

My arms thrashed wildly as my legs reared up, trying to push myself away from him or at the very least hurt him. He reacted quickly, dodging my sluggish limbs with ease before trapping them at my sides. He pushed his knees against the inside of my thighs, immobilizing them painfully with his full weight.

I let out another scream, but it immediately died away as a fist struck my jaw, throwing my head to the side violently. I spat blood onto the sand, feeling my skin split open against my teeth and a radiating pain consume my face.

"You're supposed to be out cold, my love," Ricardo

muttered, the edge in his voice sending a chill of fear racing up my spine. "No matter."

I felt him shift as hands latched around my throat and after a second of fighting it, desperately searching for air, the world fell into darkness.

———

LUCKILY OR UNLUCKILY, the tranquility of oblivion didn't last long.

Searing pain and the incessant muffling of voices roused me, echoing amongst the shadows. I didn't know how much time had passed, but as the seconds wore on the voices grew clearer until—

"Fucking calm down man!" *His* voice made my stomach churn violently.

"Calm down? Fucking calm down!" It was Leon's voice I was hearing next, and it brought me some hollow form of comfort. "You fucking rapist!"

Everything apart from the voices remained shrouded in disorientating darkness.

Sand.

I could feel sand beneath me, my numb hands buried in the grains.

A second more and I could detect the smell of salt in the air, just as I had before. I couldn't taste it this time though.

No—I could only taste something metallic. Bitter. *Blood.*

Flashes of Ricardo's menacing face. The roughness of his hands.

My senses snapped back with ferocious clarity and I gasped, throwing myself upright. My eyes flicked open but only one of them complied, the other seemingly swollen shut. Something hot and sticky ran down my face and black spots once again danced across my vision.

I need to RUN!

"Adalyn, it's okay. *You're* okay," A voice murmured some-where close by, before shouting, "I need a medic!"

I recognized it as one of my cousins.

The relief was instant, and I collapsed back into the sand, unable to hold myself upright any longer. I was in so much pain I couldn't tell where it hurt worse. My face or my neck or m-my—

I turned my head to the side just as bile spewed violently from my throat.

I once again succumbed to oblivion.

CHAPTER
TWENTY-SIX

PRESENT DAY

"When I woke up in the hospital, my father told me what had happened. They beat him for what he did to me but left him alive... I was in a private hospital in Cancun for a week before we flew home. He'd fractured my cheekbone, damaged my vocal cords and left me with some minor internal bleeding." I wiped away a stray tear.

My eyes fell to my hands, quietly trembling in my lap.

Telling Marco had been just as disturbing and excruciating as I had anticipated. The emotions from that night swirling back with unwelcome clarity, as well as renewed waves of vulnerability and weakness.

I had never spoken about that night—to anyone.

Not when my mother pressed me for details in the hospital. Not when the Doctors wanted answers. *No one.*

And while I had anticipated, at least to some degree, the discomfort that recounting the story would cause, I hadn't anticipated the sense of release that it would also bring. Somehow, getting it out into the air made me feel *stronger*. Not so alone.

I looked across to Marco. He was still sitting on the edge of the bed, facing away from me now. Motionless and taut.

The silence continued to hang in the air, heavy and suffocating, until I couldn't stand it anymore. I reached out my hand tentatively, caressing his shoulder.

"Say something," I said gently, desperate to hear the comforting tenor of his voice.

He launched himself off the bed, pulling away from my touch with startling force. Marco stormed across the bedroom and began pacing furiously. The muscle in his jaw twitched violently against the skin, as he ground his teeth. His hands latched onto his hips as his blazer strained against the tightness in his shoulders. His head jerked side to side incoherently as he muttered vehemently under his breath.

He was incensed by anger. Almost *deranged*.

I shrank back into the headboard, fearful of what this version of Marco was capable of.

"Say something. *Please*," I begged. When he continued to pace as if I hadn't spoken, my voice became strangled. "Marco, you're scaring me!"

"What would you have me say!" he shouted, spinning toward me. "That everything's alright? That *fucking bastard* strangled you. *Raped* you. NOTHING IS ALRIGHT!" he roared, causing me to shrink away from him.

"Don't you think I know that?" My voice trembled as I fought through the tears.

A hand tore down his face. "I've got to go," he muttered, stalking toward the bedroom door.

"Where are you going?" I demanded, jumping off the bed.

"Mexico," he answered simply, not bothering to even look over his shoulder.

"ARE YOU FUCKING KIDDING ME? I've just told you

what happened to me, and you're *leaving*?" I shrieked, outraged by his callousness.

He wheeled back around. "You expect me to allow that fucker to live?"

"No! I don't." I stumbled to him. "I just—please. *Please* don't leave m-me." My voice was broken and desperate by the end.

I couldn't face being alone right now. Not with everything that had happened during the course of the day.

I *needed* him to stay.

A fresh wave of tears spilled down my face. "Please stay with me."

His eyes softened as he observed my vulnerability and pain.

He puffed out a long, faltering breath. A solid minute ticked by, but finally he walked back over to me. The second he was close enough, my arms wrapped around his neck, and I buried my face into his chest. Breathing in his comforting and familiar spicy scent.

His strong arms encircled my waist, and his cheek rested against my hair, the stable pounding of his heart calming and grounding me as the minutes drifted away.

"I'm so mad." Marco spoke softly, sounding exhausted. "I'm so pissed I don't even know what I'm maddest about."

I just nodded against him, not sure what to say.

"You should have told me before," he sighed.

"It's just... I didn't want you thinking less of me for it." My ears burnt with the confession.

I could feel his head shaking. "Never."

His hands came round to cup my face, tilting my chin so his eyes could search mine. A gentle finger traced a line from my temple down to my jaw.

"I'll sort this. I'll do what your family should have done. I'll kill him." Suddenly a dark look clouded his eyes. "Though, I have no clue why they haven't done that already."

"Because it would have been bad for business..." I shook my

head, unwilling to say the words as sickening images flashed back to me. "They weren't as forgiving the second time," I added darkly.

No.

My father had shot Tyler when he burst into my bedroom that day. Shot him right between the eyes. Then Leon and another cousin had dumped his body at the bottom of Lake Mead and put a suicide letter through his mother's door.

A growl resonated in Marco's chest, his voice taking on a biting and revolted tone. "You mean to tell me that *Ricardo* was the one that took your v—"

"Yes." I interrupted, unwilling to talk about it anymore. "Please can we just talk about something else. *Anything* else."

I heard his teeth grind together and a tremor move through his body.

I sighed, knowing that unless I changed the subject that moment, he was about two seconds away from marching off to Mexico again.

Then I remembered something.

"You said earlier that we were engaged. That a marriage contract had already been signed. Is that true?"

I felt his tense body relax infinitesimally. "Yes."

I pulled away to look up at him. "That's not much of a proposal," I teased, but then my smile faltered.

What if he regretted it? Would he, *could* he even want me after everything I'd told him?

But after a short minute, a small smile stretched across his face and my insecurities melted away.

"Well, I was getting to that part. Besides, was there even a point in asking? We all know you are desperate to marry me. You did sleep with me at *a wedding* after all," he finished mockingly, referring to my conversation with Jesse and Enzo at his cousin's wedding in Sicily some months previous.

I rolled my eyes. "As usual, your overwhelming arrogance

no knows bounds, Don La Torre. Who's to say I don't have another, more powerful Don out there pining after me?" I challenged.

"You most probably do, but I doubt he's as handsome," he toyed, the last of his anger finally melting away.

"Arrogant. So, so arrogant."

"Can I take that as a yes to you marrying me?" Marco asked still smiling, eyes softening.

"Hmm..." I sighed, pretending to be deep in thought for a moment. "I don't think I've got anything planned for the next year. I suppose I could marry you."

His charming, boyish smile flashed across his face making him so devastatingly handsome it hurt.

Knowing that my secret was safe with him and that he would protect me—*love* me despite everything I told him... It made my heart ache with happiness.

And fear.

I tried to ignore the unsettling feeling that I would meet Ricardo again as it pressed against my sanity like a cloud of sleet and snow. I didn't doubt that Marco would protect me or that he had the means to deal with Ricardo just as one would swat a fly... But it didn't make my father's words any easier to forget: *Make no mistake, he will stop at nothing to get what he wants.*

I held Marco a little tighter as a gnawing sense of dread coalesced in the crevices of my heart.

CHAPTER
TWENTY-SEVEN

ADALYN

In the days following the meeting with my family, a new wave of conflicts had begun in New York and some of Marco's other territories. The cartel had been the instigators of some of them, and my father's warnings were starting to ring true.

It appeared that the La Torre's had another enemy poised on the horizon, and I couldn't help feeling entirely responsible for it.

The niggling feeling of dread had since saturated my bones with fear and tirelessly kept me up at night.

That and the fact that in two weeks, I was set to become Mrs. Adalyn La Torre.

Marco had insisted we get married as soon as possible given the escalating conflict at our door, and I had no qualms in agreeing to it. I loved the man with everything I had and a small part of me hoped that once Ricardo knew we were married, he would disappear from our lives forever.

It turns out that two weeks was not a huge amount of time

to plan a wedding for over three hundred people in Sicily. Though...by La Torre standards that was still considered a *small* wedding, according to Eliyana.

I spent most days on a long-distance call to Marco's mother arranging it all. She was so ecstatic about the wedding that her enthusiasm was contagious, lifting the heaviness that had settled within me a little.

She had hired numerous wedding planners to take care of the preparations on their side of the Atlantic, leaving me with the less stressful role of picking my favorite colors and design elements I wanted to include.

Marco even involved himself in the preparations more than I had expected. He chose the evening entertainment, sorted suits for the men and attended the wedding cake tasting session the planners had arranged.

There was something oddly sexual about seeing a lethal, ruthless man tasting different flavored frosting with a handgun tucked into his trousers.

My mouth had watered, and it *wasn't* from the decadent cakes before me.

"Everyone out!" He had shouted at the staff in the kitchen. "I need to have a word with my future wife."

They had all scuttled like bugs under a log. Exiting the room in seconds. The doors shutting ominously behind them.

"You've been looking at me like you want to fuck me for over an hour," he'd said sternly, unbuckling his trousers and my eyes tracked the movement viciously. "That's really not appropriate with a room full of staff, is it?"

"No, it isn't Don La Torre," I responded submissively, moistening my lips as my stomach pooled with arousal.

"Now," He started, freeing his erection from his trousers. "Bend over so I can lick frosting off your ass as I punish you."

Then he did as he said, delivering my punishment swiftly and deliciously.

———

"THIS HAD BETTER BE FUCKING GOOD." I sighed and then shrieked as I stumbled forward.

Marco's hand caught my arm, steadying me as I tentatively put one foot in front of the other.

I could feel the cold spring breeze against my face and knew we were somewhere outside, but where exactly I wasn't sure. A blindfold obscured my view.

"Watch it, Ada." He muttered before dropping his hold on the material over my eyes.

My mouth fell agape, and I gasped.

"What the fuck is that?"

A dark purple-mirrored paint-job reflected my stunned expression back to me.

"A car." Marco offered sarcastically.

But it wasn't just *any* car—it was a Lamborghini Aventador.

I balked as I took in the vehicle, parked pride of place on the driveway.

I took a step toward it, feeling that somehow the car was familiar...then it dawned on me.

I turned to him questioningly. "This is exactly like the car at the garage. The one I showed you on the phone." I accused. My mind immediately cast back to the luxury vehicle I'd spotted at the car dealership and had shown him on a video call. This car looked *exactly like* the one I had jokingly asked him to buy me.

"It *is* the car you asked me buy you," he chuckled, understanding my frown of confusion and answering my unspoken question.

"It was still for sale?" I was only half listening as I took in the beautiful vehicle.

It had been almost eight months since I—*well, Marco*—had bought the Brabus...

He didn't answer for a moment, stepping forwards to look around the car.

"No, I bought it the day your Brabus arrived."

Shock must have been evident on my face as he snickered in response.

"And why exactly would you buy your hostage a Lamborghini?" I questioned, skeptical that he was telling the truth. It didn't make sense for him to have bought me the car all those months ago.

He shrugged simply. "You'd looked so happy when your car arrived, I guess I just wanted to be the reason you'd smile like that again."

I smiled in sudden understanding. "That's why I couldn't park in the garage wasn't it?"

He shot me a sheepish look and I laughed, wandering over to him and wrapping my hands around his waist. I pressed my face against his silken shirt until his smell of spice hit my nose.

I sighed in contentment. "I love it. Thank you, baby."

————

THE NEXT DAY, I had auctioned off my Hellcat and donated the money to charity. There was no need for me to keep all three cars. Even as spoiled as I was, I didn't need three cars on the driveway just for me to get to and from work.

Jesse and my usual parade of security guards had come with me that afternoon when I went to try on wedding dresses from a local designer. It was too short notice to have something custom made like Marco had wanted, but I was happy to have something simpler. My tastes had changed over the course of the last few months and perhaps the old me would have wanted a $10,000 bespoke dress by a renowned designer, but something about it just didn't sit right anymore.

The ladies at the boutique couldn't quite believe their eyes when the four of us piled into their tiny store and I snorted out a laugh as the hulking great big men were forced to share a dainty little sofa opposite the pedestal.

They had watched me try on various gowns one after the other all afternoon. Jesse had been enthusiastic enough, though his tastes were questionable at best...Tom had passed out cold after he'd eaten his way through half the finger sandwiches and drank most of the champagne. Thankfully, Alonso was the most helpful of the bunch and actually made some insightful suggestions.

I surveyed my reflection in the mirror, certain that I had found my wedding dress but also certain of something else too.

I walked out of the changing room and over to the pedestal, just as I had with the numerous dresses before. Jesse let out a low whistle and Alonso's smile almost touched his ears.

I grinned excitedly at both of them. "I think this is the one."

"You look bea—" Alonso began, but was quickly cut off by an exuberant and over the top Jesse shouting,

"ARE YOU SAYING YES TO THE DRESS?!"

Tom stirred and groaned, still half asleep. "Shut *up*, Jesse!"

I chuckled as Jesse reached behind the man and smacked him on the back of the head, jolting him awake. Tom's gaze focused after another second, and he finally looked over at me, letting out a quiet '*wow*'.

The dress was stunning. It was a simple A-line dress, made of liquid white satin. A strapless modern corset allowed the material to hug my features, before fanning outwards at the waist into a simple skirt with a slit that rose up to my thigh. An elegant train fanned out behind me, rippling like water.

It was simple and elegant...and I had never looked so beautiful.

I looked over to the man that had become my closest friend over the course of the last few months.

"What, Bandit? You said it's the one!" He enthused, standing and coming over to me.

I patted away a few stray tears and stepped down from the pedestal, enveloping Jesse in a hug. "It's not that, I just figured something out is all."

"That you're...getting married?" He guessed and I felt him place a kiss on my head before pulling away.

I smiled, "It's not that. For some time now I've been trying to think of some way to help other people."

"Like your fundraiser?" He responded, retrieving a glass of champagne and bringing it over to me.

I took a small sip and nodded.

"I don't want to just do a fundraiser, Jess. I want to help people who have gone through trauma or are at rock bottom. I want to give them a fresh start in life, like what Marco has given me."

He eyed me skeptically a moment. "So...you're going to kidnap addicts and hold them for ransom too?"

I smacked him on the arm playfully, unfazed by his obvious lack of enthusiasm.

"The Cosa Nostra has done its fair share of creating the drugs epidemic facing this country. It's time that we do something to help some of the lives we have damaged and give back."

Jesse's seemed to contemplate my words for a moment longer before he nodded. "It's a great idea."

He took my glass and downed the rest of the contents as I headed back inside the changing room.

"Are you sure you don't just want a horse or something?" He yelled through the door on the other side. "That would be *so* much easier to arrange!" He whined jokingly.

"Animal therapy? I love it! We can add it to our list of services," I yelled back tauntingly, and he groaned in mock defeat.

———

WHEN WE HAD REACHED the house that afternoon, I spoke to Marco about the idea, and we'd somewhat refined the details. Surprisingly, it didn't take much to get him onboard with the whole idea, and we agreed to sit down after the wedding to work out the logistics.

Suddenly, I couldn't wait for the future.

Marco had held me in his arms as we stood on the terrace that evening.

We had come out to watch the sun dip behind the horizon, the spring air mild and fresh, his warmth keeping the slight chill at bay.

"You know I never thanked you, Marco, for this exceptional and beautiful life," I murmured into the quiet as I looked out across the grounds of our home. "I know our world is not perfect, but I am glad to be here and to share it with you all the same."

"It was far less exceptional and beautiful before you got here," he remarked, brushing his nose against the shell of my ear. I felt him take a deep breath, his chest brushing my back.

"I don't have many regrets in life, Ada, but I do regret that our love story was not more *conventional*. That you have had to see the bad parts of me more than any of the good...but I'm working on it."

My heart fluttered in my chest.

"I don't regret it." I caressed the back of his hand with my fingers. "Our love story may not be conventional but that's how I know it's real."

CHAPTER
TWENTY-EIGHT

ADALYN

To say I was a nervous wreck was an understatement.

The biggest understatement of the fucking century.

I had been just about ready to duck and roll right out of the cathedral when the ornate wooden doors had swung back, revealing the masses of people congregated inside and watching my every move. If it hadn't been for Eliyana's gentle grip on my hand and the fact that I didn't know Sicily half as well as I should have by now, then I would have given into my crippling fear and rolled the hell back out the doors.

But I didn't.

Instead, I focused on keeping one foot in front of the other until Marco's handsome face came into view. The moment I met him at the end of the alter, happiness replaced my anxiety and everyone else seemed to slip away. Leaving only the two of us captivated entirely by our love for each other.

I had gasped in awe when we'd arrived at the villa for our reception. The wedding planners had done a magnificent job. The large, ornate villa looked more like a palace than I would have ever thought possible and boasted more marble columns than I had ever seen. It was beautiful and sophisticated, yet simple and elegant. It wove the expected La Torre opulence with my more modest tastes seamlessly, and I was overjoyed with how everything had turned out.

It wasn't long before the celebrations began after dinner and once again, my nerves had my stomach clenched with unease and anxiety spiking in my system. More guests had arrived for the evening, and I internally cursed myself for wearing such god-forsaken high heels for the day. Dancing in front of that many people would have been nerve-wracking enough in sneakers rather than the sky-high heels I was sporting for our first dance.

"Why are you concentrating so much?" Marco—my *Husband*—had asked me as we swirled gently across the dance floor.

Unlike me, Marco moved effortlessly. *Lucky bastard.*

"I am just trying not to break anything. Damn shoes." I muttered, my attention caught between my balance and not getting my heel hooked on the dress.

He just laughed and held me tighter, supporting some of my weight and relieving the pressure off my toes.

While I enjoyed having a moment alone with my new husband after the craziness of the day, I was still relieved when the dance was over and I was no longer at the center of a ball-room packed full of people.

We went around greeting guests together for a while and afterwards I sat with Eliyana and Marco's aunt Catarina. They were both a little louder than usual, having commenced their celebrations earlier than the other guests.

Apparently, the canapés, a four-course meal, and a slice of wedding cake had done little to slow down their alcohol-induced buzz and my anxiety was diminishing rapidly in their amusing company. We danced, talked about

Marco's childhood, and joked about the various men of the family.

I slowly sipped at my second glass of water for the night. My nerves had been all over the place for most of the week and my stomach had been tempestuous at best all day. Making alcohol a bad mix, and eating food certainly hadn't helped.

I glanced up from the table and looked around the room, my eyes searching for Marco's familiar dark features amongst the crowd. It had been some time since I saw him last.

It was only then that it hit me that something was wrong.

Very wrong.

The numerous security personnel that had lined the entirety of the room for the evening were gone. Only four remained now and they were gathered by the main doors, frowns etched into their faces as they hunched in muted discussion. The older men of the family, including Benny and Marco's Uncle Leonardo were stood off to one side and engaged in tense, albeit heated, discussions.

The tension in the air had escaped the attention of most of the less *involved* guests in attendance or those who were too intoxicated to notice...but it was obvious for anyone who dared enough to look.

Panic started to latch itself onto my chest and I rose from my seat, looking about the room for Marco.

He's not here.

Nor was Jesse, Alonso, Tom or any of the others.

Before I knew it, I was half-way across the room.

"Benny! What is going on?" I questioned, approaching the man whose shoulders were taut as another man spoke with him.

He looked warily from the unfamiliar man to me, but he didn't say anything, his mouth settling in a grim line almost as if contemplating how much to say.

"Tell me, now! Where is Marco?" I demanded, fear and panic leaking into my voice.

The older man let out a short sigh, "There has been a... *confrontation* at the gate. It is being dealt with as we speak."

Confrontation.

Fear dripped down my spine.

I immediately knew that my family were not behind it.

My family were not callous enough or naive enough to attack on Sicilian soil. The heart of the La Torre family dynasty. My father was a proud man that hated being outsmarted, but he wouldn't have sent his people into a slaughter.

No.

This attack did not sit within the constraints of reason and certainly wasn't the product of exceptional, unrivalled power. This attack was reactive and crude in design. A product of hatred or some other emotion that questioned the boundaries of sanity... and could only mean one thing.

He's here.

A whisper of panic shuddered violently through me.

Flashes of Marco and Ricardo standing opposite one another with weapons drawn had me instantly racing toward the grand double doors, heavily guarded by unfamiliar men. One of the burlier ones intercepted me as I approached, holding up a hand in front of him placatingly, while the other rested on his gun.

"No one is to leave this room, Ma'am. It isn't safe," The six-foot-something Italian man said as I slowed, switching over to English.

"My Husband is out there. Let me out. NOW!" I ordered, making a move to go past him.

In truth, I didn't know whether Marco's men would listen to an order from his new wife, but fear was making me desperate.

An outstretched arm barred me from moving any further

and I glared up at the man who couldn't have been much older than me with a look of pure outrage.

"I'm sorry, Ma'am. Don La Torre has ordered that no one, especially *you* are to leave this room."

My teeth snapped together in frustration.

I knew Marco was trying to protect me by keeping me here. I knew that and yet...rejection had me sucking in a heavier breath of air. He had never shut me out before, and regardless of whether or not it was for a good reason, now was *not* going to become the exception to that rule.

I had had enough of being shut out by my own family and that certainly wasn't going to repeat itself within my new one. Regardless of whether it put me in danger or not, I *needed* to be part of this.

I would not be shut out anymore.

Marco didn't know the kind of man Thrasher was as well as I did, or what he was truly capable of. The fact that he was here meant that not only was he a fool—he was desperate. Desperate men were always the most dangerous.

Thrasher might have nothing to lose—but *I* did.

I need a plan.

I turned on my heel and as calmly as possible, careful to avoid bringing any further attention to myself and attempted to disappear back into the swarm of guests.

Forcing myself to slow my steps, I wandered over to the now vacant table Jesse had occupied with a few of the others for the evening. I slid into his chair for the night after recognizing his familiar black jacket slung across it. I placed my hands against the table and forced myself to breathe. To *think. Think of something.*

Out of the corner of my eye, I noticed Benny and the others turned toward me from across the room.

They're watching.

It wasn't all that surprising. Benny knew me better than to just assume I would be content sitting on the sidelines...

I picked up Jesse's discarded flute of champagne and took a slow swig, while subtly, underneath the table, working my hand around to the back of the chair. I weaved my hands between the material of his jacket until my fingertips slipped against smooth silk. I felt around a moment, seeking the interior pocket I knew he always kept his keys in. I dug my nails down into the pocket and relief flooded my stomach when they hit something hard.

I made quick work of pulling them free of the pocket and onto my lap, before replacing his glass on the table.

I wasn't a fool. I knew I wouldn't be much help to Marco or anyone else in this family if there was a fight. As much as that thought irked me, it was the ungracious truth of my situation. I wasn't physically strong enough, trained or experienced enough to make a damn difference on a physical level.

But I had to do *something*.

I might not be hard, tough or bullet-proof...but Jesse's G-Wagon certainly was. While *I* might not be able to do anything when faced with a lunatic man with a gun, Jesse's car certainly could. It wasn't much of a plan, running over a Mexican drug lord, but it was all I had.

I just needed to get out of this damn hall and preferably be armed when I did it.

I didn't have to check Jesse's jacket again for any signs of a weapon. I could tell from the weight of it that whatever firearm he'd had was most probably with him.

Forcing myself to appear calm, I hooked the keyring over my finger and hid the rest in my palm as I got back to my feet.

I headed swiftly past two nearby tables, searching for any firearms laying around unattended. Finally, after a few seconds of looking across the expanse of room, I found one of Marco's distant cousins, a man who I had only met once when Eliyana introduced us at the restaurant, passed out cold with drool creeping down his chin. His handgun rested against his waist, obvious despite the distance between us.

I calmly stalked over to him, then feigned finding something on the floor beside him. I quickly dropped to a crouch and slid the gun free of the holster, his snores not so much as stuttering with the sudden change in weight.

Not a well-trained Mafioso. I observed, grateful for his apparent alcohol-induced coma.

I unclicked the mag and slid it out to check the bullets. Fully loaded. *Thank the goddamn Lord...* Then I slid it back into place and cocked it.

Adrenaline began making my hands more frantic as I gathered the material of my dress until the blue garter at the top of my thigh came into view. I slid the bitterly cold metal against my skin, fighting the flinch as I quickly pulled my skirts back into position and got to my feet. The unforgiving metal now pressed firmly against my thigh and stored securely out of sight.

Without a second of hesitation, I ducked into the nearby hallway leading to the toilets and a back stairway. Once out of view, I ran down the corridor and silently prayed there would be an emergency exit of some sort that could get me outside.

I need to get to the car. NOW.

I all but screamed in frustration when I was confronted with nothing but a window. I threw myself against it and fought against the lock, shaking the godforsaken pane to try and wiggle it free.

"Adalyn?"

My hands stilled on the against the frame, and I turned toward the source of the voice. Biting back my sigh of bitter irritation.

Sofia.

Who the fuck let her in?

As if reading my distaste, the beautiful brunette held up her hands in a placating gesture. "My Mamma insisted I come as her plus one."

Did I care? No. And did I want this discussion right now? Also no.

I needed to get outside. NOW.

"Look Sofia, I really don't care about this right now." I swiped away the sweat starting to gather on my forehead, the adrenaline making standing still feel unbearable. "I've got to get outside," I muttered, turning back to the window and trying the pane again.

"Why?" I heard her ask, barely audible over my puffing as I shoved and pulled at the window with my full strength.

"There's something going on outside and I need to get out. NOW!" I shouted, slapping my hands against my thighs. Frustration and desperation were making my temper flare as helplessness settled in.

I heard the click of heels as Sofia approached the window beside me and also tried pulling at the ancient wood. She gave up after a second and then reached a hand up to her hair, pulling out a pin that allowed her curls to fall free. I watched as she wiggled the pin into the lock, freeing up space enough to create leverage for the pane to slide free.

What is happening right now? Why is she helping me?

Her dark eyes met mine and she shrugged gently. "I wouldn't want to be married to someone that shuts me out of the important stuff either. I get it."

I swallowed hard against the ghost of pain that danced in my chest.

Now really isn't the time, I reminded myself.

I shook it off and sprung into action, pulling up the infuriatingly intricate layers of my dress and bunching them in one hand. I all but hauled myself through the window, landing ungracefully on the stones on the other side.

The night air was silent sans my steps crunching against the gravel. *No gunfire or shouting.* I didn't know what that meant...or what I might find as a result of it.

My footsteps echoed loudly as I stepped away and turned toward where I assumed the guests' vehicles were parked for the night.

"Where are you going?" Sofia called, climbing out through the window and scrambling to find her footing on the stones.

Why the hell is she following me?

"Car." I grunted, not stopping a beat for the insolent party crasher.

"You're going the long way." She called. "There's a shortcut."

That had me pausing as I half turned back toward her, desperate for anything that would get me to Marco sooner.

She pointed out across one of the sprawling topiary gardens. "The gardens will get you there quicker. I can get you to it." She nodded. Almost as if reassuring herself as well as me that she could.

Unease made me hesitate. "Why should I trust you? You hate me." I pointed out.

She smiled softly and cocked her head to the side. "Guess I'm sick of being overlooked too." She then sighed dramatically. "You coming or not? I would much rather be hunting for a rebound right now than helping you anyway..."

I sighed. "Fine."

Ignoring the curdling feeling of distrust in my stomach, I followed after her as she set off through the garden. Her steps confident and measured as we passed by the various bushes. It was as if she knew the place well...which I most certainly did not.

Our steps crunched loudly against the gravel as we followed the pathway. The eerie silence hanging in the air set my teeth on edge.

The thudding of music from the hall was much quieter out

here, sounding almost muffled somehow. It was the only thing that disturbed the eerie quiet that enveloped the grounds, and it had me wondering whether the danger had already passed.

Until shouting erupted in the distance.

The sound ringing out someways behind us, the other side of the mansion. It felt like worlds away from where we were, hidden amongst the garden and topiary.

"That's from the gate!" Sofia shouted.

The panic in her voice mirrored the panic in my chest and we immediately quickened our pace, running along the path as it trailed through the darkness.

Gunfire erupted not a moment later, decimating the night air. Adrenaline leaked into my bloodstream and had me pushing myself to move faster, kicking off my shoes as I ran harder across the stones. The sharp edges of rock nothing but a burning caress as I pulled up the skirts of my dress, lengthening my stride.

"How much longer Sofia?" I demanded, frustrated that her shortcut was starting to feel like the wrong way to the cars entirely.

Wait...

We rounded the corner of a low-lying wall, and I skidded to a stop, the stones tearing against the soles of my feet as I came to an abrupt halt.

Terror.

Sharp, violent, consuming *terror* crashed through my veins like an excruciating poison.

"Adalyn, my love. I'm so glad you could finally join us."

CHAPTER
TWENTY-NINE

MARCO

"Fucker's not even here," Jesse growled, shoving back over the lifeless body of one of the men.

Fifteen of Thrasher's men were dead. It had been a blood bath. A massacre.

But the fucker knew it would be.

Only one of my men had been injured in the gunfire and even then, it had been a lucky shot. They were untrained, unskilled, and more importantly, outgunned.

Jesse's observation only confirmed what I had already begun to suspect.

"It was a set-up," I seethed.

Thrasher may well be a savage or a drug-fueled fool, but he wasn't an optimist. He knew he and his men wouldn't get out of this attack alive. He knew he would never get close to the reception. To Adalyn.

Yet he had sent his men here anyway.

It didn't make any sense.

Then it hit me.

"It's a distraction." My voice was hollow even to my own ears.

Most of my men were with me by the gate, leaving only a few left back at the hall. I knew Thrasher didn't have enough men to attack or get close enough to the guests inside—*to Adalyn* but he was a man without anything to lose and they were the hardest to predict.

Alberto Mannino's warning reverberated in my skull: *'He will stop at nothing to get what he wants.'*

"Get to the hall. NOW!"

————

ADALYN

"Adalyn, my love. I'm so glad you could finally join us."

My heartbeat pounded in my ears, and my stomach lurched sickeningly. I stumbled back a step, struggling to keep my footing as I tried to move away from the looming presence of the monster before me.

He looked just the same as I remembered.

For a moment it was as if it had been only days rather than years since I'd last seen him. Then I noted the change in his eyes. They were predatory, *deranged* as they ran over my body, silhouetted against the darkness.

Sofia sauntered toward the man without hesitation.

"Sofia, no—" My strangled voice rang out, trying to warn her.

"I did as you asked, Darling. I brought her here for you," Sofia cooed to him.

My stomach fell to the floor.

It was a set-up.

She had lured me outside to face a monster. To my death.

I gagged when a wicked smile contorted her lips as she approached the man, stroking his chest lovingly and gazing up at him adoringly.

He leaned down and sealed his mouth to hers. She all but threw herself at him, latching onto him passionately and moaning into him. Ricardo showed no such enthusiasm, his eyes remaining trained on me the entire time, with an intensity that made me feel like I was being hunted.

I looked away and closed my eyes, not wanting to see any more of the disturbing display before me.

"Now. Kill the bitch." Sofia's words had my eyes immediately springing back open.

She was standing before Ricardo, his arm possessively wrapped around her shoulders as she looked at me with unrestrained hatred unfurling in her eyes.

I gulped as another wave of fear sliced through me.

Part of my brain screamed at me to run, but I knew it would be futile. Ricardo was not only stronger than me and faster—he was also armed. I would be dead before I could even get to the gun at my thigh.

I watched wide-eyed as Ricardo reached his hand across Sofia's face and yanked her head suddenly to the side, the movement so violent that a sickening snap obliterated the silence.

Her body fell limp immediately, and he tossed her to the floor as if she were no more than a bag of bones, her glassy eyes frozen in the night.

A strangled cry tore from my throat and I fell to my knees. Bile rose in my throat and this time I couldn't keep it down. The world swirled before me as my stomach emptied itself.

I hardly registered a presence kneeling beside me on the floor until a large, calloused hand pulled my face painfully to the side.

"You should have known this was going to happen, my love." Ricardo said softly. His dark, soulless eyes piercing into me. "You've always been mine."

The smile on his face suddenly dripped into a hateful grimace as his eyes fell to my dress.

"It seems you forgot that," he spat, shoving my face away from him as he rose to his feet.

He turned on his heel, pacing the distance between me and Sofia's lifeless body agitatedly.

My hand subtly searched for the hard edge of my gun through the fabric and a tear trailed down my cheek as I realized how impossibly trapped it was under the material. A sob bubbled in my throat as the last of my hope extinguished.

"Imagine my surprise when after all these years of waiting for my ridiculous father to die, I find you *kidnapped* by the La Torre's. How *dare* he take what is MINE!" He roared, swinging around to face me so ferociously I flinched and braced for impact.

"No, no, no, no!" Ricardo cooed, kneeling beside me once again and taking my face between his hands. I tried to wrench myself away from his touch, but he latched onto my skin with a bruising force. "Don't be afraid, my love. I am here to save you."

I couldn't fight him as his lips crushed fiercely against mine. Silent tears rolled down my face and I wanted so much to fight him off, to push him away, but I couldn't.

I was frozen. Terrified and caged by absolute and inescapable fear.

"You see, my love, I have always wanted you. You caught my eye the moment our fathers joined forces all those years ago. You are such a beauty, Adalyn." He murmured, tracing his hand down the side of my cheek and I fought the urge to spit in his face. "I demanded my father broker our marriage the moment you turned eighteen, but both him and your insolent father refused. So...I took what was mine on your eighteenth birthday, regardless of what *they* wanted. It still wasn't enough to force them into a deal though." He spat.

I choked on a sob as understanding made me realize the depravity of the situation. Of the man before me.

I am going to die today.

Whether it was a primal instinct or perhaps an unconscious recognition of the inevitability before me, the second those six words materialized in my mind, a deep-seated sense of tranquility eclipsed the unrelenting chaos inside me.

If I was going to die today, I was going to die being *me*.

Not a pawn in a battle amongst men.

Not a spectator to my own past trauma.

I was going to die with the truth on my tongue and the love of one incredible man in my heart.

I wasn't going to be afraid anymore.

"I don't need to be saved. I chose this," I said softly the moment he pulled away.

He paused, fixing me with a maniacal look. "No! It's not true!" he shouted, viciously shaking his head from side to side and releasing my face.

I didn't flinch this time.

"I was never yours, Ricardo. You drugged me, strangled me, and *raped* me on that beach when I was eighteen."

"Liar!" He thundered, pulling back his elbow and striking me across the face.

My head whipped to the right. Stars danced across my vision and my ears rang deafeningly. My body collapsing to the side. I took in a ragged breath, trying to steady myself as the world tilted around me.

When my vision grew steadier, Ricardo was pacing backwards and forwards again like a wild animal.

I let out a painful breath, "I wasn't yours to take that night."

"SHUT UP!" Ricardo bellowed. I felt the impact of his boot

as it slammed into my back, winding me instantly and pushing me violently into the stones.

I struggled to find my voice—my breath.

But I would. I would not be a pawn in this game of chess any longer.

"I have only ever belonged to one man." My breathless voice was a mere whisper on the breeze. I pushed myself slowly onto my knees. "A man that is kind. Who loves fearlessly. Who is loyal and brilliant and a better man than you will ever be—"

"SILENCE!" Ricardo screamed, darting toward me and striking me again across the face.

Blood flowed into my mouth and the world tilted and ghosted before me. My eyes fluttered closed as I temporarily blacked out. When they re-opened, my face was against the stones and my body was painfully twisted to the side.

I knew the end was near when Ricardo's form loomed over me, engulfing me in his shadow. The barrel of a gun pointed straight at me.

But I wasn't afraid anymore.

I smiled as tears trickled down my face and I thought of the only person in the world I never wanted to have to leave.

"I'll see you on the other side, my love."

I love you, Marco.

When the bang rang out, I didn't even flinch.

———

MARCO

Everything around me blurred into obscurity as I ran through the gardens toward the distant shouts of a man on the brink of sanity. A skin splitting crack rang out amongst the night air, and I too found myself slipping into madness as I sprinted to the source of the noise.

The instant I turned the final corner, I saw two things simultaneously. The first: Ada laying crumpled in a pool of blood. The second: Ricardo Lopez with a baretta pointed directly at my wife.

The anguish and hatred that filled me coalesced into a roar as I slammed against the man who threatened to extinguish the life of the only person I had ever truly loved.

The gun exploded somewhere near my head as I tackled Ricardo to the floor. Trapping him beneath me as I beat into his face with my bare fists. His blood splattered across me as I smashed my knuckles against his skull over and over again, the contours of his face disappearing beneath them until nothing but a bloody mass of grotesque skin and bone remained.

I knew he was dead, but I couldn't stop. I was as deranged as the man whose brain was now scattered across the stones before me.

"Marco!" Jesse's voice registered somewhere in the back of my mind, but I scarcely even heard it.

I was too late to save her.

Tears clouded my vision, and I howled in anguish, completely lost to the madness.

"MARCO!"

I felt myself be dragged backwards, away from the bloody stump of a man I'd created.

Jesse's face swam in front of my eyes, but I couldn't make out what he was saying, the world and his words muffled as if submerged in muddy water.

My head jerked sharply to the side and the pain of the blow drove the delirious silence away in an instant.

"ADA NEEDS YOU!"

Ada.

Ada needs you.

It was enough to snap me out of my insanity.

When I stilled against the hands restraining me, Jesse

nodded to the men and I fell to the floor, crawling to the crumpled body of my wife.

Blood stained her white dress and grew bigger with every second. Her beautiful, delicate face almost unrecognizable amongst the damage Ricardo had caused.

A sob tore through my chest as a pain worse than death consumed me.

CHAPTER
THIRTY

ADALYN

Beep. *Beep.*

The distant sound of automated machinery cut through the quiet.

I turned away from the noise, desperate to fall back into the serenity of silence and I winced. In the back of my mind, I noted the glaring light threatening to perforate the peaceful darkness. I sighed and a sharp stab of pain broke through my senses.

Ricardo. The garden. The bang.

My eyes flew open, and I gasped in sudden panic.

I was in an unfamiliar room, dominated by bright white light. My heart fluttered in my chest and the whirring of machinery nearby picked up its pace.

It took me a moment to recognize it as a hospital.

I made a motion to sit up when a gentle hand on my arm prevented me from moving any further.

"Ada, calm down. You're alright. You're safe."

Relief, so potent and pure, washed through me as I stilled. Tears immediately pooled in my eyes.

Marco is okay. Marco is here.

The second I saw his beautiful face, the tears spilled down my cheeks and my chest heaved in happiness. I opened my mouth to say something, *anything*...but he shook his head.

"I was so scared, baby," he said gently, his words trembling with emotion.

A single tear trickled down his cheek as he raised a hand to caress my face. I turned into the warmth of his skin, truly grateful that he was alive and by some divine intervention, so was I.

"I thought I was too late. I thought you were dead." More tears leaked from his eyes and his voice sounded more broken than I'd ever thought possible.

"I'm here," I whispered, my voice coming out strangled and strained as if from disuse.

"Try not to talk. You need to rest." He murmured, tucking a piece of hair behind my ear. I shook my head slightly, and he continued, seeing the questions in my eyes.

"You've been in a coma for two days, baby. You were shot in the chest..." His face contorted in pain. "They rushed you into surgery and managed to stop the bleeding. By the grace of God, the bullet only just missed your heart."

I instinctually glanced down toward my chest but was grateful that it was covered by gauze and blanket. I didn't think I could manage seeing the wound just yet or relive the memories that went along with it.

"Your face and back are badly bruised, but nothing is broken. It'll go down in the next week or so." He continued, dropping his hand to hold one of mine as they trembled.

"Where is h—" I began to ask, but the words were burning in my throat.

He searched my face intently. "I killed him."

I nodded slightly, drawing comfort from the fact that Ricardo could never hurt me or anyone else again. That he was gone. And that this time it was for good.

"S-Sofia was behi—"

"I know. Ricardo used her to get to you. I should have seen it," Marco said, glancing away. "I let you down. I'm so sorry. I will never fail you again."

"You didn't fail me." I cupped his face with my free hand, wiping away another tear as it tracked down his face. "You *saved* me."

A sad smile contorted his face, and he shook his head in quiet disagreement but didn't fight me on it any further.

I dropped my hand from his face and held his strong hand in both of mine, content to be touching his skin. Relishing in the fact that I could; after thinking I may never get the chance again.

"Ada, there is something else I need to tell you." Marco's voice broke through my inner thoughts, and I frowned at the sudden uncertainty in his voice.

My eyes drifted up from the dirty, blood-splattered shirt he must have been wearing since the wedding. Coming to rest on his exhausted face. He looked like he hadn't slept in days.

"Are you okay?" I half whispered, half mouthed to him.

"I'm fine," he said with a gentle half smile. "Now, stop being cute and let me get this out... baby, I'm not sure how you're going to react to this, but I need you to stay calm. Everything is going to work out fine, I promise you."

The intensity of his words and the concern in his gaze had the heart rate monitor picking up speed once again, as my heart fluttered.

"You're pregnant, Ada."

What?

I tried to think through the remnants of drug-induced fogginess clouding my mind.

"I don't know how it happened, and I thought we were being careful, but...we're going to have a baby," he whispered, and excitement like I had never seen lit up his face and twinkled in his eyes.

My shock was quickly overshadowed by other, much stronger emotions, and a fresh wave of tears trailed down my face. This time for an entirely different reason.

"We're going to have a family?" I asked, warmth spreading in my chest and soothing gaps within my soul I never knew existed.

Marco nodded. "Our baby is fine. Happy and strong, just like their Mamma."

His smile was so radiant with unconditional love, loyalty and absolute contentment, that in that moment I knew that we could do it. That we could raise this child and be the family we had always wanted but never quite had.

That he was my soulmate, and by some crazy miracle I wound up being his.

His lips pressed a delicate kiss to my forehead, wordlessly promising me a lifetime of unconditional devotion and safety.

"I love you, Ada."

"I love you too, Marco."

ACKNOWLEDGMENTS

The Devil Can be Kind has been a long journey, and there were times I wasn't sure I'd ever make it this far. But here I am - the story is finally out there!

None of this would have been possible without the incredible support of my Husband, family and friends. My confidence to pursue this now, has come from each and every one of you. Thank you for everything.

To my Street Team and my readers, I am so incredibly grateful that you are here and sharing this journey with me. I could never have called myself a writer, let alone an author, without you. I am forever grateful.

To my talented editor, Shana Grogan and my fantastic designer, Sarah from Okay Creations - your patience and hard work has been invaluable in bringing this book to life. It has truly been an honour to work with you both.

And finally, to all my trauma - *what the fuck are you doing?* Nah, I'm just playing. Going through difficult times has shown me how to really appreciate the good, and how to (hopefully!) connect with others through words. Whether it is a loss that you've had to endure, some kind of abuse, or facing hell right here on earth - I hope Adalyn's story has made you realise that trauma does not have to define you.

You **are** fearless. You **are** powerful. **You have got this.**

All my love,

Elena x

ABOUT THE AUTHOR

Elena Lucas is a debut fiction writer specialising in dark romance. Her stories unapologetically dive into the depths of passion and power, blending raw emotion and humor to create characters that stay with you long after the final page. Elena's writing challenges the boundaries of love, loss, and strength, reminding readers that resilience can often be found in the most unexpected places.

Elena Lucas is also the founder of *Elena Lucas Publishing,* where dark romance novels are not just a speciality - they're a passion. Discover more of their titles, including *Obsidian Obsessions: The Dark Romance Journal,* and stay tuned...this is just the beginning.

 instagram.com/elenalucas_author